THE

Grrl Genius

GUIDE TO

[WITH OTHER PEOPLE]

ST. MARTIN'S GRIFFIN ✹ NEW YORK

www.stmartins.com

Library of Congress Cataloging-in-Publication Data

Michon, Cathryn.
    The grrl genius guide to sex (with other people) : a self-help novel / by Cathryn Michon.
        p. cm.
    ISBN 0-312-31638-0 (hc)
    ISBN 0-312-31639-9 (pbk)
    EAN 978-0312-31639-6
        1. Divorced women—Fiction. 2. Sex customs—Fiction. I. Title.

PS3613.I35G77 2004
813'.54—dc22

                                                                        2003066736

First St. Martin's Griffin Edition: February 2005

10 9 8 7 6 5 4 3 2 1

THE
Grrl Genius
GUIDE TO

[WITH OTHER PEOPLE]

Also by Cathryn Michon

The Grrl Genius Guide to Life

Jane Austen's Little Advice Book
(with Pamela Norris)

A
SELF-HELP
NOVEL

BY Cathryn Michon

This book is dedicated to my dad,
who always was enough of
an Enlightened Male to cheerfully
admit that my mother is a genius.

It is also dedicated to
Grrl Genius Nora Ephron,
who was my inspiration
because she came up with the idea first.

An Open Letter to Any Attorneys Who Might Be Representing the Ex-Husbands or Lovers of a Real Person Who Is Known as Cathryn Michon:

THIS BOOK is about a fictional character named Cathryn Michon. Everything in this book didn't happen (fiction). Even though there is also a real person named Cathryn Michon, anything that has happened to that Cathryn Michon resembling anything that happens to the Cathryn Michon in this book is, wow, a totally freaky coincidence.

Life is fully of freaky coincidences. Did you know that Kennedy had a secretary named Lincoln, and Lincoln had a secretary named Kennedy? Furthermore, what about the fact that Lincoln was shot in a Ford (theater) and Kennedy was in a Ford (Lincoln!) when he was shot?

So with that kind of coincidental stuff going on all the time, is the fact that this book is written by a woman named Cathryn Michon about a fictional character named Cathryn Michon anything but a big coincidence?

Well, that's exactly what it is, a big fat coincidence. Isn't life amazing sometimes?

Some of the items in this book are not fiction. I've included statistics, studies, and my own big fat opinion, which, although "made up," isn't really fiction per se, because I think my opinions are pretty valid—and you will, too!

The fictional things that are in this book were made up (through the power of fiction) to help you with your real-life relationship problems. Anyone who has ever been lucky enough to read *Highlights for Children* magazine and peruse the exploits of Goofus and Gallant knows that the stories of the terrible misdeeds of Goofus are far more instructive than the prissy, unbelievable claims of that champion bootlicker Gallant.

Just think of Cathryn Michon as the Goofus of Relationships. Through this character's unbelievably stupid, and yet still Grrl Geniusy, relationship exploits, you will learn everything you need to do to avoid relationship despair.

Think of this not as a "how to" book, but as more of a "how not to" book.

Although some real Los Angeles locations are mentioned in this book, they are all used fictitiously, which should present no problem for the reader, since most people know that everything in Los Angeles is fake anyway.

Besides the fictional character of Cathryn Michon, there are other fictional (fake) characters in this book. For example, at one point we meet the character of William, a made-up person who is a brilliant writer, devastatingly handsome, funny, sexy, smart, fantastic in bed, and makes incredible homemade scones. In real life, I have been involved with a brilliant writer who is devastatingly handsome, funny, sexy, smart, and fantastic in bed, but he has never once made me a scone, plus his name is not William.

Thus, fiction ensues. Amazing!

Similarly, when I tell stories about a divorce so humiliating, with details so nails-on-chalkboard-scratchingly-awful that no one could possibly make them up, please remember, I did make them up! I'm that talented!

My actual divorce could not have been more delightful.

Sincerely,
Cathryn Michon (Real Person)

P.S. And now, please enjoy the Self-Help Novel *The Grrl Genius Guide to Sex (with Other People)*.

Introduction

Literature is the lie that tells the truth.
— Dorothy Allison

MY NAME IS Cathryn Michon. I am a lifelong failure at romantic relationships. Hence I have declared myself to be a "Sex and Relationship Expert."

This is not the first time I've tried something like this. In my best-selling book, *The Grrl Genius Guide to Life: A 12-Step Program on How to Become a Grrl Genius, According to Me!* (Harper-Collins, 2001), I documented the amazing changes that occurred in my life after I declared myself to be a Grrl Genius, based on no IQ test or empirical evidence whatsoever. Since then, thousands (including many celebrities!) have followed in my well-shod footsteps.

Among the celebrities who have now declared their Grrl Geniushood are Joni Mitchell, Lily Tomlin, Margaret Cho, Merrill Markoe, Ann Magnuson, Mary McCormack, Janeane Garofalo, Marcia Wallace, Ellen DeGeneres, Sarah Silverman—and this is in no way a comprehensive list. Frankly, these people were already geniuses without my little program, but still, it was awfully nice of them to join up with the rest of us. Just as important are Maria Hjelm, Norma Vela, Patty Peppard, Fran Roy, Nancy McKenna, and countless others you probably have never heard of because, guess what: You don't have to be rich and famous to be a Grrl Genius— that's the whole point!

When I became a genius, I found out a lot of things about the oppression of women that has occurred over the last few thousand years. The first thing I found out was: It was bad! I learned that around about the time Goddess worship ended, women started getting treated like crap. Words like *bitch* (which used to be an honorific title, signifying that a woman was courageous and strong like Diana the Bitch Goddess, who ran with the wolves) evolved to mean that you were just, well, a bitch.

The second thing that I found out was that much of the oppression of women currently being practiced in this country is, actually, our own damn fault. If we, like 91 percent of women in America, feel "bad about ourselves" because we don't look like supermodels (genetic freaks), then, well, we have no one but ourselves to blame, because no one is "making" us hate ourselves. We need to get over it. We need to declare that we are Grrl Geniuses (*genius*, by the way, is actually a feminine word, derived from the Roman Goddess Juno, meaning "the Goddess within") and stop beating ourselves up for not looking like we come from the Isle of Anorexia.

I am a genius because I say I am. You can be, too.

The next step on my journey to genius is to turn my advice and attentions to the complex world of interpersonal relationships, despite having dismally failed at them for most of my adult life and a large part of my childhood, as well.

I am a sex and relationship expert, because I say I am. You can be, too.

Some people insist on leading with their strengths; I lead with my weaknesses. That's just part of my genius. Truthfully, who can better advise you on how to avoid financial collapse than someone who invested all her money in Enron because she "just loved their logo"? Who can give you better advice on how to avoid a disastrous relationship than someone whose ex-husband spent the whole ten-year marriage as a "Househusband" despite the fact that we had no children to raise, employed a housekeeper to clean the house, a gardener to take care of the yard, and I did the laundry? An ex-husband who devoted all of this time to the golf course, refusing to seek employment because it interfered with his full-time job of finding fault with everything I did?

My humiliation is your gain!

In my life, I have slept with bad boys who wanted nothing more than to crush my spirit like a jelly doughnut under a Cadillac Escalade. I have "conveniently" managed to be somewhere that was totally out of my way in order to "run into" a man who did not deserve to be run into by anything except perhaps a fully loaded freight train carrying hazardous waste. I married a man who wanted to be my husband because he mistakenly thought my family was wealthy, who in addition to never earning a living also didn't care to have sex with me more than twelve to fifteen times a year, even though, as I often tell my friends, I prefer to have sex more often than I have my period.

Yet I remain optimistic about the possibility of true love.

Furthermore, I have declared myself to be a bona fide Relationship Expert, and St. Martin's Press has agreed to publish this book, so if I'm not a Relationship Expert, well, hey, the joke's on them.

And guess what, this book actually has a happy ending! I don't want to spoil it, but here's a hint: Once you stop thinking like a loser, you'll stop being a loser.

Relationship experts are just like hairstylists. Every Grrl Genius knows that you should never trust a hairstylist with a cute hairdo. A hairstylist with cute hair is a hairstylist who plays it safe, a hairstylist who isn't willing to experiment and learn from her errors. A great hairstylist is the one who dyes her hair Ronald McDonald orange and shaves it into a reverse Mohawk, so she can learn from her mistakes, sacrificing her own looks, to ensure that you stay a perfect pale champagne blonde, with flirty side-brushed bangs and a sassy flip.

Like a great hairstylist, a great relationship expert is willing to have bad relationships, so you won't have to.

Oh, I have been working overtime for you people.

As a lifelong fan of TV nature shows, I have made an exhaustive study of the various aberrations of sexuality in both the human and animal kingdoms. I have intensively studied history and biology, and the bottoms of countless Häagen-Dazs cartons, all so that I could create various patented (pending) time-tested programs and systems that collectively form the "Unified Field Theory of Sex and Relationships" from the Grrl Genius perspective. Here's an example:

A Grrl Genius Crazy Sex Fact

Menstrual cramps have been known, in rare cases, to induce orgasm. Thankfully, in no cases have orgasms been known to induce menstrual cramps.

I will also provide extensive information on the safest and most powerful substance known to Grrl Genius–kind, the one substance that can not only enhance your sex life, but can, if necessary, replace it entirely.

I am, of course, speaking of the magical Grrl Genius Elixir. Chocolate.

A Grrl Genius "Love Is Important But Chocolate Is Essential" Handy Chocolate Fun Fact

Chocolate contains phenylethylamine, the chemical that is released in our brains when we fall in love.

I have also provided quizzes, handy charts, and graphs, assembled by using the most rigorous of scientific methods including, but not limited to, my big fat opinion.

The Official and Very Scientific Grrl Genius Evaluation of Currently Available Relationship Advice and Why This Book Is Much Better

Relationship Advice Medium	What's Good About It	What Stinks About It	Why You (and All Your Friends) Should Buy This Book Instead
Dr. Laura Schlessinger's *10 Stupid Things Women Do to Mess Up Their Lives*	Some of the stupid things actually *are* stupid.	She doesn't own up to stupid things *she's* done such as pose naked for her boyfriend who then published the pictures on the Internet.	If you buy my book and it becomes a best-seller, horrible old boyfriend who took naked pictures of me when I was nineteen will put pictures on Internet, and I will be able to see how cute I was then.
John Gray's *Men Are from Mars, Woman Are from Venus*	Excellent guide to the fact that men and women are really different, because they're space aliens!	Most people know that men and women are different. Most people aren't space aliens.	My book is about earthlings.
The Rules, the retro classic by those two girls who say the book helped them trap husbands and then one of them got divorced (no judgment, I'm just sayin')	Fantastic primer on how to totally conceal your real personality and hoodwink a man into marrying you using the very same techniques employed by used car salesmen to hoodwink buyers into purchasing a defective Chevy.	You will begin to regard yourself as a defective Chevy.	My book says you are a Grrl Genius Mercedes convertible, and any man who doesn't get your genius needs to keep his grubby mitts off your headlights. (Hey nobody ever said I couldn't stick with a metaphor.)
Dr. Phil McGraw's *Relationship Rescue*	Fantastic, kick-ass book, and what about how great he is on his TV show, where he doesn't let anybody get away with any crap whatsoever.	I took his relationship rescue quiz, failed it, and divorced my husband. (Wait, that's a good thing.) Okay, there's nothing bad about it.	Fine, buy his book *and* my book. You can afford two books. Sheesh . . .
continued	*continued*	*continued*	*continued*

Relationship Advice Medium	What's Good About It	What Stinks About It	Why You (and All Your Friends) Should Buy This Book Instead
Cosmopolitan magazine	Comprehensive and frank sexual advice dedicated to the notion that most men are incredibly finicky creatures who must be tricked, cajoled, and duped into having sex with you, and when they do, complex "tricks" and "techniques" are required to "please" them.	Actual truth is the only "tricks" and "techniques" required to "please" most men are "a pulse" and "a vagina."	My book offers comprehensive and frank sexual advice on how to find men who are concerned with pleasing *you!*

As a result of this extensive and exhaustive process, I finally found a loving, sweet, sexy, smart, funny, handsome boyfriend. (And you can, too!)

More important, I can assure you that by the time you finish reading this book, you will know the secret to obtaining the one thing you have always dreamt of, the one thing you always knew would make you happy, the one thing your soul has been crying out for, the one female longing that must be fulfilled.

Having sex with a hunky firefighter.

I feel confident that as you're reading this, you are thinking, "Cathryn is so right! The only person who can really show me the path to relationship happiness is someone who has known true, excruciating relationship despair. Ideally, this expert would have crawled like a phoenix (the mythical creature, not the city of annoyingly tanned people) from the ashes of relationship ruin into clumsy and awkward postmarital dating life, where she primarily dates closeted homosexuals. Obviously, only someone who is that big of a screwup has anything to offer me in the way of sound relationship advice that has the power to make my love life 1,000 times better (actual figure)."

Still, you may be asking yourself, "But how do I know if Cathryn Michon is screwed up enough to be helpful to me?"

Rest assured, Cathryn Michon is screwed up enough.

So now you are probably wondering what cataclysmic personal event plunged me deep enough into a trough of personal misery and failure to cause me to create the Grrl Genius Relationship Program and all the ancillary Grrl Genius Relationship Methods, Systems, and Programs.

Amazingly, all it took was a yard sale.

In my family we don't divorce men—we bury them.
                                                    —Ruth Gordon

Chapter 1

A Grrl Genius Declares Herself to Be a Genius of Sex and Relationships, Regardless of Her (Dismal) Track Record

It's the friends you can call up at 4 a.m. that matter.
—Marlene Dietrich

LEAVING MY husband was easy. Leaving my dog broke my heart.

Most people know that 50 percent of marriages end in divorce. (I suppose the other 50 percent end in death, and there was a time I would have considered this to be the better option, but it's not as easy as you might think.) I have a lot of friends who have gotten divorced, and normally, when the couple first separates, it's the man who moves out of the marital house, gets an apartment, a sports car, and a blond girlfriend, while the soon-to-be-ex-wife stays in the home and takes sleeping pills and loses weight.

But my separation wasn't normal at all, although the blond (with long dark roots) girlfriend did show up in pretty short order. My Napoleonically short, German,[1] soon-to-be ex (let's call him Kurt, because in another one of those "so strange it must be fiction" coincidences, that's his name) had refused to leave the house, even though I was the one paying for it. This had perplexed me at the time because everything I knew about divorce I had learned from

---

[1]Well, he's actually American. His ancestors were German, and he stubbornly insists that anything German is automatically the best be it German cars or German coffee makers or German people, although he has never bothered to learn the German language or even taken a trip to Germany.

the TV show *The Odd Couple* which began with a woman handing Felix Unger a frying pan and telling him to go, so naturally I thought that once you handed them their pan, they would leave.

Instead, within two months of my leaving, his towering, freakishly large-boned Hawaiian (with bleached-blond hair)[2] girlfriend whose name I didn't even know (let's call her the Triceratops) moved in.[3] Even worse, I didn't manage to lose a single pound!

"No, you leave," Kurt sneered at me after a record-breaking six-hour fight during which I accused him of never really listening to me, to which he replied, no lie, "I don't have to listen to this!" No trace of irony crossed his cruelly handsome face as he marched dramatically around the living room I had bought and paid for during his ten-year, chronic, terminal unemployment. "I'm the only one who does any work around here!" he proclaimed joblessly. "You think you can live without me, fine, go ahead and try, but I'm not going to let you ruin my house," he announced with a flip of the pretentious long blond ponytail he wore to somehow compensate for his ever-expanding bald spot. "If you stay here, you'd let the place fall apart, and we'd be bankrupt in a month."

Bankrupt!

What you need to know about Kurt is that he considered himself to be an expert on managing money, of course by "managing" he means "hoarding, confiscating, and refusing to spend a nickel" unless it was on golf. The mere earning of money is something he leaves to lesser little worker bees like me.

Yes, I was one of the thirty-five percent of American women who earned more money than her husband. In my case, when I say "more," I, of course, mean some.

---

[2] I do not know for a fact that this giantess is Hawaiian. I was informed of her alleged ethnicity secondhand by friends, and it was also posited at that time that she might be Samoan, or perhaps Balinese. Her ethnicity is immaterial to me, and I do not make any assumptions based on it. I do not judge her based on her ethnicity. I judge her based on her appallingly shoddy hair color maintenance.

[3] Having always jealously admired the overly tall, Kurt had apparently decided the next best thing to being a tall person was to mate with one.

And I had to wonder what our maid and gardener would say about the "I'm the only one who does any work around here" crack.

I was numb as I packed, numb when I woke up my best friend, Kim (at 4 a.m.), and told her I was leaving Kurt. She'd never said a bad word about him, but on hearing the news she barked, "It's about time you left that loser!" and offered me the keys to her guest-house, because she's that kind of friend. I was completely numb as I loaded my car with the handful of items that Kurt let me take.

But when I threw my arms around Thor, our giant, goofily affectionate Doberman pinscher, I wasn't numb at all. I sobbed.

"I'll come back and walk you every day, I promise," I choked, while Thor licked my face in what was his usual desperate attempt to cheer me up. I whispered into the dog's velvety ear, "It's better for you here in your big yard, Thor. But when we sell this place, I'll get a house for just the two of us, okay?"

I knew that my husband wouldn't want our pet. Kurt, who was defensively diminutive at five feet six (an inch taller than I, as he constantly reminded me) had always longed to be physically intimidating and wanted Thor to be a menacing guard dog, willing to attack on command. Instead, Thor was a clumsy affable drooler who adored me and whose only attack behavior would have consisted of driving intruders mad by relentlessly demanding they "play fetch." In fact, the only "trick" that Thor had ever learned was that whenever he sat, he would pass gas. So I trained him to sit by shouting the command, "Thor! Fart!" and he would obediently both sit and fart simultaneously. My friends and I found this hilarious. (Kurt thought it was "immature," which was technically true, but in my opinion missed the point entirely.)

Kim was waiting up for me in her giant kitchen when I arrived. She was a successful TV executive who had been my boss for a number of years and remained bossy around me thereafter. She lived on a large country estate, with many outbuildings, raising her three boys with her husband, Barnaby. Kim had wavy, shoulder-length dark hair, and the same long, coltish, lean legs as the thoroughbred horses on which she spent a fortune and kept in a large barn at her giant cozy suburban home in Hidden Hills. She also had a brittle and sarcastic personality which wasn't helped by the fact that she'd been trying (unsuccessfully) to quit smoking for the past three years. But the look on her face as she stood there in her door-way—before sunrise—was only kind and loving and understanding, and the hug she gave me let me know I was welcome to stay as long as I needed.

I don't know if other people do this, but I always think about which famous TV or movie star would be best to play the major players in the (blockbuster) movie of my own life. For example, my friend Kim would be played to sardonic perfection by Barbara Stanwyck, just as she was in the Preston Sturges classic *The Lady Eve.*

After a few months spent metaphorically licking my wounds (while physically licking my Hershey bars) I moved out of Kim's guesthouse and got an apartment in the hot and hideous San Fernando Valley, Studio City to be exact.

I kept my promise to Thor and still went back to the starkly modern, Bauhaus inspired Beverly Hills home (that I paid for!) daily, to walk him.

On a sunny California Friday, I was driving in my old neighborhood and saw a giant fluorescent sign proclaiming SATURDAY! YARD SALE! EVERYTHING MUST GO! Like any normal urban vulture, I eagerly looked for the details on the address and time of the sale, knowing fully that the domestic failures of others often resulted in absurdly low-priced barely used Cuisinarts, or delicate little cashmere twin sets whose only crime was having been purchased by some castrating mother-in-law with a big Neiman's credit limit and no sense of emotional boundaries.

Imagine my surprise when I discovered that the yard sale in question was to be held in my very own yard. The EVERYTHING that MUST GO! was EVERYTHING I HAD PAID FOR!

This called for an emergency meeting of the Grrl Genius Club.

My Grrl Genius Club consists of four strong-minded women who understand the importance of wine, chocolate, and talking a thing to death. The one rule of the club was this: We called ourselves geniuses no matter what. Our genius status was irrevocable, even when we ended up situations like the one I currently was in—contemplating having the emotional detritus of my marriage, in the form of old toaster ovens and used lawn chairs, laid out on the manicured lawn I worked fourteen-hour days to buy and have lovingly groomed by Guillermo, who in his disaster-plagued home country of El Salvador was a medical doctor, but here in L.A. was a gardener.

In thinking about the yard sale that was going to be held on the yard I had paid for, to sell things I had paid for, I contemplated the difference between my gardener Guillermo and my soon-to-be-ex-husband. Kurt was a man for whom no job was good enough, a man who believed the only reason he wasn't a show-biz millionaire was because people were out to get him. He once tried to tell me that people in Hollywood were prejudiced against him because he was Lutheran. He theorized that Hollywood was a town run by Jewish men, and they all hated Lutherans.

I should have learned (from little things like World War II) that when bossy Aryan guys start blaming Jews for their problems, logic goes out the window. Kurt truly believed that the reason he hadn't made a success of a career in show business was due to this horrifying prejudice. As the only child of a cloyingly doting mother, he simply couldn't believe that Hollywood had failed to hand him a brilliant career that required no effort beyond his mere existence. I would occasionally make the crazy suggestion that the reason he didn't have a successful career was because he didn't have, well, a job. I thought, foolishly, that a "job" would be a good place to start something like a "career."

On the other hand, Guillermo, my gardener, was grateful to work at any job, no matter how lowly, in order to care for his family. I never heard Guillermo say that the reason he wasn't a doctor in America was because he wasn't Jewish. He said he wasn't a doctor in America because he needed to pass his medical boards, which he eventually did. This leads me to my first relationship tip.

Grrl Genius Relationship Tip

When you have more respect for the man you pay to mow your lawn than you have for the man you married, it's time to end the relationship.

Grrl Genius Relationship Tip Corollary

(With the husband, not the gardener.)

Besides Kim and me, the Grrl Genius Club consisted of Vonnie and Amelia. Like many Grrl Genius Club meetings, this one was held in Vonnie's incense-infused cozy Hollywood Hills cottage. Over pinot grigio and homemade chocolate cupcakes, this matter of the Divorce Yard Sale was discussed with the grave attention it deserved.

Vonnie lounged on a pillow-strewn divan, casually running her finger through the thick, deep, dark icing on the top of her cupcake, allowing it to make furrows and ridges not unlike those that marked the acreage of her family farm back in Iowa. "Go know," she said. "That ex of yours doesn't have the good sense God gave a squirrel."

Vonnie was a widow and a TV actress in her fifties who played a plain-talkin' secretary on a famous 1970s sitcom and now made her living lending her folksy, "vaguely familiar but I can't place it," voice to ads for everything from floor wax to dessert topping. Vonnie was sassy, frighteningly honest, and enormously tall, with flame-red hair that she wore in a short, defiantly spiky hairdo. She was like an Amazonian Lucille Ball, but the kind of Lucille Ball who would have told Ricky she didn't care what he said, she was going to be in the show! Vonnie never lost her Iowa good sense, which she coupled with the fatalistic detachment she learned in her chosen religion of Buddhism. She was an inspiration to all of us, because after a long time searching, she found her true love, Eldon, when she turned forty-three. Ten years later, Eldon had the temerity to "up and die on her." Three years after his death, she still grieved his loss on a daily basis.

"I just can't believe he moved his frigging girlfriend into your house that you bought and paid for," said Kim, nervously fiddling with a cigarette as she manically chewed on both cupcake and a double dose of Nicorette gum.

"Well, I'm going to that yard sale," Amelia announced.

"I think we should all go," agreed Vonnie with typical loyalty.

"No, that's a bad idea. He'll recognize you and Kim," Amelia said. "He doesn't know me—I can be a more effective spy if I go alone."

Amelia was an exotic-looking black woman with dreadlocks, who favored starkly stylish clothing. She was a very high-end interior designer to the stars, specializing in the postmodern houses of Richard Lautner, who was the most favored architect among the wealthiest people in L.A. She had dramatic features and impeccable posture and always carried herself like deposed African royalty. In the movie of my life, she could be played by none other than Angela Bassett, who is so beautiful and interesting that she just makes everyone else (me) embarrassed to be white and dull and Midwestern. Amelia was Texas-raised, and had been for ten years the domestic partner of one of America's top female performers, the stand-up comedienne and talk-show host Clarissa McDaniels. Amelia's relationship with Clarissa had broken up over a year ago, in a flurry of tabloid coverage. I learned from Amelia a critical piece of Grrl Genius relationship advice I am going to pass along to you, gentle readers.

Grrl Genius Relationship Tip

If you must get a divorce, try to get divorced from a woman.

Grrl Genius Relationship Tip Corollary

This may not be practical for everybody.

I took another hit of frosting. I swallowed the chocolate and looked at my Grrl Genius friends. Their love and support for me was overwhelming and almost, but not quite, as comforting as the opiate of Valrona 70 percent cocoa solids cocoa mixed with sugar, butter, and pure cream. I was a rich woman to have friends and frostings like these.

"I can't believe you would do that for me, Amelia. I can't believe that you would be willing to infiltrate my yard sale," I gushed tearfully, feeling very emotional because there were only two cupcakes left.

"Well, of course. It's the least I can do. Besides, you have good stuff. If he's unloading those gorgeous wicker chairs, I want to get my bid in."

"I can't believe I am such a loser, I can't believe I'm such an idiot to have married him," I wailed pathetically.

"Sweetie, you've got to buck up, I can't hear this from you. You're supposed to be a Grrl Genius, and to me that means having the genius to admit when you've been an idiot and then learning from your mistakes," Vonnie insisted. "Now eat your cupcakes and stop blubbering."

She was absolutely right. About the cupcakes anyway.

I have a brain and a uterus, and I use both.
—Patricia Schroeder

On the morning of the yard sale, I was on a breakfast date with a man named Ben. If my life were a movie, I imagine that Ben would be played by the pasty-faced and weasely but nonetheless brilliantly talented Philip Seymour Hoffman.

Now, I wasn't a relationship expert at the time, but my instinct to make a breakfast date with Ben was excellent. Now that I am a fully credentialed (by me!) relationship expert, I can tell you that breakfast dates are the easiest way to dispense with a man who insists on asking you out, even though you know for a stone-cold fact that he is gay.

Ben was a TV sitcom writer I'd known for years who would insist on greeting me every time he saw me at the bar in the Hollywood Improv with an enormous hug, an unwelcome smack on the lips, and the following phrases: "This woman is the most amazing woman in L.A.! If she weren't married, I'd marry her, whether she wanted to or not!"

"Yeah, Cathryn is totally pretty and smart," agreed Tyler, the adorable twenty-four-year-old bouncer at the club, "but she's totally married, so, you know, back off."

Tyler was one of those people who just loved his job. He loved being a bouncer, whether it was for the club or for people's failing marriages. It was very endearing. In the movie of my life, he could be played only by Ashton Kutcher.

Ben's ridiculous "I'd marry her whether she wanted to or not" statement would normally arouse my post-feminist ire. What was he thinking, that if I was unwilling, perhaps he could clinch the deal by giving my father a goat or some shiny trinkets? I didn't take offense, though, because Ben was so totally, completely, still-in-the-closet, obviously gay.

The last time he made his proclamation, we were standing in a large clot of people and my childhood friend and surrogate big brother Tommy boomed out, "Well, Ben, it's your lucky day! Cathryn just filed for divorce!"

The look of mute horror that filled Ben's face was truly pitiable. Now he would have to make good on his boast and marry me, whether I wanted to or not. Or at least ask me out. When he did ask me out later in the evening, with all the verve and enthusiasm of a second grader who has wet his pants and must tell the teacher, I decided to let him off the hook and suggested the (much less threatening) breakfast.

Because Ben is gay.

You might be wondering how can I so surely and swiftly decide the sexual orientation of others without any empirical evidence whatsoever? It is easy, and you can do it, too! All it takes is my patented (pending):

Grrl Genius Male Sexual Preference Determinator System™

1. Face the subject in question; look him directly in the eyes.
2. Ask him whom he thought was more attractive on *Gilligan's Island*. Ginger or Mary Ann?
3. If he says Ginger, he's gay.

Ben answered "Ginger"—hence, he is gay. The reasons for this are both psychologically intricate and totally made up, but the fact is, it works, and it can save you a lot of time. (If he answers, "Gilligan," it's even faster.)

Now, if you are me (or sadly, someone like me), you need to ask yourself one more question: Do I find him sexually attractive?

If the answer is yes, he may also be gay.

Why is this? In my case, it is because when I was a mere slip of a girl, I met the man I always introduce people to as, "My best friend since second grade, Tommy." Tommy is the proverbial tall, dark, and handsome man. He's stylish, he's funny, he's kind, he's a great dancer—he is the perfect man and has always been the friend I could count on, no matter what. Of course, Tommy should be played by Rock Hudson. (Some would argue that Tommy should be played by Richard Chamberlain, but I always knew that Richard Chamberlain was gay: Tommy's gayness came as a horrifying, life-altering shock.)

I loved Tommy all my life, and when the hormones of adolescence struck like a force-five hurricane, I fell *in* love with him. He did not fall in love with me, because he is (and always has been) gay. Hence, I blame him for the fact that my brain has been prewired to fall in love with gay men.

He says he refuses to accept the responsibility for this.

So, it was while having breakfast with (gay) Ben, that I got the call from Amelia, at the yard sale. I excused myself from the table, leaving Ben with his pumpkin pancakes and the paperback David Sedaris book I brought, hoping he'd leaf through it and realize that he could still be a comedy writer if he finally and joyously declared his homosexuality and stopped torturing straight women everywhere with his appalling lack of sexual interest in them.

Amelia was in a full-blown snit. "Oh, my God, Cathryn, you aren't going to believe this! I just left the sale. You are so not going to be happy about this—I mean, it's unbelievable! You won't believe it!" she shrieked.

"Okay, I get I won't believe it, but just tell me anyway!" I said.

"Well, first of all, he is selling the most embarrassing stuff. I mean, he's selling good stuff, I got that crepe maker you told me about, but also, and I am not even kidding about this, he is selling, well, like one of the things he is selling is your dead cat's used litter box. Like, for a dollar."

I felt a rush of shame that had gone unequaled since the time I strode confidently across the stage at a high school assembly back in Minnesota, unaware of the fact that Lars Benequist had taped a sign to my back saying FAT BUTT! The idea that my fancy Beverly Hills neighbors, by whom I had always felt outclassed, were gathered around my front lawn scrutinizing a used, scratched, cat urine–stained poo receptacle was excruciating to me.

Amelia's voice continued to screech in my ear, "So this guy tried to give him fifty cents for the cat box, but Kurt said he wouldn't take less than seventy-five cents. For a used cat box! Can you believe it?"

Unfortunately, I could. I could believe it. I could hear every last word of the haggling over the German-made cat box, all of Kurt's stubborn justifications for why it was worth a whopping seventy-five cents: the durability of the plastic, the inconsequential nature of the stains and scratches. I could see him squinting his oddly pale blue eyes and hear him bragging that after all it wasn't a used cat box, it was a "vintage" cat box!

"But it gets worse!" Amelia shouted. I could hardly wait. "That big galumphing bleach-blond Hawaiian girlfriend of his is helping him. She's sitting in a lawn chair, with a ciggy butt hanging out of her mouth, surrounded by—and I don't really understand this—a lot of your lingerie. I know it must be yours, because it's all tiny and it can't possibly be hers. Why does she have your lingerie, Cathryn?"

The Salvation Army. I had gone back to the house and packed up bags of lingerie for the Salvation Army. I didn't want to keep lingerie in which I had made love to my husband, so I gave away ten years of perfect little La Perla nightgowns and Cosabella camisoles to the Salvation Army.

I had forgotten to call for a pickup.

Amelia was still ranting on. "Well she's sitting there, arguing with people about your lingerie. Some little Vietnamese woman just offered her five dollars for a silk robe. The woman was all, 'Fie dollar, I give you fie dollar!' and she was all, 'That's a hundred percent silk Cacharel robe. That robe goes for a hundred and fifty at Saks, I could go sell that at a high-end resale shop for at least fifty dollars, so I'm not taking less than ten!' Can you believe it? The Triceratops is all uppity about your lingerie!"

"At least my underwear is going for more than the cat box," I said, dully.

"What kind of woman is she?" Amelia continued. "I mean, so was he all, 'Hey, wanna come spend Saturday selling my ex's underwear that she used to wear to have sex with me?' and then was she all, 'Oh, my God, I would so totally love to sit in a lawn chair and haggle with poor immigrants about the price of my boyfriend's wife's underwear—honestly, what could be more frigging delightful!'"

As Amelia yammered on about the Jerry Springer–esque bacchanal taking place on my front lawn, I was frozen in horror. Sometimes people use the expression "like a deer caught in headlights" to describe a person who is struck immobile. I felt more like the deer after the headlights had hit it. I was that stunned.

"Amelia, thanks, thanks a ton," I said, "but I've got to go." I hung up and shut off the phone.

My gay date came over from our table to see if the fact that my face was flushed, my eyes were wild, and that I was punching the wall meant there was something wrong.

"Are you okay?" Ben asked tentatively.

"My soon-to-be-ex-husband's girlfriend is selling my old underwear on my front lawn. Apparently, she's getting good prices for it."

He shuffled uncomfortably. "Um, oh, I should probably go," he stated hopefully.

I decided to let him off the hook. "Yeah, that's probably a good idea," I agreed. "You know, I know you didn't really want to go out with me, but it was nice of you to ask me, seriously."

He suddenly radiated the kind of relief you see only in freed hostages. He quickly leaned in for another of his unwelcome mouth kisses, but I deftly turned my cheek, and that's where his rubbery, insincere, not-even-close-to-being-heterosexual lips landed.

"I hope you find a nice guy," he said. "Really I do."

"I hope the same for you," I countered. Either he didn't get it, or he had just joyously embraced his obvious homosexuality, because he merely nodded his head and picked up the check like it was a pardon from the governor and left to pay the cashier.

I'm just a person trapped inside a woman's body.
—Elayne Boosler

It was at this very moment in my life, as I sat in an outdoor café, listlessly cramming cold pumpkin pancakes into my mouth, that I had a life-altering revelation.

Not enough chocolate is served at breakfast.

A Grrl Genius "Love Is Important But Chocolate Is Essential" Handy Chocolate Fun Fact

To the Aztecs who first discovered it, chocolate was a source of spiritual wisdom, energy, and enhanced sexual powers. The drink was thought to be a pre-Viagra-era aid to sexual pleasure and potency for both men and women. Montezuma, who is sadly best remembered for a virulent strain of tourist diarrhea, reportedly always drank flagons of chocolate before entering his harem in order to fortify his libido for lovemaking.

After ordering a large hot chocolate, I had another, even bigger life-altering revelation.

I was a complete failure at sex and relationships. My life was a relationship disaster area. Too bad FEMA didn't provide emergency funding for failed relationships, because nobody qualified more than me. I had married the kind of man who pimps out his girlfriend to sell his wife's used lingerie. I was a failure at sex and relationships, an idiot, a loser.

A Grrl Genius "People Who've Made Worse Relationship Mistakes Than You" Moment

A jury in Nashville, Tennessee, convicted Raymond Mitchell III, forty-five, of tricking women into blindfolding themselves and having sex with him by

21

claiming to be their boyfriends. Prosecutors said that most of the hundreds of women that Mitchell called hung up, but of the thirty who reported the encounters to police, eight said they had sex with the caller.

———

"Admit when you've been an idiot, and learn from your mistakes," Vonnie's voice admonished in my head.

She was right. I had made so many mistakes with men that I was qualified to be an undisputable expert, a Grrl Genius of Sex and Relationships. Now, as a fully credentialed (by me!) expert, I made the executive decision that I needed ten laws, the Grrl Genius Laws of Sex and Relationships. I decided on ten laws because I vaguely remembered that in Girl Scouts there had been ten laws (Girl Scouts being the only endeavor in my life I ever signed up for knowing from the outset that it would involve terrible outfits) and I figured that if ten laws were good for the Girl Scouts, well it was good for the Grrl Geniuses, too. Each of these laws, which were made up exclusively by me, conveniently makes up a chapter in this "Self-Help Novel."[4]

Right there in the café, I spoke the first law out loud: "A Grrl Genius declares herself to be a genius of sex and relationships, regardless of her (dismal) track record."

Then I ordered a big slice of their very excellent chocolate cake—for breakfast!

———

Test Your Grrl Genius Relationship IQ

When meeting a man for the first time, you know he is a potential date if he
  a. Actually listens to what you say and gives thoughtful responses.
  b. Seems sullen and moody, like he is waiting for the right Grrl to draw him out.
  c. Breathes oxygen and exhales carbon dioxide.

———

[4] This book is a "Self-Help Novel" because (a) it is full of practical tips and information that has the power to make your love life 1,000 times better (actual figure) and (b) it's a novel because the story part of the book is not true (fiction). Hence, "Self-Help Novel."

Your ideal relationship with a man can best be described as something that includes
- **a.** A passionate but intellectually stimulating friendship.
- **b.** Verbal interplay that causes you to question the obviously artificial value system of your parents and the false gods of your hypocritical religion.
- **c.** No restraining orders.

The best time to meet your boyfriend's family is
- **a.** After the first time you sleep together, secure in the knowledge that although you don't know his middle name yet, you are obviously soul mates who made an agreement on an astral plane to run into each other getting smoothies at the Jamba Juice.
- **b.** After he breaks up with you and you decide to "drop in" on his family on Christmas Eve, just because you had an "errand to run" in central Ohio.
- **c.** As soon as his dad is up for parole.

The best way to know if the man you are dating is the man you should marry is
- **a.** If you are sure that you are sexually, emotionally, financially, and spiritually compatible.
- **b.** If you can honestly answer yes to the question, "Would I risk my own life for this person's safety?"
- **c.** If there was that one time that he saved a baby bunny that had fallen in your parents' swimming pool and he was so nice to the bunny and it made you think hey, if he was nice to a baby bunny, he'd probably be nice to a baby person.

For Each a Answer: Score 10 points
For Each b Answer: Score 5 points
For Each c Answer: Score 1 point

20 to 40 points: You're a Grrl Genius of relationships and should probably be writing this book instead of me.

10 to 20 points: You're a Grrl Genius of relationships, but really need this book.

4 to 10 points: You're a Grrl Genius of relationships because I say anybody can be a Grrl Genius of whatever she wants, as long as she declares herself accordingly; but seriously, read this book, live it, or your life will be an endless vale of tears, and I'm not just saying that to sell books, although I do have a lot of debt. The point is, don't let yourself be trapped in a series of bad relationships—declare your genius, so that you, too, can find an adorable, Enlightened Male of your very own!

———————

I can't mate in captivity.
—Gloria Steinem

———————

The Grrl Genius Wild Sexual Kingdom

The diminutive and graceful male sea horse *(Hippocampus breviceps)* is the greatest Enlightened Male of the animal kingdom. Often referred to as the "Alan Alda of the Ocean" (as opposed to the pansexual and hedonistic bonobo chimp which is often referred to as the "Andrew Dice Clay of the Jungle") the male sea horse is the only male on earth known to gestate and birth live young.

The transfer of the sea horse fetuses from the Grrl Genius sea horse to the Enlightened Male sea horse occurs during a delicate and beautiful mating dance, in which the female deposits the fetuses into the male's gestation pouch through a small throat opening, the male "swallows" the young, and then, after they have reached maturity, "gags" them back up again.

Oftentimes, in human relationships, a human Grrl Genius has to "swallow" more than she'd care to, as well. When your own emotional gag reflex just isn't enough, that's where the rock-solid emotional backing of the Grrl Genius Sex and Relationship Laws comes in, providing you with a sound plan for navigating the treacherous waters of love, and helping you to find an Enlightened Male who really does do half the work.

———

Sex is never an emergency.
            —Elaine Pierson

The abject humiliation of the panty yard sale provided the metaphorical kick in the panties I needed to finally go see Bob Burns, the attorney that Kim had recommended, and formally file for divorce. Since leaving the house in Beverly Hills, I had continued to pay all the bills, and I was looking forward to having the court step in and force Kurt to get serious about finding a job so he could take care of his share of the expenses. It was bad enough to be supporting him, but supporting the lingerie-selling Triceratops as well was really more than I could take.

As always, the most difficult part of getting into action was deciding what to wear. As I stepped into the hushed reception area of the law firm, I was feeling very good about how I was dressed. I always draw strength in difficult situations by choosing a famous movie star fashion icon. Naturally, on the day I filed for divorce, I chose brainy and feisty Katharine Hepburn from *Adam's Rib*. My tweed checked Anna Sui suit with a flirty short skirt and a cunning little back belt evoked the perfect Hepburn-esque combination of seriousness and insouciance, reflecting exactly the impeccably tailored yet whimsically chic fashion sense you'd expect from a woman like me who is both a dismal failure at relationships and yet a self-proclaimed expert of same.

The reception area of the law office was designed so that every visible surface was either marble or wood or glass or leather. I started to wonder if this was meant to represent something metaphorical about the law. Like, how the law is smooth and shiny. Like, how the law resists stains and spills.

The artwork in the lawyer's office was that handmade paper stuff that looks as if someone took an entire roll of toilet paper, shoved it into his bathtub with water and a lot of grass clippings until the thing was completely paper soup, then scooped up the whole mess, laid it out on his back deck until it dried up real nice and crispy, then cut it into pieces, put those pieces into five-hundred-dollar aluminum-and-glass frames, and sold them for a fortune to some lawyer.

I started to wonder if the artwork was supposed to represent something metaphorical about the law. Like, how you can pay a ridiculous amount of money and in the end wind up with nothing more than a huge dried-up spit wad.

When my strangely large and disheveled attorney came to fetch me from the waiting room I began to lose confidence, mostly because he didn't look very much like Spencer Tracy in *Adam's Rib,* as I had hoped. He looked more like that Barry Sheck guy who defended O. J., the one with a nose shaped like a penis. Not that my attorney's nose was shaped like a penis. Although when I started thinking about this, I started to wonder about the idea that if you have a nose that is shaped like a penis, is the converse true, and must you therefore have a penis that is shaped like a nose and if so, would a sneeze be a . . .

"Ms. Michon?"

I realized that I had been spacing out on this whole penis-nose dilemma as my attorney had been politely waiting for me to follow him into his even shinier and more stain-proof inner office.

At this point I began to regain my senses, and exactly as Katharine Hepburn would have done, I began to crisply outline the essential facts of my very good case. I explained, with all the professionalism my Anna Sui suit implied, the basic fact that my ex-husband had been chronically unemployed for the ten years of our marriage. "Obviously," I stated rationally, "this indicates that the money that was earned would obviously belong to the person who earned it, which would obviously be me. We have no children, but I would be willing to consider sharing custody of our dog, though, to be honest, I am quite sure that Kurt is not interested in the dog at all. Obviously this is more than fair and should be relatively simple."

Having so clearly outlined the facts, I felt that we should be able to resolve this matter in one, maybe two hours of his insanely expensive attorney time.

When my (did I mention quite unattractive?) mammoth of an attorney stopped laughing, he wiped the tears from his rodent red eyes and the spittle from the corners of his mouth where it clung like fake cobwebs in a church basement Halloween spook house.

Suddenly the famous person my attorney reminded me of was Jabba the Hutt from *Star Wars*.

Jabba the Attorney turned his red puffy face toward me, where I could watch the capillaries on his nose breaking in real time, and began a ridiculous wheezing recitation of "facts" about divorce in California, based on "the law."

"California is a Community-Property State," he intoned eerily, as though it were the title of a real crummy horror movie, which later I learned it really should be. "That means that any money earned during the marriage belongs to both of you equally. Furthermore, because your husband made less money than you, and because you were married for ten years, that means he will be entitled to maintenance for life."

"Maintenance," I repeated, honestly thinking he must be talking about the car or something.

"Support payments, alimony."

"Alimony?" I sputtered, wondering why, if it's a good lifesaving idea to have heart defibrillators on airplanes to revive passengers, why then it isn't an equally good idea to have convenient squirt bottles of Hershey's chocolate syrup on lawyers' desks to revive female divorce clients? "For life?" I asked. "Like, whose life?"

"Yours, of course." The dancing capillaries on his obviously alcoholic nose began forming into little red fingers that seemed to be pointing at me and echoing "Yours! Yours! Yours!" Well, that's how it seemed to me, although I could have been hallucinating from the lack of chocolate.

"I get women like you in here every day. Completely clueless. You know, these laws were put in place to protect women. By feminists. So how do you like your feminism now?" he inquired with what seemed to me to be undue relish.

I recovered, seeing his obvious mistake. "I think you've misunderstood me," I corrected, somewhat patronizingly. "You see, we don't have children, so, you know, he could have worked. He wasn't a, you know, housewife, or househusband, or whatever. He was just a guy who refused to get a job. So obviously, he wouldn't be entitled to alimony."

"Doesn't matter," said Jabba the Attorney.

"But I'm wearing a really cute Anna Sui suit!" I screeched. "And how come there's no chocolate here!"

After that highly reasoned retort, the conversation devolved into an endless screed from the attorney as to how much everything was going to cost me, including how much it was going to cost me for him to tell me how much it was going to cost me.

As he droned on and on, I remembered that there was, I was pretty sure, half an M&M in the bottom of my purse. After burrowing through the lipsticks, perfume samples, tampons, and receipts for lipsticks, perfume, and tampons, I found the grit-covered, red, candy-coated half orb of rotten chocolate. I popped it the way a double agent pops a cyanide capsule, and it revived me to the extent that I could hear his last question to me.

"I just gotta ask you, I mean, the guy didn't work at any regular job for a decade, so, you know, what were you thinking?" Jabba asked.

In a rare and regrettable burst of honesty I said, "I thought I could fix him with my good loving."

As a newly anointed Sex and Relationship Expert I had begun to learn my (very expensive) lesson.

Grrl Genius Relationship Tip

You can't fix anyone! You'll be lucky if you fix yourself!

Grrl Genius Relationship Tip Corollary

Never go to a divorce attorney without chocolate.

Chapter 2

A Grrl Genius Stays Away from "Bad Boys"

A girl can wait for the right man to come along,
but in the meantime, that still doesn't mean she can't
have a wonderful time with all the wrong ones.
—Cher

IN SECOND grade, Kirsten Overgaard was the most beautiful girl in class. She was blond, even by Minnesota standards. In Minnesota, you are blond if your hair is the same color as the freshly fallen snow. In Minnesota, Lisa Kudrow, Jennifer Aniston, and Courteney Cox-Arquette would be known as "the three brunette girls from *Friends*." Kirsten Overgaard's silky white-blond hair fell into perfect ringlets. The boys loved her. We didn't know that her mother, Lorna, a hairdresser, spent every morning torturing Kirsten by frying her hair into sausage curls with a curling iron. We thought she was born perfect, and we (a) hated her and (b) wanted to be her.

I begged my mother to get me a perm, so my stick-straight brunette (legally blond in the other forty-nine states) hair would fall into perfect ringlets and boys would love me, too. (If all the other girls hated me, well, Kirsten Overgaard and I would exchange knowing glances, toss back our perfect hair, and probably go on national tour with ABBA.) As I sat in the beauty salon, choking and gasping from the toxic chemicals that inflamed my tender scalp, I knew that the pain would be worth it, and I would finally be loved.

Instead, the love I received came in the form of boys teasing me because I had gotten a bad perm.

I looked like my hair had been run over by a Zamboni. Kirsten Overgaard made fun of me, and I became known as "the girl with the crazy hair." (Note: In Minnesota, with their typical Lutheran understatement, "crazy" and "satanically evil" are synonymous.) What I should have learned from this is that beauty does not get you true love, but what I learned instead was that perms did not get you true beauty.

I'm tired of all this nonsense about beauty being only skin deep. That's deep enough. What do you want, an adorable pancreas?

—Jean Kerr

The Grrl Genius In-Depth Analysis of the Love Lives of World-Class Beautiful Women

Woman	How Beautiful	What Happened	How It Ended Up	Happiness Quotient 1 to 10
Princess Diana	The world's most photographed woman.	Her husband cheated on her from day one with a woman twice her age.	Two cute kids. Public humiliation, loss of royal title, divorce, giving back of tiaras, untimely death.	2
Audrey Hepburn	The most elegant and stylish movie star ever, plus no cellulite.	Her husband cheated on her with less attractive actress who was starring in the same movie as she.	One cute kid. Divorce. But she still got to be a movie star with no cellulite, died gracefully at 63.	5
continued	*continued*	*continued*	*continued*	*continued*

Woman	How Beautiful	What Happened	How It Ended Up	Happiness Quotient 1 to 10
Marilyn Monroe	An icon of femininity, still referred to as the original sex symbol.	Married 3 times, slept with the president.	Divorced 3 times, may have been killed for sleeping with the president. Had cellulite but no one noticed due to tremendously large breasts.	1
Jackie Kennedy	Often considered to be the most fashionable woman of the twentieth century.	Had cool but low-paying job as a photographer, then became First Lady. Her husband constantly cheated on her with many, including Marilyn Monroe, the original sex symbol.	Two cute kids. Widowed, married old rich Greek guy who cheated on her, divorced but made a lot of money on it, went back to cool but low-paying job in publishing. Had nice boyfriend and very little cellulite when she died.	4
Elizabeth Hurley	Supermodel.	Lived with handsome English movie star who cheated on her with a hooker.	Public humiliation, breakup, cute baby by billionaire father. No cellulite.	4
Kirsten Overgaard	Prettiest girl in high school. I used to shed actual bitter tears of jealousy at night, wishing that I could be her, or that *continued*	Elected some kind of Queen, either Prom or Homecoming but how would I know since I didn't go anyway. *continued*	Married Prom (or Homecoming) King, captain of the football team who now drives the town snowplow in winter and drinks *continued*	8, oddly Kirsten seems content, but she's probably faking it. *continued*

32

Woman	How Beautiful	What Happened	How It Ended Up	Happiness Quotient 1 to 10
	she would die, or that I could be her best friend.		beer all summer because there's no snow. Kirsten has a litter of perfect white-haired children, and her husband and kids boss her around, and I'll bet she's sorry now she laughed at my perm!	

Now let's scientifically analyze some normal-looking women.

The Love Lives of More Normal-Looking Women

Woman	How Beautiful	What Happened	How It Ended Up	Happiness Quotient 1 to 10
My aunt Rita	Considerably overweight, wears the same sweatsuit in five different colors, thinks hair color and makeup are "a total waste of time." No one ever sees her thighs, so cellulite issue is moot point.	Met my uncle Roy at a bait shop in northern Minnesota. He fell in love with her when he watched her gut a walleyed pike.	They've been married for forty-six years and travel the country in an RV with a bumper sticker that reads, IF THE RV'S A ROCKIN', DON'T COME A-KNOCKIN'	8
My mother	A beautiful woman who has aged normally without	My dad fell in love with her, saying she was the most	My dad says that she is still the most beautiful woman he	9
continued	continued	continued	continued	continued

Woman	How Beautiful	What Happened	How It Ended Up	Happiness Quotient 1 to 10
	plastic surgery, a size 12 (the average size of a woman in America and considered a "plus size" by the fashion industry). Has gray hair. Has cellulite like everyone in our family.	beautiful woman he had ever seen. He also said she was the smartest person he ever met.	has ever seen. He still says she is the smartest person he ever met. They go on romantic getaways and appear to have an active sex life (but only to humiliate me).	
Cheryl, the lady who owns the deli down the street from me	Her doctor says she is "morbidly obese." She says that's crazy because she is actually "cheerfully obese," and it's the doctor who's acting all morbid.	Her husband Eli is fifteen years older than she is and refers to her as "my child bride."	Eli can't believe Cheryl loves him. He worries that she is "wasting away." Husband wishes she had more cellulite.	9
Me	Certainly no supermodel. Spends a fortune on trying to look better. Can't really do anything about her cellulite.	Married a man who didn't have a full-time job for years on end and who refused to go to counseling when his wife said she was miserable due to his lack of ambition, unwillingness to have sex, and constant criticism of her.	Got divorced. Has yet to lose postmarital virginity. Terrified of making the same mistake again. Feels that if she were as beautiful as Audrey Hepburn, her life would have worked out differently but is obviously wrong. (See chart above.) Accepts that beauty is not the key to true love but still would like to get rid of cellulite.	3

So, setting aside for the moment the false notion that I was a failure at relationships because I wasn't beautiful enough, I was forced to consider other causes for the never-ending train of agony that was my love life. Maybe, just maybe, it had something to do with my choice of men. Maybe it had to do with the fact that when I wasn't falling in love with gay men who would always admire my outfits but never want to take them off me, I was falling for "bad boys."

Here is a little quiz to help you determine who is a bad boy, and who is not.

The Grrl Genius Bad Boy Identifier Quiz

Who Is the Bad Boy?

    a. Doug, a heroic firefighter who runs into burning buildings in a very cute outfit to save lives, doesn't smoke, drinks very sparingly, and works out every day.

    b. Ian, a research scientist who is working on a cure for a rare kind of bone cancer. He loves to cook gourmet meals and go to the symphony. His shirts have a very high thread count.

    c. Steve, a former (so he says) drug addict with a lip ring who now works as a drug rehab counselor, spending all his time with other people who have lied and cheated and stolen to support their repulsive habits. His hobby is reading weirdo science-fiction novels.

The answer is . . . *They are all bad boys.*

Do you know why? Because every single one of them does the same thing. Says he will call, and then doesn't. Doug is always too busy "saving lives" to call, except other firefighters manage to make phone calls when they aren't running into burning buildings in *their* cute outfits.

Ian claims to be too caught up in his, you know, "cancer curing," to return a phone call, and then calls at the last minute to see if you're free to join him and his high-thread-count shirt help him unwind from, you know, "curing cancer."

Steve is always running off to bail some addict out of the pokey, but he uses it as an excuse to never commit to a plan with *you*. Probably the only way he'll return your call is if *you're* calling from the pokey. Plus, have you ever tried to kiss someone with a lip ring? Eeew!

Do not be discouraged. It is easier than you think to spot a nice man who is not a bad boy.

A nice man is the man who treats you nicely. He calls you and returns your call. He shows up when he said he would.

Most important, he says the three little words that every Grrl Genius longs to hear. He is able to say, "I am sorry."

––––––––

Of course, saying you'll stay away from bad boys, as Grrl Geniusy as it is, is easier than actually doing it. I mean, remember Doug, the hunky firefighter who was Bad Boy A. in the patented (pending) "Grrl Genius Bad Boy Identifier Quiz"? Suppose he brought his hose over to your house, could you really, truly not let him in?

––––––––

The Grrl Genius Wild Sexual Kingdom

There are many peaceful and monogamous birds in the Animal Kingdom who provide a model for loving human relationships. Mourning doves, sparrows, and finches all have tender and caring courting rituals and share jointly in the nurturing and protecting of their young.

There are, however, a few bad birds. And the baddest of the bird world Bad Boys is the rare male great tit *(Parus calioptrus)*. Ornithologists are usually excited when they see a pair of great tits in the wild, as you can well imagine.

It should come as no surprise to anyone who's ever had to suffer through an episode of *Benny Hill* that great tits make their home in England. While there are also blue tits and mouse tits, it is the great tits who are notorious for being among the very few songbirds that actually murder other songbirds. Male great tits have actually gotten so aggressive that they will steal food from humans, using their sharp beaks to open freshly delivered bottles of milk on people's doorsteps.

You'd think great tits would have their own milk, but of course, they don't.

This tendency for great tits to go wrong (thus becoming killer tits) is avenged only when they themselves become victims of larger birds of prey like hawks or owls. There is almost no sight in nature as ugly as a battle to the death between a pair of big hooters and some killer tits.

It is unfortunate to note that female great tits respond sexually to the most aggressive males, consistently preferring to mate with those males who sing the loudest and longest and generally never let any of the other, lesser tits get a note in edgewise.

Because of this behavior, there is less pair bonding and more promiscuity among great tits than there is among other songbirds, proving that even in the animal kingdom, preference for bad boys gets you nowhere.

The human female also displays a tendency to be attracted to males who are bullies and braggarts, who never shut up, and who take stuff that isn't theirs. Fortunately, it is the wise Grrl Genius who looks past these types of bad boys, remembering that no good comes of loving Bad Boys, and the only killer tits you need are your own.

Of course, I am not the only female who ever fell for a Bad Boy. Let us consider the story of the following two women—women who, against all sense and reason, decided to marry tennis-playing, bad-toupee-wearing brothers Lyle and Erik Menendez after they were both convicted of double homicide!

It serves me right for putting all my eggs into one bastard.
                                        —Dorothy Parker

Yes, amazingly, while broke, in prison for life for double murders, and without their trusty hairpieces, both of these charmers managed to find women who would marry them, even though these marriages would never be consummated and the odds of these guys doing half their share of the household chores were incalculably low.

I don't want to say Mrs. Tammie Menendez and Mrs. Anna Menendez are not Grrl Geniuses, because of course Grrl Geniushood is something that all of us can obtain at any time, though I have to say while these girls are potential Grrl Geniuses, they are also complete morons!

Sure, I was stupid to stay married to a chronically jobless man who constantly criticized me and my career, but anyone who marries a convicted killer is, I am sorry, even less Grrl Geniusy than I was!

Tammie has stayed with Erik, and recently sold her home to help pay for his continued legal defense. At least Anna had the good sense to leave Lyle, but her reasoning may have been a little flawed, she left him not because he was a confessed double murderer, but because she found out that he was writing to another woman from his double murderer's prison cell. In my book, that is a somewhat lesser offense.

In researching this topic, I found out that there are many women who have married felons serving time in prison. There are entire Web sites devoted to finding a man in prison; my personal favorite was Penn Pals, although I was surprised to discover that there was no Match.Con. The Web sites featured all kinds of testimonials from women about why they loved being prisoners of love.

These women are crazy.

Pros and "Cons" of Dating a Convict

Pros	"Cons"
He always calls.	He always calls collect.
Writes long romantic letters.	Ends long romantic letters with requests for naked pictures of you and your friends.
Never leaves the toilet seat up.	Doesn't have a toilet seat.
Understands commitment.	Is already committed.
Works out regularly.	Gets knifed regularly.
Is able to form intimate, caring relationships with other men.	Is forced to form intimate, caring relationships with other men.
Loves to make things by hand.	Things are usually shivs carved out of toothbrushes.
Has a big house.	Is in the big house.

Grrl Genius Relationship Tip

Don't date or marry convicted prisoners.

Grrl Genius Relationship Tip Corollary

Well, maybe you could make an exception if you are one.

All the members of the Grrl Genius club left calls of support before I made my way to the Beverly Hills Courthouse for my first divorce hearing from Kurt, the bad boy I had married.

New message, sent Sunday, June 17, at 6:14 p.m.: "Hey, doll, it's Vonnie. Remember, he can only take your money; your genius is yours to keep. Look, just remember, whatever it costs you, it's worth it! Oh, yeah—and be sure to dress ugly. You need the judge to feel sorry for you. It's like, I know you think the key to everything in this world is looking cute, but in this case you could not be more wrong. The key is to look ugly, dowdy, and poor. Seriously dowdy, like Iowa dowdy. Surely you must have something awful you can wear, or maybe you could borrow something from Kim. All the money that girl has, she always manages to look like year-old Spam on a two-year-old cracker. Whatever. Call me when it's over. . . ."

New message, sent Sunday, June 17, 7:26 p.m.: "Cathryn, it's Amelia. . . . Good luck tomorrow—I know it's all going to work out just fine. Listen, Vonnie told me about the clothes thing, and of course she couldn't be more right. I think you should wear that sort of hideous baggy flowered dress you have that's the color of baby diarrhea. You know, the sort of Sissy Spacek *Coal Miner's Daughter* one that makes your tits look all saggy? Or what about the other one you have that looks like Sissy Spacek in *Carrie,* after the bucket of blood fell on her? Anyway, point is, I know how you always have to dress like a movie star, and I say Sissy Spacek is the way to go on this one. And maybe you can borrow some of that horrifying giant jewelry that Kim's always wearing these days. . . . Just a thought."

New message sent Sunday, June 17, 8:09 p.m.: "Hi, it's Kim. Heard you need to look like shit in order to kick ass at the hearing, so, you know, feel free to borrow anything you need from me. . . . And don't forget to take chocolate!"

A Grrl Genius "Love Is Important But Chocolate Is Essential" Handy Chocolate Fun Fact

Psychiatrists have suggested that the reason that women are the greatest consumers of chocolate, the reason that women are twenty-two more times likely than men to choose chocolate as a mood enhancer and why 50 percent of all women say they would choose chocolate over sex, is because the mechanism that regulates the level of phenylethylamine (a mood-enhancing endorphin) may be faulty in some women. This would explain why women (wisely) have a tendency to binge on chocolate after an emotional upset. It's an instinctive (geniusy) attempt to self-medicate. It's also cheaper and faster-acting than Prozac, without the side effect of loss of sexual desire.

The Beverly Hills Courthouse is one of the many places in Los Angeles that you feel like you have been to a thousand times before, and the fact is, you have. You have seen Erik Estrada standing in front of it as he flashes fluorescently white teeth the size of Sub-Zero refrigerator doors, his massive and impossibly firm thighs striving to break free of the cruel bondage of his standard-issue *CHiPs* khaki pants. You've seen Dick Van Dyke as an elegantly mustachioed doctor, heading through its ornate doors in order to testify in the trial of one of his many murdered friends. You've seen Heather Locklear weeping prettily in front of it as the Mother/Sister/Girlfriend of a Kidnapped Child/Teenage Prostitute/Wrongly Accused Killer in a movie of the week on Lifetime/Lifetime/Lifetime.

As I headed into the courthouse, I was dressed in a chokingly high-necked, snot-green blouse that had the effect of forcibly smashing my breasts so that the nipples pointed in vastly different directions, sort of like the arms of the beloved scarecrow in *The Wizard of Oz.* I wore a heavy, long black skirt that clung to my rear end in such a cruelly tenacious fashion that it looked as though my buttocks were conjoined twins fighting viciously for the window seat in their parents minivan, and I finished it off with the kind of thick-soled loafers that city workers wear when they descend into sewers to hunt alligators.

Today was very important, as it was the preliminary hearing for my divorce. I took the practical measure of calling the daily advice hotline of a genuine Santeria witch who lived in Miami—Rosio the Seer. The recorded voice had a thick and mysterious Puerto Rican accent that reminded me of *West Side Story*, one of my all time favorite movies.

"Hello, *mi'ja*," the recorded voice began. "Today I tell you that if you have problems with someone in your life, someone who is not respecting you, here is the spell of the day for you, *mi'ja*. I want you to take like a piece of tape, write that person's name on it, and then put it on the soles of your shoes, so you are like walking on that person. You will see amazing miracle results from this spell through the power of Rosio and the Blessed Virgin Mother. I will pray for you, *mi'ja*. Good luck!"

Obviously, it was excellent and practical advice.

A Grrl Genius Crazy Sex Fact

A woman successfully sued the city of San Francisco after a cable car accident, which she said turned her into a nymphomaniac who had sex as many as fifty times a week, thus giving new meaning to the phrase "the San Francisco treat."

I was late to my first divorce hearing, as I often am, because I had been having a panicky last-minute pep talk with Kim on my cell phone. As I raced up the courthouse steps, I was conscious of the odd, sticky presence of the bands of tape on the bottom of my shoes.

After accidentally going to traffic court and what looked to be a murder trial, I finally found the right courtroom where Jabba the Attorney, a.k.a. Bob Burns, was waiting for me at the table where Heather Locklear would normally be crying nonstop and somehow managing to not run her mascara. As usual, he looked unnaturally damp and appeared to be wheezing loudly. What appeared to be a decent enough suit appeared shabbily crumpled because of the way he awkwardly shoved into various pockets his PDA, cell phone, notepads, beeper, and something that looked, and smelled, suspiciously like a leftover tuna sandwich.

Kurt and his fifty-something, silver-haired, nattily dressed attorney Drake Nimmer, from the celebrity law firm of Mountebank, Nimmer, Gibson, and Suarez, were ensconced at the table where Dick Van Dyke would normally be sitting. Kurt was wearing a new Armani suit, which had been impeccably tailored to his feather-weight proportions, and naturally had been paid for by me. The judge was seated at the bench. She was a very tall black woman with gorgeous tiny braids of hair elegantly looped into a ponytail that trailed halfway down her back.

"Remember, let me do all the talking. Where have you been, anyway? I tried to call you," Jabba whispered moistly into my ear.

"I know, I know," I said, cutting him off.

The judge began the proceedings. When she spoke, her voice had a British cadence, and a deep, authoritarian timbre, to me she sounded almost freakishly like Sidney Poitier, handsomest man ever, in *To Sir, with Love*. She looked amazingly like the bronze statue of Winged Justice that graced the lobby of the building, and I felt quite certain that her Grrl Genius would guarantee that fairness and truth would prevail, which meant she was on my side.

So naturally I could not have been more wrong.

Jabba looked at me, and I noticed small tributaries of sweat beginning to pour down his face. He leaned over and whispered in my ear, "There's been a few changes, and well, in addition to half the marital assets, which we knew about, they filed a motion for support, because Kurt is an alcoholic . . . ," he dribbled off.

"What!" I shrieked.

Alimony! There had been no mention of alimony from Kurt's attorney up until now. We had assumed that he was going to be content with half the marital property, none of which he'd personally paid a dime for, because he was a drunk and couldn't keep a job. That had seemed horrible enough. Now, Kurt was asking for alimony, because he was a drunk and couldn't keep a job! In a flash, my genius got the best of me as I stood up and spoke to the *To Sir, with Love* judge lady, throwing myself on what surely must be her infinite mercy.

"What does being an alcoholic have to do with it?" I raged. The judge gave me a severe warning look, and I immediately shut up. On the outside, that is; inside, I continued raging. "Alcoholics can get jobs!" I thought. "I've known alcoholics who are millionaires! Alcoholics built this country! The president of the United States admitted he's an alcoholic, so is at least half the Congress, and what about Teddy Kennedy? I mean, I wouldn't want to drive with the guy, but you can't say he wasn't valuable. In fact, I'll bet you probably everybody who signed the Declaration of Independence was looped on flagons of mead or whatever!"

Kurt sat quietly, oblivious as he always was of the screaming that was going on inside my head, no doubt contemplating the vile and insidious disease of alcoholism that kept him from getting a job and forced him to make his biweekly journey to Costco, where he helplessly stocked up on flats of Milwaukee's Finest, which was, in fact, the worst but also the cheapest beer ever to emerge from that great brewing city.

Although Kurt was "not an earner," it could certainly be said that he was "not a spender," either.

Jabba motioned frantically at me to stop talking.

The judge began questioning Kurt about his job skills.

"What is your line of work, Mr. Bremerhoffen?" the judge asked.

"I am a finish carpenter, Your Honor," Kurt said proudly.

"Who never finishes anything," I snarled under my breath (but apparently not far enough under).

"Mr. Burns, please advise your client to control her outbursts," the judge warned my attorney. Jabba gave me a stern look, and I somehow managed to keep my mouth shut.

"Ms. Michon, I'm a little confused. I've seen you on TV, you host a program where you show old movies, but it looks in this paperwork as though you have more than one job. Are you a writer, or an actress, or a TV hostess? . . ."

"Yes, Your Honor. Due to my husband having no jobs at all, I have been forced to have more than one job."

The judge, my former imaginary ally, then addressed the group of us. "Due to the fact that Ms. Michon has been the sole wage-earner in this relationship, Ms. Michon is under order of this court to continue paying the bills as she has been until we set a further hearing to determine whether support will be awarded."

"But, the bills have gone up, he's living in my house with his girlfriend, I'm paying for both of them now, why can't she pay the bills, now that it's all like a big Sadie Hawkins dance with the girls paying for everything?" I sputtered uselessly.

"That's not the business of this court, Ms. Michon. Any further motions?"

Everyone sat silently as a high-pitched scream echoed in my head, although apparently I was the only one who found it troublesome.

"Fine, then we are adjourned," the judge said sonorously, tapping her gavel.

As everyone gathered up papers, I obsessively ground the soles of my hideous Agnes Gooch-y shoes into the shiny linoleum, hoping that the black magic from the masking tape Santeria spell would do something to make all of this just go away.

So naturally, I was disturbed when the only result of this spell was that as I got up from the table, the now-wadded clump of masking tape caused me to stumble and make a brief but disastrous flight that nearly landed me flat on my face in front of the judge, not unlike the way Dick Van Dyke would have done it in the opening credits of his classic sitcom. I recovered my balance, if not my dignity, and strode purposefully out of the courtroom.

Jabba the Attorney rushed to my side as I clumped on my horrible shoes outside into the daylight.

"Uh, you okay?" he asked, mopping his brow.

"How come I have to pay for Kurt and his Jurassic girlfriend to shack up in my house? Plus maybe alimony? This can't be serious!"

Jabba shrugged. "Well—"

"Let's tell them I'm an alcoholic . . . ," I interrupted.

"Doesn't help," Jabba told me. "If you're an alcoholic and you don't pay, they send you to jail. I know that seems unfair, but don't forget, these laws were designed to protect women—"

I cut him off with a withering glance. "You need to stop talking. Now. I have to go. Call me if they decide I deserve the chair."

I marched off, and just as I was about to dial my cell phone and alert the Grrl Genius Club that an emergency meeting needed to be convened at the nearest cozy watering hole, I realized that I didn't have time: I had to make my way to the airport to fly to Chicago, where I was supposed to appear on a TV talk show, giving relationship advice "from the Grrl Genius perspective."

Unfortunately, at that moment, the only relationship advice I could think of was

DON'T!
EVER!
HAVE!
A!
RELATIONSHIP!

We had a lot in common, I loved him and he loved him.
—Shelley Winters

46

A Grrl Genius Guide to Festive Divorce Customs in Many Cultures and Native Lands

Culture or Native Land	What They Do	Why It's Festive
The Ndeble tribe of Africa	When a woman is married, her husband gives her a series of necklaces, which artificially lengthen her neck, are a demonstration of his wealth and power, and cause her neck muscles to atrophy. If she divorces him, he takes back the necklaces.	Woman is reminded that a literal pain in the neck is better than being married to a pain in the neck.
Ancient Judaism	Requires that each party in a religious divorce give each other a "get" (permission to divorce), and then they spit on each other's shoes.	Acknowledges the awesome importance of shoes.
Philippine Tausugs of Jolo Island	Only men have all the rights to legal divorce, but a woman may divorce if she goes to the headman and places a curse on her husband, if the husband finds out this has happened, he risks contaminating the tribe by defying her curse and so he grants her the divorce.	Curse against husband actually works.
The State of California	"No-Fault Community Property Divorce" ensures that the person who did not contribute financially to the partnership, regardless of reason, is regarded by the state as a financial cripple who becomes the permanent lifetime responsibility of the person who actually worked for a living and whose only (Enormous! Irrevocable!) mistake was marrying such a person.	Talk about festive! The ex-spouse can have a party every day! In fact, it's better if he does, because it makes him disabled!

The only men with whom I have ever had a truly honest conversation have all been cabdrivers, and the oddly twitchy man who drove me to the TV studio in Chicago was no exception.

"So now," I whined from the backseat of the pine-scented cab, "because I earned all the money—and furthermore because he's supposedly so 'disabled' from being an alcoholic—now I'm supposed to support him for the rest of his life!"

Anthony Spreccace, my cabbie according to the mug shot on his hack license, was enraged. "That is just effing crazy, pardon my French."

"No problem, I am French."

"I mean, that is just effing nuts," he said. "Can't get a job 'cause he's an alcoholic, what a load of crap! Look at me, I'm an alcoholic, I've got a job!"

Since his job was driving me around at high speeds in a poorly maintained automobile, I was less than enthusiastic; still, I wanted to give him the benefit of the doubt.

"So, I guess you're sober, then," I ventured hopefully.

"Well, I am now, obviously."

I breathed a sigh of relief.

Anthony continued. "I mean, you know a few beers at lunch or whatever, but I know what the rules are, a man of my bodyweight can drink up to two-point-five ounces of pure alcohol an hour and still be legal to drive. And believe you me, I stick to that two-point-five-ounce rule. I'm responsible, not like your piece of shit ex, pardon my French."

The car whizzed through a yellow/red light and made a sharp squealing turn to the right.

"You know, Anthony, I'm really not in an enormous hurry or anything."

Anthony, fueled on righteous anger and, apparently, no more than 2.5 ounces of pure alcohol, pulled the cab up to the TV studio and screeched to a halt. Shakily, I reached into my wallet for the fare.

Once inside the TV station, I was greeted by Derek, a ridiculously young and enthusiastic producer with Drew Carey–sized horn-rimmed glasses and a shaved head, despite having what was obviously the potential to sport a full head of hair. "We are so glad you're here. I just loved the book! The whole Grrl Genius philosophy is so funny and so true, and I definitely am trying to be the Enlightened Male! And you are so much more beautiful than you look on the cover of your book," Derek blurted out at breakneck speed.

His enthusiasm was both encouraging and exhausting on a day when I felt anything but Grrl Geniusy. Derek, who appeared to be all of twenty-one, fell into the (very small) category of males who are instantly attracted to me. These males are also known as "children." Men my own age can sense that I have more backstory than a Spanish soap opera and wisely run for cover. "I'm glad you enjoyed the book," I said warily.

"I'm just trying to find a Grrl Genius of my own, you know? I mean, I'm so about smart women, I think smart women are great. I think, they're, well, geniuses, you know?"

"Right, of course. Keep saying it, I promise you, calling women geniuses is a great way to get laid," I advised. "Even if it's a lie, it doesn't matter. Women lie to men all the time—all we are asking for is a little mutual insincerity."

Derek laughed like it was the funniest joke ever made, and not a quote from my press release. "Oh, my God—that's hilarious. That's, that's . . . hilarious!" he gasped, sucking air in and out of his lungs and staggering as if I'd literally punched him with my punch line. He led me up the stairs into the green room, where another author was waiting, holding a cup of coffee in his hands. Apparently we were both guests on the show.

As I walked into the room, little did I know that the man standing there would eventually be cause for all my friends to accuse me of never learning from my past mistakes. He was dressed in a preppy-looking sweater and khakis. He was of average height and had the fit build of a privileged white guy who had grown up with tennis lessons and had never stopped playing. He looked about forty, and had short, dark hair shot through slightly with strands of gray, and an easy, kind smile that he shared with me as he shook my hand. He looked like—well, he looked just like Kevin Kline, whom I have always found to be devastatingly attractive because he's that rare combination of handsome and funny. His dark brown eyes were traced with the kind of charming laugh lines that point up the essential unfairness between men and women in the aging process: the adorably crinkly eyes that are impossibly endearing in the face of a forty-something man are, in a forty-something woman, just cause to inject deadly botulism toxin. For this very reason, at age sixty, Sean Connery was the sexiest man alive, and at the very same age, Shirley MacLaine was lucky not to be cast as Sean Connery's wizened mother. The Grrl Genius philosophy demanded that I refuse to take this ridiculous double standard to heart.

"William, this is Cathryn Michon, she's the Grrl Genius, I'm sure you've heard of her, she is so amazing!" Derek gushed.

I could see that he had not, which was perfectly understandable, I hadn't heard of him either. We were just two authors, pretending to be famous until someone actually decided we were, which is what authors do to sell books.

"Cathryn, this is William McCall. He's from Soda Springs, Idaho. He's a humor writer, too. He wrote the book *How to Be Ignored by Your Kid*. It's a book on parenting."

"It sounds funny," I observed dubiously.

William smiled at my tone.

"And Cathryn wrote *The Grrl Genius Guide to Life*, plus she's very attractive!" spurted Derek, whom I had sort of forgotten was in the room. He was staring at me the way you stare at a zoo animal.

"I can see that," William said dryly. I felt my face flush, and Derek giggled. It was obvious that he intended to continue hanging around like a bad cooking odor.

"Listen," I said to Derek, hoping to use his youthful eagerness for something more useful than pointless conversation, "I don't suppose there's dinner for us?"

"Uh . . ." Derek gestured weakly toward a table of half-eaten day old bagels and dried, crusted, bacteria-ridden cream cheese. He shuffled his feet like a fidgety two-year-old. He seemed to be growing younger by the minute. I had to fight the urge to tell him to "Use your words, Derek."

"Oh, that's not real food," I scoffed, assuming my best diva manner by imagining myself as Diana Ross in *Mahogany*, a bad movie to be sure but an excellent primer on how to access your inner pop princess. I had learned on the road that when it came to being fed, I was never willing to be a martyr, especially not to a television show. "I need something in The Zone, anything with chicken and vegetables. Aren't you hungry, William?"

"I'll get you something, get you both something . . . ," promised Derek as he rushed out of the room.

William turned to me in disbelief. "How did you do that? I tried to get food, but they said—"

"You've just got to be a diva. These shows are so cheap, but the fact is, they don't have a show without us, and a little bit of chicken and vegetables is not going to bankrupt them."

Shortly, Derek returned with an enormous amount of chicken and vegetables and what looked to be a UNICEF shipment of rice. His age regression seemed to be continuing, when he left us alone, I though I saw him actually stick his thumb in his mouth. I worried that soon he would become fetal, and perhaps not be viable outside the studio.

As we ate, William told me that he was starting to get calls from people in Hollywood about turning his book into a sitcom.

"Do you think that's—oh, I don't know—sort of cheesy?" he asked.

"Maybe, but it can be worth a lot of cheese. Of course, they'll probably take all the credit and try and try to have you killed, but other than that, you should do it."

"I wouldn't have to move to Hollywood, would I?"

"Well, it would probably be a good idea, and why not, I mean, aren't you dying to get out of Cola Falls?"

"Soda Springs," he laughed.

"Whatever," I said dismissively, "I mean, wouldn't it be fun to come to the big city?"

"Well, I don't know, I sort of like living in the sticks. I'm not a huge fan of cement," he ventured politely.

"Hey, everything's got its good sides and bad sides. I mean, I'm not a huge fan of ax murderers, and they always live in the sticks."

"Is that so?" he asked innocently.

"Well, sure," I rambled on, "there's the Unabomber—"

"What about the Boston Strangler?"

"Okay, fine," I admitted, "but what about the Green Acres Strangler?"

"You mean the Green *River* Strangler."

"Whatever. Point is, and I think you have to agree with me, almost one hundred percent of ax murderers live in rural areas," I stated factually.

"As opposed to the city, where they use guns," he said. I pouted. "Okay, fine, you tell me, what's so great about L.A.?"

"Uh . . ." I faltered. "I know! Did you know that in L.A. you can get a bank loan for fake breasts? It's considered like, a solid investment."

"Oh, hey, that's great, I'm there." William said, with the kind of smile that let me know that he was sort of kidding and sort of a typical man who thought that large breasts, regardless of origin, were a welcome addition to any metropolis.

"Really, you should come just for the plastic surgery. Women in L.A. get the fat sucked out of their butts and injected into their lips."

"You're kidding," he said, looking astounded.

"It's true," I affirmed.

We both reflected silently on the idea of women sitting around in L.A., their lips plumped with butt fat.

I smiled into his dark brown eyes. "Sort of gives a whole new meaning to the phrase, 'Kiss my ass!' Doesn't it?"

He threw his head back and laughed. It was endearingly attractive. Then he regarded me very seriously.

"So, can I ask you, why do you have the name *Kurt* taped to the bottom of your shoes?" he inquired politely.

I glibly recounted that morning's events in divorce court. Having now told it to two cabbies, I had the whole story honed to be both witty and shocking, but William simply listened.

It turned out that he was divorced. Only in his divorce, he and his ex-wife had stayed friends, which sounded pretty freaky to me.

"Divorce is sad," he said simply. "But we're both happier now."

Suddenly I didn't like him. He was being honest, and I was so not in the mood. He was implying that divorce was something that was both people's fault, and I was so not on board with that. My divorce was caused because I married a Bad Boy—it was as simple as that.

I was grateful that just at that moment, Derek (who was still old enough to walk on his own) came in and took me to the stage to tape my segment.

After both of us finished our taping, they sent us in a cab back to our hotel. William chatted perkily about the show, about how the audience had hated him, and how unfunny he was, all of which was untrue and revealed a talent for self-deprecation that I didn't run into very often in the ego-inflating hot air of Hollywood. As I watched him, I thought, he seemed so unusual to me, almost like he was another species. Then I realized what was so strange about him: He wasn't a Bad Boy.

I felt the way I felt the first time I saw a bald eagle in the wild, incredibly privileged just to catch a glimpse of such a rare creature. "This is what a normal guy looks like!" I thought. Unfortunately, normal guys live in fishing shacks in Utah or Idaho or wherever it was he lived, and I lived in one of the most populous cities on earth. You would think that in one of the most populous cities on earth, there might be one or two normal guys, but I hadn't run across any as of yet. I started to get very depressed about the idea that I would never find, date, and fall in love with one of these elusive creatures. Or maybe I was just depressed because it seemed that I might go bankrupt supporting the Bad Boy who was now my financial responsibility for life.

We got out of the cab and walked into the elegant grandeur of the Drake Hotel. William asked me if I'd like to stop in the bar for a drink. The truth was, there was nothing I would have liked better than talk to him some more, have a drink with him, have him take me dancing and give me foot rubs. Then I had a vision of myself living in a log cabin in Bubble Brook, Idaho, wearing bison skins and grooming lice out of my hair. What was I thinking? In two minutes, I was fantasizing about throwing away my whole glamorous life for some strange combination of Kevin Kline and Jethro Bodine. He might be a normal guy to most women, but to me he was just as bad a Bad Boy as anybody! How many times did I need to learn this lesson?

"No, I'm tired, but thanks," I replied, regretting it the moment it came out of my mouth—and secretly hoping that he would try to persuade me.

He looked disappointed, but accepted my refusal graciously. "Well, then," he said, "I guess I'll just go up to my room and read your book. It was great meeting you, Cathryn. You're a very unusual woman." He gave me another one of his warm smiles, shook my hand rather formally, and turned to go. Feeling indecisive, I watched him walk away with my book tucked under his arm, knowing that I could call after him, change my mind, but for some reason unable to do it. My Grrl Genius instincts had either failed me or rescued me, I couldn't decide which.

I went back to my room, where my increasingly dark mental state resulted in my raiding the mini-bar, not for liquor, but for medicinal chocolate, eating both the seven-dollar package of Oreos and a ten-dollar Kit Kat, which I don't even like, before finally falling into a deep, depressive sleep.

When I left the hotel the next morning, I glanced around the lobby, wondering if I might see William again, and then reminding myself that I wouldn't. Why would I see him again? We were just guests on the same talk show. Obviously I would never see him again. That's part of being a grown-up, I thought.

Being a grown-up sucks.

A mistake is simply another way of doing things.
—Katherine Graham

Naturally, the four members of my Grrl Genius Club had a lot of opinions on romantic mistakes, having made a few themselves. While I was not the only one who had slept with Bad Boys, I was the only who had actually married one, which gave me a special if unwanted distinction in our club. The following weekend at Kim's enormous western ranch mansion, we sat around in the early evening taking advantage of her Martha Stewart–wanna-be obsession and eating her famous brownies, which were practically flourless and made entirely out of butter, sugar, and chocolate, and talking about the Bad Boys we had slept with.

Amelia, reflecting on her lesbian marriage to Clarissa, would sum up her biggest romantic mistake as having committed to a monogamous lesbian relationship when she all along felt she was bisexual, something none of us could relate to in the least, and actually sort of made her the Bad Boy of that relationship.

Kim always said her biggest mistake was in marrying Barnaby way too young. "I should have been more of a slut before I settled down. Cathryn has slept with too many bad boys, and I haven't slept with enough of them!" she reflected bitterly.

Kim's husband, Barnaby, was a nerdishly handsome research chemist at a food conglomerate who wore geeky but somehow sexy glasses and specialized in creating artificial smells and flavors. If you ever enjoyed a trout-scented scratch-and-sniff sticker, you probably have Barnaby to thank.

Vonnie felt her biggest mistake was just the opposite. In her days as a '70s sitcom star, she slept with, "anybody with an X and a Y chromosome!" including a long bad affair with a married guy.

Still, Vonnie said her out-of-control behavior taught her some things and allowed her to recognize her true love, Eldon, the airline pilot, when they literally ran into each other at the baggage carousel of LAX. So in the end, she thought bad boys could be useful because they taught you to look for something else.

As we ate and drank in Kim's big living room, Vonnie was trying to make me feel like less of a loser by talking about all the people that had blown it worse than I had in the area of love. "I mean look, doll," she said as she ran her fingers through her spiky red hair, "it's not like you're the first person in history to make an enormous mistake by actually marrying a bad boy."

"I know, I know that," I said. "But the thing is, I just feel like I should have known. I should have known he was the kind of guy who would end up selling my lingerie on the front lawn."

Kim was knitting, with what can only be described "a vengeance," as the furious whipping up of pink baby booties was her latest way of preoccupying her cigaretteless hands. For whom these booties were being angrily created was unclear, and apparently unimportant. The way she knit made you realize that knitting needles would make a pretty good murder weapon if you found yourself needing such a thing. "You couldn't possibly have known that Kurt would sell your lingerie on the front lawn," she spat. "I mean, it just wasn't knowable. If you marry Hannibal Lecter, you don't know until way too late why you have such low grocery bills."

"My mistake wasn't not knowing my partner; it was not knowing myself," Amelia added. "Look, I sincerely thought I was a lesbian when Clarissa and I got together, I just wasn't being honest about the fact that I'm also sexually attracted to men."

"Amelia, angel, no offense, but it's hard to draw conclusions from your situation," Vonnie observed matter-of-factly. "Most women know what their sexual menu is, they just choose the same crummy entrée over and over."

I took an enormous bite of a brownie that seemed to become one with me the moment it entered my mouth. "The whole thing about being a Grrl Genius is that being an idiot is just part of your genius," I said. "But you have to admit, women have always had a lower status in society, and so they have made their romantic choices from a feeling of being 'less than.' I'm sure that's what happened to me. I'm sure I knew better than to marry Kurt and just didn't have the self-confidence to stick up for myself. And so I'm kicking myself."

"Well, that's incredibly useful," noted Vonnie, with irony caked on as thick as Tammy Faye Bakker's mascara. "I'll tell you who should have kicked themselves, the five wives of Henry the Eighth."

"He had six wives," I corrected her snottily.

"I know that doll, but I'm givin' the first one a pass. She didn't know. If a guy cuts off his wife's head, and then wants to make you his new wife—well, that's really sticking your neck out." We all groaned but Vonnie continued, undaunted, "But here's the thing: He still had four more wives! Four more women who were willing to marry a guy who cuts off his wives' heads!"

Kim's knitting needles clacked like samurai swords. "Women are such idiots when it comes to men. Why do we do it? Do we really think they're going to change for us?"

"Look at O. J.—he can always get a date," Amelia said. She downed the last of her brownie, eagerly licking her fingers and shaking her dreadlocks in delight. As I watched her, I realized that there was something about the way Amelia ate that made you think about sex. Truthfully, there was something about the way Amelia did pretty much everything that made you think about sex. It wasn't so much that she was sexy, it was just that due to her omnivorous sexuality, it never felt like the topic went away with her.

I wasn't prejudiced, I hoped, but bisexuals just made me a little nervous. I just found it somewhat off-putting that by their very nature, whether they were hanging out with all men, or all women, they were never "off duty." Amelia finally finished her finger-licking and spoke. "Look, I think that you should take it as a positive sign that in Chicago you found yourself actually attracted to what appeared to be, for all intents and purposes, a nice man, not a bad boy."

"Not that you were willing to have even one drink with him," chided Kim, clacking away with her needles.

"Not that we can even be sure that he actually was a nice man. No offense, baby doll, but you thinking he's nice is not exactly the Good Housekeeping Seal of Mental Approval," Vonnie added.

"Oh, piss off," I retorted, that being my usual response when someone I love is uncannily right.

"Oh, Cathryn," said Amelia, "don't you think it's time you started dating? You know, for real, like, guys who aren't gay. Would it have killed you to have one drink with a quote-unquote nice man? Aren't you getting tired of, you know, not having sex? Why do you have to be so prickly and difficult?"

It would not have killed me. I was achingly tired of not having sex. But I certainly wasn't going to admit it. "Why do I need sex when there's food like this? Food is the new sex!"

"Right! And angry is the new happy!" sang out Kim with an insanely flamboyant gesture that sent one of her knitting needles flying like a poison dart and landing squarely in the sofa cushion across from her.

We all just stared at her for a moment, until Vonnie said, "Um, are we talking about her, doll? Or are we talking about you?"

"Her obviously!" snapped Kim.

"Really," said Vonnie knowingly, "and how *are* things with Barnaby these days?"

"Fine!" Kim answered way too angrily, even for her caustic demeanor. We all stared silently for a moment—a storm was brewing there in Kim's vivacious eyes, but at this point all we could pick up was the rumble of distant thunder.

"Right," said Vonnie, looking less than convinced. "Anyway, I think Amelia might have a point. Cathryn, you might want to think about getting back into dating, you know, for real."

My Grrl Genius posse could not have been more right. It was time for me to step back into the tiger pit of dating, and see if there were some heterosexual non–Bad Boys I could manage to get through a meal with.

A Grrl Genius Quiz

HOW DO YOU KNOW WHEN YOU ARE READY TO START DATING AGAIN AFTER A BREAKUP?

If you were on an airplane that was in the process of crashing, knowing that in mere moments you will be dead from what the FAA calls "traumatic decapitation" (as opposed, apparently, to the more pleasant "not all that upsetting decapitation") would your final thought be

a. Maybe I shouldn't have been so rude to that businessman sitting next to me who offered to buy me a drink even though he's one thousand years older than me.

b. I should have had the chocolate cheesecake instead of the mixed berries for dessert!

c. This sucks, but at least now I don't have to date.

If you were kidnapped by aliens, and once on board the mother ship they began to perform invasive, probing medical experiments on you, you would probably be saying to yourself

a. Ow!

b. Their skin is so smooth, I'm against cruel medical experimentation on any living creature, but if the result of all this is some kind of miracle cellulite cream, these bastards better give me some before they wipe my memory banks.

c. This sucks, but it sure beats dating.

If your friend Vonnie invited you to a birthday party that was being held in a swanky bar with a lot of cushy leather sofas that was being thrown by some fancy friend of hers and she tells you that it will be "fun" and there will be a lot of "nice men" there do you

a. Try to kill yourself.

b. Pretend to be already dead.

c. Say, "I'd rather stick poison darts in my eyeballs because the only thing worse than dating would be going to a place and looking like I was interested in dating."

SCORING
FOR EACH a ANSWER: 10 points
FOR EACH b ANSWER: 5 points
FOR EACH c ANSWER: 1 point

20 to 30 points: You are on the road to recovery, and should begin dating immediately.

4 to 19 points: You are still wounded and bitter, but you should begin dating immediately.

3 points or fewer: You are not a well woman, but what are you going to do, become a nun? (This is a valid option). Begin dating immediately—you have nothing to lose.

———

I took the fact that I had found the fish-snaggling mountain man and potential non–bad boy William McCall attractive as a sign of progress. It was an almost infinitesimal (and of course ultimately pointless) step forward, but it was positive nonetheless. I had actually been attracted to a man who had a job, and no obvious substance problem, and excellent manners, and what looked to be more than adequate hygiene. Granted, it was a low bar, but William had sailed over it effortlessly.

The way I saw it, if I continued to obey the second Grrl Genius law of relationships—A Grrl Genius Stays Away from Bad Boys— things were bound to look up. Because, as usual, they could not possibly get worse. Or so I thought . . .

You must change in order to survive.
                                        —Pearl Bailey

Chapter 3

**A Grrl Genius Tries to Learn from Her Romantic Mistakes
and from the Romantic Mistakes of Others**

**Mistakes are part of the dues one pays for a full life.
—Sophia Loren**

WHEN I WAS twelve, I was shamelessly addicted to the *Ladies'
Home Journal* feature "Can This Marriage Be Saved?" I could never
get enough of this feature, the drama, the blame, the explicitly
described outfits. I can clearly remember lying on my mother's bed
reading the story of Irene Peters, "a carefully made up, soft-spoken
delicate blonde with a stylish feathery shag that flattered her fine,
high cheekbones, and elegant swanlike neck. Irene, who nervously
wrung her perfectly manicured hands around a single sheet of
Kleenex, looked trim and fit dressed in a blue Quiana shirt and slim
camel slacks." How could I help but swoon over prose like that?

The women whose marriages needed to be saved were always,
without fail, "trim and elegant," as well as being "soft-spoken and
nervous."

They were nothing like the women in our neighborhood whose
marriages needed to be saved. Not like Mrs. Nelda Halverson over
on Holton, who, if she appeared in "Can This Marriage Be Saved?"
would have been described as "a blotchy, angry harridan with a
voice like a broken car alarm. Nelda, who was dressed in stretched-
to-the-tensile-limit sweatpants, nervously twisted a stray tendril of
hair that had escaped the curlers that she perpetually wore preparing for some miraculous event, perhaps the second coming, that

would register as socially important enough to compel her to finally release her rodent brown hair from its endless pink foam rubber bondage."

The article always began with the wife's point of view. (This was, after all, a women's magazine.) By the time she was finished, you were convinced that her husband was a rat bastard and a hateful tyrant who should be "taken to the cleaners" in a victorious divorce settlement. In this magazine, the wife, regardless of how lazy or dull or prudish, was always right.

The wife always "worked her fingers to the bone trying to make a nice home" for a husband and children who seemed to regard her as their personal servant just because taking care of the house was her only job. If she was too tired to give in to his constant animalistic demands for nonprocreative sex, was it any wonder? And why did he touch her only when he wanted to be "serviced"? Why couldn't they take long walks on the beach? Was it any surprise she didn't enjoy the brutish, clumsy fumblings of such a gruff and self-obsessed workaholic? Why didn't her husband appreciate what a strain it was trying to "keep up with the Joneses" on his constantly fluctuating salary? Why couldn't the husband have been a better businessman and taken the well-paying management job his father-in-law had so kindly offered in his sewage treatment plant instead of selfishly insisting on going into brain surgery?

When it came time for the husband's turn, he always made some pathetic defense, claiming that he thought that marriage meant you would have sex more than once every six months, and that he was sorry that he didn't have time to take long walks on the beach with his wife because (a) his time for recreation was short due to his forty-eight-hour shifts at the hospital and (b) they lived in Nebraska.

These lame, weasely excuses from the husband gave the article the appearance of fairness, but it was always so obvious that the man was selfish and wrong.

Then it was the counselor's turn. Amazingly, the counselor could always manage to save the relationships with a few simple psychological techniques. Usually, each member of the couple learned how to make his or her needs known to the other in a nonthreatening manner by employing the use of "I statements." For example, instead of the husband saying, "Why do you have to be such a frigid bitch?" he would say, "I don't appreciate it when you are such a frigid bitch." (See? Amazing!)

In a truly great "Can This Marriage Be Saved?" the husband was always miraculously transformed into what basically amounts to an emotional porn star who constantly expressed his innermost feelings, because the counselor had a searingly brilliant psychological insight into the husband's twisted psyche, and confronted him with the fact that his mother was (a) dominating, (b) emotionally cold, or (c) inappropriately needy, causing him to regard his wife with (a) anger, (b) anger, or (c) anger.

It was all because of his horrible mother! The wife could not agree more.

The husband then constantly bombarded the wife with affection, flowers, and even gooey love notes, because, of course, this whole thing was not a realistic article about marriage counseling, but was, in fact, science fiction. After being assaulted with Hallmark sentiments from the newly emotionally available husband, the wife (who really *was* a frigid bitch if you were being honest about it) became wildly passionate about her husband. She was suddenly a shameless wanton harlot who, having spent the children's college fund on alluring and uncomfortable lingerie, eagerly demanded to be sexually satisfied by him daily in the bedroom, the laundry room, and even in the rumpus room (no double entendre acknowledged).

Oh yes, and all of this all happened in three or four sessions. Because this is the most unrealistic form of female entertainment ever devised. After reading it, I would dreamily lay my twelve-year-old body on my mom's bed and picture the strong, handsome, emotionally expressive man who would someday be my husband, spending every minute showering sentimental affection on me (when he wasn't out fighting fires).

Which is exactly what made it so delicious.

As an adult who has been through, and flunked, marriage counseling, I can tell you that this stuff does not happen in four sessions. Occasionally marriages do get fixed, but only if people get into counseling right away. People who have been romantically miserable all their lives do find happiness, but it takes time and endless chocolate and wine-fueled discussions with our girlfriends. Which is why the third Grrl Genius Law of Sex and Relationships is so very crucial. We have to constantly focus on (some would say *obsess*, but why quibble) our romantic mistakes and those of others. This is the only way we can learn, and it's also the best form of entertainment around.

A Grrl Genius "It May Be a Small World But It's Chock-Full of Big Weirdos" Festive Global Dating Sampler

THAT'S ONE WAY TO GET STRAIGHT GUYS TO GO DANCING

If a woman from the Goajiro tribe of Colombia is successful in tripping a man during a ceremonial dance, he's required to have intercourse with her.

LIKE MIDOL'S GONNA HELP THAT

At her first menstruation, a Biman-Kuskuman tribeswoman is subjected to a ritual involving the piercing of her nose and left earlobe, as well as extensive ritual scarification achieved by over one hundred inch-long incisions on her abdomen.

THEY SHOULD GO TO THE MALL OF AMERICA

African Hottentot men find women with large fatty buttocks to be the most sexually attractive, preferably three feet wide or more.

KURT'S SHIRTS WERE ALWAYS WELL PRESSED

The average American married couple makes love 133 times a year. The average French couple makes love 168 times a year. The global average is 119 times. Eleven percent of Americans would rather iron in the morning than have sex.

BUT HOW MUCH DOES IT COST TO FLY THERE?

Pacific Islanders of the Marquesan tribe teach their young men the art of prolonging their erections indefinitely until their female partner has had two or three orgasms.

GIVES NEW MEANING TO THE PHRASE "G'DAY MATE!"

Among the single women of the world, Australian women are the most likely to have sex on a first date.

UM, THANKS, BUT, OW!

The Patagonian Indians employ a ringlike device called a *guesquel*, which is fashioned from the coarse stiff hair of the mule and fitted around the penis and which they believe produces intense orgasms in women.

LIKE A RHINESTONE COWBOY . . .

Sumatran men have been known to insert small stones into incisions in their penises to make them more lumpy and pleasurable to women.

———

The day after the Grrl Genius Club's flourless-brownie-and-wine extravaganza at Kim's, I was very surprised to find there was an e-mail from William McCall, the attractive (but what was the point of him being attractive?) author who lived under a rock somewhere in Nicaragua or Utah, or whatever.

I was oddly excited to see his return address in my in-box. I had been thinking about him ever since I met him, then chiding myself, because I knew I would never see him again.

From: William@backwoodswriter.com
To: GG@grrlgenius.com
Subject: I am home . . .

Dear Cathryn:

First let me tell you how delightful I found your company the other
evening—I must have, because I really don't ever use the word
"delightful" under any circumstances. It was fabulous talking to you.
There, see? Fabulous, what kind of word is that?

I was fortunate enough to be returned to my home after only being
held hostage by an airline for half a day: apparently there was
something wrong with the engine, which they didn't so much fix as
decide was unimportant. That this decision was made by the
mechanics who were staying on the ground gave me less comfort than
I would have wanted.

While sitting in the airport I opened the copy of your book that
you gave me and was immediately captivated, yes, delightfully,
fabulously captivated, by the wonderful humor you use to describe
your everyday life.

In this case, I do not mean "everyday life" to mean "normal
existence." Clearly, your circumstances rarely stray into a state
of affairs which could be described as "normal."

Anyway, the book is well written and I can't wait to see how it turns
out. Well, except that I DO know how it turns out: the heroine becomes
a lovely, successful, kindhearted woman who spends several hours
helping a neophyte understand the ins and outs of a Hollywood
project.

Thank you, thank you Cathryn, for all of your advice. I really
appreciate it!

66

I'm back home in Idaho now. I have a view outside my window of a lake and of my neighbor's disabled truck. I find at least one of these sights very pleasing to the eye. My dream is to take the foothold I have established in the business of show (is that how you fabulous people say it?) and turn it into a way to make a living without having to leave the shores of this little lake more than once or twice a year. I love it here, the views are great, there's hunting and fishing, and, as you pointed out, in Idaho it is fairly easy to find a good potato.

Yours,
William

Men aren't usually attracted by my mind, they're attracted by what I don't mind.

—Gypsy Rose Lee

William was as disturbingly charming in a letter as he was in person. Surely there had to be (available) men like that in L.A.

I estimated, after extensive Google research, that the odds of meeting and dating this type of man within your time zone were roughly the same as those of lying in a Barcalounger, eating Jell-O, and having a meteor plunge through the roof of your trailer home and bore a molten hole in your floor as you sit there unscathed, a small blob of Jell-O hanging suspended off your slack-jawed lips as you stare in amazement.

Yet, this is exactly what happened to Mrs. Lydia Beauchamps of Sylacauga, Alabama, in the year 1973—and well, if she could beat the odds that spectacularly, surely I could, too.

I decided I would write him back, but it could certainly wait, as there was no point, and I was late for a shopping adventure with Amelia, who had asked me to be her beard-date at a gay and lesbian fund-raiser. When it came to her sexuality, Amelia liked to keep people guessing. Because the gay community had seen her breaking up with Clarissa as a defection of sorts, she had taken a lot of abuse. Amelia was still an ardent supporter of the charity in question, GAY/LA, so she opted to show up with a "gal pal" in tow. As everyone who has ever read the *National Enquirer* knows (and really who hasn't read it at least once?) "gal pal" means "lesbian lover who can't admit it."

Sex appeal is fifty percent what you've got and fifty percent what people think you've got.

—Sophia Loren

"Okay, going with you to this fund-raiser might be the dumbest move I've made yet," I announced to Amelia as I randomly pawed through the hangers of whisper-thin Cosabella teddies in The Farm, an improbably farm-themed clothing store that sold lingerie and dressy clothes in my little neighborhood of Studio City. At The Farm, there were pitchforks draped with glittery dresses, big milking buckets full of thongs, and a life-size scarecrow clutching ridiculously expensive bra and panty sets in his straw fists, looking for all the world like Ray Bolger at one of J. Edgar Hoover's famous cross-dressing parties.

Amelia, every inch the former celebrity lesbian wife in Herman Munster chunky boots, one of her many thousand-dollar leather jackets, chicly distressed Diesel jeans, and a tiny pink tee that said BITCH GODDESS, responded in the voice that she uses when she is annoyed, dropping her cool L.A. attitude in favor of the Texas drawl of her childhood, "Oh, Lordy," she sighed, "I'm so not hearing this from you."

"You're the one that says I should get back out there, start dating again, and then you want me to be your fake lesbian beard at some gay fund-raiser. Like I'm gonna meet a guy there . . ."

"Well, what the hell, since you seem to prefer dating gay men, you should be right at home, since if there were nice, straight men there, you would probably refuse to have a drink with them," said Amelia judgmentally as she ran her fingers through her dreadlocks.

"That William guy sent me a very nice e-mail . . . ," I ventured.

"That I'm sure you haven't bothered to answer."

I squirmed at the deadly accuracy of her prediction. "Who comes up with the idea that a clothes store should look like Ma Kettle's milking shed?" I demanded as though I weren't desperately trying to change the subject.

"Don't change the subject. Here, you should try these on, if you are ever going to lose that postmarital virginity of yours, you're going to need new lingerie," Amelia pronounced as she handed me a—no kidding—$345 French lipstick-red satin-and-lace bra-and-panty set. I snatched it from her hands just to shut her up and stepped past the burlap sack curtain that provided privacy in the tiny dressing room. Tossing my clothes onto the complicated-looking wheat thresher or horse gelder whatever farmy geegaw it was that was sitting in the corner of the tiny room, I quickly got naked and put on the lingerie.

I was really not prepared for what happened next. I looked at myself in the mirror, standing there in an entire car payment's worth of underwear and the simple fact was, I looked hot. I mean, I literally found *myself* attractive.

Maybe it was the lighting, or the farm equipment, but I didn't think so, I was pretty sure it was the underwear. It was a kind of rich maraschino cherry-red silky satin that made my skin suddenly look like French vanilla ice cream. In a miracle that defied modern physics both the bra and panty fit me perfectly. For me, panties always seemed to involve a lot of, well, strife. But these panties seemed to effortlessly agree with my ass, instead of arguing with it like belligerent in-laws trying to make it through one round of Trivial Pursuit without killing each other.

The bra straps, instead of mercilessly cutting into my arms and seemingly screaming the phrase "Fat arms just like Grandma!" instead gently glided along my back and shoulders, but it was the cups of the bra that truly transformed me. They were reembroidered lace that extended gingerly beyond the bra, so that the bra itself looked like elegant crimson gloved hands that were gently lifting and cradling my breasts in exactly the way that up-and-coming movie starlets always do when they coyly pose in *Vanity Fair,* holding their own perky breasts as though they had just noticed them and were examining them for the first time with an "Oh, my, what on earth are these darling things doing just sitting here on my chest!" sort of way.

I have no idea how long I stood there staring at myself. At some point Amelia pulled aside the gunnysack curtain and peeked her head in the room.

"Oh, my God." She seemed as stunned as I was. "You look hot," she breathed.

"I know."

"I mean, I'm not kidding, you look hot. You're buying that."

"It's too expensive," I argued without conviction.

"Don't be ridiculous. I'll tell you what will be expensive, the therapy you're going to have to undergo for not buying the one thing that has made you feel sexy in two years," she countered.

It made sense. Well, not really, but I honestly didn't care.

"I will buy these panties on one condition," I said, making a promise to myself even as I was saying it, "I'm not wearing these with a guy until I find one that's deserving, even if it means I never wear these with a guy. From now on, these panties are like the Holy Grail. A guy isn't allowed to see me in them until he has endured various tests and trials, until he has proved that he is honorable and worthy."

"Or at least that he's not an asshole," Amelia added.

"No, he has to be much more than 'not an asshole.' He has to be officially deserving of red panties."

"DORP!" blurted Amelia.

"Huh?" I glanced at her to see if she needed the Heimlich maneuver or something.

"Deserving of Red Panties. He has to be a DORP," Amelia said.

"Total DORP," I agreed.

Amelia was getting swept up by the whole idea. "I'm getting

some, too, not the same as you, but very expensive red underwear. For the right guy. Not necessarily the first guy, but for the right guy, not the 'compromise' guy."

"I want a hunky firefighter," I stated for the record.

"Of course." Amelia nodded absently. "Hunky firefighters are probably the whole reason I couldn't stay strictly lesbian."

Naturally, the "right guy" was a firefighter. Every woman I knew agreed absolutely, usually after countless viewings of the crap movie *Backdraft*, which we always watched with the sound off. The sexiest thing a man could be in the whole world was a firefighter. Although, I held out (impossibly) for a Harvard-educated firefighter/novelist/gourmet chef who studied Thai foot massage for fun.

When I would wax rhapsodic about hunky firefighters, their physical bravery, their selfless sacrifice, their incredible buffness (but not for vanity—they were buff to save kittens and old ladies!) my male friends always felt the need to tell me that "real" firefighters "weren't like that."

As if they were firefighters. As if they knew.

"Firefighters are just a bunch of beer-guzzling, sexist, blue-collar lunks that resent women and wouldn't know a good book if it bit their dicks off, much less write one," my friend Tommy said to me bitterly one night at the Improv, looking out for me in that big brotherly way of his.

"Well obviously some firefighter turned you down, and now it's soured you on the whole thing," I theorized, and from the look on Tommy's face, I could tell I was deadly accurate in my assessment. "My fantasy firefighter isn't like that," I said earnestly. "He's a true intellectual who loves being a firefighter and writing closely observed novels about love and modern manners. Plus he can cook and give foot massages."

"Really, I'm surprised he doesn't tat lace, too. Please, he sounds like Jane Austen in a rubber coat and suspenders!"

"Exactly," I agreed, shocked that Tommy was finally beginning to understand what I was looking for.

But Amelia and all my other Grrl Genius friends understood. "The thing about firefighters," I told her, "is that they represent a total change of archetype from the men I have always chosen. If I sleep with a firefighter, I will finally be breaking the pattern. If I sleep with a firefighter, I will finally have learned from my mistakes."

"Plus, you will have slept with a firefighter." Amelia sighed.

If I had to live my life again, I'd make the same mistakes, only sooner.
—Tallulah Bankhead

The Grrl Genius "Who Do You Love in the Band?" Romantic Mistake Analysis System™

Like all my genius systems of personal insight, The Grrl Genius "Who Do You Love in the Band?" Romantic Mistake Analysis System™, is based on a blinding flash of brilliance that came into my genius brain while eating a chocolate product. The simple fact is, all your mistakes and bad choices about men stem from the crucial moment in your life when you first had a crush on the member of a rock band. It was then that your "romantic type" was imprinted on you, and from that day to the present, every choice you have made about men has been influenced by that first rock-and-roll crush.

Now let's look at the four male archetypes of my system.

THE DRUMMER

You know the "drummer" first of all by his incredible, impossibly buff forearms. (It's important to remember that the "incredible forearms" are actually a metaphor. Your "drummer's" "incredible forearms" may in fact be his twinkly blue eyes, or his poetry writing, or his BMW convertible, but the point is the "incredible forearms" are the quality that he has that makes you overlook his more obvious flaws, like his annoying tendency to take fatal overdoses.)

The "drummer" type of man can be counted on to "keep a steady beat" (if he manages to make it to the gig, that is!). If he "drowns in a pool of his own vomit," well, you picked the wrong little drummer boy.

When you think of the "drummer" type, you think of someone like Ringo Starr, or Charlie Watts, or Alex Van Halen. Guys who are not the flashiest or most attractive, or even the most talented, but nonetheless are "part of the band."

If you are attracted to "drummers," it is because you are insecure and don't think you deserve any better. You want a man to "set the pace" for you, but you can't commit and are always looking to "march to a different drummer." Your choosing a drummer is unfortunately a "cymbal" of your unwillingness to "get on the stick" and make your own choices!

THE GUITAR PLAYER

The single most notable thing about the "guitar-player" type is that he is "moody." He is the boy in the band that is most likely to churlishly smash his instrument in a hotel room. (Although I'll admit this is probably because the other guys in the band have instruments that are too heavy to throw.)

The "guitar player" is the "misunderstood brooding intellect" of the band. He is the one who is most looking to be rescued and brought out of his darkness by a princess of light and love. That's you!

If you love the "guitar player," you are a rescuer. Instead of focusing on yourself and your goals, you are willing to sacrifice everything in order to cheer him up. If you love the "guitar player" you need to learn to "get picky!"

THE LEAD SINGER

The lead singer is, of course, the "star" or the "front man" of the band. He wears the "tightest pants" and "jumps around" the most. The lead singer is all about confidence and being "center stage." The most noticeable thing about the lead singer is that he doesn't notice you at all!

The lead singer is not interested in anyone but himself, which is, of course, what makes him so incredibly attractive. He expects that the most beautiful women in the world will love him, and amazingly, they do. He marries supermodels like Jerry Hall and Christie Brinkley and then cheats on them with younger supermodels.

If you love the "lead singer," it's because you are secretly a rebel but don't have the guts to break the rules yourself. You want to be an outlaw, but you settle for dating or marrying one instead. You need to learn to "take the lead" yourself, fire the lead singer from your life the way Eddie Van Halen fired three lead singers from his band, and get your own time in the spotlight!

THE BASS PLAYER (SEE ALSO: THE KEYBOARD PLAYER)

The most noticeable thing about the bass player (or the keyboard player, I mean, whatever, they're basically the same thing) is that with the exception of Paul McCartney, who, let's face it, was really a lead singer pretending to be a bass player, nobody cares about them.

Come on, be honest, can you name even one famous "bass player" who isn't Paul McCartney?

If you love "bass players," you probably have the ability to see beyond surface qualities and into the true qualities of a person. You understand that although the bass line is the most boring part of the song by itself, if there were no bass line, everything would sound tinny and hollow and dull.

Unless of course, you only loved the "bass player" because you were pretty sure he was the only one who would love *you*. If you loved the "bass player" because you were unwilling even to try for the "drummer" or the "lead singer," well, you're not quite as together as you seem, are you? It's time for you to "get back to BASSics, missy!"

———

After my shopping binge with Amelia, I walked in the front door of my apartment clutching a bag so light, it seemed impossible that it contained almost four hundred dollars' worth of underwear. Underwear that gave me a sinking feeing of doom because I knew I could no longer afford it. Underwear I was going to have to return. As I walked into my kitchen, I reached into my "chocolate drawer" (the same drawer that less practical people reserve for fripperies like silverware) and grabbed a handful of Hershey's Kisses. I turned on my computer to check e-mail, because even though I couldn't be bothered to answer his e-mail, I was secretly hoping that William McCall might have written me again, and when I opened my e-mail tool and saw a message from him, I felt as foolishly giddy as I felt in fourth grade when I shook the Valentine mailbox we all kept on our desks in February and heard the tell-tale rattle of a card.

I was pathetic.

From: William@backwoodswriter.com
To: GG@grrlgenius.com
Subject: Your book!

Dear Cathryn:

I finished the book! Your book, of course, and I found it to be exactly as I expected, a wonderful, funny, and ultimately revealing romp through your life. You truly are a genius, you know. It was so insightful and hilarious.

I have a little trouble buying the low self-esteem thing . . . because how could you, of all people, have low self-esteem? You've accomplished so much in your life. I'm what, 10 or so years older than you, and I have come up with very little that I can point to as life accomplishments. Well, I did fix the screen door last week.

Some things are happening in your neighborhood, the west coast one, I mean, that I just don't understand having to do with my own humble attempts to write. What exactly is a "development deal"?

They are agitating for me to come back out to L.A. again already, and I am not sure why. Last time I was there, all we did was sit in a big conference room and drink water out of a bottle. I drank an awful lot of water during that meeting, so I was glad I hung on to the empty bottle.

I hope you don't mind giving me a little advice on dealing with these Hollywood people, if they are, in fact, people. I'm somewhat confused as to what they mean when they say, "We plan to screw you out of this deal." Are they sincere?

I'd like to thank you for your advice by buying you dinner when I'm in L.A., which will be happening in two weeks. I'll be out there for four nights, so hopefully one of them would work with your schedule?

I hope to hear from you soon!

William the Conqueror

Because of my book, I had gotten some pretty strange e-mail from guys. Men had written to me, telling me they were in love with me, sending me suggestive e-mail, wanting to talk about what I was (or wasn't) wearing, offering to send me plane tickets to come meet them and fall in love with them. True to my Grrl Genius law of learning from past mistakes, I needed to proceed with caution when it came to this William person. There was something rather off-putting in his perky, upbeat demeanor. I decided to respond, but I would be formal and polite, because what would be the odds of me having a long-distance relationship with some older, divorced guy who is committed to living under a hay bale in the middle of the forest? But I liked him, so as far as dinner went, "Sure, why not?" I thought.

Besides, he was funny, and that is the one thing I can never resist.

From: GG@grrlgenius.com
To: William@backwoodswriter.com
Subject: No, YOUR book . . .

Dear William,

Thank you for reading and enjoying my book. I read your book, and although it is against my Grrl Genius philosophy to say so, your book is much better than mine, because it is funny and endearing and relatable and true and mine blows chunks as does everything I do on the planet.

What was your question about my low self-esteem again?

As it happens I am feeling very low because I have just spent way too much money in a fancy store, something I can now no longer afford to do because I am forced to pay for my slacker alcoholic ex-husband to live in a luxurious Beverly Hills home with a woman whose only job seems to be selling my old lingerie on the front yard I have to pay to keep up, but can no longer enjoy.

Not that I'm bitter.

As to your question regarding development deals, they are a thing where some big rich entity like a movie studio pays you a lot of money to take very good things you've written or might write and turn them into the unrecognizable dreck that currently clogs your cable box.

Note that I'm bitter.

If at all possible I suggest you feel free to take the development deal. I also suggest that you feel free to take a leak during boring meetings in conference rooms, but by all means excuse yourself from the table, as peeing in water bottles will only get you a reputation as a guy who pees in water bottles.

I hate to seem craven and bitter, but believe you me, when those "Hollywood Types" say they're going to "screw you out of the deal," well, they're not kidding. The only mistake you're making is that if they are interested enough in you to even want to screw you over, well then you should be thinking about moving to L.A., because you are clearly on the very cusp of being the new hot writer in town. But since you seem to be committed to your whole Unabomber-esque comedy writer lifestyle living in your little cave and snaggling trout with your bare hands for supper, you probably won't do the practical thing and move to L.A. to take advantage of the truckloads of money they are obviously dying to give you.

But best of luck!

Don't worry about me, I'm going broke but I have plenty of chocolate.

Cordially,
Cathryn Michon

P.S Um sure, we could have dinner.

Just then the phone rang. Caller ID was registering "unknown caller," but as usual I was unable to resist finding out who the unknown caller was.

"Hello?"

"Hi, it's Amelia. I know that you are sitting there feeling guilty about buying that underwear, but you can't return it—it's a spiritual investment in your future."

I could just tell that Amelia, who was very into everything from numerology to rebirthing, was about to spout one of her New Age–y proclamations.

"We're going to learn from our mistakes, Cathryn. Isn't that the Grrl Genius philosophy?" she asked.

"Exactly, I agree," I said warily, wondering what kind of faux

Hindu mumbo jumbo was headed my way. Sure enough she started in. "We all create our own realities, Cathryn. You need to create a reality where you have a good reason to wear that underwear. And you need to start creating that reality by not returning it."

"Great," I said, "next time I'm creating a reality, remind me to create that I drive a Mercedes like you, instead of that piece-of-shit Volvo of mine, you know, the empty-wombmobile, the car that Kurt and I bought when we were going to be normal and have kids."

Amelia, who was a sensible person except for all the crazy stuff she believed in, was undeterred by my sarcasm. "When you go to bed tonight, I want you to wear that fancy red underwear. You have to stop being so prickly, so afraid of showing your softer side, I really believe the underwear is symbolic of that."

Sometimes Amelia was so airy-fairy, I just couldn't stand it. I knew underwear was important, but I didn't think it was going to turn my love life around. Still, Amelia had an uncanny ability to be right about things often enough that you couldn't completely dismiss her opinion.

"You keep calling me prickly—what did you mean by that?" I asked hesitantly.

"Oh, Cathryn, I don't know how to say this to you, but . . ." I could just tell I wasn't going to like what was coming. "I know marrying Kurt was a mistake, but, well, every man in the world isn't Kurt, and um, sometimes, well you come off like kind of a, well . . . a man-hating bitch. Please don't be hurt."

I didn't know what to say. I was, according to one of my best friends, a prickly man-hating bitch.

"Oh, why should I be hurt?" I replied faintly.

"Also, you, uh, I thought you might want to think about getting a bikini wax, before you, you know, go pubicly public, so to speak . . . and you might think about getting a Brazilian, because, you know, the regular ones are sort of out of fashion. I'm sending you a gift certificate for Arabella's in Beverly Hills. You'll go to Ludmilla—she's the best."

I instantly flushed on hearing this advice. It had not escaped my notice at the gym that the old-fashioned bikini wax was as out of fashion as the poodle skirt. A really small poodle skirt, but still. Now you had to have the little landing strip, or that strange Hitler mustache, or a swoosh, or, nothing at all! The thought was horrifying.

I didn't want to argue with her about the politics of pubic hair, or the life-changing opportunities of really good panties, and I did feel like sleeping in the underwear, so I said I would go see Ludmilla and sleep in the red panties. I would be less prickly and try not to be hurt that one of my best friends thought I was a man-hating bitch with shaggy pubic hair. I would imagine the fireman of my dreams coming toward me. I would imagine the two of us together, as close as we could be.

I would never have guessed how soon it would happen, or how it would happen. If I'd known, believe you me, I'd have returned that underwear, but of course, I didn't.

The Grrl Genius Wild Sexual Kingdom

The American porcupine *(Erithizon dorsatum)* whose Latin name roughly translates as "irritable back" is well known to be a prickly creature, but is even more prickly when it comes to mating and love. About thirty thousand quills cover the female porcupine's back, and they are apparently a formidable threat against predators and boyfriends alike.

During mating season, the female porcupine is often pursued by males who call to her and (not unlike certain divorcing human females) she tends to reject them with a series of guttural grunting noises, preferring instead to eagerly rub herself on her "play sticks" or really any handy, hard object, since although she may be prickly, she's not picky. The rejection of the male by the female often results in "stick-riding behavior" on the male's part, but after vigorous stick riding, both male and female porcupines are usually observed to visibly "mope."

When both male and female porcupine are finally ready for mating, the male porcupine begins the bizarre courtship dance, which involves him approaching the female with each of them standing on their two hind legs, so their soft and vulnerable undersides are exposed to each other, and then spraying the female porcupine with his urine from head to toe. Although the porcupine's quills can be deadly, even to other porcupines, during bonded mating, both porcupines have a relaxation response, which causes the quills to lie flat and not inflict harm.

Just as in human life, female porcupines are not ready and willing to have sex until the male they have chosen has pissed on them from head to toe. Surely, for women, and porcupines both, there must be a better way.

———————

Be bold. If you're going to make an error, make a doozy, and don't be afraid to hit the ball.

—Billie Jean King

It took me forever to fall asleep that night, despite wearing the magical life-changing red underwear, and as often happened, I fell asleep with my laptop computer on my bed, as I had been surfing the Net, looking at pubic hairstyles. That night I dreamt that there was a fire in my apartment building, and I was carried out of the flames by an impossibly hunky firefighter as the sound of the smoke alarm squealed relentlessly. I awoke with a start as I realized that the fire alarm was real, my building was actually on fire!

I leapt out of bed, and in doing so, sent my laptop crashing to the floor. I scrambled to grab it, and realized that I had broken the screen. I wish I could say that this was the first time this had happened. While most people had computer "crashes" involving software, I literally crashed them, despite the fact that they were an important tool in earning my living. I was furious that I had done it again, but because I had to evacuate from my burning apartment, I didn't have time to dwell on it as I threw on a cute nightgown so that at least if I made it out alive the local firefighters would see me at my best. As I headed downstairs in my best black silk nightie, clutching the broken computer, it dawned on me that it was not the smoke alarm that was blaring, but the strange and loud doorbell of my old and funky apartment. I looked at my kitchen clock and realized it was one in the morning. I was both relieved, and disappointed, I had no desire to lose what little I had left in a fire, but being rescued by hunky available firefighters made it seem almost worth it.

Reluctantly, I staggered across the door to the intercom, which never worked, so I buzzed in the unknown visitor. As I looked out the peephole of my front door, I was surprised to see that my visitor was my stunningly beautiful and brilliant (Harvard-educated on a full scholarship) cousin Jen, whom I adored beyond all sense and reason.

Jen was slender and graceful like the ballerina she had been as a child, with long hair that had changed color so often I wasn't really sure what color it was naturally. Whatever her hair color, she was stunning. She had the winsome quality of a young Goldie Hawn, so, in other words, was a dead ringer for Kate Hudson. She could be somewhat sarcastic (it ran in the family) but unlike me, she was naturally optimistic and she usually charmed people instantly with her sincere, lovely smile. Jen was a real beauty, but as a child, she had been the ugly duckling of her family. With an immense horsey overbite and short, badly cut hair, no one held out for Jen to be pretty. Only my uncle Dick, an orthodontist, saw her potential. "You wait," he predicted, "get some braces on that kid, she'll be a knockout!"

And so she was, but I am not sure she ever really believed it. Jen had recently graduated from Harvard in cultural anthropology, so naturally she worked as a waitress. She lived with her five-star-chef-boyfriend, Rich, whom I referred to as the Tattooed Gourmet. In the movie of my life, he would be played by none other than tough guy Ray Liotta because Rich was an immense man, tall and wide, but not fat, all muscle. He was covered with tattoos, my favorite being the one across his tree trunk of a neck that read CAN'T STOP, WON'T STOP. He made the most incredible food anyone had ever tasted, and we loved him, not just for the food, but honestly, the food really tipped the scales in his favor. In my family we did not believe in marrying for money, but we were not necessarily against the idea of marrying for food, if it was accompanied by love.

My immediate family had been eagerly waiting for months for the engagement of Rich and Jen that Rich had said was imminent. He had pulled each of us aside last Thanksgiving and asked us about what we thought Jen's preferences on an engagement ring might be. When Christmas came and went with no engagement, we said nothing, but began to worry, because, well, we kept remembering the seven-course Christmas-tasting menu we had hoped would become an annual tradition, and also it seemed like Jen loved Rich very dearly, which was a good thing, on account of the seven-course Christmas tasting menu.

Jen hadn't been planning to visit, as far as I knew, but here she was at one in the morning, lugging a giant suitcase and duffle bag. I ran down to help her. I gathered her up in a big hug, and she burst into tears, which was certainly the sort of thing I was prone to do, but not like Jen at all.

"Oh, Cathy," she said, using the childhood nickname I disliked intensely. "I'm sorry if I woke you up. I broke up with Rich . . ." She huddled into my arms as she wept soddenly. I grabbed her duffle bag and gently led Jen up the stairs to my apartment, where she collapsed gratefully on my girlish lipstick-red sofa.

I didn't know what to say, and was somewhat ashamed that my brain was panicking about the potential loss of high-end cuisine, and feverishly working on how I could get these two nutty kids to work out their silly little spat, thus ensuring that all future family events would still include that faultlessly prepared grilled foie gras surrounded by braised Asian pears, nestled on a bed of steamed Swiss chard and covered in a drizzled reduction of cassis and Marion-berries, served with a crisply cold sauternes.

"And I love him so much, but when he didn't ask me to marry him, I realized that I was making a huge mistake and wasting my life, and I certainly don't want somebody that doesn't want me . . . ," Jen apparently continued.

This sounded serious. Jen and Rich had had lover's quarrels before, but they had never involved cross-country plane trips and enormous duffle bags. Usually she had encamped at my parents' place on Cape Cod, and Rich would show up with stunning food and sincere apologies. One time he had arrived with an entire three-course wild game winter menu, consisting of grilled medallions of venison stacked on Asagio polenta and smothered in a fresh lingon-berry coulis finished with a frise of shredded tempura-battered Maui onion, followed by an impeccably simple wild buffalo steak tartare served on toasted fresh garlic-and-basil-infused extra-virgin-olive-oil basted croquettes, and the third course to round out the evening was a perfectly roasted maple glazed squab, with a rosemary scented roasted winter vegetable, apple-and-currant wild rice stuffing. . . .

"So if Rich doesn't see what a prize I am," Jen was saying when I started to listen again, "if he doesn't see what a treasure I am, and he's so unable to make a commitment—which I didn't even ask him to do, by the way, I was perfectly content with just living together, he's the one who brought up the whole marriage thing, and then doesn't even have the backbone to go through with it, when it was his idea—well, there is just no way I'm going to sit there feeling rejected and unloved, and so that's why I decided to move to California."

Now I was truly shocked. And really hungry.

"You, you're moving here? Permanently?"

"Yup," she affirmed through her tears, with the world-class stubbornness she had always displayed even as a child, "that's that. I've made the big move. There's no going back."

"So, where's Rich?" I asked, somewhat mournfully.

"I have no idea. I suppose he's back in Cambridge, where I left him. I wrote him a note when he was off at the fish market getting lobsters for some stupid soup he was making—"

"The saffron lobster bisque?" I gasped. I couldn't believe she could leave him while he was making that ambrosial potion. This was serious.

I continued tentatively. "Jen, I've been thinking about this a lot lately, really trying to analyze the mistakes I made in my relationship with Kurt, and, well, you do know, in every relationship, each part-ner has the potential to bring something special to it, and well, maybe you should take a minute to remember how Rich used to cook for you, how you woke up every morning to fresh-squeezed blood-orange-and-papaya juice and perfectly poached quail eggs with that amazing crab hollandaise sauce he did over those roasted artichoke hearts and the grilled fennel. . . ."

Jen pouted. "Yeah, whatever, it was great sometimes, but you know what? Sometimes I just wanted a Pop-Tart."

I resisted the urge to slap her slender fanny. Surely, after a few days of my cooking, she would begin to see reason, so I decided it was best to drop the whole topic.

"Well, of course, you can stay as long as you want here. . . . I've missed you," I said.

It was true, I had missed her desperately. I had missed Rich, too . . . but was too hungry and exhausted to really dwell on it.

She threw her arms around me like the happy little kid I always remembered her to be. "Oh, thanks, Cath, thanks. I promise, I won't be any trouble, and then I'll get a place of my own and be out of your hair."

"So, what are your plans?" I asked.

"Well, you know—obviously, I'll get a waitressing job—"

"Hey, don't be so defeatist, you've got a degree in cultural anthropology from Harvard, for crying out loud. I mean, let's see if we can't get you a, you know . . . ," I trailed off uselessly.

"Cultural anthropology job?" she prodded.

"Right! Exactly."

"Cath, waitressing *is* a cultural anthropology job. It's kind of like the only one available, and certainly the best-paying one I could get. It's okay though, really, a restaurant is like a perfect laboratory for human behavior. When I get my Ph.D., trust me, my dissertation will be all about coffee refills as bonding rituals, or something like that," Jen asserted with her usual sunny optimism.

"I guess, if you don't mind it. Speaking of which, you want some hot chocolate? I've got Valrona. . . ."

"Oh, God, yes, please. So I'll tell you the other thing I'm gonna do out here. I'm gonna find a rich man."

I puzzled. "To help you start a restaurant?"

"No, silly, to marry!"

I stared at her, open-jawed.

"I'm dead serious," she continued. "I tell you what, I had a revelation when I was crying in the airport bookstore. See, I looked up and I saw this book, *The Rules*."

She rummaged around in her backpack and pulled out an extensively dog-eared copy of the hated retro Mamie Eisenhower dating manual *The Rules*, written by those two awful girls who trapped themselves a couple of husbands, and then (of course!) one of them got divorced, not that I was judging.

"Please, don't get me started on that, that book," I began, just getting started. "It is the complete opposite of the Grrl Genius philosophy. That book is the single most insulting, demeaning, disgusting screed on how to lie and manipulate and dupe some poor man into—"

"Into what? Into being a man? Into being the kind of guy who is willing to step up to the frigging plate and say he loves you?" Jen challenged.

I could not deal with the idea that Jen had suddenly become a "Rules Girl." It was obvious that the thought of losing Rich's love had tipped poor Jen over the edge, just as the thought of losing his cooking was about to do to the rest of the family if this horrifying tragedy of a permanent breakup could not be averted.

"Well, look, Jen, I know you're hurting . . . ," I tried to reason.

"Seriously, this book all about returning to more traditional, ritualized, and ordered methods of organizing male-female sexual interactions, according to proven social structures, which . . ." Jen continued ranting senselessly and without regard for important gastronomical considerations.

I served up the warm cocoa and trooped into my office to make up the daybed for her. As she rambled on, I went back to fantasizing about the incredibly delicate and savory saffron lobster bisque that was probably still simmering on the stove back in Cambridge. Finally, I had to put a stop to her temporary insanity.

"Jen, I just can't sit here, as your cousin, and agree with you that you should manipulate some guy into marrying you just because he's wealthy and is willing to play by your silly 'Rules,'" I said. "Marriage should be about love and partnership, and mutual trust, and sexual intimacy, and real friendship—"

"What, like yours was?" Jen rebutted.

This stopped me cold. Immediately Jen rushed over to where I was laying out towels for her. "Oh, God, I'm so sorry. That was, I'm so sorry. . . ."

"It's fine . . . ," I muttered. What would be next, more lectures on how I was a man-hater with bad pubes?

"It's just, no offense, I don't want a guy like Kurt. I want a traditional guy, a guy who wants to take care of me, a guy who if, God forbid, we got divorced. . . ."

"Wouldn't make you pay him alimony." I sighed heavily. "Well, you know what, when you put it that way, I guess I can't say I blame you."

The truth was, of course, that I couldn't blame her at all. I had to face up to my enormous romantic mistakes and learn from them, so I wouldn't keep doing the same stupid thing over and over again. I truly felt that leaving Rich was an enormous mistake, and even though I had no credibility in her eyes, I knew I had to talk her out of it. The only problem was, as usual, I had no clue how to do it.

A Grrl Genius "Love Is Important But Chocolate Is Essential" Handy Chocolate Fun Fact

Chocolate has a number of physical components that combine to make it a highly pleasure-inducing food. It satisfies cravings for both sugar and fat, it has a melting point of 97 degrees, which is just below human body temperature, so it melts immediately, and it contains a blend of over five hundred flavors, more than two and a half times more than any other known food. Laboratory experiments have determined that when we experience pleasure, the body's immune system is enhanced, causing us to be more resistant to infection and disease. In short, chocolate can save your life!

The next morning was Saturday, and Jen and I slept in, and then she made me amazing French toast that Rich had invented that was suffused with nutmeg and vanilla and each piece was improbably coated in crushed corn flakes, which sounds awful but trust me, for a recipe that contains no chocolate whatsoever, it's brilliant. She then went on her way over to Hollywood to look for a cultural anthropology waitressing job. I had a magazine article that was due in a week, and so naturally I decided to hunker down and begin procrastinating immediately by heading off to Beverly Hills to take Thor for a longer-than-usual hike. Besides, I needed to take my computer to be repaired, and couldn't possibly be expected to write the article without access to the Internet, or with anything as low-tech as pen and paper.

When I arrived at my distinctive glass and steel house, I was disappointed to see that Kurt was actually home. I had counted on him being at the driving range, which he regarded as his office, and reported to six days a week on a grueling eleven-to-four schedule. Even as a slacker, Kurt couldn't manage to put in nine to five.

I slipped my key into the front gate and walked up the strangely asymetrical steps to the stark, prison yard-like front patio. As I approached, my stomache clenched as I saw Kurt's bantamweight frame draped on one of the ridiculously expensive modern teak lawn chairs he had claimed would be "a good investment for us" when he bought them. (As though there are multimillionaires wandering around their enormous Nantucket seaside mansions clapping themselves on the back for having the foresight to have purchased two-thousand-dollar lawn chairs, thus starting family fortunes that lasted generations. "Just think, Bitsy, all this is ours because we had the smarts to spend insane amounts of money on patio furniture!")

Of course, the investment was paying off for Kurt, wasn't it?

As I walked toward the house, Kurt looked up from his crossword puzzle. "Oh," he greeted me with studied casualness, "I was working, I didn't hear you."

To Kurt, doing a crossword puzzle was "working."

"I'm just going to take Thor for his hike," I stated flatly.

"You know," he intoned preachily, "this actually isn't a good time. I really don't think it's fair that you think that you can waltz in here anytime you like."

I knew that losing my temper was not going to get me anywhere.

"Well, sorry, but as you know, my schedule's kind of erratic, besides I wasn't waltzing, it was really more of a jitterbug . . . ," I joked halfheartedly, trying not to let things get ugly, as they usually did, between us.

"That really can't be my problem. This is my home now. You have to respect that."

"I know I have to pay for it, but I didn't really see why I have to respect it!" I said, inside my own head. This was one of my many silent retorts that surely would have laid Kurt flat, if in fact I ever uttered them.

Kurt continued, "I spoke to my attorney about it, and he said it's reasonable that I ask you to let me know in advance when you are coming. I'd hate to have the lawyers get in on this, it seems like we should be able to come to an agreement without paying a lot of unnecessary lawyer bills."

As if he ever paid a lawyer bill. As if he ever paid any bill. Suddenly, I realized that the reason Kurt was sitting there was that he knew I'd be coming over to hike Thor, that he had waited for me, just so he could have this very discussion. Just so he could glory in his newfound, court-sanctioned ability to try to control me.

"Well, I am happy to call and schedule with you from now on," I lied pleasantly, "but since I'm here anyway, I might as well just take him."

"Sorry, this really isn't a good time," he declared with finality.

"Because?" I asked tersely.

"It just isn't a good time. Sorry." He picked up his absurdly large thermos of "iced tea" (actually beer) and headed for the house. "Why don't you call and let me know what time you want to come on Monday," he called out over his shoulder, "in the afternoon would be best for my schedule. You can let yourself out." He walked inside and shut the door.

I stood there, filled with useless rage, realizing that I had few good options for dealing with the situation at the moment, mostly due to an appalling lack of automatic weapons. With tears stinging my eyes, I walked back down the steps and to my car. I had to face up to the fact that it was my mistake in "helping" Kurt that had turned him into the useless slacker he was. If only I hadn't been "supportive," if only I hadn't "believed in him," he'd have been forced to get a job and be a grown-up like everybody else.

As I opened my car door, I heard a tapping sound and turned to look at the upstairs bedroom window, where Thor, who had obviously been shut away, was scratching at the window and whining mournfully, like Lassie trying to let everybody know just exactly which mine shaft Timmy had fallen down. I assumed that Thor must be very distraught, wondering why I was leaving without taking him for his usual hike.

"Because Kurt is an asshole," I said under my breath, hoping vainly that somehow Thor would understand. "And it's partly my fault."

As I drove away, I felt pathetic and helpless. And then really, really angry at Kurt, and even more angry at a legal system that seemed intent on validating his slackerhood. It was all so unfair, and it was bad enough that it was unfair to me, but now it was unfair to a poor innocent creature who couldn't begin to understand why, on a beautiful sunny day, he wouldn't be allowed to go far a walk. My anger and frustration made me literally want to tear my hair out.

So that's exactly what I did.

I decided that I might as well try to use the gift certificate Amelia had given me and go see Ludmilla at Arabella's so she could violently rip tender hairs out at the follicular level in the most sensitive and nerve-laden area of my body, since it certainly couldn't be more annoying than dealing with Kurt.

Fortunately, Ludmilla had a cancellation and so I was hustled into the deluxe and immaculate treatment room, where my abuse was apparently going to take place to the whiny strains of Enya. Ludmilla had an incomprehensible accent, and I started to wonder why it was that so many of the waxing experts in L.A. hailed from former Soviet-bloc countries. I guess once the Politburo quits hiring, you've only got one choice, come to L.A. to cruelly denude the pudenda of the rich, famous, and foolish.

I had decided that what I wanted was the "Half-Brazilian," which I had seen on-line and was really just a slightly more severe old-fashioned bikini wax. When I told this to Ludmilla, she nodded gravely and responded in her dour and impenetrable eastern block accent, "Da wanna da Bradidan."

"The Half-Brazilian," I clarified.

"Da da bradidan," she agreed.

"The Half-Brazilian," I affirmed.

"Da da bradidan," she pronounced with Stalinist finality.

She then placed a lavender-scented pillow over my eyes, which I fervently prayed had been spiked with chloroform. Warm wax was gently stroked on my nether region, and I felt slightly guilty for how pleasurable and comforting it was.

But not for long. With a loud *thwack!* there was a searing shock of mind-bending pain, and the further shock of my own screaming. I leapt off the table, tossing aside the lavender pillow and pathetically clutching my own pubis. When I looked down, I saw the rather obvious source of my distress: Ludmilla had not given me the requested Half-Brazilian, but had rendered me the senselessly vicious Full Brazilian! (Well technically, half a Full-Brazilian, since I had stopped her.) I had to get out of there, because there was no way I was going to let that woman near my genitalia ever again. Ludmilla, who was apparently used to more willing torture victims, followed me as I hastily put on my jeans and ran out of the room.

"Da gonna be da mistake! Da gonna be lobdidded for all da life!" she called out for everyone in the salon to hear.

"I don't care if I'm lopsided! I told you half! Half!" I shrieked as I staggered out the front door.

I went home, and when Jen saw me hobbling up the stairs, she asked me what happened. I told her that I was suffering from the last remaining battle of the cold war. She gave me a puzzled look, and I want to bed early with an ice pack, musing on the idea of what would be a worse mistake: possibly having someone see my Half-a-Full-Brazilian, or going back to Ludmilla.

I decided that the way things were going, there was little danger of anyone seeing my tragic waxing until it had regrown to its former fuzzy glory. But I had been right, bad as it was, the waxing was still less annoying than having to deal with Kurt.

A Grrl Genius Crazy Sex Fact

In Kentucky, it is against the law to marry the same man four times.

(Come on, they really need a law?)

When I finally got my crashed computer back on Monday, I had more than a hundred unread e-mails. There were the usual offers of Viagra and randy cheerleaders who were dying to chat with me, but there were also seven e-mails from William McCall, each with increasingly panicky subject lines like "Subject: I need your help!" and "Subject: Hey, you're not mad at me, are you?" and "Subject: Urgent! Please answer!" and finally ending with this one:

From: William@backwoodswriter.com
To: GG@grrlgenius.com
Subject: Ready or not!

Dear Cathryn,

Well, you have been entirely "Le chien de la soire" as the French
say, which either means "hiding in the night," or "the very dark
dog" (my French is at least as French as Cheez Whiz is Cheese).
Anyway the point is, you have been IMPOSSIBLE TO REACH and that
is too bad because I have made a life-altering decision. I've sent
you a bunch of e-mails, which have gone unanswered, and I
couldn't find your number in directory assistance. So I had to
decide on my own, without talking to you, but I feel like you
already made yourself clear.

I'm moving to L.A.!

Why? Because you told me to, you said it was a good idea, and I
agree.

Professionally, I have been offered a job for which I frankly don't
feel qualified: writing a screenplay for a movie, which is about a
woman living in L.A. She's single and there's a bunch of complications,
but I knew right away that even if I could write from the
perspective of a single woman (no, don't know how I am going to
do that) I still don't know how it is to live in L.A. and that sitting
here with a flannel shirt in Idaho, nursing a 10-day-old beard
(I saw it as a project I should undertake, but I shaved it this
morning) I simply was NOT going to get the vibe right for a single
woman in L.A.

So: I've made up my mind. I'm moving to L.A. Of course I have no
idea where I will be living, or parking, but I'm sure it will all work
out somehow.

I can't wait to see you again in person. I'm scared out of my mind that I might be making a huge mistake, but life is full of risks. More on that when we see each other.

As promised, and one of my first acts upon arriving, I want to take you out to dinner, you name the place, not because you are, in fact, the only person I actually KNOW in L.A. but because you are such a delight, and, of course, the inspiration behind this whole move! Hell, maybe we could even write this darn screenplay together!

You've been wonderfully supportive in all of this, and I so appreciate it! I will make it worth your while, you'll see, I promise.

William

I was shocked. I couldn't believe that William was turning out to be so strange. I couldn't believe that I randomly suggested that he should move to L.A., and then he just up and did it. Because he was going to "write a screenplay"? Was someone going to pay him for this, or was this one of the typical L.A. rip-off deals where a bunch of "producers" were "working with him," as he toiled away for free?

Did he expect me to put him up? And now he expected me to help him write it, as well. I said I would have dinner with him, not be his "only friend in L.A.!" He said I was the only person he knew here, he said that I was "the inspiration behind this whole move." It was insane! I barely knew him. I shared some rice, okay, a lot of rice, with him and we sent a couple of e-mails, and now he was saying that I had been "wonderfully supportive" and that he was going to make it "worth my while." He sounded exactly like Randy from Boston, or Dave from Seattle, or any of the other strange stalkers I had collected on my book tour, guys who, having read my book, had decided they were "the Enlightened Male I need." Now, in the course of a weekend, I had a new roommate (Jen) and what appeared to be another one on the way.

The next day I called an emergency meeting of the Grrl Genius Club to discuss what to do about William. I knew what they would say before I even got to the restaurant. I just couldn't believe that this unshaven comedy-writing potato farmer (or whatever he was) from Idaho (whom I had begun to think of as an actual normal man) was crazily uprooting his whole life to move to L.A. just because I randomly, *casually*, suggested that it might be a good idea!

We met at the bar at Musso & Franks, a Hollywood institution that, not surprisingly, served the kind of food that could only be described as "institutional." Vonnie loved it for its old Hollywood atmosphere, and the rest of us tolerated its overpriced, overcooked food. I didn't care where we met—I needed to access my club members' collective genius for advice on this "William thing," and pronto.

Vonnie weighed in with her opinion first. "Now, doll, you know I'm a hopeless romantic, but it sounds like this William person is potentially dangerous. Dangerous for you, anyway, what with your bad history of trying to rescue men."

Kim was typically blunt. "This is all your fault. I mean what on earth were you doing giving him advice on how to live his life? Can't you see how that fosters dependency on you?"

Even the ever-tolerant and experimental Amelia was against him. "Honey, I'm glad you're starting to attract non-gay men for a change, but this guy sounds like he's planning to have himself surgically attached to your thigh."

I winced at the idea of anything surgical in that still oh-so-tender area.

"You just can't start lactating for the guy, that's all," Vonnie warned. "And I don't have a good feeling about the fact that he suggests writing with you, I mean, you've got a lot of very impressive credits, and he's just some guy from the sticks. I'm sorry, but I'm really seeing shades of Kurt here. I don't trust it."

"The harsh fact is this," said Kim, who was a big fan of harsh facts, "you are facing financial ruin because you co-depended a husband, so you have to make sure that this William person, who frankly sounds sort of needy, doesn't get the idea that he's coming to town and you are going to 'take care of him.' You cannot keep repeating these same disastrous patterns with men, because frankly, I can't take the stress of it. You have got to learn from your mistakes."

"If you're going to give him the brush off, do yourself a favor," said Amelia, who, because of Clarissa's most recent live HBO comedy special, which was titled *F**ck Amelia,* was literally world-famous for breaking up with people, "be brief and businesslike."

"Not rambling and personal, like how you usually are," Kim affirmed. "And don't chicken out on this. You always think you can save every wounded bird. It will feel terrible giving him the cold shoulder, but it's just got to be done. Remember, this whole 'saving thing' is how you ended up married to Kurt, and look how that turned out!"

"So you don't think if, once he moves out here, if he seems normal . . . ," I began weakly.

"No!" roared the Grrl Genius Club in unison.

That night I sent out an e-mail William. I was perplexed and saddened by his strange behavior, but I knew that the Grrl Genius Club was right. I couldn't make it seem like I was responsible for him or his career, or his choices.

I decided that the best choice was just to lie and seem really busy with work.

From: GG@grrlgenius.com
To: William@backwoodswriter.com
Subject: I'm not ready

Dear William,

I was surprised to get your e-mail, and hear that you are moving to L.A.

I really hope it goes well for you.

As it turns out, I don't think it will work out for us to have dinner for the foreseeable future, as I find that I am really busy with a number of projects and have decided that I will keep social obligations to a minimum. I am sure as a writer, you understand.

Probably the best thing would be for me to drop you a line when things ease up for me, as I probably won't be checking e-mail much or answering the phone either, since I'll be hiding out from the people I owe writing to.

After I get out from under, I will get in touch, and perhaps we can have that dinner then.

Good luck!

Cathryn Michon

I felt just terrible writing the letter to William. I felt like a bad person, like I should help him, but my friends said this is exactly what was wrong with me, and I supposed they were right. I even, in a pique of non–Grrl Genius cowardice, tried to *unsend* it, which it turned out I couldn't because of some Internet crap I didn't really understand. It was obviously for the best, but it just didn't feel very good. When I went to bed, I started to realize that I had done the right thing: I had finally learned from my past relationship mistakes. I couldn't afford to rescue men anymore; I had to finally learn to rescue myself.

A woman needs a man like a fish needs a net.
—Cynthia Heimel

Chapter 4

A Grrl Genius Does Her Best to Maintain a
Positive Attitude

I love men, I love sex, and I don't care who knows it.
—Margot Kidder

IT HAD BEEN a few weeks since Jen had arrived, and I had given William the brush off. I decided that the way to turn my life around was to cultivate something I'd never really had before—a positive attitude. I told Vonnie all about my new rosy outlook on life one afternoon as I sat glumly on my big red sofa. She was supportive, if somewhat skeptical.

"Being positive would be the best thing in the world for you, doll," she cooed, patting me (rather dismissively, I thought) on the knee. "So what's new with the mountain man? Is he lurking in your bushes?" Vonnie wanted to know as she sipped her tea.

I sighed. "William? No, he's stopped stalking me. I wrote him an e-mail a few weeks ago saying something like, 'I'd go to dinner with you, but I've got plans for the next four years,' and he wrote back and said 'okay' and that's it, I haven't heard from him since."

"Sounds like you dodged a bullet with that one!" Vonnie pronounced heartily.

"Maybe," I said doubtfully.

"Honey, you were not put on earth to rescue men."

"I know, I know. Being a Grrl Genius of relationships isn't as easy as I thought it would be. It just makes me sad not to hear from him anymore—"

"Sad you don't have a man showing up on your doorstep wanting you to create a career for him, sleep with him, and fix him breakfast, to boot? Please! That's not being positive, hon. Let's move on. What's new with cousin Jen—you two still getting along?"

"Oh, please!" I sat up, surveying my uncharacteristically neat apartment. "She's a miracle! Except for her endless screeds about *The Rules*, we get along perfectly. Not only does she insist on pulling her weight with the housework—which turns out to be pulling my weight, as well—but when she couldn't find a job at any fine-dining restaurants in L.A.—"

"I guess the actresses have sewn those up," Vonnie said wryly.

"Right. So she took what she refers to as a 'waitressing/cultural anthropologist job' at this horrible Astro Diner dive."

"Oh, my God!" Vonnie blurted.

"You know the place?" asked cautiously. I couldn't imagine the tiny, scummy, hole in the wall on Hollywood Boulevard (notable only for the fact that a majority of the clientele were either hookers, drug addicts, pimps, bums, transvestites, or sometimes a festive combination of all of these) was a hangout for an ex-Iowa beauty queen like Vonnie.

"Doll, I'm going to have to leave that story for another day," Vonnie replied mysteriously. "But we've got to get her out of there!"

"Oh, I tried to talk her out of working there, but she insists on contributing to the household expenses, which is sort of refreshing, given the whole Kurt experience. Plus she's got this whole crazy idea that working there is 'research' for her dissertation involving the habits and customs of people who live outside of mainstream society."

Vonnie scowled "Bums."

"Exactly. Jen is teaching me a whole new definition of being positive."

"Being delusional?"

"Right," I concurred. I told Vonnie I was even trying to maintain a positive attitude toward Kurt, who was making it increasingly difficult to schedule my hikes with Thor. He would always phone at the last minute, saying he needed to reschedule, that whatever arrangement I had made to come get the dog would be "inconvenient." My positive attitude toward Kurt consisted almost entirely of my not having murdered him.

"Hon, your soon-to-be-ex is as useless as a limp dick," Vonnie proclaimed with all the down-home wisdom of her common-sense Iowa upbringing.

A Grrl Genius Crazy Sex Fact

The penises of the Bushmen of the Kalahari Desert are semierect at all times. (No statistics are available as to how this affects the attention span of the Bushwomen.)

My newly adopted positive attitude really kicked into high gear when I received a horrifying request from Elaine Carriere, an old friend from Minnesota who now lived in L.A., to sing at her wedding. She and her fiancé Andy had rewritten lyrics to the Bing Crosby hit "True Love" and wanted me to belt them out in front of her family.

"I'll be happy to. I love weddings!" I gushed with newfound Grrl Genius positive attitude. Yes, I thought, I love weddings. I love weddings the way Vietnam vets love helicopters. I just hoped I could stick to the new lyrics and not appear as some kind of horrifying Ghost of Marriage Past, rattling the chains I forged in life as I warned over and over again, "Beware! Beware!"

Reality is something you rise above.
        —Liza Minelli

How to Have a Positive Attitude (in Relationships)
No Matter What

Bad Relationship Situation	What Stinks About It	What's Positive About It	How to Have a Positive Attitude
Your boyfriend of two days says that he thinks you're great but is worried that the relationship is "moving too quickly."	You probably won't be able to get the deposit back from the moving company you hired.	You hate him and wouldn't want to be in a relationship with him if he were the last man on earth.	Pretend he is the last man on earth.
All the good single men are gay.	Gay men don't like to have sex with women.	Gay men often enjoy ballroom dancing.	Go dancing, and pretend he is not gay!
You are old and fat and ugly, and nobody will ever love you.	You are old and fat and ugly, and nobody will ever love you.	There are older, fatter, uglier women than you. Aren't there?	Pretend you are not old and fat and ugly and that nobody will ever love you.
The best relationship you have ever had is with your dog.	Picking up the poop.	Everything else.	Pretend that the men you are dating are dogs (this is not hard).
You married someone who didn't really love you and he never had a job and then he got mad at you when you finally left.	You might have to support him for the rest of your natural life.	Nobody lives forever.	Pretend he is one of those Sally Struthers kids you sponsor in a foreign country and that he has flies all over his eyes and is really sad.
You have to sing a goopy love song at your friend's wedding.	Weddings make you want to kill yourself.	The cake.	Pretend that it's a funeral. Your funeral, since that's how you'll feel.

As soon as I told the Grrl Genius Club that I was going to turn my love life around by being more positive, even if it killed me, they were chock-full of suggestions. Kim suggested that instead of spending my time hoping to meet a firefighter, I should simply go out and get myself one. Or several. Because Kim is nothing if not goal-oriented, she informed me that at her kid's richy-pants school auction, they were going to be auctioning off hunky firefighters, and told me I should just "Get your butt out here and buy you some firemen of your very own."

I was very positive about the idea.

AUCTION ITEM 147
THE HIDDEN HILLS FIRE DEPARTMENT

A wonderfully festive and educational evening for you and five lucky friends with the brave firefighters of the Hidden Hills Squad 73! The firefighters will prepare a homemade firehouse meal for you and your guests, emergencies permitting. The squad will then give a fully guided tour of their living quarters, and explain the uses of all their equipment, from the Jaws of Life to power hoses.

As I've mentioned before, Kim may be crabby, but she's an excellent friend.

Kim's three boys attended a private school where the classrooms were little ivy-covered cottages and an organic gourmet lunch was served every day in a giant open courtyard. It cost a billion dollars a semester (actual figure) but tuition was just the beginning. Each parent was expected to donate money to the school, usually by purchasing normal household things that they would need to buy anyway (such as skiing trips to Switzerland or new breast implants) at the annual school auction. The funds raised at these events were earmarked to "enhance the educational environment" by providing massage therapists during exam week or by infusing the air with gold dust.

Although I knew there were worthier charities than making sure that the children of sitcom stars and heart surgeons got a new electron microscope for the science lab or a world-class Frank

Gehry concert hall for performances of "Itsy Bitsy Spider," I felt very positively about contributing what was left of my dwindling funds to help the children of millionaires become even more spoiled and privileged. I was going to get firefighters out of it.

I am the sentence, you are the word
True love, true love
I am the feather, you are the bird
True love, true love
I love to kiss you, when day is done
True love, true love
We belong together, like hot dog and bun
True love, true love!

The ridiculously bad lyrics I would be singing at Elaine and Andy's wedding ran through my mind whenever I thought of the hunky firefighters I hoped would soon be mine. To be strictly accurate, I would be buying them for only one night, but I figured that would be only the beginning. As I strolled across the velvety green school lawn, sipping champagne and listening to the string quartet, I looked again at the well dog-eared page in the auction catalog.

I used my powers of Grrl Genius positive thinking and imagined my brave and hunky firefighters as they pulled people and puppies out of burning buildings and then cradled them in their bulging biceps. I saw them frantically pounding on the chests of heart attack victims and using their full and sensuous lips to breathe the breath of life back into people who were clutched in death's icy grip. I pictured them at the end of the day, the hollows of their cheekbones manfully smudged with soot, as they slouched off their heavy yellow rubber coats and sweat-soaked shirts, revealing their well-cleaved, smoke-scented, hairy chests as they came into the cozy firehouse kitchen where I had conveniently just dropped by with warm apple cobbler, which I would learn how to make.

See how this works? With my newly positive attitude toward sex and relationships, I was no longer going to be passed out in front of my computer in a tattered bathrobe with greasy hair, little dried bits of Häagen-Dazs chocolate ice cream darkening my nails from a rather desperate late-night bottom-of-the-carton struggle, dreaming about hunky firefighters.

No, I was using my positive can-do Grrl Genius attitude to make my way to this ridiculous event where I wouldn't just be vaguely dreaming of firefighters, I would buy myself a whole squad of them!

Kim spied me obsessing over the catalog and rushed over to greet me, her immense turquoise jewelry clanking as loudly as a busboy's silverware tray. Because of her fanatical dedication to the simple, down-home values of the Old West, she was wearing a metal pendant so outrageously enormous that it could function both as a decorative object and as a bulletproof breastplate for a shootout at the O.K. Corral.

"Cathryn!" she wheezed, still suffering from the smoker's lungs that had her sucking on a Tootsie Pop as desperately as if it were an oxygen tube. "I'm so glad you made it!"

"Nice necklace," I enthused insincerely.

"Isn't it? It's made from found objects—"

"Like what, Buicks?" Her scowl told me that, once again, I should have kept my fashion commentary to myself. "I mean, I love Buicks, they're so—"

"Can it. I hate the stupid necklace, too. Barnaby bought it for me. I don't have the heart to tell him that I can't stand all this gaudy jewelry he buys me. Anyway, the silent auction is over there in the Zen garden. Let's go do a quick recon and see if anyone has bid on your hunky firefighters."

As we made our way to the auction tables, Kim outlined her plan of attack.

"Think of me as the Tony Soprano of Hidden Hills," Kim said. "I have my ways, but it's probably better you don't ask too many questions. *Capisce?*"

"Capisce," I said, as if it were something I said all the time.

Next to the phony sandbox were the tables that held the clipboards for the silent auction. They were covered in white linen and aggressively large floral arrangements. The floral arrangements were filled with the kind of garish tropical flowers that had brazenly engorged pistils and pollen-soaked stamens and served to remind us that flowers are as flagrantly obvious about their wanton sexuality as Hollywood Boulevard hookers.

Kim and I checked the silent auction sheet for the hunky firefighters. The bidding was to start at $250, and there were only two bids, one for $275 from Missy Berwin, whom I knew to be the third wife of a well-known therapist-to the-stars, and one for $300 from someone named Delores Hatcher.

Immediately I could see the wheels turning in Kim's brain as she assessed our situation. "Delores Hatcher is the librarian—she's no threat—but this Missy Berwin thing is a real problem."

"Why?" I asked, alarmed.

"Missy's a former PA turned slacker clacker," Kim sneered. In the shorthand language of cynical L.A. marriage evaluation, *clackers* were women who wore little five-hundred-dollar Manolo Blanik mules and clacked their way up and down Montana Avenue, shopping and lunching and having affairs with their Pilates instructors. A *slacker clacker* was a further refinement that meant the trophy wife in question was dedicated to, above all else, not holding down a job other than decorating her expensive house and body. "Missy is very competitive, plus very pissy from being the stepmom of two teenage girls, plus she's loaded as all hell," Kim observed worriedly.

I just couldn't hear this. I couldn't outspend Missy Berwin. "I can't believe this! Why does God hate me? Why can't I ever get anything I want?" I lamented, my Grrl Genius positive attitude maybe slipping just a tad.

"Don't worry, I can take care of this. Put in your bid. Make it four hundred so they know you're serious."

"But I can't afford—"

"Just do it," she ordered in a way that made me understand it was definitely an offer I couldn't refuse. "You just have to make sure to invite me to the damn dinner. . . ."

Shakily I wrote down my bid, following her bossy instructions as I usually did.

"But, Kim, you're married, you don't need a hunky firefighter, and there are so many deserving single women, it's not fair."

Kim pulled me in so close I could feel the front bumper of her strange necklace poking me uncomfortably in my left nipple.

Pulled in as closely as I was, I suddenly noticed that although she was very angry, her face was completely uncreased with emotions. She had had Botox! "I want to come to the dinner," she hissed. "I need to meet those frigging firefighters. I deserve it as much as anybody. Barnaby and I haven't had sex in over a year."

I was stunned.

Had I heard her right? Was this true, or was this just the poison in her face talking? "What do you mean you haven't had sex in over a year?" I asked stupidly and far too loudly.

She gave me the look of derision I deserved and again leaned in close. "Which part do I need to explain? The haven't had sex part or the over a year part?" Kim whispered fiercely.

"But . . . why? I mean, why haven't you, and he . . . ," I stammered.

"I have no idea."

"Do you think Barnaby might have, you know, like, an impotence problem?" I asked warily. Even as I said it, I imagined that for most men, the phrase "impotence problem" was the ultimate redundancy.

"I don't know! How can I know what's going on with his dick when I haven't seen it up close and personal for over a year now!"

"Sorry, I'm, I just thought . . ."

Kim looked contrite. "No, I'm sorry I'm just a little . . ."

"You haven't had sex in over a year, I get it."

"Exactly." Kim slumped heavily into a lawn chair; it seemed as though her jewelry were weighing her down like an anchor. "I still love him. I don't know if he's having an affair. I don't know if he masturbates. I know I do. Usually while I'm thinking of firefighters."

I nodded in agreement. "I hear ya, sister."

We both sat quietly for a moment, contemplating the image of firefighters that had kept us warm all the nights of the past year.

"Well, look," I said, "obviously, obviously you're in for the dinner. If I even get it."

"Oh, you'll get it—don't worry about that. Think positive!" And with that she clanked off hurriedly, leaving me to contemplate the enormity of the information she had dropped on me.

Kim and Barnaby hadn't had sex for an entire year!

How does that happen? How does a whole year go by? Even in the darkest days of my unhappy marriage, even as I spent my days earning a living writing murder stories for television—murder stories that were mostly inspired by my then husband (as I told my bosses on the show, hey, this is like free money to me, I would just be sitting home planning a murder!)—even then, we still had sex, occasionally.

I wondered, did that make me a slut? Having sex with someone I couldn't stand just because I was married to him and he was, well, there? How long does it go before you notice how long it has gone? Do six months go by and then you start leaving little lists on the refrigerator whiteboard that read THINGS TO PICK UP: MILK, BREAD, WILLING SEX PARTNER.

At that moment a giant gong sounded and an announcement crackled over the loudspeakers. "Ladies and gentlemen, there are two more minutes to complete your bids for the silent auction!"

I was not as hopeful as Kim wanted me to be. I felt confident that while I might be able to outbid Delores the librarian, there was no way that I could outgun Missy Berwin, who was sporting a $75,000 tennis bracelet on her wrist. (Although I was quite certain she didn't even play tennis.)

As it turned out, I didn't have to outspend Missy, because I had the rock solid Grrl Genius of Kim, "the Tony Soprano of Hidden Hills," on my side. As she swung into full suburban Mafiosa mode, Delores was dispatched with a simple reminder that Kim chaired the school library committee, which the very next week would be considering the matter of whether to send a representative to the Santa Fe library convention in the fall.

Missy had to be shot down with bigger guns, and Kim destroyed her with the triple threat of Natalie, Lisa, and Meagan, the three best baby-sitters in Hidden Hills. "Listen," Kim said threateningly to Missy, "I got all three girls bit parts on shows on my network, so from now on, those girls sit only for me, or my friends." Kim then smiled sweetly. "We are friends, aren't we, Missy?" Missy threw down her pen in disgust, leaving the silent auction table.

Just then the gong sounded the end of the auction, and Kim and I eagerly high-fived, her stupid pendant nearly giving me a black eye as we did so.

But it didn't matter. Squad 73 was mine, all mine. My Grrl Genius positive attitude was finally beginning to work.

True love, true love!

If you can't change your fate, change your attitude.

—Amy Tan

I still could not believe my good fortune when I arrived home to my Studio City apartment building holding my little certificate for Squad 73. Jen wandered sleepily into the living room when I opened the door. "I got it! I bought us hunky firefighters at Kim's auction!"

"For reals?" she asked as I walked in and she reflexively handed me a spoon and pulled out a carton of Ben & Jerry's Cherry Garcia from the freezer. We sat on the sofa as we silently began chopping away at the ice cream.

"Totally," I replied. "They'll cook dinner for us, and then show us around, then there's some kind of hose demonstration. . . ."

"Ha! You wish," she snorted.

"No, seriously. But here's the thing. I mean, obviously you're in, and Amelia and Vonnie and but that only leaves me two other spaces. Oh, no, I only have one because now I have to invite Kim."

"No way," proclaimed Jen. "She's married. She's got her whole perfect Martha Stewart country life with the husband and kids. She doesn't need it."

"She and Barnaby haven't had sex in a year," I instantly regretted saying.

"Get out!"

"Get in. I couldn't believe it either. . . ."

"Does he have a, you know, functional problem?" Jen wanted to know.

"She doesn't know, she hasn't you know . . . She doesn't want to ask him. They just—they just don't talk about it," I explained lamely.

Jen got that look on her face that she always gets when she thinks she's having a great idea. "Oh, man. You know what she should do? I heard about this on an episode of *Ricki Lake*. The way to find out if a man is having, you know, erectile difficulties, is to put some postage stamps around his penis when he's sleeping, and then if when he wakes up and the postage stamps are torn apart, then you know that he's getting nocturnal erections."

"That's the stupidest thing I ever heard."

"What, it works!" Jen said.

"Look, I'm sure it works, but how the hell do you explain it? I mean, presuming you could even get in there while he's sleeping, what are you going to say to him when he wakes up and finds stamps in his underpants?" I snickered.

Jen thought about it a moment. "I don't know . . . how about, 'Special Delivery!'"

We both burst into helpless giggles. "Hey, here's the good part, though," I said brightly. "If she finds out something is wrong with it, at least she's already got postage on it so she can ship it off to get repaired!"

I promised Jen I'd pass her postage tip along to Kim, because this was exactly how the Grrl Genius network worked, as we turned the world pink, one Grrl Genius at a time.

A Grrl Genius "People Who've Made Worse Relationship Mistakes Than You" Moment

Darryl Washington and Maria Ramos of New York City were injured at New York City's Bowery subway station when a train plowed into them while they were having sex on a mattress they had thrown on the tracks.

High on my success in buying firefighters I decided to use my positive can-do attitude to do something else good for myself. I was going to rob my own house.

After two weeks of Kurt blowing me off nearly every time I scheduled Thor's walk, and then having to frantically restructure my day, and then sometimes not being able to see Thor at all, I had simply had it. Thor was a creature of routine, and I knew that every day our regular walk time came and passed without me, it stressed Thor out as he anxiously waited until I finally showed up. Sometimes, as I made my way up the steps, he was actually trembling with relief, and it broke my heart. Thor missed me, and the truth was I was aching for Thor and missed him every hour of every day I didn't see him. The plain fact was, I knew that if you can't find a good man, you need to find a good dog.

Reasons Why Dogs Are Better Than Men

What's Great About Dogs	What's Great About Men
You can train them not to scratch themselves in front of guests.	They wear pants.
Dogs are absurdly grateful for everything you do for them.	They can drive.
Dogs are absolutely loyal to their mistress.	Sometimes they don't have a mistress.
A dog will protect you and defend you against all enemies foreign and domestic.	Sometimes the pants they wear are clean.

My plan was simple: I would wait till two in the morning and then sneak in the back gate of the house, climb in through the dog door, and get Thor. I would make it look like Thor had shoved his way through the spindly wooden fence in back of the house, as he often did, and had run away. I knew that Kurt would deny me permission to take the dog if I asked him, but also that he wouldn't be willing to expend much effort to find the dog if he thought Thor had just run away. Even without a yard, I knew that Thor would be happier with me, and Kurt would be none the wiser.

Like everything I ever did, the majority of my planning for my heist involved thinking about the outfit I would wear while doing it, and what famous movie star I would most resemble. Whenever I had to plan an important outfit, my main method was to imagine what a beloved classic movie star would wear if she were in the situation I was in. For the dognapping, it was obvious that the ideal ensemble would be something like the little black capri pants and matching boatneck blouse Grace Kelly wore in *To Catch a Thief*. Unfortunately, due to steady doses of the Grrl Genius healing elixir of chocolate, I was having some difficulty fitting into my *To Catch a Thief* capri pants, and so had to go instead with my Linda Hamilton in *Terminator 2* cargo pants. As a Grrl Genius, it is my devout belief that clothes are everything. I felt okay about this look, though it was definitely my second choice.

The Grrl Genius Pretend You're a Famous Movie Star Do-It-Yourself (and Doesn't That Feel Good!) Disaster Fashion Response System™

Disaster du Jour	High-Maintenance Grrl Genius	Medium-Maintenance Grrl Genius	No-Maintenance Grrl Genius
Tornado	Judy Garland in *The Wizard of Oz* impeccably coiffed and ruby lipped and wearing *the single greatest pair of shoes ever!* And by the way, is it not one of the greatest Grrl Genius cinematic moments of all time that on her way to see the mighty and powerful Wizard she has the presence of mind to stop for a spa treatment? That's Grrl Genius in action, people!	Margaret Hamilton as the Wicked Witch in *The Wizard of Oz*. Her look isn't everyone's cup of tea, but at least with a crisply starched pointy hat and flowing black robes, she made a choice. ("All my beautiful wickedness!") Besides, it's never fully explained why her face is green, and might it not be that it's merely because we have caught her in the middle of a facial?	Helen Hunt in *Twister* rushing around trying to warn innocent potential tornado victims about oncoming cyclones but unwilling to take even the smallest amount of time to prevent herself from becoming a slovenly fashion victim. She doesn't even take 10 seconds to apply under-eye concealer or so much as a swipe of lip gloss. All because of some stupid childhood incident with a storm cellar and a deadly twister. Whatever. (Oh sure, she winds up with Bill Paxton in the end but *only because* she invokes the name of Dorothy. I rest my case.)
Trouble with Water	Marilyn Monroe in *River of No Return*, on a raft with fully boned push up lingerie, false eyelashes, and a Dacron wig that makes it impossible for her *continued*	Kate Winslet in *Titanic*, who unlike Marilyn did consent to getting her hair wet (what with it being a sinking ship and all) but never backed down on her lipstick, which stayed fresh *continued*	Look, I'm not trying to beat up on her or anything, but Helen Hunt in *Twister* was also deluged with torrential rains and didn't make the slightest effort to wear decent underwear even *continued*

continued

Disaster du Jour	High-Maintenance Grrl Genius	Medium-Maintenance Grrl Genius	No-Maintenance Grrl Genius
	hair to get wet, even underwater!	and lovely as she kissed poor Leo good-bye forever. I'm sure he was grateful.	though she surely knew it would show under her rain-soaked, shapeless, style-free outfits. I suppose that's all because of some alleged childhood trauma, too. Whatever.
Nuclear Meltdown	Jane Fonda (who learned her fashion lessons well in *Barbarella* and has only that horrifying Florence Henderson–esque shag haircut in *Klute* in her style demerit column) in *The China Syndrome,* who manages never to have a hair in her enormous hairdo or a single false eyelash out of place, even as she is doing her best to prevent a nuclear core meltdown. Go, Jane!	Tracy Reed who plays the mistress/assistant to General Turgidson in *Dr. Strangelove,* and who, despite the threat of total nuclear warfare between the U.S. and the USSR, remains coolly elegant in a casual (but sexy) bikini and big (but not as big as Jane's!) hair.	It's not like I hate Helen Hunt (who has never been in a movie about a nuclear meltdown). But how come Helen Hunt never has big hair? Helen Hunt can't even manage to back-comb her hair when she wins a frigging Oscar. (Which she deserves, but still, hair is about height, and she should know that or pay someone to tell her that, and I am totally saying this with love in my heart and I think she knows that.)
Marooned on a Desert Island	Any one of the ladies on *Rescue from Gilligan's Island* (what, it's a legitimate movie!) all of whom managed to keep their outfits varied and perfect with just what they brought for a three-hour *continued*	Doris day in *Move Over Darling,* who comes back from five years marooned on an island without so much as a sunburn and who manages to convince hubby Rock Hudson that even though she *continued*	Helen Hunt's boyfriend, Tom Hanks, was marooned on a desert island in *Castaway* and she *didn't even go!* Plus I hate that one sweater she wore. *continued*

Disaster du Jour	High-Maintenance Grrl Genius	Medium-Maintenance Grrl Genius	No-Maintenance Grrl Genius
	tour. (Plus coconuts and indigenous flowers, and really, doesn't Dawn Wells have a few things to teach all of us about the importance of the simple, classic, lung collapsingly tight tied man's shirt?)	was shipwrecked with hunky Chuck Conners, she never even kissed him once. (Never? Never kissed the frigging Rifleman, for crying out loud?)	

I parked around the corner and was struck by the irony of having to sneak up like a (albeit smartly dressed) thief on a house for which I was still paying the mortgage. I eased in around the back, opened the rickety wooden gate Kurt never cared to fix since it wasn't "architectural" and "didn't show." The fact that the fence was "functional" and kept the dog from "running away" was not of interest to him. I made a plausible, Doberman-sized opening in the fence with a hammer that I had brought in my fake Kate Spade shoulder bag.

Thor's absurdly high-tech German temperature controlled dog bed/throne sat in a far corner of the kitchen, directly next to the dog door. The bedroom where Kurt and the lingerie-selling triceratops slept was at the far other corner of the house, so I knew that even when the dog did his customary happy dance upon seeing me, Kurt wouldn't so much as stir in the lizardlike embrace of his hideous girlfriend. The only trick would be getting Thor to go outside, because he hated going out the dog door and preferred to be let out the front door. With this in mind, I had brought along plenty of name-brand Milk-Bones to coax Thor out of the house.

Kurt, in his perpetual cheapness (with the money I earned) insisted on buying our pet generic dog biscuits, which Thor refused to touch.

Outside the kitchen door, I twisted myself corkscrewlike through the aluminum dog door. As I slid into the house, I felt the cool white ceramic tile on my belly. The über-high-tech kitchen was done entirely in white and brushed steel and looked not so much like a kitchen, but more like the set for an autopsy show. Needless to say, Kurt had overruled me on all issues of décor. When I had gotten about halfway through, Thor heard me and came clattering clumsily toward me and began licking me with his usual obsessive enthusiasm. For a moment I was content to sit there, enjoying his slightly funky, musky doggy smell and feeling his furry face as it happily brushed against mine. I fed him a Milk-Bone and it was at that moment I became conscious of the full implications of (once again) having chosen the wrong outfit.

As I grabbed Thor's collar and started to ease him out the door, after me and I realized that nothing that could be described as "easing" was about to take place. The same chocolate situation that had necessitated the wearing of the ugly cargo pants had in fact caused my butt to be wedged firmly in the dog door. As if my extra chocolate-enhanced girth wasn't enough of a problem, the stupid pants with all their paramilitary zippers and toggle snaps and rip cords that had slid *in* the door so perfectly were far less inclined to allow me to slip out. I contorted and shoved and groaned, and yet nothing was moving.

I tried, according to my newly minted Grrl Genius laws, to look at the bright side of this ridiculous situation. All I could think of that was good about it was that maybe it would save me money on the expensive and pointless phony New Age rebirthing weekends that Amelia kept trying to con me into doing with her.

Keeping in mind that there is nothing to fear but fear itself, I began to panic.

I then remembered that I had tucked my cell phone into the pocket of my jacket. As humiliating as it was, I was going to have to call someone, and get them to come rescue me. Vonnie's name was the last number dialed on my cell phone, so she won the late-night phone-call lottery.

"Listen, Vonnie, it's Cathryn, don't hang up!" I whispered fervently into the phone when Vonnie finally answered.

"Huh?" she mumbled incoherently.

"Look, I'm sorry to wake you up, but it's an emergency and you've got to help me."

"Okay, doll, I'm there for ya, kid," she agreed vaguely, a true blue Grrl Genius, even when unconscious.

"The thing is, I'm stuck in the dog door of my house, I mean the house Kurt is in, I'm stealing Thor and, I, I need you to come help me get out."

"That's fine. Can we do it tomorrow?" she asked, clearly not getting it.

"What? No! Now! You have to come now!"

"Okay, okay, okay, I gotcha, I'm coming now. Don't worry, hon, I'll be there in two shakes!" She hung up. I had no idea if she had understood any of it, not that it actually made sense, and as I had had conversations with her in the past where she had been totally asleep, there was no way to know if she would really come.

Just then, I heard a loud thump and a sudden stream of expletives which I recognized as Kurt making his nightly knee slam into the sharp steel corner of the bedroom dresser. Kurt, perhaps to make up for his lack of stature, had an improbable fondness for oddly shaped pretentious German contemporary art furniture that was both hideously ugly and wildly impractical. Lying there on the kitchen floor, I remembered how much I used to enjoy hearing the solid thunk that meant his enthusiasm for "important" furniture and his congenitally weak bladder had met on their nightly rendezvous of doom.

I was absolutely terrified. If Kurt found me, I wouldn't put it past him to call the cops, and I certainly didn't care to have my first meeting with the Triceratops in this humbled position.

Of course Thor immediately began barking his head off, sternly warning the offending dresser and any other furniture in the house that he was on duty and ready to defend. I was still holding on to Thor's collar, and tried to get him to stop barking by literally holding his jaw shut, but it didn't work. Finally, I held open his jaw and threw in a Milk Bone.

"Thor! . . . Goddamnit, shut up!" Kurt called out. Although Thor almost never obeyed him, this time he did, due to being rewarded with fistfuls of nongeneric doggy treats.

As I lie there breathing shallowly and feeding name-brand Milk-Bones to the dog (I had paid for) and was now trying to steal from the house (I had paid for) my (apparently now much larger) ass solidly stuffed into a doggy door, I wondered if, in fact, this was the lowest moment of my life.

I then realized that I could think of at least a dozen moments that were at least this humiliating, and oddly, that gave me some comfort.

I heard Kurt stumble back into the bedroom, and I began breathing more deeply. I don't know how long I lay there, but I almost let out a scream when I felt a hand on my ankle, and then stifled it when I realized it was, thank God, Vonnie.

We quickly determined that the only way to get me out of this new low was for Vonnie to take off my pants, despite the fact that I was pantyless underneath them, thus bringing what was admittedly a low situation for me to a new, even lower low.

I have always devoted far too much of my brainpower worrying about my butt. God only knows what diseases I might have cured or Middle East peace treaties I might have brokered with the time I have wasted worrying about my ass. How many times had I asked others, "Does my butt look fat in this?" I realized, that in this particular situation, naked and wedged firmly in a dog door, I need not ask, since the answer was obviously a resounding, "Yes!"

Vonnie yanked, twisted, and pulled on my naked, freezing ass, as I could imagine her doing when birthing calves during her days as a farm girl in Iowa. Suddenly, her tugging went slack. "Uh, doll?" Vonnie inquired in an urgent whisper.

"What!" I whispered back.

"Uh, I know it's none of my business, but, um, you're kind of, well, you've got a hair situation down here that's . . ."

Oh, right, it wasn't enough that my naked butt was hanging out a dog door, I forgot that I was still in the full flower of my newly inflamed disfiguring Half-Full Brazilian.

Just as it seemed that things could not get more humiliating, amazingly, they did. I heard a weak but kindly voice cry out in a reedy whisper, "Hello? Are you all right? Do you girls need some help?"

It was my dear neighbor, Mr. Trilling. Mr. and Mrs. Trilling were a frail and sweetly devoted couple in their late nineties. Although Mr. Trilling certainly didn't recognize me from that angle, he had fortunately seen Vonnie a number of times, and didn't seem at all frightened to see a woman pulling on another woman's half-plucked naked body at three in the morning. In fact he really seemed genuinely sincere about wanting to help us do—whatever the hell it was we were doing.

"Oh, hey, there! Um, we're fine, we're just, you know . . . doing Pilates!" Vonnie, always the friendly Midwestern gal, whispered cheerfully.

"Pilates. Hmm, that's a new one on me. . . ."

Vonnie, who was on a big health kick and was very into Pilates, began enthusiastically to explain, "Oh, gosh, you should try it for sure. It's this wonderful series of exercises that both stretch and strengthen—"

At that moment, I kicked her, hard.

"Ow!" she gasped. "Gol darn it! Okay, okay, okay . . ."

"Looks more like judo to me, but I'm sure you girls know best. . . . Good night, then!"

"Good night!" Vonnie shot back as she made her final tug and I landed into her lap just in time to watch Mr. Trilling feebly pick his way over the paving stones to his back door. About fifty Milk-Bones later, we got Thor into my car, and I gave Vonnie a grateful hug good-bye as she called out, "You better get back to that Ludmilla gal or your gonna end up lopsided down there for the rest of your life!" and then made my way back to my apartment.

I had successfully stolen my own dog. I had never felt more proud.

When I brought Thor home to Studio City, he could not have been happier. He did his crazy little Doberman happy dance as he crashed through the much smaller living quarters, breaking a new lamp and knocking over the few scraggly plants I had as he, well, doggedly followed me wherever I went, which of course wasn't far. He was unwilling to be separated from me even when I peed (into what he had always regarded as his punch bowl) and he insisted on watching me shower, nosing the opaque shower curtain aside with his big muzzle until I relented and replaced it with a clear one so he could see me. Frankly, I was happy to have any male that excited to see me naked.

Thor loved Jen, too, though she wasn't home much because she had started to pull double shifts at the crazy horrible diner where she stubbornly insisted on working. She improbably claimed she was on to some really exciting cultural observations by spending her days and nights serving patty melts to crackheads.

The day after I stole Thor, Kurt called to tell me that Thor had run away, but he didn't seem particularly upset about it. I told him I would put up signs around the neighborhood, with my number on it, but that whole week Kurt never once called to see if there had been any response. The three of us, Jen, Thor, and I, were very happy in our cozy, crowded little life, and my optimism began to be less fake, and more real. I began to feel actual hope about the future.

Hope is the feeling that you have that the feeling that you have isn't permanent.

—Jean Kerr

Until Kurt called again, that is.

"I know you have the dog, Cathryn. Adam from across the street saw you take him," he accused.

"Damn," I thought. "You know what, Kurt, Thor's my dog, too, and it turns out he's actually happier here . . . ," I began shakily.

"Oh, really, and how are you going to prove that, Cathryn?"

"Well, I can just tell, I mean, he was getting very upset with the irregular schedule—"

Kurt cut me off. "I see, and did the dog tell you that he was upset? Do you speak to dogs, Cathryn?" he asked, implying as he always did that I was completely out of my mind.

"No, Kurt, obviously, it's just, he was trembling uncontrollably the last time I came to hike him there, he was so stressed out from waiting," I pleaded.

"Then maybe you shouldn't come at all if it stresses him out so badly. If you can't manage to organize your time so that the dog can count on you, then maybe it's best that you don't see him at all!" And with that he hung up.

I wasn't really surprised to hear from Jabba the next day. Apparently, the next divorce hearing had been postponed because Kurt's billion-dollar attorneys needed more time to "review Ms. Michon's outstanding contracts." In other words, they needed to try and figure out exactly how much money I had, and how much I was likely to have in the future, so they could take as much of it as legally possible. However, we were still going before the judge on the appointed date because now Kurt was, no lie, suing me for dog custody. He had discovered that if the court awarded him formal custody, I would, in addition to having to pay all his bills, further have to pay him "dog support."

"You've got to be kidding me!" I yelled at Jabba into my cell phone.

Jabba mumbled a lot of gobbledygook about "laws" and "facts" and other things that were completely irrelevant as far as I was concerned, so I hung up on him. And then called back with an apology, which Jabba, at $350 an hour, was only too happy to accept.

About a week later, I was once again seated at the "Heather Locklear Memorial Crying Table" at the Beverly Hills Family Court, where my rumpled, sodden attorney once again advised me to be sure to let him do all the talking. I was again dressed very badly, this time in the Sissy Spacek–esque *Coal Miner's Daughter* dress Amelia had so lovingly suggested.

I also made a quick call to the Rosio the Santeria Witch hotline before I left the house.

"*Mi'ja*," the familiar voice purred into the phone, "If you are having troubles today, you must have faith that by the power of Rosio and the Blessed Virgin Mary you'll triumph in the end. Here is the spell for the day, whoever is preventing you from your heart's desire, you get a lunch sack, write that person's name on the sack, and then crumple it up and put it in the freezer. This is a very traditional spell back in Puerto Rico. It will work," she promised.

So I did it of course, wrote "Kurt Bremerhoffen" on the bag, crumpled it up, and tossed it in the freezer as I kissed Thor goodbye on my way out the door. Although as I drove to the courthouse, I began to wonder how this spell could be "very traditional." I didn't know anything about Puerto Rico except for what I had learned from Oscar-, Emmy-, Tony-, and Grammy-winning Grrl Genius Rita Moreno's extra spicy rendition of "I like to be in America, okay by me in America . . ." but I was pretty sure that they hadn't had freezers in Puerto Rico for all that long, since, as I understood it, that's exactly why she "liked to be in America."

As usual, Judge Riananne Hunter-White disappointed me by already being on the bench when we arrived. I was let down because I'd always liked the whole "All rise!" thing, even on the *People's Court* they did it, and it seemed a shame to drop the pomp and circumstance, since it cost nothing and was sure to add a little extra much-needed pizzazz to the otherwise depressing event.

"Mr. Bremerhoffen is petitioning the court for full dog custody as well as an award of pet support of the family dog, a Doberman pinscher named Thor, which he contends was removed from his residence and is now residing in the apartment of the plaintiff—"

"His residence!" I blurted out. "His residence, that I bought and paid for with my own money and continue to pay for with my own money, where he and his giantess of a girlfriend drink champagne I bought in my hot tub which I bought! Oh, but I forgot, it's fine that he drinks champagne because, since this court decided he's going to get paid by me for being an alcoholic, that's like, his *job* now!"

The judge banged her gavel and tossed her hair with a Cher-like verve I couldn't help but admire even as I was hating her. "Ms. Michon, I have asked you not to speak out of turn in this courtroom, and I don't want to have to ask you again." Jabba gave me the classic little brother "I told you so" look.

I dug my fingernails into my palm as I had learned to do when I was a small child who could not refrain from inappropriately shouting out questions and comments in quiet, adult places like church or the DMV, the idea being that the pain would focus me on the goal of keeping my mouth shut.

"I have read the petition," she continued, "and I would like you to tell me, in your own words Mr. Bremerhoffen, why you feel you should retain custody of the pet in question."

Kurt stood, rising to his full five feet six inches. Like many men who are short of stature, Kurt overcompensated with impeccable, almost military posture, and as he walked briskly to the bench I began to imagine there was an almost, well, the only word I can think of to describe it would be *goose-steppy* quality to his gait.

I had been married to him for a decade, and had never been able to figure out exactly who Kurt's movie star twin separated at birth was until that very moment, when I suddenly realized it was Rolf, Liesl's endearingly formal suitor in *The Sound of Music*. Rolf was, of course, one of the great movie Bad Boys of all time, the tender crooner of "You are sixteen going on seventeen," one minute and a heartless Nazi whistle-blower the next.

Rolf *was* Kurt.

"Your Honor," Kurt said with the precise, Germanic politeness he reserved for people he was trying to charm, "ever since Cathryn, since Ms. Michon abandoned the marriage and the home . . ."

My nails dug into my palm so deeply, I was afraid they would press through to the other side. I had not "abandoned" the home. I had asked him to move out and he refused.

Kurt continued with unctuous condescension. ". . . the dog has remained in my care, in the surroundings he is used to, in a spacious yard, so I believe I am acting in the dog's best interest by wanting to keep him in his home."

"I see" the judge said, her mind obviously already made up. "Ms. Michon, would you like to state why you feel you should have custody of the dog?"

"The dog likes me the best!" I blurted out uselessly. "I'm the

122

one who walks him every day, and I have, every day, even though it means I have to go back to the house. Kurt doesn't even like the dog, he's only doing this to get back at me, and apparently to get more money. Why don't we bring the dog in here, see who he goes to?"

"Ms. Michon, I wouldn't even let you bring *children* in here to see who they prefer, so we're not going to do it for a dog. It seems as if there is compelling reason for the dog to remain where it can run free in a yard, and for dog support to be awarded. We will set that amount at the hearing on the twelfth."

"But he won't even buy name-brand Milk-Bones!"

"I beg your pardon?"

"If he's going to get money for stuff for the dog, can't you like, stipulate or whatever, that he has to buy the name-brand of Milk-Bones? Thor hates the other ones—that's how I got him to go out the dog door when I took him—"

Jabba the attorney actually poked me in the ribs, hard, at that moment, and then I realized he had a point, as I was sort of admitting to stealing the dog.

"Your Honor," Kurt oozed, "that is the other matter I would like to discuss, the fact that Ms. Michon broke and entered into my place of residence, which was very disturbing to me, and caused me great emotional, um, distress and threatened my sobriety, which as the court agrees is a serious disability—"

"Mr. Bremerhoffen, I believe this is territory that you would be better off leaving alone, or perhaps to your attorney," the judge interrupted, finally showing Kurt some of the harshness she had previously reserved for me. "If she entered, as you claim in your motion, through the dog door, then nothing was 'broken,' so there is no 'breaking and entering.' There's only trespassing, and since she is co-owner of the property, and there is no restraining order in place, that seems to me to be a specious claim."

Feeling the tide turn my way, I leapt in. "Your Honor, I did not abandon the home as Mr. Bremerhoffen is claiming. I left because he refused to leave when I asked him to, as any normal man would have, like on *The Odd Couple*—"

The judge cut me off yet again. "I must ask you both to let your very able attorneys speak for you in these matters, unless I question you directly, is that clear?"

It all seemed so unfair; it all seemed so unlike *The Odd Couple*.

I nodded my head quietly in response to the judge's question.

For a moment, I thought I saw a glimmer of sympathy in the judge's eyes, but she remained all business.

"As to the issue of the spending of dog maintenance funds on name-brand dog treats, as with child support, it is not up to the court to stipulate how these monies are going to be spent. Unless negligence is demonstrated, the disbursement of those funds remains the sole discretion of the recipient."

Well, there it was. No name-brand Milk-Bones for Thor.

"I will, however, order that Ms. Michon gets private access to the marital residence once a day, at a time of her choosing, for a period of two hours in which to have daily dog visitation."

"But, Your Honor—" Kurt began.

"That's my final word on the subject, Mr. Bremerhoffen, and if the presence of Ms. Michon in the home is a threat to your undoubtedly precious hold on sobriety, I would suggest that you remain far away during those two hours. We will reconvene on the twelfth."

As she banged her gavel, I could see the anger welling up in Kurt and was hoping for one of his world-class temper fits to show itself, but he said nothing.

Things were bad, but I felt that I had heard the faint but steady strains of Grrl Genius sarcasm in the measured voice of the judge, and I began to feel optimism stirring within me, for I knew, where there are two or more sarcastic women (three if I counted Rosio the telephone Santeria Witch) gathered in the spirit of Grrl Genius, miracles can take place.

The only way to enjoy anything in this life is to earn it first.
—Ginger Rogers

The Grrl Genius Wild Sexual Kingdom

In the "Wild Sexual Kingdom," male slackers are rare indeed. Basically, throughout nature, the well-adapted female animal demands that her mate not only be a good provider but also be dynamite in the sack.

The Human Grrl Genius would do well to take a lesson from her sisters in the wild.

A female African lioness in heat demands that her paramour make love to her as many as 157 times in a forty-eight-hour period, and she will not ovulate if her lover does not satisfy her sexually.

Stick insects (not to be confused with supermodels) have sex for as long as ten weeks at a time. But perhaps the most demanding Grrl Genius in the animal kingdom is the female honeybee, who is surely the insect world's most popular bachelorette. Usually up to twenty-five million bees are trying to get a date with a single queen, and whichever one succeeds will be rewarded with an all-expense paid honeymoon ending with him having an orgasm so thunderous that he literally explodes as his genitals are ripped from his body with a loud snap.

Hey, love hurts.

As to providing a living, most female animals (except humans) will simply not put up with deadbeat husbands or boyfriends. The male hunting spider not only brings food to court a female (a good idea for any species), but he also takes the trouble to wrap the snack in silk. Surely the hunting spiders that can also manage to include a card are the most likely to succeed in their quest.

None of the females mentioned are incapable of feeding themselves and earning a living, or even sexually satisfying themselves. (Female bonobo chimps are dedicated masturbators and prove that man is not the only "toolmaker" with the wide variety of sex toys they are able to fashion with just ordinary things you'd find lying around the jungle.)

Reasonable females of all species just want to know that their prospective partner will do his part, sexually *and* financially once they have children, and there aren't going to *be* any children, unless he proves himself worthy. And if he can't, well, maybe he'll explode next time he has an orgasm.

Hey, a girl can dream.

———

Thor loved to drive my car. Like most dogs, he drove from the backseat, and I was mostly unaware of his efforts, but he kept a steady eager focus on the road and was thrilled to be in control of a high-powered Volvo sedan using only his doggy will. He loved the smack of the wind on his face and the feeling of his own cold slobber being blown out of his eager panting mouth and forming an endless contrail of dog spit that landed on the side of the car, surely impressing everyone.

I was driving Thor back to the house in Beverly Hills, as the judge had ordered me to. The night before, I had allowed Thor to sleep with me in my bed, something he had tried to do all his life and had never been allowed to. It had been a restless night for both of us, as Thor's glee at finally being allowed up into a big human bed with an actual human actually in it made it impossible for him to sleep, as he didn't want to miss a precious second of such a delectable and forbidden treat.

For my part, I didn't mind the lack of sleep, as I was dreading giving him back and was already feeling a real physical ache for the dog. Having Thor for even a week reminded me that for years he had been the only living creature in my house who was truly happy to see me at the end of the day.

When I pulled up to the house, Kurt was once again sitting in his teak lawn chair. He eased himself up and rose stiffly. Thor did not seem particularly excited to see Kurt, but then, I couldn't be expected to judge that accurately. Kurt marched to the front gate brusquely and opened it (for a moment I imagined he had actually clicked his heels together like Colonel Klink on *Hogan's Heroes*) and I reluctantly handed him Thor's leash. I didn't ask to enter the property I had bought and continued to pay for, and he didn't offer. All I said was, "Um, I'll be by tomorrow at two to pick him up for his hike."

"Fine, I'll be out," replied Kurt icily. I said nothing else and turned to go. As I got back to the car, I saw Thor's giant fresh trail of slobber as it traced across the smog-encrusted exterior of my car. I was suddenly overcome with embarrassing, heartbroken, racking sobs, which I pretended was a fit of coughing for the benefit of the still-watching Kurt. I didn't want him to see how much I was suffering at the loss of the dog; I didn't want to give him the satisfaction. I quickly got in the car and drove down the street, pulled over, and cried in the horrible, hiccupy, drooling, gasping way that people never do in the movies, but I always seem to do in real life.

After a long while, I tried to pull myself together. I had to be positive, I had to believe that no matter what, I would eventually get the dog—and my life—back.

When I was able to control myself, I drove the fifteen minutes back to my apartment. I instantly rushed to the freezer, where I kept a box of Marshall Field's delectable chocolate Frango mints for emergencies just as this. Somehow, I could bear the loss of the hopes and dreams of the marriage, but after having Thor living with me again, the loss of the dog seemed like it would kill me, even though I believed it was only temporary. I needed the Grrl Genius elixir of chocolate to give me the strength to think positively about everything that was happening.

Being divorced is like being hit by a Mack truck. If you live through it, you start looking very carefully to the right and to the left.

—Jean Kerr

The next morning was Saturday, the day of Elaine and Andy's impossibly corny retro wedding. I was still in a deep depression over Thor's absence, but did my best to buck up as I put on a bias-cut, sexy-yet-somehow-perfectly-proper, chartreuse silk Betsey Johnson dress that had cunning little silk chiffon cap sleeves, and took out of tissue paper the impeccable Manolo Blahnik beige kidskin mules that were a reminder of happier financial times.

If I had understood the divorce laws better during my long and unhappy marriage, I would have realized that every penny I spent on shoes was money that couldn't eventually be divided up with my soon-to-be-ex-husband. The only assets of the marriage that he couldn't touch were the ridiculously expensive shoes I had "thrown money away on" (in his nonearning opinion). It wasn't until the morning of the wedding, as I slid my manicured toes into those hand-sewn shoes that I realized why shoes are an important totemic object for Grrl Geniuses everywhere. Shoes are the one thing no one can take from you. Shoes are yours. Suddenly, the lessons that Grrl Geniuses from Cinderella to Dorothy to Imelda Marcos had been trying to teach us became blazingly apparent.

Grrl Genius Relationship Tip

If you can't have a good relationship, have good shoes.

Grrl Genius Relationship Tip Corollary

Even if things start looking up, still have good shoes—you never know.

As I drove to Elaine and Andy's wedding, I felt a growing sense of discomfort, a feeling of being trapped and even suffocated, that I could not entirely attribute to the fact that I was wearing pantyhose for the first time in over a year.

So it was, as I drove around the corner onto the street in Santa Monica in front of the 1940s-era Moose Hall, where Andy and Elaine were getting married, I thought about the one thing that seemed to calm me down lately and give me comfort, the Hidden Hills firemen. I tried to do what Amelia had advised me, back when I bought the infamous red panties. I tried to imagine a firefighter of my very own, a firefighter who was truly DORP. As I slowed down to look for a place to park, I was imagining, in exquisite detail, the perfect merging of me and a dark-haired, dark-eyed firefighter, as our bodies joined together eagerly in a spectacular conflagration of passion and emotion.

It was at just that very moment when the truck slammed into my car from behind. I heard the horrifying sound of my own voice screaming as glass and metal smashed together and changed shape (but certainly not for the better) and my body was jolted violently forward, activating the kind of fight-or-flight adrenaline surge I usually experience only in life-and-death situations such as someone suggesting that they set me up on a blind date.

I'm proud to say that true to my Grrl Genius program, even as I was experiencing the shock of the crash itself, I tried my best to remain optimistic, my final plucky and upbeat thought as I watched the cars coming together was, "Sure, this is bad, but maybe the fire department will have to come! If this involves meeting hunky firefighters, well, it can't be all bad!"

The way I see it, if you want the rainbow, you gotta put up with the rain.

—Dolly Parton

Chapter 5

A Grrl Genius Is Always Open to the Possibility (However Remote) of True Love

If love is the answer, could you please rephrase the question?
—Jane Wagner

THERE REALLY IS no more "high impact" way to make a dramatic entrance at a wedding than to have a car crash in front of the place where the ceremony is to be held. As I hobbled out of the car, a gaggle of bridesmaids dressed in 1940s padded shoulder peplum dresses screamed in unison while ushers in zoot suits rushed toward me.

"Oh, my God, Cathryn, are you okay?" Elaine's brother David asked me as he grabbed my arm and hauled me away from the wreck.

"I'm fine, I guess, I mean, I have no idea what happened. . . ."

I began to feel woozy and sort of slumped into a low crouch. Just when I thought I might be passing out, I felt a strange mixture of comfort and excitement as a tall well-built man with wavy blond hair in a Los Angeles firefighter uniform rushed toward me. He was a dead ringer for the impossibly delicious Matthew McConaughey. "How on earth did the hunky firefighters get here so quickly?" I wondered happily to myself.

But this was no hunky firefighter here to gather me up in his sinewy arms and throw me over his perfectly sculpted shoulder and carry me off to safety and ecstasy. I could see from the name sewn on his shirt that he was LUTHER J. BURTON, the Los Angeles firefighter who had just slammed into me with his aptly named Subaru Brat and who now pierced my mental fog by screaming at me.

"What kind of idiot are you? What the hell were you doing! You just stopped, right in the middle of the goddamned street! That's illegal!" Luther J. Burton shouted.

My brain, which was trying to decide if it wanted to over-rev on adrenaline or flame out from shock, couldn't seem to process what was happening. I was reeling from the trauma—not the trauma of the high-speed impact, the shattering of the glass, or the twisting of the metal—but rather the trauma of having my most cherished sexual fantasy, an actual firefighter (who looked like Matthew McConaughey no less!) in his cute uniform, yelling at me like, like, a bad ex-husband. It was an unbearable thought and a horrifying vision. It was like being a child and having Santa Claus tell you to go to hell. It was like seeing Mother Teresa beating her dog; it was like seeing Brad Pitt in a padded bra and panties.

This just couldn't be happening. Could I have suffered brain damage and somehow be hallucinating this obscene perversion?

I tried to speak. At first only vague moans emerged, but finally my confused thoughts sputtered into language, "I, I didn't stop, I, just pulled over to the curb, to park—"

"Don't tell me what happened," he raged. "I'm a firefighter, I am trained to observe traffic, I drive a fire truck!"

"But, I didn't slam on my brakes. I didn't—" I protested weakly.

"Of course she didn't—we all saw it!" David said.

David's sudden support helped me to recover my native genius. "And, um, look, even if I had slammed my brakes, well, then, you must have been following me too closely, because in a rear-ending accident, well, it's always the fault of the person who does the rear-ending."

"Oh, that's ridiculous, what are you talking about, how can it be my fault if you slam on the brakes!" Luther J. Burton scowled.

"I'm talking about traffic laws, which I am surprised that someone who is licensed to drive a high-speed heavyweight vehicle wouldn't be more familiar with! Rear-ending is the fault of the person who rear-ends you. Besides, I didn't slam on the brakes, and I have witnesses," I said with a sudden, adrenaline fueled burst of confidence.

"She's right! You're wrong, and you owe her an apology," added Elaine's brother, causing me to wonder, just what exactly was David Carriere's story, and why did he suddenly seem so devastatingly handsome?

Luther J. Burton began strutting around like, well, like a black-crested tit during mating season, swaggeringly confident that all the other tits thought he was top tit. He puffed out his chest and leaned in toward me.

"Well, we'll just have to see about that. My girlfriend is in the truck, she's a witness, too, and I'm sure she'll be happy to back me up. And the cops will back me up. I'm a firefighter—they know I know how to drive."

"We get that you're a firefighter—that's been duly noted," replied David attractively, "and no one said you didn't know how to drive. You just apparently don't know how to stop."

I glanced into the windshield of the truck, where Luther J. Burton's girlfriend was rubbing her neck and tentatively working her swollen mouth. She looked like she was in considerable pain.

"Um, is your girlfriend okay?" I asked. "It looks like she has a fat lip or something—"

Luther J. Burton jabbed an accusatory finger at me. "Hey, are you making fun of my girlfriend?" It was then that I realized that her lip was not swollen—it was just your basic ass-fat-injected L.A. lip—and that her tortured mouth movement was the standard one I had seen in a thousand Beverly Hills coffee shops as recent plastic surgery victims tried to cope with their newly inflated "Clutch Cargo" rented lips.

"No, I'm—I was just concerned. Fine . . . Let's just call the cops and see what happens," I said, carrying on bravely despite the potential devastating loss of a lifetime's worth of sexual fantasies. We then exchanged insurance info after calling the cops, who refused to come since neither of us was dead. I did get the wedding photographer to take a few pictures of the collision, and then we all headed into the wedding, where we agreed not to tell Elaine and Andy about what had happened out front until after the ceremony, lest I become what I had often been accused of, some freaky combination of both the bride at every wedding and the corpse at every funeral.

When I got up to sing "True Love" at the wedding, I cried my eyes out. What no one knew was that I was not crying because of the true love between Elaine and Andy. I was crying for the idea that my personal vision of true love, the helpful, rescuing hunky firefighter, who would willingly risk his life to protect and save me and then carry me away for an evening of inflamed passion might in fact be not a vision at all, but an illusion, a lie, a sham, the reckless driver of a Subaru Brat with a girlfriend with lips like braunschweiger, for heaven's sake.

The rest of the wedding was charming, personal, romantic, corny, and in every way a full-on mascara ruiner.

A Grrl Genius Crazy Sex Fact

During the fifth century B.C. the Nasmones of Libya required the bride to sleep with all the male wedding guests at the party. (There was, gratefully, no requirement that she write them all thank-you notes.)

I could only hope that my upcoming hunky firefighter dinner with the brave men of Hidden Hills Squad 73 would somehow repair this now-tarnished erotic firefighter dream of mine. I fervently fantasized that the firefighters I bought would cook for me, demonstrate their hoses for me, and slide down their big brass pole for me, so that this horrible psychosexual wounding would heal, and my "go-to" sexual fantasy could return to normal.

In the meantime, wandering around Elaine and Andy's reception, I was suffering from a tremendous shock. To say that I "drank a little" at the reception would be like saying that Janis Joplin "partied a little" during the '60s. Since my car had already been towed to the dealer, I knew I wasn't going to have to drive. Elaine's brother David was kindly attentive, bringing me an endless supply of strange, sugary sweet martinis that tasted like the candies of my childhood: Jolly Ranchers, Tootsie Rolls, Hot Tamales. Since I'm much more about sugar than I am about alcohol, these drinks seemed like the perfect antidote to the events of the evening, although truthfully, I'd have preferred a fistful of Jolly Ranchers, Tootsie Rolls, and Hot Tamales rather than their pale alcoholic imitations.

As the evening wore on, David and I danced to Tommy Dorsey and Stan Kenton. I tried to remember what it was Elaine had said about her eligible and now devastatingly handsome (when viewed through the lens of a pure alcohol version of a Tootsie Roll) brother. I noticed as I held on to him that he had lovely well-muscled shoulders, elegant strong hands, and was wearing some quaintly old fashioned aftershave that smelled delightfully heterosexual. Surely, in the movie of my life (which would now take place in the 1940's) David would be played by none other than Cary Grant! I began to nurture random thoughts about whether everything in my life had in fact been leading up to this one car accident, which would bring David and me together at this wedding, which would be the perfect story to tell our grandchildren at our own twenty-fifth wedding anniversary, which we would have in this very Moose Hall.

I managed to corner Elaine in the ladies' room, where she needed help lifting up her enormous 1940s vintage wedding dress over her head so she could pee. "Oh, Cathryn, my brother David is a mess," Elaine said when I asked her about the witty, single David whom she was always quoting but oddly refused to set any of her girlfriends up with. "Every relationship he's ever had has just been a huge disaster. He's a total nightmare."

I handed her the toilet paper under her skirt. In this position, she looked oddly like a giant roll of toilet paper herself.

Some would assume that as a Grrl Genius who was now a sex and relationship expert, I would have taken this vehement nonrecommendation of handsome David from Elaine, his own sister, as a fortuitous warning, a well-timed harbinger of romantic doom.

Naturally I took it as a challenge. If I was going to be open to the possibility of true love, no matter how remote, wasn't I going to have to stop being so picky? Wasn't everyone always telling me that I was being too picky and negative, that I was out of hand rejecting every man that came my way, deeming them to be inferior? Didn't everyone always say that in order to meet your prince you had to kiss a few frogs?

The Grrl Genius Wild Sexual Kingdom

The male American green frog *Amphibusverte americanum* is not particularly discriminating when it comes to mating. Quite often it has been observed in the wild mistakenly trying to mount and mate with a floating leaf, perhaps thinking that the leaf is a particularly anorexic and winsome frog, sort of the amphibian equivalent of Lara Flynn Boyle.

Eventually the male frog realizes (as did Jack Nicholson) that the leaf is too thin and fragile for any kind of vigorous sexual congress, and it moves on until it finds an actual, more substantial female of its own species.

Since male frogs are rather awkward and unskilled lovers, they have developed specially adapted hooked thumblike appendages that allow them to hang on to the female's back with what amounts to a death grip if she gets bored (as she apparently often does) and tries to hop away.

In human life, males have also developed strategies for hanging on to a bored female who is trying to hop away. These include repeated phone calls, self-pitying statements, and the sending of stuffed bears wearing small T-shirts embroidered with messages like I WUV YOU, so that when the human female attempts to end mating rituals, she is forced to confront a sad little red felt mouth that seems to be pleading "Don't go!" and is compelled to turn away from little button eyes that seem to be glassy and tear-filled but are in fact just glassy because they are made of glass.

As in human life, female frogs often find it is less trouble simply to complete the courtship ritual and mate with a male who has "gotten his thumbs into her" than to risk the trouble of trying to "get him off her back."

It's not the men in my life that count, it's the life in my men.

—Mae West

Mere hours after the wedding, I found myself walking along the beach near the pier in Santa Monica with David. Fueled on the alcoholic equivalent of a Halloween bag full of candy, I babbled happily as he took my hand, and moments later he pulled me into a resolute kiss.

Kissing. Oh, dear God, it had been over a year since I had been kissed, and I had truly forgotten what a thrill it was. Oddly, kissing had not been a huge feature of my married life, as Kurt had a whole list of foods that he felt made kissing an unpalatable activity, and eventually, the forbidden foods began to be more appealing than the remote prospect of being kissed by my husband.

Of course, I hadn't told David that I regarded him as sort of an amphibious starter kit, one of a series of frogs I would need to liplock on my way to finding, if not an actual prince, at the very least a somewhat normal guy. I didn't mention that his sister said he was "a total nightmare" or that I was graciously giving him a chance to prove otherwise. Even though she was my friend, as the kiss went deliciously on, I began to believe that perhaps Elaine was a big liar, that her brother was a dreamboat and that she just didn't think that anyone, not even a true friend, was good enough for him.

David began kissing me more insistently, and as much as I was enjoying feelings of sexual guilt from public making out that hadn't been a part of my life since a long-remembered basement rec room make-out session at Melanie Lindstrom's eighth grade (supposedly girl-only) slumber party, I was feeling increasingly panicky about just how to keep this making out at a solidly prepubescent level that never progressed beyond sweet torture, as opposed to the kind of decidedly adult evening that ends up with an arrest for indecent exposure in a public place.

I "came up for air," as we used to call it back at Pleasantview Junior High, and pulled away from David slightly. I was relieved to note that he did not display the American green frog's infamous death-grip capability and that he loosed his hold on me easily and graciously. Some things had changed since junior high.

"I can't believe he ran into me!" I said, obsessing once again on the boorish behavior of alleged firefighter Luther J. Burton, whom I had decided, using my considerable skills of denial, might in fact not have been a real firefighter at all. Maybe he was on his way to a costume party! Maybe he was some kind of a psycho who wanted to be a firefighter, but couldn't pass the tests, who dressed up like a firefighter and drove around bashing into women and delighting in destroying their sexual fantasies. . . .

"He's—" (small kiss) "—a—" (tiny kiss) "—jerk—" (deep, complex, distracting kiss) affirmed David.

I pouted. "And then he yelled at me!"

"Mmmm." David kissed.

"He sounded exactly like my husband."

David pulled away rather abruptly.

"I mean my ex-husband, to be . . . ," I corrected abruptly.

"Well, you know, some guys are just awful like that," he cooed.

"Holy crap, don't I know it!" I agreed heartily, and now that we had taken a little break from the kissing portion of the evening and were moving into the chatting portion of the evening, I then proceeded to regale David with my best hilarious sardonic divorce anecdotes, all my same tales of ridiculous legal decisions and bare-assed dognappings that I had told many cabbies and limo drivers to such great effect, figuring that it would provide us with a welcome respite from all the increasing sexual tension from which we were suffering.

At some point, I became aware that he was no longer kissing me—or even trying to kiss me. He was staring rather desolately at his hands, which were now folded on his lap. Although it was clearly obvious that he was no longer interested in kissing me, I leaned in again for another kiss, which he almost seemed to dodge slightly as he began to rise off the sand. I did this because, like Groucho Marx, I only want to belong to those clubs that don't want me for a member. David's sudden lack of interest made him all the more interesting. It also made me wonder if, like so many of the men I find attractive, he was actually gay. Maybe he had stopped kissing me because he didn't really want things to go further. It certainly couldn't be that talking endlessly about my divorce was (as my friends constantly had warned me) the single biggest sexual turn-off of all time.

"I, uh, it's getting kind of late, we should probably go . . ." David said.

I rose to join him, casually throwing my arms around his neck and giving him a sassy little peck on the lips. He stood woodenly.

"Look, I, uh, I've just been thinking," he mumbled, retrieving his jacket, dusting off the crusty blobs of sand. "It probably wasn't a good idea for us to do this. I mean, you were in an accident, you were upset, you had some—well, you know—quite a few drinks at the wedding. I wouldn't want you to think that I was trying to take advantage of you. . . ."

Gay, I thought to myself. He's either gay or else impossibly old-fashioned. I was really hoping for the second option.

"Silly man," I whispered into his ear as I nibbled slightly on his earlobe. "That is so sweet, really, but I'm a big girl, I know what I'm doing."

He cleared his throat. "Well, um, the thing is . . ."

Now it was me who pulled away.

"The thing is, well, I'm just starting to think that maybe it's not a good idea that we, you know, 'start anything' here," he said.

"What do you mean?" I said evenly, or what I liked to imagine was evenly. Hadn't things *already* started?

He ran his fingers through his tousled curly hair with what seemed like genuine anguish. "It's not that I don't think you're pretty—"

I suddenly felt as though I were being broken up with, or about to be, and I tried to remain neutral even as I felt my old childhood eye tic starting to rear its ugly, well, eye. Some things *hadn't* changed since junior high.

"It's just, I've recently started group therapy, because, well, apparently I don't make good choices when it comes to relationships, and my therapist, she gave me some, you know, sort of trigger words and phrases that I'm supposed to really pay attention to whenever I hear a girl use them, and when I do hear those words and phrases, I'm supposed to, sort of, 'just say no.'"

I was completely shocked. "Well what kind of 'trigger words and phrases' do you mean?" I said.

"Well, I'm not sure it matters, and it's kind of personal anyway. . . ."

By this point, I had pulled away from him and had grabbed my little beaded evening bag from where it was sitting in a pile of seaweed and beer cans.

"I think I certainly have the right to know what kinds of offensive little 'trigger words and phrases' are part of my lexicon," I shot back angrily as I rummaged in my bag for lip balm. "That way, if I meet any other guys who are in your culty little therapy group, I can avoid saying them so they don't have to 'not start anything' with me, so that their Guru-Therapist-Boss-Mommy won't make them drink the poison Kool-Aid or whatever punishment she doles out for kissing girls who say 'trigger words and phrases'!"

I was so agitated that as I tried to shove the lip balm back in my bag, I managed to spill the entire contents of my purse on the beach. Expensive Chanel lip glosses, and tampons, and purse-size spray samples of pricey perfumes I could no longer afford tumbled gaily along the sand, collecting grit that would surely not wash out of their wands and applicators for months on end.

"Dammit!" I cursed as I dropped to my hands and knees, trying to gather everything up before it all became permanently sand encrusted. David bent down to help me, but I waved him away.

"Don't!" I snapped. "It's kind of personal!"

David kneeled near me, looking very contrite, a position that made me find him annoyingly appealing.

"Okay, I mean, I guess maybe you do have a right to know," David conceded slowly. "The thing is, I have a tendency to date women who sort of, you know, don't like men, I mean, not lesbians, but women who are just sort of—"

"Prickly man-hating bitches?"

"Exactly!" he said with obvious relief. "And I notice you say a lot of things like—oh, you know, like—'All men are jerks' and 'We'll he's just a typical man' and 'Men, you can't live with 'em and you can't kill 'em!'"

"Obviously those are jokes."

"Well, you know, that may be, but to me they're not so funny maybe."

"Fine," I said in clipped tones, having gathered up my now-ruined makeup and tampons. "This works out fine for me, and I really thank you for sharing, because as it happens, my therapist has told me I need to avoid men who don't have a sense of humor and who constantly try to censor what I say."

My therapist had said nothing of the kind, but it sounded very convincing even as I was making it up, thus, as was the case with so many things I make up, I began to believe it.

Conveniently, by the time David dropped me off at my apartment, on some level I began to remember the entire incident as involving me wisely heeding my therapist's advice, and putting the brakes on a potential romance that was ultimately going nowhere and was psychologically unhealthy for me.

Well, that's what I allowed myself to think, until I remembered all the sweet beach kissing, and the awful truth that I needed to have a Surgeon General's warning posted on my forehead, easily able to be read by anyone so foolhardy as to get close enough for a damp, salty beach kiss.

A Grrl Genius "Love Is Important But Chocolate Is Essential" Handy Chocolate Fun Fact

Chocolate contains theobromine, a substance similar to caffeine (but with fewer side effects) that affects brain function in a positive way by increasing alertness, concentration, and cognitive functioning. Obviously, chocolate is essential to your genius.

The morning after Elaine and Andy's wedding, I awoke feeling as if I had a combination of an adult alcohol hangover and a child's post-Halloween candy binge tummy ache.

As I stumbled around the apartment, making espresso, for the adult hangover, and cinnamon toast, for the child's tummy ache, the phone rang. I assumed it would be David, calling to apologize for his boorish behavior and probably wanting to make some sort of plans that would include falling madly in love with me, fathering my two perfect children (the girl, Sophie, a concert violinist who studied at Juilliard, and Cameron, the boy, who is a really great accountant and loves doing my taxes for free and doesn't get mad about having to pick through hundreds of crumpled, chocolate-stained receipts). I resolved to forgive him instantly, as I really needed to give birth to that brilliant and indulgent tax accountant as soon as possible.

Unfortunately, the call was from my car insurance agent, Randy, who informed me on my answering machine that Luther J. Burton was not only an unreconstituted jerk and an embarrassment to brave, hunky firefighters everywhere—unfortunately for my imaginary sex life, it turned out he really was a firefighter, after all, and not just some sort of obsessed Village People fan who wandered around in uniform—but he was also uninsured.

Apparently I had uninsured driver coverage, so the extensive repairs to my car would be covered, and all I would have to do was drive a crap rental car for over a month, pay my absurdly expensive deductible and what was likely to be a whopping increase in my insurance rates.

Lucky me.

Both Jen and I had the day off, and so we spent it kicking around the Rose Bowl flea market, as part of my ongoing quest to find various household objects I had lost in my divorce. Not long after I left Kurt, I wandered into the housewares department of Macy's, looked around, and realized, "This is the department of the stuff I used to have!" I couldn't afford to replace all the wedding gifts of high-end toasters and blenders and juicers at Macy's, so I decided I would gradually find them used in antique shops and flea markets.

As we walked around Old Town, I endlessly hassled Jen with questions about Rich, whether she'd heard anything from him, how he was doing, what he might be cooking. The stalemate between them was apparently ongoing, as he hadn't called once, and she certainly hadn't called him. She stubbornly declared, "I don't care if I never hear from him again!" in a tone of voice I recognized from a three-year-old tantrum she had thrown once when she fell down in the middle of a crowded intersection, was lifted to safety by her father, but then insisted that she should have been allowed to walk across the busy street by herself, so she declared, "I do it myself!" and hurled herself back into the traffic to prove she could walk across the street unaided. It was a suicide mission that she was not allowed to complete, and for me it had obvious parallels to her situation with Rich. I knew she loved Rich dearly, but true to her personality, she was too self-destructively stubborn to admit it. What was worse was that when you got Jen on the topic of relationships, she endlessly spewed forth dogma from her newfound romantic religion, *The Rules*. She told me that from now on, "I'll make sure that any man who is interested in me is under the impression that I am only mildly interested in him, because all men want what they can't have." I told her about David, and what had happened the night before, and she advised me, "Don't speak to him, even if he calls, for at least a week."

In direct violation of *The Rules*, I kept calling on my cell phone whenever her back was turned and obsessively checking my voice mail all day, constantly disappointed to find no call from David about our future life together.

At the end of the day, Jen and I were sitting down to a gorgeous meal that she had prepared, a cozy and homey dinner of meatloaf and mashed potatoes, with a copy of *Backdraft* in the VCR and a fresh box of chocolate-glazed Krispy Kremes sitting seductively on the counter. It was then that I realized that despite everything, I was a lucky, lucky person, and that your girlfriends are everything. I didn't need a man; I just needed meatloaf and doughnuts and hunky firefighters that I could watch with the sound off.

Just then the doorbell rang. I went to the door and saw a man in shorts carrying a hotel lobby–sized flower bouquet as he unsteadily mounted the crooked stairs of my funky apartment building.

David had sent flowers! I was right to believe in the possibility of true love, after all!

The rather hunky delivery man, who looked oddly like the sort of delivery man made popular in countless porn movies, (and since this was L.A., he may in fact once have been the star of one of those movies) handed me the card that came with the flowers. It wasn't the usual cheap and tiny complimentary florist card; it was a large and creamy envelope, big enough to contain a detailed and guilt-ridden apology for bad make-out behavior.

It was, I discovered in the very next moment, also big enough to contain a summons. A court summons.

From Luther J. Burton.

Despite the fact that he had rear-ended me, in an accident that was 100 percent his fault, and the fact that he had no insurance, he was suing me for his injuries, and for pain and suffering.

Pain and suffering. Was Luther J. Burton talking about the pain and suffering of a failed marriage followed by having my car destroyed by a non-self-sacrificing, unbrave, admittedly hard-bodied, yet hard-hearted firefighter?

I looked forward to making Luther J. Burton understand the concept of pain and suffering, and I felt confident that I was just the Grrl Genius to do it.

A Grrl Genius Crazy Sex Fact

In Saudi Arabia, a woman may divorce her husband for failing to keep a steady supply of coffee in the house. It is, however, not "grounds" for divorce if he "forgot to put extra foam on your latte."

The following morning, Jen drove me to pick up a rental car from Rent-A-Wreck, which was all I could afford given the ridiculous amount of money my insurance allowed for a rental car. The car was some horrible thing from the '90s called the Dasher or the Blitzen or something like that, and it was tiny and ugly and had the kind of automatic seat belts that are constantly trying to garrote you as you get into the car.

Delightful.

After Jen left for her afternoon shift at the Astro Diner, I called Rosio the Santeria Witch's hotline, as I was supposed to have a meeting the next morning with Jabba the Attorney so he could explain to me some more petitions that Kurt's billion-dollar attorney firm Mountebank, Nimmer, Gibson, and Suarez had filed in preparation for the upcoming alimony hearing.

"Hello, *mi'ja*," cooed the familiar voice on the recording. "Today I get that there are many obstacles in your path, so today I give you an extra-strong spell. Whoever is in your path, preventing you from your heart's desire, you must put this person in your mind very strong, *mi'ja*. Now, go to a butcher's shop, and you get the foot of a pig; then you take a pair of your underwears, *mi'ja*, and you wrap it around the foot of this pig, all the while you concentrate on how this person needs to cooperate with you. This is a very powerful spell, but I'm telling you this for your own good. Do it. You won't be sorry. Don't do it, believe me, you'll be more sorry. Rosio and the Blessed Virgin Mary hears your prayers and wants to give you all you desire."

Well, what with Rosio and the BVM (Blessed Virgin Mary), at least I had two people I could count on.

Love is a fire. But whether it is going to warm your hearth or burn down your house, you can never tell.

—Joan Crawford

It wasn't until the next day when I was already in my irritating rental car, with the crazy automatic chokehold seat belts, heading down the canyon and off to Jabba's office that I remembered that I hadn't gotten the pig's foot from the butcher. I wanted to blow it off, but something about Rosio's whole Love Potion No. 9 vibe creeped me out enough that I was afraid not to do what she advised at $7.99 a minute.

I raced back to the house, sure that Jen and I could improvise some kind of jury-rigged version of what I needed to cast a spell that would make Kurt bend to my will. So it was, that ten minutes later, I was back in the car, racing down the boulevard with a stuffed pig doll from the movie *Babe*, who had two strips of over-cooked leftover breakfast bacon duct-taped onto his little plushy cloven foot and a pair of my worst underwear on his head, all shoved hastily into my large purse.

As I sat in Jabba the Attorney's marble conference room, it occurred to me suddenly that the reason the decor was so marble-centric was to get the client used to the feeling of being in a mausoleum, used to the feeling of being buried alive, because, in fact, that was exactly what was happening.

Jabba was already precipitating heavily, which he always did when things were not going his way, so this could not possibly be a good sign.

"Uh," he began inauspiciously, "Nimmer filed a motion, and, well, it looks like they are gonna go for the IP—"

"The IP? What's that, the Idiot Plan?"

He took out his handkerchief and began to squeegee his leaking face. "*IP* means 'intellectual property.' I'll, I'll sort of, uh, summarize the petition, 'Mr. Bremerhoffen, upon further consideration blah, blah, blah, specifically regarding his disabled status due to his alcoholism, not only seeks spousal support blah, blah, blah, also his rightful share of joint intellectual property created or conceived, during the marriage, blah, blah, blah, Ms. Michon's writing or performing, and any income derived from same blah, blah, blah, et cetera, et cetera.'"

"The things I make up are joint property?" I asked astounded, hoping that I had misunderstood all the *blah, blah, blah*s.

"Yeah, it's property, same as the house. But there's another part here." Jabba seemed reluctant to go on. I, too, was reluctant for him to go on, because I didn't get the feeling that there was any good news to follow.

"Uh, well," he continued as a small reflecting pool of sweat began to form on the desk under his dripping chin, "Kurt is also claiming ownership of any future work of intellectual property you might finish after the marriage ends, but which you 'conceptualized' during the marriage. Do you understand what this means?"

"You mean, like, if I create something after the divorce, but I *thought* of it during the marriage, it's half his?" I ventured carefully, through clenched teeth, hoping that I was wrong.

"Right. That's right!" Jabba seemed excited that I had so cleverly guessed the worst. "So what Nimmer will want to do is depose you, in order to inventory, your—well, you know—thoughts and ideas—"

"He wants to catalog every thought I ever had during my marriage?" I exclaimed. "Do you mean to tell me Kurt actually owns half my thoughts? In America?"

"Well, he doesn't own your thoughts per se," Jabba demurred.

"No, I get it, he only owns the thoughts after I do the hard work of turning them into a book, or movie, or TV show, or whatever!"

Jabba was silent, except for the steadily increasing drips of perspiration that cascaded off him, making him look like nothing so much as a human version of the Trevi Fountain. I pointed my finger at him accusingly. "Well this is ridiculous, obviously. I mean, can't we—you know—object or whatever?"

"Well, you know, it's perfectly legal. . . ."

Then Jabba explained what else was "perfectly legal." It seemed that "jointly owned property"—like my ideas!—was awarded separately from any consideration of alimony. So Kurt was pressing a claim for "his half" of the "IP" along with any income that might be generated by "his half." And then, as if they were not connected, Kurt was demanding alimony in the amount of half my yearly income—the other half, in other words.

One hundred percent of my income for Kurt. No percent for me. So much for the power of the bacon panty-pig.

Even as it was beginning to sink in, I was remarkably calm. Because this meant that I could lose everything. The idea of losing everything can sometimes be almost comforting. Once bad things start happening, human beings have an amazing ability to absorb and accept bad news. I am convinced that this is why, when you see a woman in big pink rollers standing in front of her decimated trailer home that a tornado has just pulverized, as she stares glassily into the camera and speaks into the CNN microphone that has been shoved in front of her, she is usually calm, and is sometimes almost giddy. When you lose everything, but aren't dead, it almost seems like a good deal. That was how I was starting to feel.

I also began to take comfort in the idea that if I literally had no income, the noninsured, rear-ending Luther J. Burton, whom the law also felt deserved a piece of my income, could sue me all day long and there'd be nothing left for him. Apparently, the State of California felt that the needs of a slacker alcoholic husband superseded the needs of an abusive, bad-driving, sexual fantasy-ruining, off-duty firefighter.

"Let me understand this," I said with uncharacteristic calmness to Jabba the Attorney. "If what you're saying is true, then I could end up literally giving him one hundred percent of my income."

"See it's this thing called 'double dipping.'"

"Well, that sounds sort of, illegal—"

"Yeah, I know!" he agreed excitedly. "In fact, I got that question wrong on my bar exam, funnily enough."

"No kidding, that's hilarious," I replied darkly, wasting valuable sarcasm on Jabba, who seemed impervious to it.

"But even though double dipping is legal," Jabba went on to explain, "no judge is going to actually make you give him a hundred percent of your income, I mean, that would be crazy."

"But of course the whole thing is crazy!" I shouted crazily. "I mean, can you *guarantee* that the judge won't do it?"

"Well no," he waffled, "I can't guarantee anything, because technically, legally—"

"I know! I know! Technically, legally I'm his slave! How the hell did Lincoln miss out on this one!" It was absurd, and yet the whole disaster that had become my life was so bad, it was almost thrilling for me. I really felt as though I might spontaneously combust from the sheer drama of it, which might have been another reason the law office's walls and floors were all marble and glass—it probably made for easier hosing-down of melted clients.

I knew that I was spinning out of control, and so I tried to calm myself by popping in one of the Godiva Pastilles I had learned to keep in my purse for all legal occasions. They were very high-quality chocolate, a minimum of 40 percent cocoa solids, and fully medicinally capable of doing the job.

Jabba ended the expensive silence. "The good news is that alimony is tax deductible," he proclaimed.

"Say, that *is* good news!" I replied with faux spunk.

"I'm glad you're starting to see the bright side!" Jabba said cheerily. "And look, maybe you'll start to get more work—"

"Which Kurt gets half the money from, if he can prove I thought about it during our marriage!"

"Right, but still, you know . . ."

"Half is better than nothing?" I guessed impishly.

"Exactly! But it's extremely unlikely he'll get the full fifty percent."

I sat quietly, monitoring my heart rate and breath, trying to determine at exactly what core temperature blood would come pouring out of my eyes and ears. Obviously Jabba didn't understand that things that were extremely unlikely happened to me every single day!

"So, we have this court date on the twelfth, and if the judge awards him the future intellectual property, then we will set up a deposition—" Jabba said.

I cut him off. "Is there anything more you have to tell me?"

"Well, no," Jabba mumbled, "I mean, that's the main substance of—"

"Fine," I spat back. "Then I have to go, because I can no longer afford to pay three hundred fifty dollars an hour to have to you tell me about how I'm losing all my money. I'll just go home, where at least there's plenty of chocolate, and try not to think of anything valuable, because if I do, I have to go to court and have it sucked out of my brain so it can be used to treat Kurt's disability with cases of Costco beer!"

I began to gather up my things because I had to get out of there. With all that had happened, suddenly, amazingly, things had actually managed to get worse. My life was becoming like a demonic Ronco infomercial, an endless chorus of, "But wait, there's more!" I had gone from dreading losing half my income to dreading losing all of it. Rosio the Santeria witch had utterly failed me.

A Grrl Genius Legal/Sexual "Fun Facts" Chart

It's Actually Legal	It's Not Legal
To be forced to pay lifetime alimony to an able-bodied spouse who has a graduate degree (you paid for) just because he could never manage to get a job.	To give or receive oral sex in the city of San Francisco.
To increase the amount of spousal support paid due to a spouse who claims he is unable to find work due to having the disease of alcoholism or any other disability (including but not limited to cutting off his nose to spite his face).	For moose to have sex on the sidewalks of Fairbanks, Alaska.
For a spouse to claim ownership of the intellectual property of another spouse (including but not limited to notions, musings, random sexual fantasies about hunky firefighters, thoughts, ideas, and feelings that might subsequently be turned into works of art or products).	To have sex in a butcher shop's meat freezer in Newcastle, Wyoming.
For a spouse who earned no income to claim half of all pension benefits earned by the spouse who did earn an income.	To masturbate while watching two people have sex in a car in Clinton (!), Oklahoma.
To receive "pet maintenance" funds and refuse to buy name-brand dog bones.	In Middle Eastern Islamic countries, to eat a lamb that you've had sex with.

After my meeting with Jabba, my emotional situation was dire. I faced financial ruin, I was unloved, untouched, and dangerously low on chocolate.

My heart was aching and, as much as I believed in Grrl Power, I could feel a sad and lonely emptiness within me that only being held in the arms of a man could fill. Kurt had a (hideous) girlfriend, but I had no one to hold me or reassure me that however unlikely it looked, eventually things would be all right.

I wanted a man. David's kisses on the beach had started a slow fire within me that wasn't burning itself out. I wanted to believe in the possibility of true love, but I worried that in my ragged state, I needed to try to remember not to throw myself at the first man to come along, but at the best man to come along.

The job was Beach Blanket David's to lose, but when two weeks went by with no call and no flowers, I decided that enough was enough. My Grrl Genius spunk reasserted itself, and I decided that he wasn't good enough for me, anyway!

I decided I needed to consult with the Grrl Genius club on the topic of my postmarital virginity, but probably not as a group. Vonnie still wasn't dating—she said she felt like she wasn't ready, felt like she couldn't bear the disappointment of dinners with a parade of men who were nothing like her beloved Eldon. She was still grieving. Her therapist and her friends all felt that it was fine to give it time, so I didn't want to bother her with my dilemma. Kim—well, endless discussions had been held about Kim's sexual stalemate (what an apt word!) with Barnaby, so naturally she was out of the running for giving sex advice. Amelia was the genius I needed to consult; pansexual, freewheeling Amelia, who was actually famous for her sex life, must surely have some good advice on the topic.

I wished I was like the girls on *Sex and the City*—breezily confident about shagging a variety of different male archetypes. I felt like the *Sex and the City* girls, who regularly slept at a man's apartment with no more luggage than a small lipstick-size evening purse, were so unlike me. I felt that in order to do such a thing I would have to show up with not only metaphorical, but also actual baggage: a chic leather backpack at the very least.

The truth was, I wasn't a sophisticated, urban, sexual adventuress. At heart I was just a dull, awkward girl from the Midwest. I further hated to admit that I was, at age thirty-four, actually nervous about the idea of going to bed with a man. Nervous about him seeing my body, seeing my cellulite, nervous about the actual logistics of sexual congress, which people were always saying was something you remembered, it was, they said over and over, "like riding a bicycle." Because of this, I had actually gone so far as to go to Santa Monica and rent a bike down on the boardwalk. When I managed to ram it into a cement parking barrier and scrape the skin off my knees and elbows, well, the bike metaphor no longer provided me with any sense of sexual confidence. I wasn't so sure anymore that the man needed to be my true love, to be DORP as I had hoped for, but I did want him to be someone—well—someone not too messed up.

In other words, someone not like me.

To say something nice about themselves, this is the hardest thing in the world for people to do. They'd rather take their clothes off.

—Nancy Friday

Brilliantly, my first step in finding a man was to attend the GAY/LA fund-raiser with my famously bisexual friend Amelia. She came to my apartment to pick me up and I tiptoed precariously down my front steps in the three-inch stilettos, a giant curly updo, and a hot pink, skin-tight, Nicole Miller cocktail dress that looked like something out of a Doris Day movie and which I felt sure would let any eligible non-gay men at the event know that while I was with Amelia, I wasn't, actually "with" Amelia, and was exuberantly heterosexual. As I got in the car, Amelia took one look at me and exclaimed, "Oh, my God, look at you, you are the perfect lipstick lesbian!" Which was not what I was going for at all.

Things were a little "off" at the fund-raiser from the moment we

arrived. Everyone seemed to be snubbing Amelia, and conse-
quently, me. I had not heard so much furious and bitchy whispering
since I last ate in a high school lunchroom. As we waited for drinks
at the bar, a girl in a leather Suzy Wong dress "accidentally" spilled
a Bloody Mary on Amelia's white silk pants. As we attempted to
mingle, the whispering grew louder, and I heard quite a few people
cough loudly as they said, "Bitch!" Amelia was determined not to
let it get the best of her as the cocktail hour dragged on, but in the
ultimate high-end charity snub, the waiters simply refused us
access to the passed hors d'oeuvres, endlessly claiming the tiny
slivers of cucumber, topped with crème fraiche and three measly
caviar eggs were for "somebody else."

Events finally came to a head in the ladies' room, just as they
did in my favorite trashy movie of all time, *Valley of the Dolls*. As
Amelia stood at the vanity mirror, arranging her dreadlocks and
refreshing her lipstick, a woman in a pink cocktail dress almost
identical to mine and another woman with a crew cut (wearing an
electric blue sharkskin suit) shoved their way in front of us and got
right into Amelia's face.

"I can't believe you have the balls to show your face here after
what you did to Clarissa," barked the woman with the crew cut.

"Hi, Phil," said Amelia coolly, "it's good to see you again, too."

"If you're not gay, what the hell are you doing here, and what's
she supposed to be," Phil demanded harshly, jerking a finger in my
direction, "some kind of dyke beard?"

Amelia didn't seem fazed in the least. "Phil, I'd like you to
meet my friend Cathryn."

Phil's glance didn't waver, and she began poking an insistent
thumb into Amelia's chest. "Why don't you get the message that the
gay community wants nothing to do with opportunistic fake lesbians
like you who sleep with girls only to get a little press and help their
interior design businesses."

Amelia calmly grabbed Phil's hand and removed it from where
it was poking her chest.

"Phil," Amelia said evenly, "last time I checked, there was no

Gay Sex Commissioner, and if there were, I doubt you'd have been elected to the position, so why don't you be a nice girl and mind your own frigging business."

Phil, true to the high school spirit of the whole event, then perfectly executed the classic bully shove, accompanied by the requisite, "Oh, yeah? You gonna make me?"

Amelia's patience was clearly wearing thin. "Phil, there's no reason for this to get so ugly—"

"It's already ugly. You made it ugly when you dumped Clarissa for a guy," Phil said as she lunged for Amelia's dreadlocks and began yanking on them. Phil may have looked like a man, but apparently she fought like a girl. Amelia began to struggle to get her hair free. Before I realized what was happening, Phil's pink-clad prom date shoved me, I stumbled away, breaking the ridiculously thin heel of my shoe. I was terrified and thought, Do they expect me to fight? I'm the lipstick lesbian!

As I crawled on the floor, trying to find the broken heel, I quickly concocted a plan. I sneaked up behind Phil and Amelia and took my battle position.

"Stop it right now or I'll shoot!" I commanded, shakily aiming the spray canister I had for just such emergencies at Phil and her pink ladyfriend.

Phil looked very shocked and hurriedly scrambled away from Amelia. "Hey, take it easy," she warned in her best *NYPD Blue* cop voice. Clutching Pinky, she began backing toward the door.

"Just go!" I ordered.

"If you want to go nutso, we'll take this up another time, breeder girl," Phil shouted at Amelia as she slammed out of the ladies' room, followed by her date.

Amelia turned to me and clapped me on the back. "Nice going, I didn't know you even carried Mace!"

"I don't, it's just a purse-size Aqua Net for my updo, but I guess it did the trick, huh?"

Amelia laughed and gave me a limp high five, and then we straightened ourselves up, so to speak. As Amelia touched up her lipstick, I noticed that her lip was trembling, and I saw her angrily wiping away a tear. Amelia was always so tough. It was surprising to see her looking so vulnerable. When I put a tentative hand on her shoulder, she choked out a small sob and curled into my embrace.

She sniffled. "Oh, Cathryn, I don't care what people think of me, I really don't, but I know they're acting this way because Clarissa is still so mad, and you know what, I do care what she thinks of me. I really did love her, you know."

"I know, I know you did, Amelia, because I know you, you would never pretend to love someone you didn't truly love."

I held her for a minute, and it felt strange, but good, because most of the time it seemed like Amelia was the Grrl Genius comforting me.

"Let's get the hell out of here," she said abruptly, drying her tears like a kid who was mad at herself for having cried.

"Good idea," I agreed.

We were starving, so we ended up at the infamous Rock and Roll Denny's on Sunset Boulevard. It was near Guitar Center and jam-packed with freaks 24/7. Finally, I could ask Amelia's advice about my postmarital virginity dilemma.

Though Amelia had been remarkably closemouthed about her new sexual situation, sleeping with men after a decade with Clarissa, I asked her to spill personal details about the logistics of her first man after her lesbian marriage.

"Well," she began somewhat tentatively, "he was my friend, Julie's nanny. He'd been taking care of her kids part-time for years, so I knew he was . . . kind. He's a grad student at UCLA, twenty-six, adorable. I mean, I knew that he was too young for us to be serious, but it was the perfect reentry, so to speak. He was a white guy, so now I suppose in addition to the lesbians being mad at me, black people are going to be mad at me, too."

Amelia was always remarkably old-fashioned when talking about sex, considering her own sex life had been supermarket tabloid fodder for years.

"Here's the deal," she continued, "I don't want to be crude, but you've just got to get this over with. And honestly, I would suggest someone, younger, someone less complicated, right?"

"Well, I don't know. I mean, I don't want to be like some Mrs. Robinson cliché," I demurred.

"It doesn't have to be like that, but the thing is, you just have to think of the first guy kind of like the first waffle. I mean, you just have to throw it out. But it does get the iron ready for the other waffles."

As often was the case with Amelia, she seemed to have a good point. I needed to find the man who would be a good first waffle, and as I contemplated that idea, I just went ahead and ordered some waffles, because frankly, after everything that had happened, I was starving.

A Grrl Genius Crazy Sex Fact

A recent survey determined that black women are 50 percent more likely than white women to have an orgasm when they have sex. No mention was made of whether or not this was because they were more likely to have sex with black men.

The sex-waffle image was still strangely on my mind one evening when Tyler, the adorable twenty-four-year-old bouncer at the Improv, was walking me to my car, as he always kindly insisted on doing after I finished hosting the Friday late show. I always said I would be fine, but he always said he would never forgive himself if something happened to me.

Tyler had brown, wavy hair that always seemed to have its own opinion about which direction it ought to be going. He wore pants that perpetually seemed to be falling off his body, not for the fashion effect, but because he seemed genuinely incapable of looping a belt through them—too much bother, I suppose. He ambled around the club cheerfully, giving out hugs and backslaps to people he sometimes didn't even know. He was like a big friendly Labrador retriever, just genuinely excited by everything that was happening, no matter how dull and ordinary it actually was. He had been very kind to me when he heard what was going on with my divorce. It incensed him, as it incensed most men, that my slacker ex would take any money off me at all.

"Hell," he had said at the time, "I'm a total slacker, but there is just no way I would ever live off a chick I wasn't even balling. That is all, like, so morally wrong!"

Tyler was a twenty-first-century gentleman. A true Enlightened Male.

This was further illustrated by the great idea he came up with for me earlier in the evening. He knew I was under serious financial pressure and had come up with a great scheme for me to make a little extra pin money. (A term that he wouldn't have understood, because only people who were a thousand years old know the term "pin money"—I didn't even really know what it meant.)

"The thing is," Tyler had said, "you are a totally pretty person, I mean the truth is, you're actually hot, if you want my opinion. And, well, this will probably shock you, because you're too classy to get this, but there are guys on the Internet, like on eBay, who will pay money for panties from pretty women. They don't even have to be nice panties. So I like checked it out at the Costco, and you can get like a pack of thirty cotton panties for eight ninety-nine. Just to keep it honest you could wear each pair of panties for like five minutes, so they'd be, you know, genuinely used. And I figured in the costs of mailing and everything, and even with all that, you'd be clearing ten bucks on every pair of panties. That's like, serious money."

Tyler and I had differing definitions of "serious money," but I was very flattered that he had gone to all the trouble to construct a used-panty business plan for me, and I thanked him profusely.

As we were walking to my car that evening, Tyler was talking about something I had said in the bar that he felt I should put in my act.

"Well," he said a little shyly, "you're like, a totally good comic, but sometimes you don't even notice how funny you are, so I feel like it's my job to remind you, or whatever . . . ," he trailed off, since we had reached my car.

Suddenly I froze in my tracks. I realized, all of a sudden, that here was this very attractive man who was genuinely interested in me, genuinely admired me, genuinely cared about me, genuinely thought I could make a fortune selling used underpants. I wondered if I should flirt with him a little.

"Um, Tyler," I began nervously, "did you mean that, what you said earlier, about me being pretty?"

I thought maybe Tyler would respond affirmatively, would then perhaps ease in a little closer, but I had neglected to consider the effect of twenty-four-year-old testosterone. This tentative question was all that was required for a major make-out session to begin. I had forgotten that fresh testosterone is rather like newly distilled whiskey—raw and not yet mellow, but full of intoxicating effect. It was both exhilarating and sweet.

Exhilarating and *sweet* were two adjectives that also applied to what took place once we got to Tyler's place in Hollywood. It was decorated in a style I recognized, Early Deadhead Frat. It actually reminded me of my brother Teddy's dorm room in college. My brother and I had been into the Dead, but it seemed bizarre to me that Tyler, who undoubtedly was too young to ever have seen Jerry Garcia, unless of course he'd been in a stroller, was a fan of both the Dead and the Other Ones (the Dead without Jerry). I tried not to dwell on how paleolithically old that made me feel. As we kissed our way to his tie-dyed-covered futon, Tyler was exuberantly passionate and adorably affectionate, and once we arrived in bed, he brought his puppylike enthusiasm to love-making, as I should have expected. I tried not to think about how young he was, but it was, given the activity at hand, hard not to be aware of it. When he was gently savoring my breasts, it occurred to me that if someone that young was going to pay that kind of extensive attention to my breasts, perhaps I ought to be lactating, but I let the thought go.

We are always the same age inside.
                              —Gertrude Stein

Probably my favorite moment of the whole evening was when suddenly a giant happy grin crossed his face and he said, "Isn't this fun!" as though we had just test-ridden a new roller coaster at Disneyland.

Of course, the downside of twenty-four-year-old testosterone is that sometimes the coaster comes to a stop before everyone has really gotten all the thrills the ride has to offer. But Tyler was more than attentive to my needs and really, if I were writing about the evening in a folksy Minnesota Christmas newsletter, I would merely say, "A good time was had by all!"

Briefly the next morning, I lived in the fantasy part of my head that was willing to consider that Tyler and I might actually have a serious relationship. That ended when, over a frosted Pop-Tart he had toasted for me, we were talking about my last book, which he had not read.

"So, I get that it's about your life, but is it fiction or nonfiction?" he asked.

I thought perhaps that he wanted to talk about what Michiko Kakutani had just discussed in a column in the *New York Times Magazine* the previous week: the current trend of a blurring of the differences between memoir and novel. She had been musing on what has now become the standard for how "true" something needs to be in order to be classified as nonfiction, and further, what about these alleged "novels" that are just cleverly disguised reportage, true in a way, but not necessarily accurate.

"Because," Tyler continued, "I am always getting those two screwed up. I mean, fiction, that's the one that's, like, made up, right?"

In that moment I realized that I probably couldn't have a "serious" relationship with someone who couldn't remember if fiction was the one that was "made up."

It wasn't that Tyler was stupid—far from it. We were just in very different times in our lives. He was in the time where Cocoa Puffs and Pop-Tarts were a good breakfast, and I was in a time where if I was going to be intimate with someone, he needed to know the difference between fiction and nonfiction.

What was amazing was that, although we never slept together again, we just sort of went back to how we were before our night together. Tyler never pressed the point—his life seemed to be an endless series of "hookups" with girls—and he didn't place a lot of importance on "how it turned out." He stayed my friend, my protective little brother when unwelcome guys hit on me at the club, and he continued to point out when I said something funny, that I hadn't really noticed.

I felt that I had been true to my Grrl Genius philosophy of being open to true love in choosing to go to bed with Tyler. He was gentle and fun and kind. Although it wasn't going to become a long-term relationship, at least I hadn't repeated what I had identified as my two classic relationship mistakes: I hadn't tried to "fix" a bad boy, and he hadn't been gay.

It was the perfect reentry, so to speak.

Men reach their sexual peak at eighteen. Women reach theirs at thirty-five. Do you get the feeling God is playing a practical joke?
—Rita Rudner

There was plenty to discuss at the next Grrl Genius Club meeting, and fortunately it took place at a lengthy Sunday brunch (with alcohol). The disastrous GAY/LA fund-raiser was the first topic on the agenda. Amelia was still very worked up about the whole thing and wanted to know what she should do about being the tar baby of the L.A. lesbian community. "I mean," she said, taking a healthy slug of her Bloody Mary, "there's Phil, attacking me in the ladies' room, for crying out loud, accusing me of not being a 'real dyke,' saying that I had been with Clarissa because it was good for my business!'"

"Well, doll, I'm just playin' devil's advocate, but *wasn't* it good for your design business?" Vonnie asked in her direct, no-nonsense Iowa fashion.

"Yes, it was," Amelia said with no obvious sense of reluctance. "But that's not why we were together. I loved her. I still love her. I'm just—I'm bi, and I wasn't going to lie to her about that, and if that makes me a jerk, well then, so be it."

"Then your conscience is clear, and you don't owe anybody an explanation. Those lesbian PC sex Nazis have no right to tell you who to love. I wouldn't pay any mind to them," Vonnie concluded.

We all sipped our cocktails in steadfast agreement. Then the topic turned to Kim and her lack of sex life, which had become a major obsession with all of us. The truth was, we were kind of ganging up on her. Our intentions may have been good, but our manner was relentless. I had decided finally to suggest to Kim that she find out whether Barnaby's problems were physical or psychological— told her all about Jen's brilliant idea of giving Barnaby the postage-stamp test.

"You want to explain to me how I'm supposed to get the stamps on there?" Kim demanded.

I hadn't really given that a lot of thought, but I remained enthusiastic about the idea, "Well, I don't know, I mean, you always said Barnaby was a heavy sleeper. I mean, I know it's potentially embarrassing if he wakes up, but this is your sex life we're talking about—"

"God!" Kim exclaimed. "You people act as if sex is everything! I love Barnaby, and there are a lot of good things about our relationship. He's a great dad, he works hard, he's nice to be around—sex isn't everything in a relationship."

Vonnie, who was apparently feeling very much the wise woman, piped right up. "It's true, sex isn't everything, until sex isn't anything. When the sex is fine and dandy, it's ten percent of a relationship at best. But when it's bad, it becomes like eighty percent."

"I hear ya, sister," I agreed. "Call me crazy, but I like to have sex more often than I have my period!"

"We know. You told us. A thousand times," said Kim.

Vonnie suddenly got misty-eyed, as she often did when she was thinking about her beloved Eldon, her handsome airline pilot husband. "Goddamn that Eldon for up and dying on me," she murmured, taking another sip of her champagne cocktail. "God knows, he was the sexiest man I ever knew, and I knew a few. You know what was amazing about him when we had sex?"

We all wanted to hear it. We loved hearing about Eldon, the love of her life whom she didn't find until she was forty-three, thus making her the role model for all of us. Vonnie's love affair and marriage to Eldon was the thing that made us all believe that a Grrl Genius really did have to remain open to the possibility of true love, wherever she might find it.

Vonnie continued, "In bed, my Eldon—well, he just smiled. Smiled the whole time. Most guys I went to bed with would make all these tough, grimacing, sort of macho faces, but my Eldon, he would just grin his fool head off. In bed, he always looked like a kid on Christmas."

There was nothing more to say about that, except what we always said.

"What a bastard he was, dying on you like that," I said quietly. Of course, Vonnie didn't take offense; it was our standard line.

"I am so gonna give him what-for when I see him next," Vonnie added, because her Buddhism was the kind that allowed her to recognize people right away in her next incarnation and yell at them for leaving her behind.

Toward the end of brunch, I told the geniuses about Tyler, and they all congratulated me, and agreed that I had made a good choice, that he was the perfect "first waffle" for me, and that I was now ready to heat up the iron and start having waffles for real.

Less than a week later, I had no appetite for waffles, real or metaphorical. I was wandering around Brentwood, buying Christmas presents, when I got the worst phone call you can get in show business, the phone call that always begins with your favorite network executive from the channel you host a TV show for saying, "You know, Cathryn, I hate making phone calls like this. . . ."

Ten minutes later, I was sobbing in the Gap, on the phone with Kim, drying my eyes on the ridiculously long scarves that were all the rage that season.

"I can't believe my TV show got cancelled!" I wailed.

"Well, they fired the network president—you can't expect they were going to keep you," she pointed out with annoying accuracy.

I sniffled noisily. "But it's Christmas."

"Prime TV-firing season, you know that."

I did know that, but it didn't make the news any easier to take.

"Listen to me," Kim said with her customary bossiness. "You've got to head over to Camparte, that handmade chocolate shop over on Barrington, I'll call over and let them know you're coming. They'll have the fudge sliced and waiting. Don't make any rash decisions until after you eat the fudge. Okay?"

"Okay," I agreed, knowing even in my shock and grief that this was sound advice.

The fudge helped, but as I sat there, puffy-eyed in front of the little chocolate shop, and evaluated my situation, I realized that things were pretty grim.

I was under court order to support Kurt in the lifestyle to which he'd become accustomed, which meant sending him close to five thousand dollars a month.

Alimony hadn't yet been set, but Jabba had warned me that even without my "intellectual property," Kurt was going for "half," and not half of the zero I was suddenly making—I made a quick $350-an-hour phone call to Jabba, who warned me that the judge could view this sudden loss of income just before alimony was to be awarded as "malicious underearning" and an attempt to reduce a future alimony obligation.

Sometimes the court believed you couldn't help losing your job; sometimes they didn't. Amazingly, the court could award your maintenance support at the level the judge thought you *should* be earning, and if you didn't pay what they awarded, they could put you in jail for contempt of court. How you were supposed to scare up any dough in the big house was beyond me.

I had no savings, and Kurt, always a skinflint when we were married, had gone on a credit-card spree at the end of our time together, and though they were his purchases they were legally my problem. I wouldn't be extracting my half of the equity from the house any time soon, because Kurt was making it difficult for the Realtor to show the house, and the market was slow.

I had exactly one month's severance on my contract, exactly a month to find a job that would get me out of this jam.

Vonnie was sympathetic as always when I called her.

"I'll tell you what," I began, "Tyler's Internet panty business is starting to look pretty good."

"Oh, doll, you'll find a job. You've always gotten work—you're gonna be fine," Vonnie soothed.

"Well, I've got to make some kind of big score, because if I can make some real money, I can move into a place with a yard and maybe get Thor back."

"I cannot tell you how it frosts my cake, the way he uses that poor dog as a pawn. He doesn't even like the dog—he never did!" Vonnie declared with rare, righteous anger.

Her anger matched my own. "Oh, it's bad all right. I see Thor every day, but he gets so upset when I go. And that's not just me projecting, because last week he was limping really badly after our hike, and I just hauled him off to the vet. Once we got there, he was so excited to be with me that he jumped and ran around the waiting room banging his head into all the chairs, because apparently he'd been faking lame just to try and get me to stay. Of course the vet thought I was completely nuts. Oh, and get this, now Thor fakes lame every time I have to go," I rambled in my usual chatty fashion.

Vonnie laughed. "That dog should get a special Oscar."

I couldn't believe how low things had sunk, in the course of a morning I was unemployed, broke, and as a "malicious under-earner," I was now a potential felon.

Merry frigging Christmas to me.

A Grrl Genius "Love Is Important But Chocolate Is Essential" Handy Chocolate Fun Fact

On an average day, 20.5 million Oreo cookies are consumed worldwide. On a bad day, 20.5 Oreos are consumed in my apartment.

Christmas, which Jen and I spent together, was a blur of baked goods and naps, but somehow I survived. Now it was January, and show business emerged from what I always referred to as "Lampshade on Head Season," in which no decisions could be made, no jobs offered, and no career progress made. When my Hollywood agent told me that he had a meeting for me at Warner Brothers, for a writing job on a TV pilot, I was thrilled. It wouldn't be my intellectual property, which was great.

When I got to the meeting, it became apparent to me that there was no big money job at all, only yet another producer who wanted me to work for him "developing" (in other words writing for free) his brilliant idea for a TV show. The producer, the appropriately named Delbert Fink, was one of those fired network executives who is given what is known as a "studio housekeeping deal," which basically amounts to no operating budget and an office to die in. The Fink's dazzling TV show idea was based on a female superhero who drew her amazing powers from her own menstrual cycle. As he described her she was, "Sort of like, 'Super PMS Woman!'"

I thought it was an insanely stupid idea. My attention wandered the entire meeting and I couldn't stop thinking about lunch. I was seized with an overwhelming craving for a BLT. As I left his office, I had to admit I felt angry and bloated, and remarkably like "Super PMS Woman" myself, so I decided to go to the Warner Brothers commissary and have a damn BLT before I ripped someone's head off with my bare hands, using only the power of my incredibly bad cramps and dire financial situation to fuel my superhuman strength.

As I paid for my meal, I realized the source of my sandwich

yearning was the month-old Santeria bacon panty-pig in the bottom of the large purse I had not used since that fateful meeting with Jabba the Attorney. I threw away the bacon, and the plush toy, but when I glanced back and saw the stuffed pig's sweet little pink satin snout buried in the refuse, as though struggling for life, I snatched it back and shoved it deep into my purse. I then settled into a corner booth with my sandwich, a book, and my deepening self-pity.

"Hey, Cathryn!"

I looked up, and there was William McCall, the Idaho bumpkin and e-mail stalker.

He looked tan and fit and preppy and not at all—as I had rewritten him in my mind—like some Depression-era starved and unshaven Steinbeck character desperately clutching dirt-covered Idaho potatoes in his hands. I was completely flustered, embarrassed, and worried that maybe he was still stalking me, so I glanced around for security. But when I looked into his face, I just saw that he was . . . happy to see me.

And I was . . . happy to see him. I couldn't help it. The guy was just too goofily friendly.

He was standing with Elsbeth Hixton-Cooper, a particularly odious development executive with a very prestigious film and TV production company. Her personality was as phony as her breasts, which tilted heavenward like missiles on a launch pad from her nearly skeletal frame. She also had the (apparently now regulation) butt-fat-injected lips. She had arrived in Hollywood as Beth Bernstein ten years ago, but a brief early marriage and a quick rewrite on her first name gave her the kind of WASPY cache that Grrl Genius Martha Stewart, née Kostyra, obtained in the same fashion and turned into a home-improvement empire. I don't even want Elsbeth in the movie of my life, but if she had to be in it, she would be played (badly) by Pamela Anderson in a cheap brunette wig.

Of course, despite the fact that Elsbeth had personally killed a pet project of mine, she greeted me like we were long-lost sorority sisters.

"Oh. My. God. Cathryn Michon!!!!!" she trilled as she hugged me to her rock-hard pleasure globes. "How *are* you! It's been *forever!*" Of course she did not care in the least how I was, which was fine because I didn't care how she was either. "Do you know William McCall?"

"I do," I admitted. "We met on a talk show on our book tours."

"Oh. My. God. How hilarious is *that*?" she squealed. "William is our newest overnight sensation at Sit Down Prince, and I *discovered* him!"

Sit Down Prince Productions was the prestigious production company she worked for. As to her having "discovered" William, I highly doubted that it had occurred before his book had been published, or that her "discovery" process had included reading anything more than the book jacket, which frankly would have been a lot of words for Elsbeth to absorb. William looked uncomfortable at all the gushing, and I found that refreshing.

She continued her inane babbling until her congenitally short attention span demanded that she go pretend to be someone else's best friend, and she finally left us alone.

William stood there awkwardly for a minute. "Hey," he said, "that sandwich smells really good!"

I smiled nervously and clutched my pork infused purse tightly closed.

"Mind if I sit with you a minute, I mean, unless you're busy . . ." he tapered off politely.

I winced at the reference to my allegedly busy life. In the time my calendar had been supposedly been too busy to see him, I had accomplished absolutely nothing new, had in fact lost a major source of income, even as he had apparently become the "overnight sensation" of Sit Down Prince Productions. He was a huge success, I was a huge failure, and yet I had believed that he was trying to use me to get ahead in show biz. I had never felt like more of an idiot and less of a genius. I couldn't imagine why he even wanted to talk to me.

"I guess you're doing great!" I enthused, trying to sound cheerful.

"Well, it seems to be going okay, but I have to say, I really feel sometimes like I'm in town on the egg money. I mean, people here are, well"—he seemed to be gesturing vaguely in Elsbeth's direction—"different from what I'm used to."

"Yeah," I agreed. "Tell me about it. I just met with a guy who wants me to help him create a premenstrual superhero."

"Huh," he said, considering this carefully. "So I guess she strikes fear in the hearts of criminals because she's, like, in a really bad mood?"

I laughed. "Something like that." He seemed to be deep in thought, perhaps considering the future capers of "Super PMS Woman."

"You know, all she'd have to do is start talking about 'heavy flow,' and male criminals would be surrendering like crazy," he observed.

"Right," I bantered. "She retains power—and water!"

"Maybe chocolate could be her Kryptonite!" he said.

"I'm not taking the job, you know."

"Oh," he said, suddenly shy, and I regretted that I might have made him feel foolish for giving actual consideration to such a ridiculous proposition. "I never know what to take seriously here," William continued. "I made a joke in a meeting the other day about a great idea I had for a movie where there is a serial killer on a Greyhound bus, sort of a cross between *Speed* and *Silence of the Lambs,* and now they actually want to develop it!"

"Well, you're officially 'hot' in Hollywood. Everything you say is officially 'a great idea!'"

I didn't tell him it wouldn't last.

"Well, obviously that won't last," he said sarcastically. "But, my God, what are these executives thinking? Imagine this movie, there's bodies dropping left and right, and then there's Jodie Foster or whoever and she says, very seriously, 'Dammit, Steve, I think it's someone on the bus!'"

"I'm not taking the PMS job mostly because it isn't a job at all," I confessed, feeling like a genuine loser. "Just a lot of free work that will go nowhere, and I can't really afford it right now." I knew I was rambling just as my girlfriends were constantly warning me not to do, but I seemed powerless to stop it. "I'm trying, well, I'm trying to crawl out from under this divorce. Kurt is going for my intellectual property, and I lost my TV hosting job, so I've got to get a job, but it has to be something I can prove isn't my idea, because if it *is* my idea, Kurt will get half the money automatically. If I can get enough money to get a new place with a yard, the court might give me my dog back," I blathered, feeling I had said too much and instantly regretting it.

"Huh," he said, again seeming to be pondering something. "So I guess your divorce isn't final?"

"Yeah. I'm just hoping for a deal where I can keep my brain and give away all the money," I proclaimed with mock eagerness.

"That would be a good deal," he said.

"Are you being sarcastic?" I asked defensively.

"No, Cathryn, not at all," he reproached gently. "I have the utmost respect for your brain, *your* brain is a treasure. Money is just money."

"Yes, well, it comes in handy, though, doesn't it?" I retorted somewhat bitterly.

The question hung in the air. Suddenly, William seemed very energized as he reached into a large leather computer backpack.

"Listen," he began, "I'll be honest with you. . . ."

"Whenever someone says that, I am usually convinced it's because they are about to start lying to me," I stated dourly.

He threw his head back in that joyous way of his and laughed. "Oh, my. Well, that's a very cynical attitude, and probably very wise. But seriously, here's the thing: I'm on this TV-film overall deal with Sit Down Prince—"

"You're on an overall deal?" I blurted, my customary bitterness creeping in, annoyed that I was being offered free menstrual jobs as he was luxuriating on what was surely a fat three-picture deal.

"Well, yeah, and believe me, I get that's a good thing, everyone keeps telling me that I am very lucky, and I believe them. Anyway, they want me to write this movie. It's a romantic comedy about a single woman in L.A., and frankly, it's not going all that well. They want me to partner with someone, because I've never written a screenplay, and they suggested some guy named Norm Vela, who's really hot right now—"

I involuntarily let out a disgusted *"Ha!"* which William ignored.

"—but I suggested that since the screenplay is supposed to be about a single woman living in L.A., that maybe I could find a great woman writer who was, you know, a single woman, living in L.A.," he continued.

I said nothing.

"And it occurs to me that you are a great writer, and a single woman living in L.A., who's written a lot of screenplays. . . ."

I said nothing.

"It's not on spec—it would be guaranteed. Your half would be a hundred twenty-five thousand dollars, and since it's my project, it wouldn't be your intellectual property. So I was wondering, do you think you'd be interested? You'd really be helping me out. I've got the scenes figured out—it's just the woman's voice, you know? I can't find her voice."

I literally could not speak. Which anybody who knows me can testify is a rare freak event of nature along the lines of a tidal wave or a good Ben Affleck movie. I also had to take a minute for my irony meter, which was solidly in the red zone, to pipe the hell down. Because, of course, here was the guy who was supposedly so needy that my fellow Grrl Geniuses said I had to refuse even to eat a meal with him, offering me the biggest job anyone had put in front of me in five years. I couldn't understand why he was even speaking to me, considering how I'd blown him off, but I was in no position to question his kindly attitude toward me.

William seemed to take my silence for reluctance, and he continued to press his case.

"I mean, you'd really be doing me a favor. It's just one of the projects I have with them, but it is sold, and they said whoever I wanted was fine with them," he pleaded.

I thought about what that hundred and twenty-five thousand

dollars could do. If I had that kind of money, I would finally be able to move to a place where the court might allow me to keep Thor, and I missed Thor so much, it literally made me ache inside. I still couldn't talk, because I was afraid if I opened my mouth, I would burst into grateful tears. I could just see everything coming together.

Finally, I spoke. "Well, you know, sure, I mean, yeah, why not," I said in a low tone, trying to pretend like he wasn't saving my whole life. The guy I wasn't supposed to rescue was rescuing me.

"Well, great, that's really great, then." He smiled with that endearingly goofy grin of his. "It's due in six weeks, though. Is that okay for you?"

It was fine for me. The truth was, my calendar could not have been more clear.

We exchanged numbers and agreed to meet for breakfast later that week as William gave me another of his very professional handshakes and headed toward Elsbeth, who was motioning to him that it was time for them to go. Still in a state of shock, I watched him jauntily rush off, following Elsbeth's gigantic breasts like they were twin compasses pointing due north.

I sat there in the commissary, feeling truly amazed. A lot had happened, and a lot of it had been very bad. I realized that the last few weeks had indeed included some stressful events, including but not limited to a major car accident, the potentially devastating loss of the one go-to sexual fantasy that I could always count on (hunky firefighter), a beachside sexual arousal followed by an almost instantaneous rejection and breakup, both a new roommate and the loss of perhaps the greatest single source of amazing cooking I had ever encountered, the loss of my postmarital virginity and the exciting prospect of a new business selling my used panties via the Internet, the additional and unexpected expenses associated with being hit by an uninsured driver, the fact that I would be without my safe but dull car for over a month with only the not-very-encouragingly-named Rent-A-Wreck as my sole source of transportation, getting yelled at by lesbians for being with my friend who wasn't enough of a lesbian, and finally, in addition to the fact that I was going to have to give up half my assets as well as most likely have to pay for the support of my slacker ex for the rest of his life, I also had to adjust to the concept that I was now potentially going to have to divulge and catalog, at great financial expense, the entire scattered contents of my brain so that the man who had promised to love, honor, and cherish me could fully and completely co-own any future revenue from any thought I ever had in the last ten years, without having to do a lick of work himself.

But then, suddenly, with the reappearance of a man I had, quite frankly, been awful to, in one hour, my whole life seemed to be suffused with a strange substance I faintly recognized as true hope. It wasn't just that the job he had offered was the exact perfect job I had needed at the exact right time, it was more than that. It was the idea that suddenly, out of the manure of life, a beautiful fragrant blossom can manage to appear out of the stinky muck, unexpected and delightful. To me this was the absolute proof of the validity of the Grrl Genius philosophy. Things are bad only if you admit they're bad. You're only an idiot if you call yourself an idiot. You're never completely an idiot any more than you are completely a genius. You are going to be lying to yourself some portion of the time, so why not lie and say you're a genius? Why the hell not? Besides, sometimes, good things happen—they really do. If the exact perfect job could appear this suddenly, if I could suddenly feel true hope, could true love be far behind?

Love is or love ain't. Thin love ain't love at all.
—Toni Morrison

Chapter 6

A Grrl Genius Realizes That She Cannot Let Bitterness (No Matter How Well Justified) Get the Best of Her

The hardest years in life are those between ten and seventy.
—Helen Hayes

WILLIAM NEVER questioned me as to why I had so rudely refused to see him when he moved to L.A., and I didn't really feel it was worth explaining that it had been because I thought he was a pathetic needy loser who was trying to use me.

William and I had agreed we would work out of his apartment in Santa Monica. It was a huge drive for me, but I wasn't about to complain; I was so grateful for what he had done for me. William had managed, without my codependent help, to get a very nice, spacious, stylish apartment right on the sand in Santa Monica. (That was rent controlled!) Well, so much for him being a toothless bumpkin "in town on the egg money."

Obviously I had read him wrong, but, in my defense, his relentless "Aw, shucks, m'am" self-deprecating attitude could certainly lead a person astray. He acted like his book, which I found out had sold a hundred thousand copies in hardback and was now being turned into a TV show, was just some big fluke. William loved to lead people into believing that he was just a big ol' Jed Clampett country feller from Booger Holler who done turned his "'ritin" into a new-fangled career.

It was very annoying, because I had completely fallen for it. I'd been afraid to have dinner with him, for God's sake, lest he end up camping out in his pop-up trailer in front of my apartment building and cooking possums over a can of Sterno that he would then drink as an amusing aperitif.

The truth was, he had lived in the sticks, but it turned out that had made his living as a top executive at a life insurance company, and not as a hardscrabble potato farmer/trapper/fish snaggler as I had imagined. He was incredibly dedicated to his writing, and for the last twenty years had gotten up at 5 a.m. every single morning to write. That's the kind of thing people often lie about, but the fact was that he was obviously incredibly prolific, as he had completed nine unpublished, rejected novels before his tenth, which had been published.

I knew, because I could see the big thick manuscripts on his shelf. It was both inspiring and intimidating.

William's "shack" in Idaho turned out to be a ski-in/ski-out condo on a lake, where he spent every fourth week, since that was when he had custody of his sixteen-year-old son, unless he and his ex-wife (who was remarried to a guy he claimed to actually *like*) needed to change the schedule, which they usually did after a reasonable discussion, according to the easy terms of their friendly and very respectful divorce.

Since the movie was his project and he liked to work in the early morning like the simple country farmer he had hoodwinked me into believing he was, I got in the habit of beating the rush-hour traffic to Santa Monica at sunrise. Because I was an ungrateful wretch, I cursed having to adjust my body clock to rising at the ungodly hour of 4:30 a.m., but couldn't help feeling awe every time I drove down Ocean Boulevard and saw the morning sunlight on the sparkling surf, the sky lit in the kind of electric pinks and purples you normally see only on drag queens.

I would arrive at William's apartment, where he was always relentlessly cheerful and unfailingly polite. He just loved getting up early and writing, and really couldn't believe he was lucky enough to get to do it full-time now.

It was a little nauseating. He would always greet me sunnily.

"Hey there, you! Wasn't the sunrise incredible!"

"I suppose," I admitted sleepily, "although I might point out it looks almost the same as the sunset, which comes at a far more civilized time."

Even I don't look like Cindy Crawford in the morning.
—Cindy Crawford

It turned out that William was a great cook, and sometimes he had baked the most incredibly moist and perfect currant scones or buttery wild blueberry muffins, or sometimes he even made the homemade caramelized cinnamon rolls I have always worshiped, suffusing his apartment with the warm yeasty smell of true happiness expressed through the miracle of cinnamon, fat, and sugar. William had learned that the easiest way to tame my early-morning crabbiness was with home-baked carbohydrates.

All other crabbiness was obviously best deflected with chocolate, and he kept a good supply on hand the way lion tamers always keep a good supply of chairs on hand. He even, after I mentioned their existence only once, tracked down a box of my beloved chocolate Frango mints for me. It made me weepy with gratitude. He didn't understand why, but he seemed pleased anyway.

William was a nice man.

He was more successful than I was, had better work habits, was neater, was more polite, was a better cook, had a nicer apartment, nicer car, nicer divorce, and frankly, a nicer personality. He was, in fact, so together that it was hard not to despise him, except for the fact that he was now my writing partner, so all his irritatingly good qualities were actually of benefit to me, especially with my upcoming divorce court battle.

My prospects for the impending court date with Kurt were pretty grim. Jabba had told me that we should plan for the worst-case scenario of Kurt getting both an alimony award and a significant portion of my intellectual property. "But probably not as much as half, although, you know, technically . . . ," Jabba repeated himself in yet another $350-an-hour rerun of the horror movie I'd already sat through in his office.

Jabba suggested that I wait to pursue dog custody until after all the financial decrees, because if I moved into a nicer place with a yard before alimony was awarded, Kurt's attorneys would assume that I had more money hidden somewhere and would then force me to hire someone called a forensic accountant, who would cost me a lot of money, so that I could prove that I don't have any money. Even if I moved, for as long as Kurt was encamped at our house, his attorneys could make the argument that the dog would be happier in the home he'd always known. So, for now Thor and I had doggy visitation when we hiked at 5 a.m. which was when I collected him from his doghouse in the front yard, where he'd been relegated to sleeping due to Kurt's girlfriend's allergies. Apparently Triceratops are allergic to Dobermans. As my friend Vonnie would always say, "Go know."

Naturally, given my prickly personality, I had to find something to fight about with William, if only to prove to myself that he wasn't perfect. So we fought about New York City, which he hated and I felt was the greatest city on earth.

"It's the world's largest monument to cement," he would say.

"It's a city! Cities are made of cement! It's the greatest city on earth!"

"Okay, if you like cities, which I don't, by the way, how about Kansas City?" he suggested. "Clean streets, low crime—"

"High boredom, no good Chinese food!"

"Hey, there are lots of great Chinese food restaurants in Kansas City, and I've been to both of them!" he would protest with a grin.

Then, at the mention of Chinese food, like a couple of dogs who suddenly have a Liva Snap waved in front of them, we would forget about the argument about New York and begin the complex process of ordering Chinese food for lunch.

At least he understood that meals were more important than anything else.

Unlike almost every man with whom I had ever worked,

William was incredibly professional and never made cheesy little sexual comments at my expense. He just treated me like someone he really respected.

The only problem was that I occasionally found William, well, attractive. Usually when he was handing me homemade baked goods, but sometimes when he was just sitting there thinking, or when he made me laugh, which he often did. However, William did not seem in the least bit attracted to me. Which normally would have made me think he was gay, but was far more likely due to the fact that, like David, he had been in therapy and knew enough to avoid obvious emotional train wrecks like me.

Or maybe (and this was painful for me to contemplate) it was just because he didn't find me attractive. God knows my husband hadn't. And surely this was a good thing, because our business partnership was essential to me now. And yet, it bothered me that he never seemed to notice me as a woman. It became a little drama in my mind where I would really go to a big effort at 4:30 a.m. trying to pull together a cute look, so that William would find me attractive, and maybe even make a pass at me, so that I could then take the moral high ground and give him a big lecture about the inadvisability of business partners becoming romantically involved.

Of course, I would be looking really cute the whole time I gave the big lecture.

Despite all my obsessing about choices of outfits and hairdos, William never seemed to notice one way or the other. It didn't really matter, because we worked together so well, writing scenes in the movie and then trading them back and forth for rewrites. We often seemed to be eerily on the same comic wavelength, sometimes coming up with the same joke at the same moment. We even misspelled the same words.

"How do you spell *bureau?*" he called out as we were proofreading a scene.

"I have no idea. I spell it so badly I can't even find it in the dictionary," I confessed.

"Well, it's a dumb word, anyway. Let's just make it a—a—"

"Dresser!" we both cried.

Sometimes hours would go by and I wouldn't notice, we were so "brain to brain." His love of writing was infectious, and oftentimes, much to my shock and dismay, I realized that I was having fun, and that this wasn't simply a more lucrative financial solution than selling my used panties on eBay.

A Grrl Genius "Love Is Important But Chocolate Is Essential" Handy Chocolate Fun Fact

Chocolate does not promote tooth decay as much as other high-sugar foods do. An antibacterial agent has been recently found in chocolate that inhibits plaque formation. Eating chocolate is practically the same as brushing your teeth!

William had an expense account in his big fat studio deal, so we always ordered good lunches to be delivered. The only time things got really dicey between us was when we argued about what music to play while we were writing, although sometimes his taste in music surprised me. After sticking in a CD I was sure he would hate, I watched for his reaction, and was surprised to see that goofy grin of his spread across his face.

It's fun to stay at the
YMCA!
I love to stay at the
YMCA!

"I love this song!" William cried out improbably as he leapt up, grabbing my hand and pulling me out of my chair. We began dancing around the apartment like idiots. William hated Madonna but loved the Village People. Go know!

Perhaps the best thing about William was his willingness to tolerate what I would call "my hobbies" and what some—well, really all—of my friends insisted on referring to as "my nutty obsessions." One day at lunch, over chopped salads that had been delivered from La Scala, he regarded me carefully as I diligently arranged and rearranged the roasted peppers on top of my salad in what I regarded to be a rather intriguing basket-weave pattern.

"You know, I have to say, my favorite part of your book was the whole salad-competition thing, and I've always wondered, was that true?" William asked shyly.

"Yeah. It's true," I replied bitterly. "Only, I'm done with all that. It's all so political, and there's no way they'll ever let me win, even though I'm always the best. The salad competition is in two weeks, but there's no way I'm going to go through that humiliation again."

Every year for the last four years I had participated as a contestant in the Live Salad Making Competition at the Santa Barbara County Fair. Every year I concocted a salad that somehow expressed my deep internal emotional struggles or my impassioned opinions about sociopolitical trends. Every year my salad had a theme (as I often said, there was always a message in my roughage) and I always wore an outfit that reflected the theme, along with my trademark tiara. Every year, despite putting in Herculean effort, I always ended up in third place, due entirely, I felt, to the political chicanery of one craven, corrupt home arts judge, a certain Mrs. Peggy Keefer, who had taken a dislike to me (because I wasn't a stay-at-home mom) and had been my saladic nemesis for four long years. The bitterness I felt toward Mrs. Peggy Keefer knew no bounds. "I'll tell you one thing I know for sure," I stated dourly, "Mrs. Peggy Keefer wouldn't know an innovative, important salad if it bit her unstylishly Dacron-polyester-clad arm off, and I'm not going to work my butt off just to watch someone else get a blue ribbon and a twenty-five-dollar gift certificate to the Sizzler."

I pouted as I picked at my salad in a desultory fashion. William got that very focused look on his face that he always had when he was concocting a plan.

"Cathryn," William began, looking adorably like Kevin Kline as he earnestly regarded me. "You are having a rough year. Because of a very unfair system, you may be losing a fortune to an alcoholic ex-husband who clearly never appreciated you or your genius. So, the way I see it, the need for some kind of victory in your life, no matter how trivial, no matter that it consists only of a blue ribbon and a twenty-five-dollar gift certificate to the Sizzler—which I'm going to go ahead and assume you don't even like—is, well, essential."

He could not have been more right. I needed to win at something, anything. I agreed to enter the world of live salad making once again.

Over the next week, William eagerly took on the task of helping me with my salad planning, as though it were as important as any real job.

"But, Cathryn," he said earnestly during one of our high-level strategic salad sessions, "what is you're salad about, really? What are you trying to say, vegetatively, at the core level?"

This was how we'd come to talk about the whole thing, and yes, it was slightly crazy.

"I think," I said, truly deep in thought, "I think that I want my salad to be about my new life as a single woman, I want it to be about my belief in true love, my blossoming single sexuality . . ."

I noticed that William was beginning to blush—he had the admirably old-fashioned tendency to express his squeamishness on certain topics by dilating the blood vessels in his face. So few people care enough about anything to blush anymore, and I found it charming.

I continued, undaunted that his face was as red as the heirloom tomatoes I had decided would be lining the rim of my salad bowl. "I think that my hope, my optimism about men is best expressed by my ability to remain positive on the topic of the hunky and brave American firefighter, despite everything that has happened with this Luther J. Burton person."

"Luther J. Burton is a horrible human being and a disgrace to firefighters everywhere," he agreed emphatically.

"So if the salad could somehow be, like, a passionate tribute to firefighters, their bravery, their selflessness, their biceps—"

William suddenly leapt out of his chair.

"I know! I've got it!" he exclaimed. "You could set a salad on fire. You could make a salad flambé!"

It was perfect, absolutely perfect.

"Yes, yes!" I agreed. Suddenly, I was on a roll, a salad roll. "Oh, my God, yes, that's it! And, I'll wear, I'll wear a bikini, expressing my vulnerability, my ability to be comfortable within my own skin, and, yet, I'm frightened I'm scared of getting hurt, so, so it will be a chicken salad!"

"Oh, God, that is so great!"

"And it's about passion, so I'll have passion fruit, and a bunch of other tropical fruits, and then I'll set everything on fire, and I'll call it, Cathryn's Grrl Genius Flamingly Passionate and Yet Ultimately Chicken Salad!" I declared, all my synapses firing at once.

William threw his head back and laughed and laughed. "Oh, Cathryn, that is so great. Oh, my, there's no one like you—"

"Well, we'll see," I said with false modesty, "but I have to admit, I think it's pretty good. Besides, it was your idea to set a salad on fire."

"That's nothing. I'm a guy—we live to try and blow things up, but you, well, you're just a Grrl Genius, and that's all there is to it."

Sometimes, I felt like he actually meant it. He was a good friend to me.

A Grrl Genius "People Who've Made Worse Relationship Mistakes Than You" Moment

Carmen Friedewald-Hill, twenty-six, shot boyfriend Ryan Gesner to death in Frederick, Maryland, during an argument over which one of them loved the other more.

Confronting Mrs. Peggy Keefer was nothing compared with the post-traumatic stress disorder I had suffered from the vehicular and emotional assault on my cherished firefighter fantasy from one Luther J. Burton, but I was determined to swallow my bitterness and let nothing ruin the night where I and five of my luckiest girl-friends would be prepared dinner by the brave and hunky firefight-ers of Hidden Hills Fire and Rescue Squad 73.

I had received a lot of desperate phone calls from women I hadn't heard from since forever, all of whom wanted to be invited to the hunky firefighter dinner. On the day I was to extend the final invitations, I got a phone call from Tommy, my proverbial (and actual) gay best friend, the true love of my life, the man whom I bit-terly blame for a lifetime of disappointments about men. It bothered me that attractive women in movies always have a gay best friend, but they always managed to meet their gay best friend when the guy knew he was gay, not in second grade as I had, when nobody knows anything. The women in the movies never had to suffer through confused adolescence or awkward fumblings. They just met as adults and went to swanky bars and got great outfit and man advice from their gay best friends with no remaining sadness that every-thing would have been fine if the love of their life hadn't turned out to be gay.

Friday 9:18 a.m. "Hey, Catherinabell, it's Tommy. I know that this firefighter thing is supposed to be some kind of 'Grrl Genius Only' affair, but the fact is, I really think my fantasy needs should be considered, too. Plus, I'm your oldest friend. Let me rephrase that, I'm the friend that's known you the longest. When you're mak-ing up your little dinner party list, how about you try to remember who it was that helped you clean off that little pink-and-lime-green Lilly Pulitzer sundress when you sat in that big dog turd during second-grade recess? I'm just sayin'. What about how I remember that it was a Lily Pulitzer dress? Don't I get points for that? I know, I'm normally not this queeny, you're always complaining I'm not 'gay enough,' whatever that means, but I'm willing to do it for the chance to eat the hunky firefighter spaghetti. I know you don't want to hear it, but statistically one in ten of them is gay, and that's all I'm asking for, just a shot at the one in ten. Call me, 'kay?"

Although I had intended it to be an all–Grrl Genius affair, I decided to take Tommy's request under serious advisement. After all, he was my oldest friend, and at some point I was going to have to stop holding it against him that he didn't like to go to bed with women, and had thus ruined my whole life. If one of my Grrl Genius goals was to let go of bitterness, I reasoned this might actually be a good place for me to start.

The Grrl Genius Wild Sexual Kingdom

Perhaps the bitterest female in the entire wild sexual kingdom is the female European praying mantis *(Mantis religiosa)* who is notorious throughout the wild sexual kingdom for giving new meaning to the phrase "high maintenance," by electing to bite her lovers' heads off during mating. Apparently, once the male mantis has had his head bitten off in the middle of intercourse, he thrashes about in a "highly stimulating sexual frenzy." Although metaphorically "biting his head off" by starting an argument is also a behavioral pattern seen in bitter human females, it is less likely to result in a "highly stimulating sexual frenzy" and much more likely to result in a conversation about how the female is "such a freakin' bitch."

This behavior is not unique to the praying mantis. Over eighty different animal species have been observed whose females consume their lovers during sex. For example, the midge, which is a small (and apparently very bitter) fly, entices her lover to lick her genitalia, and by way of thanks, she smashes a hole into her unsuspecting boyfriend's head, injects an enzyme that liquefies his internal organs, which she then consumes by drinking until she's sucked him dry (although certainly not in the way he had hoped for) and discards his eviscerated exoskeleton like an empty diet Coke can.

While no evidence exists to prove whether the vivisected male midges "were asking for it," one may in fact hypothesize that the liquefied boyfriend may have been a little too much like the midge's no good ex-husband, who is perhaps bleeding *her* dry by taking half her net worth in a divorce, plus has a lot of annoying habits like never trimming his nose hairs and yelling at the contestants on *Wheel of Fortune* for refusing to buy a vowel.

Of course, this theory has yet to be tested in the wild.

———————

We never worked late, so I had no idea what William did with his evenings or weekends. He was very professional that way. Of course I wondered, but I never asked. William was, I came to learn, a rather shy and socially awkward person at heart. I decided that was why he always wanted people to think he was a big unsophisticated hayseed, so he could exceed their very low expectations of him socially. I thought he might even be a little agoraphobic, since he never wanted to go out for food, always preferred ordering in. Usually we knocked off at around four so I could go to my yoga class and he could go mountain biking, a truly inane sport that involved taking a device that was obviously designed to be driven on a road and proving to yourself that through sheer force of will and relentless stupidity you could make it go up a muddy, rock-strewn path, slower and more painfully than you could walk up it. Yoga versus mountain biking was one of our favorite topics.

"Why is it fun to try to kill yourself?" I demanded.

"It's challenging on the way up and then it's exciting on the way down."

"Plus it gives you a good story to tell in the emergency room!" I declared.

"Well, I don't know. It's certainly more fun than choking back incense while some old hippie yells at you do Downward Thrusting Turkey, or Downward Facing Flounder," he replied.

"They don't yell in yoga. And it's Downward Facing Dog, for your information."

"Rancid Beetle Pose, Angry Hamster Pose," he mocked.

"Those aren't real—"

"What about corpse pose—you told me they have a corpse pose," he said.

"Well, sure, but they have corpse pose in mountain biking, too, it's like, the whole goal of it. At least in yoga the corpse pose is temporary."

It went like that.

Hunky Firefighter Day dawned bright and sunny, like nearly every other day in Los Angeles. After all the phone calls and e-mails were considered, the choice of who was to attend actually came down to the people I liked the best.

And so it was that on that Saturday, Jen, Vonnie, Amelia, Kim, and Tommy all piled into Kim's gigantic minivan and headed to Hidden Hills.

Kim, whose keenly competitive nature and caustic sarcasm usually made her an unlikely candidate for giddy behavior, was as excited as a Make-A-Wish kid headed to Disneyland.

"Do you think that they will actually slide down a big pole?" Kim asked excitedly, and then burst into actual giggles, a sound I had never heard come out of her head before.

"You're frightening me, doll," said Vonnie, although she looked pretty excited as well. We were all . . . very excited.

As we drove, the assembled Grrl Geniuses squealed and talked all at once like a Brownie troop on its way to day camp, while Tommy, the lone Enlightened Male, who had grown up with four sisters and was accustomed to being drowned out in a chorus of estrogen just sat back and let us babble.

The most important topic of conversation naturally was all about the lingerie we had decided to wear.

Amelia, always a devoted shopper, answered the question in one word, "Cosabella!"

Amelia had gotten me hooked on Cosabella, the crack cocaine of expensive lingerie that was whisper thin, thin enough to fit on a microscope slide, and yet amazingly supportive.

Kim, who was ridiculously practical, didn't get the whole Cosabella obsession. "I don't know why you are always on about that Cosabella stuff. It looks like nothing and it costs a fortune."

"It looks like nothing in the store, but on your body, it's a miracle. It instantly makes your breasts as perky as when you were sixteen," I said defiantly.

Kim snorted. "I don't care about lingerie. I never have sex anymore, so what's the point? Half the time I wear his briefs—" She snapped her nicotine gum impatiently.

"What! I'm shocked. You're a successful executive; you could afford all the Cosabella you want," protested Amelia.

"Tell me you're shocked when you've got two kids to get off to school, and you're racing out in the morning looking at piles of undone laundry you haven't finished, and the only clean underwear are his," said Kim.

"Well, I don't understand, if you both work full-time, why don't you both do the laundry?" Amelia asked.

"Because," Kim replied, suddenly sheepish, "because, well, I don't like how he does it. He's incapable, he puts in the wrong soap—"

"Oh, please," I scoffed. "Barnaby's got a Ph.D. in chemistry, if he can figure out how to make a scratch-and-sniff hamburger sticker, don't tell me he can't figure out how laundry detergent works. You don't let him do the laundry so that you can be a big martyr and make him feel guilty. Maybe that's why you guys don't have sex."

Kim glared at me. "My sex-free marriage is not the topic here. The topic is underwear, which I don't give a rat's ass about," Kim retorted. "Why? I'll tell you why. My breasts were never perky. Remember the pencil test? To see if your breasts were sagging? You weren't supposed to be able to hold a pencil beneath your breasts, but I always could. Now I can hold a stapler in there."

"Kim," I began preachily, "you have got to learn to be less bitter. A Grrl Genius cannot be bitter—that's one of my Grrl Genius laws."

Kim picked up her cell phone as though it had just rung and started speaking into it. "Oh, hi, it's the black kettle, calling for you, Mrs. Pot!" she bleated, tossing the phone at me.

"Fine, fine," I said, "I'll be the first to admit that I can be bitter about things that I obviously have every right to be bitter about, because they are so very unfair. But at least I am trying to get over it! At least I have the good sense to move ahead with my life! At least I wore cute lingerie to the hunky firefighter dinner!"

Jen, who was so effortlessly beautiful that even women loved to look at her, spoke up. "I don't know why you all went to so much trouble. I'm wearing my pink cotton camisole from Target. It's adorable and it cost only ten dollars."

Vonnie gave Jen one of her classic eye rolls. "Oh, honey, you could wear a *bag* from Target and look adorable." She patted Jen on the hand. "But I knew enough to wear sexy underwear to this shindig. That's why I'm wearing a black silk satin merry widow that was made for me when I played Dolly Levi on the national tour. I'm so hot in it that *I'd* do me."

"Besides," Jen added, "according to *The Rules,* there would be no possible chance of any of these guys getting anywhere near my underwear until we'd had at least seven dates, so it really is a moot point."

Everyone in the Grrl Genius club always ignored Jen when she started spouting off about *The Rules,* which we all thought were ridiculous. Because she was my cousin, the geniuses politely ignored Jen's ravings with the sort of "Isn't that nice, dear!" attitude reserved for family members who've gone temporarily insane and joined cults that involve the wearing of saffron robes or the selling of Amway.

"Just think," I said, trying to shift the focus from Jen and her nutty and retro *Rules.* "What if there was some kind of a huge disaster while we were there, like, say a big earthquake, which could totally happen because, you know, it's California, and we got like, conscripted into the fire department, as volunteers, and we had to go into the, you know, changing room part of the fire station, you know, that part where they slide down the big pole half-naked because they are in such a big rush and all, and we had to put on this special equipment, or whatever, and because it was such an emergency, we'd all be racing around, tearing off our clothes at the same time and getting into our special equipment, which we really wouldn't be that familiar with, right? So they'd be all half-dressed, and so would we, but they'd have to help us get dressed, and then they might see our underwear!" I suddenly became aware of a space-vacuum-like silence in the minivan. "So, that's why we'd want to be sure that we had cute underwear, obviously. . . ." I trailed off, realizing that, as usual, I may have given out more information than people needed or wanted.

Everyone just stared at me dumbly.

Finally, Vonnie spoke. "Doll, did anyone ever tell you that your mind is a dangerous place to be?"

Tommy took advantage of the stunned silence to finally get a word in edgewise.

"I'm wearing new blue-plaid Gap boxer shorts," he stated simply.

We said nothing.

"Look, the statistics are one in ten men is gay—you can't blame me for that," he argued.

"I don't blame you for the one in ten," I responded sullenly, "I blame you for the fact that the one in ten is always the one that's handsome, witty, smart, and kind. The one in ten is always—well, he's always just like you. That, I will never forgive you for."

"Oh, Cathryn," he said as he pulled me into a hug, smoothing my hair gently. "You know that if I hadn't been gay, I'd have married you and I'd have loved you all your life. Just like I do now."

"Except we'd have sex . . . ," I pointed out.

"Right," he agreed, kissing me on the top of my head distractedly.

Tommy was a nice man.

"There's one thing I know for sure," I stated with the authoritative tone I always use when I'm about to make up some facts. "I have determined that the ideal man is what I like to call the 'gay straight man.' He is gay in every way, except sex. He's just like you because he cooks, he has good opinions about outfits, he likes to dance, he's gay in every way except—and this is key—except sex. In sex, he's straight."

Kim glowered at me in the rearview mirror. "Well of all your nutty obsessive little relationship theories, this is the nuttiest."

"I am absolutely right about this," I insisted. "Why do you think that *Queer Eye* TV show is such a hit? It's just everyone acknowledging what I have been saying all along, gay men are just . . . better men!"

"Here, here," said Tommy.

"It's true," I continued. "If a man could be gay gay gay twenty-three hours a day, and then go hetero for like, one whole hour—"

"Not seven minutes, which is the statistical average," added Amelia.

"Exactly, a full sixty glorious straight minutes and then poof, he's a big Nancy boy again, well, then he's the perfect man. The gay straight man," I concluded.

"Doll, I thought the whole idea was that your ideal man was a firefighter. I thought that was the whole purpose of this whole hoot-enanny," Vonnie said.

"Well," I said defiantly, "right, the ideal man is obviously a gay straight firefighter."

"Except in sex," said Amelia.

"Exactly," I agreed happily.

Amelia got a worried look on her face and said to me, "Cathryn, you didn't wear the red underwear, right? I mean, you're still waiting for someone DORP before you wear it, right?"

"Of course. The red underwear is about true love. It's obviously very powerful, and I've got to be careful with it. I wore it to bed by myself one night, had the intention in my mind of 'getting together' with a firefighter, and the next thing you know, I'm rear-ended by that jackass Luther J. Burton."

"You don't really think that happened because of underwear." Kim frowned.

"No, I think it happened because of lingerie. Lingerie is not underwear, Kim; lingerie has the power to change our lives," I lectured stubbornly. "It should be obvious, but if you are so negligent in the lingerie department that you end up wearing your husband's briefs, well, it should come as no surprise that your sex life comes screeching to a halt. Frankly, the way I see it, the only way you're going to get into your husband's briefs is for you to get out of them."

"Oh, I don't want to talk about this anymore," Kim muttered, driving and chewing on both her nicotine gum and the very good point I had just made.

Brevity is the soul of lingerie.
    —Dorothy Parker

If anything went right at the hunky firefighter dinner, I am hard-pressed to remember what it was. As we pulled into the fire station parking lot, we were all nearly panting with anticipation.

It went downhill from there. It turned out that the hunky fire-fighters were anything but. They were all paunchy, married, and unbearably sincere with a statistically impossible ratio of handle-bar mustaches and Elvis sideburns. Each and every one of them chain smoked, because they said it "conditioned their lungs for the fire." They endlessly listened to country western music with a spe-cial and horrifying emphasis on a person I have sadly come to know as Billy Ray Cyrus. They mistook our excitement at being at the fire station for an actual interest in the coma-inducingly dull tech-niques and methods of modern firefighting. They fed us a wretched, inedible meal composed entirely of gargantuan portions of over-done spaghetti, in a sauce that tasted like hot Heinz ketchup and cowspit, only less flavorful. The dinner conversation consisted of a heated debate on which was the best motor oil, centering primarily on a lot of impassioned arguing about viscosity, a term that, when pressed, not a single one of them could begin to define. Apparently, as a group, they felt strongly that the primary tool of dental hygiene was the toothpick, and that it must be used ceaselessly throughout a meal. They had heard of Amelia and knew all about her lesbian divorce from Clarissa, and they slyly asked if she was "still into lezzie action!" At the end of the meal, Hose Mechanic Bo "Did-dley" Dawson gave a sentimental toast, because apparently it was the twentieth anniversary of his mustache and he was just so happy that we could all be there to celebrate it with him. It looked to me like he had stopped trimming it around year twelve.

After dinner, they dutifully showed us every picture that had ever been taken of their mawkishly adoring wives and toothless grinning children. Then, as the grand finale to an evening that was already about as fun as a five-hour mammogram, they took us into the "lecture hall," where they presented a slide show on the new generation of foam units, digital mini-pumpers pro or con (they were rabidly pro), the proper angle for maximum snorkel effectiveness, and, of course, a long diatribe on the infamous "dry sprinkler–wet sprinkler" controversy.

No one slid down a pole, no one aimed a hose, no one was single, hunky, or even mildly interesting. I had spent half my rent money on an evening that epitomized the kind of senseless torture that usually prompts an indictment by Amnesty International.

The only redeemable thing about the night for me, was that every one of the firefighters agreed that Luther J. Burton was obviously a raging asshole, and if they ever saw him, they all promised to beat him up for me, which was hardly worth seven hundred dollars but was the only consolation prize I was liable to get.

Grrl Genius Relationship Tip

Not all firefighters are hot and hunky.

Grrl Genius Relationship Tip Corollary

That doesn't mean there aren't hot and hunky firefighters out there! Don't be so negative!

On top of everything, we were starving. So on the way home, we all piled into a Denny's for some gourmet food, or what certainly seemed like it after the gluey noodles and Orange Fanta we had choked down earlier.

In the cruel fluorescent glare of the Denny's, we gratefully ate patty melts and chocolate shakes and macaroni and cheese, and big slices of French silk pie and every other comfort food we could get our greedy little hands on.

Vonnie looked up from her single-minded dedication to a hot fudge sundae. "Well, hon, I hate to say it, but maybe it's time we give up on this whole firefighter fantasy."

"No!" I protested vehemently. "That is *not* the lesson in this— that is not the point. For one thing, the salad competition is next weekend, and I have already planned my whole presentation to be about my willingness to give up bitterness about men and every- thing, and my whole salad is about learning to be vulnerable and optimistic, which is totally exemplified by my belief in the ideal of the Hunky American Firefighter."

In the last four years, Jen had spent a lot of time dealing with the whole "salad thing" primarily because I was always calling Rich for consultations. At best, she was wearily tolerant of my obsession, but in the past week she had been extremely helpful with the salad proj- ect, particularly in the area of outfit consultation, having helped me buy a bikini on-line that, through the use of water-filled push-up pads, increased my apparent breast size by a cup and a half.

"Look, Cath," Jen began with a sigh, "if you really go out there in a bikini and a tiara and set a salad on fire and win the blue ribbon, do you think you can let this thing go finally, because, you know, it really seems to take a lot of your time. Maybe," she added, "that's time you could better spend, you know, working . . . or in therapy."

"Well, yes," I replied. "The whole thing is about winning. If I can just win it once, I'll be happy to retire from professional salad- making forever."

"Well, Cath, it really isn't professional. I mean, please, winning a gift certificate from the Sizzler is hardly going to disqualify you from entering the salad Olympics, or whatever," Jen added unhelpfully.

"If we're done talking about foods that crunch, I have an important announcement," said Kim.

I leapt in excitedly, "You did it! You put the stamps around Barnaby's penis! What happened, did the stamps come apart, did it work, does it work, you know, his penis, I mean?"

Kim gave me the kind of look she normally reserved for when one of her sons insisted on making fart jokes at the table, and then replied, "Well, it's none of your business, but since you are so rude to ask, and since no one in this particular group ever seems to have any notion whatsoever of the concept of personal boundaries, or the wisdom of not sharing every last detail of our intimate lives, I will tell you that, yes, I did put stamps around my husband's penis in the middle of the night."

Kim stopped abruptly, as though she had finished, which was, of course, completely unacceptable.

Amelia finally broke the silence. "Oh, come on, just tell us, you know you're dying to."

Kim frowned and swallowed a huge dollop of French silk pie. "Oh, fine, its not the announcement I wanted to make, but I'll tell you since you're being such big whiny babies about it."

We all sat wide-eyed, eagerly awaiting the results of the penis postage experiment like nervous newlyweds watching the indicator on a home pregnancy test.

"So, I of course couldn't sleep, because once I got the stamps on there, I realized that I didn't know how to get them off before he woke up and found out that he was postmarked for a very special delivery. Finally, at four in the morning, I went back down under and found that, yes, indeed, the equipment is fully functional. And that's when I took the stamps off. And he never knew a thing."

"Maybe I'm missing the point, but couldn't you have just, oh, I don't know, asked him?" said Tommy dryly. "It would have saved postage."

Jen gave him a dismissive look. "Oh, right, she's gonna be all, 'Honey, we haven't made love for a year, and I was just wondering is your, oh, I don't know, penis not working by any chance?'"

"But if she's married to him," Tommy argued, "I mean, they are familiar with each other. What is it with women? Why can't they ever just come out and ask men things? Why can't they just be honest about—?"

I cut him off. "Right, 'cause guys are super into really open, honest conversation about what might be wrong with their penises. And then why not finish the evening with a size comparison with every guy you ever went to bed with, because they love that even more."

This was one of Vonnie's pet topics, so she leapt in, "I will never understand why men are so obsessed with the whole 'bigness' thing. I'm a gal that's been having sex for goin' on forty years now, and I am here to tell ya, bigger is not better. Longer is better. Not in inches, in time. He can have a number-two pencil eraser for all I care, just let it last longer than the average Budweiser commercial is all I'm sayin'."

We all agreed on that topic. Even Tommy.

The books say we're supposed to have penis envy, but look who wrote the books.

—Yoko Ono

"Anyway, do you want to know what my actual announcement was?" Kim asked.

"I'm guessing it's not that you're pregnant," I observed.

"Well, I've finally decided to spend the money and get the interlocking paving stones for my driveway."

This brought the conversation to a complete standstill.

Finally, Vonnie spoke up. "Huh," she said, really speaking for all of us.

"I—I can't believe it," I sputtered. "I can't believe that's your big announcement! Your marriage is in crisis because your sex life is nonexistent, you don't know if your husband is having an affair, and instead, you focus your time and attention on interlocking paving stones for your driveway!"

"Well," said Tommy dryly, "at least her driveway will be rock hard."

"Exactly," said Kim, "exactly right. I don't know how to fix my marriage, so I'm just going to fix my driveway. That's just part of my genius."

I had to admit it, but that was Grrl Genius in action.

THE GRRL GENIUS WILD SEXUAL KINGDOM OFFICIAL "PENIS FUN FACTS" CHART

Animal	What's Interesting About Its Penis	Other Interesting Facts	What We Can Learn from This
Blue Whale	Largest penis on earth, 10 feet long and 1 foot in diameter.	Whale sex lasts approximately 10 seconds.	Size isn't everything.
Banana Slug	Banana slugs have both penises and vaginas, and although their bodies are only 6 inches long, their penises measure over 32 inches.	They mate for 30 hours and then chew off each other's male sex organs.	Never underestimate the importance of having good postcoital snacks on hand.
Gorilla	Although they weigh upwards of 500 pounds, their penises are a third the size of the average human male, and the typical mating session lasts 15 seconds.	Female gorillas are in heat for only 6 days every 4 years.	Can you blame them?
Swans	Swans are the only birds that have penises.	Swans mate for life.	Apparently all other birds still looking for a better deal.
continued	*continued*	*continued*	*continued*

Animal	What's Interesting About Its Penis	Other Interesting Facts	What We Can Learn from This
Red-Billed Buffalo Weaver	Although this bird has no penis, it has evolved a pseudophallus, a rod of tissue that does not deliver sperm.	During sex, the male rubs the rod against the female's genitalia for about half an hour, and then ejaculates from his genital opening.	Creativity is the name of the game.
Human Male	The average penis is 6 inches in length when erect. The average American man believes the average penis is 10 inches when erect; the average American woman believes it is 4 inches when erect.	The average human male ejaculates within 3 minutes of penetration; the average human female requires 11 minutes to reach orgasm.	See *Red-Billed Buffalo Weaver*, above, for some helpful ideas.

"So, how was that firefighter dinner of yours? Did you meet the Jane Austen–loving hunky hero of your dreams?" William asked slyly the next day at work.

"No."

"I see," he replied. "So maybe all your guy friends who said that firefighters are mostly a bunch of sexist lunkheads were right?"

"Fine. My dream has been dashed," I agreed petulantly. "You don't have to rub it in—all I wanted was to resurrect my fantasy of falling in love with a brainiac firefighter, and now I know that it's a dumb fantasy because it could never happen in real life."

"Never say *never*, Cathryn. Remember, you're the one who said a Grrl Genius has to learn how not to be bitter, right?"

God, I hated it when people used my own philosophy against me.

Whenever you see food beautifully arranged on a plate, you know that someone's fingers have been all over it.

—Julia Child

So it was that at two in the morning on the night before the Live Salad Making Competition at the Santa Barbara County Fair, I was helplessly banging around my kitchen, trying desperately, for about the seventeenth time, to set a chicken salad on fire.

"Why doesn't lettuce burn?" I fumed. "Aren't they leaves? Leaves burn all the time. Aren't there forest fires like, all the time?"

"Yeah, but not forests of romaine," Jen muttered.

Jen sat blearily in the corner, surrounded by bottles of gin, vermouth, rum, brandy, and various assorted alcohols, none of which had proved to be capable of immolating a salad. Nothing seemed to work.

"Maybe if you just mixed in a tiny amount of lighter fluid," Jen suggested, sounding truly exhausted.

"I hate Mrs. Peggy Keefer, but I'm not going to actually poison her, tempting though that would be . . ." I trailed off, even as I imagined the plebian low-brow County Fair judge moving the plastic salad fork filled with poison salad to her coral-frosted lips, I imagined her clutching her clawlike hand to her Be-Dazzled sweatshirted chest, gasping for air as . . .

"I think the lighter fluid would burn off. It wouldn't be poisonous," Jen argued.

"Yeah, well, I can't take that chance." I steeled myself to ask one more time the question I'd been asking all night: "Don't you think we could call Rich? It's five in the morning there—he gets up early—"

"I told you before. I don't care what time it is, we're not calling him," she stated defiantly.

"God, you are so stubborn. . . . Fine, I'll try looking it up online again."

I went on the Internet and tried various Google searches, but the Internet—the supposed miraculous superhighway of information—was nothing but a roadblock. It turns out that if you want to have sex with a farm animal or enjoy making love while wearing diapers, there are resources aplenty, but if you want to cremate a salad, you're apparently some kind of a freak, and there isn't word one of advice available to you.

As I searched uselessly, suddenly there was William, who was back in Idaho with his son, sending me an Instant Message.

BACKWOODSWRITER: Hey! You up?

GRRLYGENIUSGRRL: Yes! Desperate! Can't set salad on fire!

BACKWOODSWRITER: Hmm, might have an idea. . . .

GRRLYGENIUSGRRL: Yes! Please! Thank you!

BACKWOODSWRITER: You're up late, don't you need your bikini sleep?

GRRLYGENIUSGRRL: I know, I know, but the thing is Jen and I have tried everything and I cannot get this salad to go on fire! Help please . . .

BACKWOODSWRITER: Kirschwasser is what you want. It's made out of cherries and it's the highest proof alcohol you can buy. It not only burns instantly, but if you drink it on an empty stomach, you'll wind up puking on the lawn of the Sigma Chi house . . . or so I've heard.

GRRLYGENIUSGRRL: Kirschwasser! That's great! I'm going to the all-night liquor store, thank you so much! Bye!

BACKWOODSWRITER: Hey, don't forget to call me or send me an e-mail after the contest. I have to hear everything that happens. . . .

GRRLYGENIUSGRRL: I will! You rock! You are the best, the absolute best! Bye!

"Kirschwasser!" I exclaimed as I signed off my computer and started scrambling for my purse and keys on the counter while Jen snored cutely in my big pink easy chair.

I immediately ran out to the all-night liquor store, got some

Kirschwasser, and it worked like a charm, setting my chicken salad solidly ablaze like Sherman torching Atlanta.

William McCall was turning out to be a very useful person.

A Grrl Genius Crazy Sex Fact

Men from the Siwa tribe of North Africa believe that if they lace a woman's food with their semen, women will find them irresistibly attractive. Not surprisingly, women of the Siwa tribe are remarkably willing to do all the cooking.

At two in the morning the next night, Jen and I finally rolled in from the bacchanal that was the Live Salad Making Competition. Jen was exhausted and went right to bed, but I was still adrenaline fueled from the competition and the leftover Kirchwasser, so I decided to check my e-mail before I went to bed. When I opened my mailbox, there was a message from William, as I had thought there might be.

From: William@backwoodswriter.com
To: GG@grrlgenius.com
Subject: Semi-naked truth

Dear Cathryn,

I've just spent five straight hours playing a video game against my son, so my nerves are jangling and I'm feeling aggressively homicidal. Gosh, whatever did parents do before the invention of Total Annihilation? The game is supposed to take only half an hour but we had to replay several times because I couldn't figure out how my son was cheating. Eventually, I discovered he was using his faster reflexes, which is clearly against the rules. I was able to beat him in the final game (which I declared, after it was over, to be for the "all-time championship of the world") by waiting for the strategic moment and then attacking him with pillows.

Anyway, now it is late and, having electronically laid waste to the entire virtual planet, I'm restless and answering e-mail, even spam offering to help me grow longer and/or extra appendages.

But what I don't see is an e-mail from you! And surely even more important than being the all-time champion total annihilator of the world is the outcome of the flammable salad competition! Please don't leave me hanging out here. I want to know, did you win? Did you set things on fire and the firefighters rushed in, so that you not only won the trophy but were sprayed with fire hoses? Write me back, I really want to know! Really!

William

From: GG@grrlgenius.com
To: William@backwoodswriter.com
Subject: Re: Semi-naked truth

Oh William,

It's three in the morning, and I've had enough Kirschwasser that I'm finding it hard to say Kirschwasser (no worries, Jen drove) but I got your message and so here, as promised, is everything that happened at the Live Salad Making Competition.

As we strategized, I knew that my salad would be an accurate representation, in vegetable form, of my new single life. I knew that the salad would be telling the story of my unwillingness to let the actions of one Luther J. Burton make me cynical and bitter about all firefighters (and I suppose, by extension, men in general, even though every male friend I have, my friend Tommy, you, everyone, is always telling me that firefighters aren't that great, and certainly the ones I bought weren't, but must my dream of the hunky, intellectual, kind, firefighter really die? Must it?) and of course my fear of pain and rejection. As I told you, CATHRYN'S GRRL GENIUS

199

FLAMINGLY PASSIONATE BUT ULTIMATELY CHICKEN SALAD would be surrounded by a mélange of tropical fruits of passion, and then, at the last minute I got the inspiration to have it be festooned with edible nasturtiums, which would perfectly depict my transition from being a bitter, angry woman, blossoming, if you will, into a Grrl Genius who is filled with hope about life and love. I knew of course, that I was preparing it in a rather cunning black bikini with my customary tiara. Other than that, who knew!

When you left for Idaho, I retired to my test kitchen and began to create the magic. I tried to remain confident and not be mired in the bitterness of all the third-place ribbons from the past, even though I knew that everything that happens up there at the Earl Warren Showgrounds (Earl Warren was a man who dedicated his life to justice, and yet, is there real justice being carried out in the judging of fair entries? I think not!) is always so very political, and I personally no longer had the time or inclination to spend my year kissing the substantial ass of a certain judge, Mrs. Peggy Keefer.

Life is too short and that woman wouldn't know an innovative salad if it grew directly out of her (undoubtedly) unshaven armpit.

By this point in this letter I know you must be anxious for me to tell you what actually happened, so I will get to the point and tell you. . . .

I WON! I WON! I WON!

After four long years, I finally won first place at the Live Salad Making Competition at the Santa Barbara County Fair!

Did I win because, after her three-year despotic reign of terror, a certain Home Arts judge named Mrs. Peggy Keefer has finally been ousted and exiled to whatever fetid trailer park she currently calls home?

Possibly.

Did I win because I wore a little black bikini and soaked my salad up with a ton of 90 proof Kirschwasser (thanks to you and your amazing suggestion! Go Sigma Chi!) and set it on fire? Is this win due to the fact that it wasn't enough for me to have a salad flambé, I had to make a salad that was immolated like a tenement in the South Bronx, thus raising the "Presentation" portion of the judging to the level of big-budget Hollywood special effects?

Certainly plausible.

Did the fact that this salad was so loaded up with alcohol that it was both savory and sweet and could knock you on your ass with one bowlful have any effect on the usually narrow-minded philistine judges who determine saladic excellence there at the Earl Warren Showgrounds?

Does the fact that I have devoted four years of my life to winning a cheesy contest at a second-rate county fair, the fact that I would willingly chop vegetables in a swimsuit in front of leering strangers, the fact that I have honestly had hurt feelings, and been unaccountably bitter every time I clutched yet another white ribbon in my tiny little hands that were begging to hold the elusive silky blue, does any of this indicate that I have a dangerously distorted work ethic and a delusional need to win at all costs, regardless how pointless and stupid the contest?

Highly probable.

Is it possible that contemplating supporting chronically unemployed ex-husband who never supported either my dreams of show business stardom or my quest for saladic glory for the rest of his natural life or until someone else is foolish enough to marry him has left me so beaten down that I have sublimated my desire for revenge and justice into a hatred for one poorly coiffed, soiled-polyester-clad Home Ec judge which borders on the maniacal?

Who gives a rat's ass? I WON I WON I WON I WON I WON I WON I WON I WON I WON!!!!!

I am choosing, William, not to see this victory as a ridiculous misappropriation of time and ambition that could have perhaps been spent on such rewarding endeavors as rewriting our movie, or in-depth psychotherapy. I chose to see this blue salad ribbon as a metaphorical triumph, the sort of symbolic victory that will inexplicably translate into such real life benefits as an end to the expensive legal wrangling on my divorce so I can start to build my financial life back up so I can eventually build a new happy life for myself and my beloved doggy Thor.

I'm trying to learn to be less bitter about my genuine failures in the past, to move forward into the future, and I honestly feel, regardless of how silly it seems, that this victory puts me one step closer to the elusive goal of mental wellness and financial solvency.

"How does this happen?" you may be asking. Well, how it happens is less important than my belief in the idea that it *will* happen. As a Grrl Genius, I have to believe that the ripples that are passing through the collective unconscious due to my defeat of one Mrs. Peggy Keefer are sure to be felt on a cosmic level.

In other words, I haven't the faintest idea.

The other thing this represents for me is that, and please don't think this is the Kirschwasser talking, is that not only are you the best writing partner I have ever had, you are a real friend to waste your time helping me with something as silly as this. If it weren't for your prize-winning suggestion, I don't think I'd be sitting here at three in the morning drinking alone in my kitchen wearing a blue ribbon.

That was more of a compliment than it sounded. I guess I'm getting pretty tired and need to go to bed, but seriously, thank you for indulging me.

You really are a good friend. Right?

Sorry if this was too long and crazy . . .

Yours in Geniushood and Saladic Excellence.

Cathryn Michon (Grrl Genius)

On the day after my triumphant victory in the Live Salad Making Competition, I slept in, and when I woke up, I found this e-mail from William.

From: William@backwoodswriter.com
To: GG@Grrlgenius.com
Subject: Flaming Victory!

So let me get this straight, did you win?

That's a joke.

Congratulations! I always knew that you had it in you to be a bikini-garbed flaming salad champion, I just never knew how to tell you without you thinking I was flirting with you.

I think I've discovered a way to up your word count every day, and that way is "Kirschwasser." You did take heed of my advice not to drink on an empty stomach, didn't you? If not, your stomach will soon be very empty—not all of the explosions Kirschwasser produces are the flaming kinds, though they usually feel like it. . . .

I digress. I wanted to tell you several things. First, that you are very silly, but I like you like this. Kirschwasser for breakfast! Second, I am proud of you for digging in and keeping focused and doing what you wanted to do no matter what it took, up to and including the courage to wear a bikini on stage, which I could never do (not that I wouldn't do so in private if asked). Kirschwasser for courage! And third, that I was touched by your alcohol-driven paean to me as writer and partner. Kirschwasser for friendship! Kirschwasser forever!

You're probably the funniest person I have ever met, you know.

William

Okay, William was teasing me, of course, but still his e-mail left me wondering about a few things. What did he mean about not wanting me to think that he was flirting with me? Did that mean he wanted to flirt with me and somehow thought I wouldn't want it? And what did he mean about wearing a bikini? Did that mean he wore bikini underwear, which my ex-husband had worn and I always disliked? I had always figured him for an adorable plaid boxer type of guy, but of course had no information on this.

Clearly the only way to end this useless speculation was to get the day going with some of my famous chocolate chip banana pancakes. As always, chocolate was the obsession that distracted me from my even more destructive obsessions, like uselessly wondering what kind of underwear my writing partner wore.

The Grrl Genius club was indulgent enough to want to take me out to dinner that night to celebrate my finally having achieved salad victory, after five long years. I convinced them it would be nice to meet at the hideous Astro Diner, so we could be supportive of Jen, who was much more comfortable with her crummy job than I wanted her to be.

When we arrived, Vonnie admitted that she had in fact once gotten a Coke to go at the restaurant back in the '70s, and as a result, Doc, the cadaverous, praying-mantis thin, drug-addled, aging biker who owned the place, had cajoled her into signing a head shot, which he hung on the wall, along with the head shots of other people who had been on television and tried to get away from Doc as quickly as possible. When she arrived, he greeted her effusively, clutching her in his greasy embrace.

"Look, everybody, it's TV's own Miss Vonnie Watkins in the house!" Doc called out in a deep, gravely voice that sounded like a strange combination of a talk show host and a troll under a bridge. A couple of transvestites in the corner looked up, but the junkie at the counter, not a TV fan apparently, remained unmoved.

"Oh, dear God," Vonnie gasped, having finally escaped his clutches and staggered over to our booth, "that guy hasn't aged a day. Of course, that's the benefit of looking truly decrepit in your twenties. When you look decrepit in your fifties, everyone says you haven't aged a day! Go know!"

Amelia nodded knowingly. "Keith Richards, Mick Jagger, they looked terrible then; they look terrible now. It's definitely not a bad aging strategy."

Kim, suburban to the last, was horrified that Jen was working in such place. "We have got to get her out of here."

We all nodded our heads in agreement, breathing in the heady aroma of a grill that hadn't been cleaned since *Starsky and Hutch* was a top-ten TV show.

Jen came over to the table in a major snit. "I have horrible news, Rich is here!"

"Rich? Do you mean, your Rich?" I asked.

"He's not *my Rich*, I broke up with him!" she corrected. "But yes, it's my Rich."

"Well, what's he doing here?" I demanded, genuinely confused.

"He came back to try to convince me to get back together with him. Not that he asked me to marry him or anything—he just wants me to go back to living with him, which in no way am I gonna do because that is so not *The Rules*. So now, he says he's gonna stay and convince me, and that idiot Doc has hired him to be the cook here, can you believe it?"

"Jen, that's, really, wow, that's a lot of information. You must be shocked."

"I'm furious! What makes him think he can just barge in on my new life!" she said, sweeping her arm grandly around, gesturing toward a panorama of squalor that I was hard-pressed to believe she could be defensive about as a "new life." Then I had a thought, a sudden, happy thought.

"So," I began tentatively, knowing it was always a delicate subject between us. "You mean, you mean, Rich is the cook? So he's cooking? Here?" I said, almost not daring to believe it.

"God!" Jen fumed. "I should have known that would be your reaction, it's always about the food with this family. What about me?"

She stormed off, and I felt terrible, because I cared deeply about her and knew I had to give this whole problem some serious thought, which I would surely do after I had perused the handwritten menus she had slammed down onto the table.

The Grrl Genius club members seemed perplexed by everything that had happened. Amelia particularly had a look of concern on her face. "Listen, this is awfully—you don't think this guy is some kind of a stalker, do you? I mean, look at him!" she said.

"No, of course not," I protested. "I mean, he's big and scary looking, but if you tasted his pomme soufflé you'd—"

"God, Jen's right, you are pimping her out for the food. That's awful!" Kim snapped scornfully.

Just then Rich approached the table. I had forgotten what a hulking colossus of a person he was, tattoos covering his hamlike forearms, and yet he moved with an almost mincing grace. He carried a cracked dinner plate on which was arrayed an assortment of delicately wrought hors d'oeurvrey–looking things.

"Ah, hey there, Cathryn, ladies," Rich began awkwardly, "this here's just a little *amuse-bouche*. Uh, I didn't have a lot to work with here, but what you've got is yer simple ratatouille of garlic, olive oil, onion, mushroom, tomato, and zucchini, flavored slightly with a little bacon, but the surprise there is, I found some wild fennel growing out in the parking lot, so I grilled that and threw it in, and then that there is on yer homemade puff pastry, which, face it, is nothin' but water and flour and butter, which even this joint has plenty of, and then the other one is a pork chop, sliced real thin and then pan seared and then topped with an apple, lemon, prune confit, and that's on a fairly decent polenta that I made out of yer Quaker Grits there." With that he shambled back to the kitchen.

The Grrl Geniuses looked at the departing giant with genuine fright. "She should be able to get a restraining order," Kim insisted. "I know he hasn't done anything, but look at him, he's like Frankenstein put together out of other people's tattoos." She picked up one of the *amuses-bouches* and eyed it cautiously. "Believe me, the LAPD isn't going to be any happier with having a creature like that in this neighborhood than we are." Kim popped the concoction into her mouth and chewed, her eyes widening in surprise.

"You really think we should get a court order?" I asked skeptically. "I mean, doesn't a person have a right to work where he wants?"

"Not when he follows you all the way across the country!" said Amelia.

"Just a second," Kim murmured, holding up a cautionary hand. "Maybe a restraining order is a little much." She gazed down at the plate of appetizers. "Are there any more of these ones?" she asked earnestly and then, seeing her object of desire, placed the *amuse-bouche* into her waiting mouth as gently as someone taking Communion.

Amelia shook her head. "We have to hit him hard, shake him up. I know a lawyer, feeds guys like Rich to the killer fish in his aquarium." Amelia absently reached for a small square of something with bubbling cheese and bacon and bit into it. Her eyes, watery with deep pleasure, met mine. "Oh, dear God," she moaned.

Vonnie nodded. "I'm with you gals—let's run him out of town on a darn rail."

"This food is amazing!" Amelia breathed.

"Try the prune thing," Kim urged.

"What are you people talking about?" Vonnie snapped. She picked up "the prune thing" and popped it into her mouth like a pill. Her expression turned soft, eyes going half-lidded.

"Why can't these two crazy kids just work it out?" Kim wanted to know.

"I think it's darn gutsy that he followed her out here. I like a fella with gumption," said Vonnie.

The food kept coming. Oh, God, it was magical, stunning. Without our meaning to, little sighs of pleasure escaped our lips, and we all removed every molecule of every delicious sauce from our plates like alley cats left alone with a can of tuna.

Vonnie finally spoke. "Don't let anybody tell you any different—food is so the new sex."

Rich came back over to the table, looked at me very seriously, and then spoke. "I, uh, I wantcha to know. I love yer cousin. I do. I'm here to make this thing work. I'm here for as long as it takes. I'll do penance and cook in this dump for as long as it takes, ya got my word on that. I want her to come back to me, but I want it to be her idea. I'm not gonna force anything. So, you know. *Bon appétit!*"

With that he quickly turned and lumbered back to the kitchen. Kim gave him a long look.

"I have to say, I might have been wrong. I like the guy."

We all licked our chops in agreement.

The meal proceeded with Jen sullenly banging down plates of ever more incredible food made from the most humble of ingredients. Eggs, bacon, ketchup, potatoes, chicken, macaroni, cabbage—all the usual mundane diner staples became flights of gastronomic fancy under the ministrations of his giant tattooed hands.

Doc, sensing that something special was happening, even took our bribe of twenty dollars to go to the liquor store and get us a decent bottle of wine.

"I ain't gotta liquor license," he admitted cheerfully, "but what the hell, I got junkies shooting up in the bathroom, so if I'm gonna get narced, it might as well be for friggin' Beaujolais, right?"

Since Jen refused to talk to any of us, we greedily kept accepting whatever Rich made and washed it all down with the Beaujolais Doc brought us. The conversation, as usual, settled into what we thought each other should be doing to fix our lives. As was often the case, I had the most drama on my plate, due to the divorce hearing that was scheduled for that coming week.

"Why can't we just threaten Kurt, get him to drop this whole intellectual-property thing? Don't you have any dirt on him at all?" Amelia asked as she sneakily ran her finger around a finished plate, trying to gather up every last DNA strand of the chicken that had been there.

"You don't get it," I explained. "The way the system works, all his dirt actually *helps* him. It helps that he's an alcoholic who can't hold down a job. The more that's wrong with him, the more he's my financial responsibility."

A puzzled look crossed Vonnie's face. "You know, hon, I guess I didn't really realize he never did *anything*. . . ."

Amelia laughed. "Oh, no, he was some kind of an inventor for a while, right, Cathryn?"

I rolled my eyes.

"It's too bad he doesn't have any of that—whadyacallit— 'intellectual property' so at least you could make money of *his* ideas," Vonnie said.

"Ha!" I snorted. "Of course, he always had a million ideas on how he was gonna get rich without getting an actual job. He had a million 'inventions,' like—oh, this was a great one—the Five-Year Diaper."

"What the hell was that?" Kim sneered.

"It was some kind of a vacuum pump device that you'd attach to the kid's butt, with a sort of industrial-grade sealed diaper, so you know, you wouldn't have to change diapers for five years," I explained.

"Eeeew! That's disgusting," Amelia said, wrinkling up her nose.

"You wouldn't think so if you had kids," Kim said. "I don't suppose it actually worked?" she inquired with what looked to be genuine interest.

"Oh, please—he never even built the thing. And then, here's another one, because he was so cheap, he invented this thing called the Tip-O-Meter which was this sort of calculator thing that would compute exactly how much to remove from a waitress's tip, based on if she was rude or didn't refill your coffee fast enough, or whatever." Just the thought of his ridiculous inventions made me dig deeper into the dish in front of me, a hearty, savory cheesy concoction that looked amazingly like macaroni and cheese, and yet was not macaroni and cheese at all, but some higher incarnation of macaroni and cheese that could never be duplicated by mere kitchen mortals.

Amelia made a disgusted face. "God, Kurt is horrifying. I love how he was cheap, with your money. Of course, I suppose he never had to wait tables. Why should he, when he could live off you!"

"It just figures that his 'inventions' would be as worthless as everything else about him. So he gets to own half your life's work, and you get to own half an imaginary Five-Year Diaper. There's justice for you," Kim snorted.

Jen resentfully, and with great clanking, proceeded to clear the last set of dishes.

Vonnie leaned in conspiratorially. "I don't suppose Miss Jen would be doing very well on the old Tip-O-Meter."

"She'd owe us, according to cheapo Kurt," I responded. "I just—I just can't believe my powers of Grrl Genius have completely failed me. I can't believe the courts can consider allowing a negligent uninsured firefighter and a slacker, no-good ex-husband to take all my money. I'll tell you one thing: I decided I'm going to countersue that Luther J. Burton. My insurance company said they would pay for it, and he frigging deserves it!"

"Look, doll, I know you're pretty bitter right now, but you don't want your whole life to be about fighting men in court, right?" Vonnie reasoned gently.

"Whatever," I said, trying so hard not to be bitter that it hurt. "I suppose not, but then, I'd have to meet some men who didn't deserve suing, wouldn't I?"

"Oh, they're out there, hon. They just aren't the first guys you're attracted to, that's all," Vonnie rambled on. "You need to learn to see the guys you don't notice right away, the nice guy, the guy who doesn't come in the package you expected, the guy who isn't perfect or flashy, or exactly what you thought the ideal guy was, that's the kind of guy who doesn't deserve suing. It's just . . . you're not ready for it yet."

"Do you think I'll ever find real love? Is it even possible?" I lamented.

"You know what? I do. I believe in real love. I had real love." Her eyes grew misty, and her voice got thick with emotion. "Then my Eldon goes and blows the whole thing by getting cancer and dyin' on me, but the love, the love I had with him for ten years was real, can't nobody talk me out of that."

I didn't want to talk her out of it. I wanted desperately to know what the hell she was talking about, and I didn't have a clue. I had never felt it.

If I had been telling myself the truth, I'd have admitted that I wanted what Vonnie had with Eldon more than anything. But I knew she was right, I would never find it until I could let go of my bitterness.

Then, Rich brought dessert. Somehow, with only ordinary Hershey's chocolate, and Folger's restaurant coffee, he managed to make a mocha soufflé that was as light as a true lover's impassioned whisper and yet was deeply, urgently, achingly, infused with flavor.

As often happens when chocolate, fat, sugar, and coffee begin flowing through my bloodstream, the bitterness began to drift away, and it was right then that I finally had a long-delayed flash of pure Grrl Genius. I leapt up from the table and started dancing around crazily.

"I know how to do it! I know how to do it!"

Everyone looked at me, startled, except for the two transvestites in the corner, who looked as if it would take a lot to surprise them.

"It just came to me. I know how I can trick Kurt!"

"Well, spill it, doll!" Vonnie urged.

"It's just like that one episode of *Star Trek!*" I exulted.

"Oh, dear God . . . ," Kim sighed.

"You don't even like space shows—you hate science fiction," said Amelia.

"Seriously, hear me out. Remember the episode where Captain Kirk saves the ship by harnessing the power of some other planet's gravity to fling the starship out into orbit and return them on their voyage?" I continued.

"I thought that was in *Apollo 13*, I remember, because Gary Sinise, who is so hot, was the one who figured it out," Amelia said.

"Okay, fine, whatever, it was in *Star Trek*, too, but the idea is the same. Here's the thing I just realized: It doesn't matter that Kurt's inventions are crap. *He* thinks they're valuable! I'll have my lawyer write his lawyer a letter, demanding my half of all the future revenue from all his lame-ass inventions, like I think they're super-valuable! He's such a cheap control-freaky egomaniac, he'll think I know something he doesn't, and he won't want to share them with me, so I'll get him to drop the whole thing. I will, just like Captain Kirk and Gary Sinise, harness a great natural power. I will harness the power of Kurt's planet-sized ego and use it to defeat him and to fling myself away from him and his whole stinky orbit!"

My friends, my dear wonderful friends, even precious Jen, who was still mad at me but who couldn't help gathering around to hear, all looked at me, every last one of them, with a look that said, "She's crazy."

Finally, Vonnie spoke. "Well, here's what, she's crazy. But it's genius, it's pure Grrl Genius, and I think it will work. Just like in *Star Trek*."

"And *Apollo 13*," insisted Amelia.

I felt the resentment from all the slights I had endured melting away, because I was right. Vonnie was right. It was going to work. I had (with the divine intervention of a chocolate mousse) let go of my bitterness for a few precious moments, and it caused me to have a true flash of genius.

I was going to kick Kurt's ass and have him think, at the end of it, that he had won.

After all, I had won the salad competition; surely, victory in court could not be far behind.

Cooking is like love; it should be entered into with abandon or not at all.

—Harriet Van Horne

Chapter 7

A Grrl Genius Is Willing to Take Risks in Order to Have the Relationship She Deserves

You can't be brave if you've only had wonderful things happen to you.
—Mary Tyler Moore

JEN AVOIDED me for two days after the Grrl Genius Club's food orgy at the Astro Diner, which was no mean trick, considering we were living in the same apartment. I knew she would eventually forgive me for eating all Rich's incredible cooking, and perhaps even be willing to ease up on her ridiculously rigid *"Rules* Girl" stance and give Rich the second chance he deserved. I couldn't understand why she couldn't risk being hurt by him, in order to gain the love (and perfect béchamel sauce) of such a wonderful man. I thought sooner or later she would weaken, if nothing else, just from the incredible smells that wafted from his stovetop at the diner.

I had severely underestimated her resolve.

Finally, on the third day, she spoke to me, and what she had to say was more terrifying than anything I could have imagined.

"I have signed us up for an on-line dating service," she announced. "The *Rules* girls came out with a book on on-line dating, and I think it's the way for us to go."

"What are you talking about, *us?* I don't want to be on any on-line thing!"

"Well, you already are. It went up yesterday. According to *The Rules*, you aren't supposed to answer any e-mails until twenty-four hours later, but it's been twenty-four hours, so now you can answer them," she said simply.

"How could you do this without my permission? I can't believe you did this!" I was truly incensed.

With her customary stubbornness, she ignored me and prattled on. "I picked the best site. It's called Millionaireboyfriend.com. The men who are registered on the site must have a net worth of at least a million dollars, and they have to be seriously marriage minded."

"Jen, Jen, earth to Jen, I am not even divorced yet!"

She gave me the even, patient stare I've seen her give rude and belligerent diners time and time again. "Don't you even want to see if you got any e-mails? Don't you even want to see what I wrote about you, and your picture?"

Of course I did. I opened up my laptop and went on-line to her ridiculous site. She showed me how to call up my listing. I could not have been more horrified.

There I was, on Millionaireboyfriend.com, where Jen had posted a digital picture of me taken just a week earlier, smiling happily, which would have been fine, except that I was also wearing a bikini and holding a flaming salad and a blue ribbon.

My screen name? LETTUCEMEET!

There were also forty-seven e-mails in my in-box. Forty-seven millionaires who wanted to meet me. Forty-seven millionaires, who, judging by the subject lines of the e-mails, had spent an inordinate amount of time trying to be as bold and witty about chopped vegetables as I had been with my inane picture and absurd screen name that I didn't even choose!

You've Got Mail Millionaireboyfriend.com Subject: You're a diamond in the roughage!

You've Got Mail Millionaireboyfriend.com Subject: Please, Don't Leaf Me!

You've Got Mail Millionaireboyfriend.com Subject: Let's see your UN dressing!

You've Got Mail Millionaireboyfriend.com Subject: Nice tomatoes, salad girl!

You've Got Mail Millionaireboyfriend.com Subject: You love lettuce, I love head!

And the other forty-two were even worse.

"Listen," Jen argued, "you're the one who's always studying ancient tribal customs or the love lives of cheetahs trying to figure out how to have a good relationship, but you always ignore the obvious solutions because you always have to do everything the hard way. There are over twenty-five hundred dating sites on the Internet. More and more people are meeting this way, so how can you possibly not try this yourself, just try it?"

She paused a moment, and then she went for the jugular.

"At least," she informed me archly, "they won't be like Kurt. At least they'll have a job and won't be dating you for the money."

If there was one thing that annoyed me about Jen, it was what a freaking genius she was, and how she always managed to use my own arguments against me. She was right—I had no choice but to date a few of these millionaires, so that I could prove to her that the whole concept of chasing millionaires according to the on-line *Rules* was completely bogus.

And the trouble is, if you don't risk anything, you risk even more.
—Erica Jong

I called Jabba to tell him about my brilliant idea of tricking Kurt into thinking I was aggressively going to pursue my rightful half of his genius inventions like the Five-Year Diaper. As usual, Jabba was cautiously pessimistic about our chances.

"I don't know," Jabba drawled in his maddeningly slow style

that seemed to add pricey pauses to every conversation we had, "I mean, could he really be so stupid as to believe a Five-Year Diaper that doesn't even exist is as valuable as a proven career in entertainment?"

"Yes, he is that stupid," I replied, trying to keep my answers short and snappy, as every conversation with Jabba was a luxury I couldn't afford and didn't enjoy.

"Even if that's true," Jabba intoned negatively, "Drake Nimmer is no fool. He's made a living being a vampire, sucking the lifeblood out of artists in show biz. He's not going to let Kurt throw away good money."

"Please, just draw up the motion. I'm telling you, Kurt's ego is a force of nature that we can harness for good and not evil. Trust me, Captain Kirk and Gary Sinise know what they're doing."

"Have you been consulting other attorneys?" Jabba asked cluelessly.

"No, sorry, they're just, uh, friends of mine," I quickly fibbed.

"Well, I think you have to realize that the opinions of people who are not practicing divorce law on a day-to-day basis are not going to be relevant when considering interpretations of the most recent statutes handed down by . . ." Jabba blah blahed expensively, so ably proving my point about the potential awesome elemental power of the male ego that I actually let him go on for a few more dollars' worth, just to give myself encouragement that my plan had merit.

"Excuse me," I interjected, interrupting his cash flow, "I have absolute faith in your skills and would never dream of consulting any other attorney, so, since we agree that it's a pretty good idea, I'll go ahead and take your advice and say, let's draw up that motion, since it was your great idea in the first place."

"Fine," he proclaimed, falling for my fake flattery as so many men had in the past. "I think we may really have a shot with this; I just don't want you to get your hopes up."

"I have complete confidence in you," I lied baldly. "So let me know what happens, gotta go, thanks a million!"

I was boldly going where no Grrl Genius had gone before. . . .

A Grrl Genius Crazy Sex Fact

Sixty-six percent of women admit to having faked an orgasm at least once. Approximately 100 percent of men believe this is true, but are pretty sure it wasn't with them.

The Grrl Genius Wild Sexual Kingdom

In March 2001, biologists Erik Petersson and Torbjorn Jarvi of the Swedish National Board of Fisheries announced that they had concluded from their observations that female brown trout regularly fakes orgasms.

Yes, amazingly, female fish are faking it!

When brown trout have orgasms, both the male and female quiver violently with their mouths open, and at that point the female fish releases eggs and the male fish releases sperm. The male brown trout, unlike some human males whom we have neither the time nor space to enumerate here, apparently won't release his sperm unless he observes that the female has had an orgasm.

The female brown trout, who is evidently one of nature's greatest gold diggers, will sometimes fake her orgasm and hold back her eggs if she sees a larger, more superior fish. She will then repeat the courtship process and attempt to mate with the "better fish." If the superior fish does not respond, she then mates again with the fish she initially tricked, thereby having what is referred to as "more than one fish on the line."

In human life, the female occasionally fakes orgasms, as well. She, too, is most likely trying for a "better fish," although she may just be what biologists often refer to as "simply dying to get the hell out of there."

In my Grrl Genius opinion, both the female human and the female brown trout should never fake an orgasm. They should either "fish or cut bait." Nor should they lie about the "size of their catch," as all this

218

will get them is a man (or a fish) who thinks he is hot stuff but is, in fact, all wet.

———————

So it was that I decided to take a risk and accepted Jen's challenge to become a shallow manipulative *Rules* girl and date the eager millionaires who obviously assumed that any female willing to publish horrifyingly unretouched photographs of herself setting a salad on fire in a bikini was the kind of good-time girl they just might like to have hanging around the mansion on a permanent basis. Jen insisted that I date my millionaires "*The Rules* way," since, as she had correctly pointed out, "if nothing else, you can prove me wrong, which you're always trying to do."

In the week following the listing on Millionaireboyfriend.com, Jen went out with ten different guys. Rich knew about it and did nothing. Just stayed there at the diner, quietly making astonishing meals from the ingredients that would normally be available to him there. Doc refused to order any different or high-end foodstuffs, but this seemed to appeal to Rich, apparently his declaration that he was "doing culinary penance" in order to win Jen's love was sincere.

As Jen's millionaire dating frenzy continued, we quickly discovered what I had secretly suspected all along: Guys who are millionaires are just like other guys, only they have a million dollars.

Eventually, Jen winnowed down her pool of eager millionaires to one guy, Malibu Jim, whose story was as unlikely as his personal hygiene was terrifying. Malibu Jim was a kind of tall, skanky, rumpled guy who bore an eerie resemblance to Fred from *Scooby-Doo*. He was a seawater-addled surfer who had clearly sucked back way too much toxic runoff.

Nevertheless, he was, as promised, a self-made millionaire. He had become a millionaire completely by accident. Apparently, he started out working to earn food money by selling sunglasses from a rolling cart in Malibu. When the guy who owned the cart skipped town, Jim was suddenly an independent businessman. As it turned out, Jim, despite his casual attitude toward bathing and laundry, was very picky about sunglasses. He was an absolute wizard of sunglass design. He instinctively knew what other people would think was cool when it came to eyewear. It was the one thing he had any esthetic sense about.

And he was now one of the most successful manufacturers of high-end sunglasses on the West Coast, even though all he did all day was go surfing and draw pictures of cool sunglasses, which is what he had always done. Other people handled the making and keeping of his millions, which was fine by him.

Though his story was fascinating, Malibu Jim was not. He was just a guy who talked endlessly about wave height, boards, the best place to find a good break, and what made sunglasses cool. Though he was well into his thirties, talking to him was like having a conversation in high school, except the bell never rang to tell us it was time for biology class. He had no other interests.

Except now he was interested in Jen. Sort of. Since Jen is truly beautiful, all men were interested in her, on one level or another, but he seemed rather blasé about the whole thing. He dated her according to her prissy little "rules" and seemed happy enough to be led by the nose and guided toward the altar in the same way the executives of his multimillion-dollar company steered him toward even greater wealth as he diversified into clothing and accessories and lip balm and a whole line of Malibu Jim products.

The first time Malibu Jim sat on my sofa waiting for Jen to appear for a date, he stared slack-jawed out the window, his fermented scent wafting around him with such olfactory violence that the urge to call in a hazmat team was almost irresistible. According to her interpretation of *The Rules*, the millionaires needed to wait at least fifteen minutes for her to appear. This meant I was forced to either hide in my room or interact with them. While Malibu Jim sat scratching at what I desperately hoped were not head lice, I stood at the kitchen counter, writing a grocery list, making a note to stock up on Lysol, just in case Jen kept dating this one.

"Uh," he said, and then paused for such a long time that I was pretty sure that was going to be the sum total of his clever repartee. "Uh," he continued, "nice pencil." He gestured at my writing implement and then gave me a big, unwashed, sand-encrusted thumbs-up.

"Thanks," I replied. "It's a number two, Ticonderoga."

"Awesome!" he declared, and then sat back, now content that he had completed what, for him, must have been a sparkling social interaction.

Unfortunately, in that first week, after only two dates with Malibu Jim, Jen had pegged him as the most promising and lowest maintenance of her millionaires and set about to make him hers. It made me heartsick. I knew I had been a terrible role model to her, but I hated the idea that at twenty-six she was completely cynical and craven about relationships. All I could do was hope that she would eventually come to her senses like the true Grrl Genius she really was.

As for me, I committed that I would date three of the prospects who had written to me. Jen was insistent that for my "research" I undertake this endeavor as a real *Rules* girl. I read the stupid book again and was horrified by its scheming approach to "love" as defined by some guy putting a diamond ring on your finger and promising to pay your bills for the rest of your life.

Since I was currently suffering from the residual effects of exactly this kind of "love" and would apparently be paying the financial price of same for the rest of my life, I remained justifiably skeptical.

As far as I was concerned *The Rules* were the opposite of The Grrl Genius Philosophy on Having Sex with Other People. I mean, sure, so far, The Grrl Genius Laws that I had come up with had yet to produce a successful relationship, or, with the exception of the sweet but inappropriate Tyler, even a good date. Yet, I didn't feel that was any reason to give up on my ideals and sell out.

The Grrl Genius "A Four-Year-Old Has Better Rules than *The Rules*" Comparison Table

Actual quotation from *The Rules* written by those two women who denied their true personalities so they could trap husbands and then one of them got divorced (not that I'm judging)	Actual quote from My Grrl Genius niece Maya Cathryn Michon (age 4) when asked for her "Rules About Boyfriends"	Why Maya's "rules" are so much better than *The Rules*
"Don't tell sarcastic jokes. Don't be a loud, knee slapping, hysterically funny girl . . . when you're with a man you like, be quiet and mysterious, act ladylike, cross your legs and smile. Don't talk so much."	"A good boyfriend is because he's funny. And he thinks I'm funny."	Maya is less concerned with how to trap a man than whether or not the man is worthy of her, and she isn't about to hide her wit or charm just to make a man feel confident.
"A playboy type who falls in love with you because you did *The Rules* will automatically mend his ways."	"I only be friends with a boy if he is nice and not angry."	Maya understands that you can't change a man. If he's not your type; no *Rules* are going to fix him.
"Don't say much at all. Let him do all the thinking, the talking."	"A boy doesn't protect you. You can protect yourself."	Maya understands that her Grrl Genius is her first priority and she can take care of herself.
"All your movements . . . are fluid and sexy, when your hair falls in front of your face, you tilt your head back and comb back your hair with your hand from the top of your head in a slow, sweeping motion."	"You don't have to act to a boy. It's more important to be brave than strong. Strong is just for picking up stuff."	Maya isn't about to turn herself into a psycho drag queen just to get a man.
"Act as if you were born happy. . . . You may feel that you won't be able to be yourself, but men will love it!"	"Matthew is my boyfriend because he's so fun and he likes to play."	Maya has chosen a boyfriend for what *she* likes about *him*, not for what he likes about her.
"Do everything you possibly can to put your best face *continued*	"It's more important for a girl to be smart than pretty. *continued*	Maya understands that her beauty is a natural *continued*

Actual quotation from *The Rules* written by those two women who denied their true personalities so they could trap husbands and then one of them got divorced (not that I'm judging)	Actual quote from My Grrl Genius niece Maya Cathryn Michon (age 4) when asked for her "Rules About Boyfriends"	Why Maya's "rules" are so much better than *The Rules*
forward. If you have a bad nose, get a nose job. . . . Men prefer long hair. . . . It doesn't matter what your hairdresser or friends think. You're certainly not trying to attract them!"	Pretty is just how you decide you want to look. You can look cool if you want to look cool, or maybe weird if you want to look weird."	extension of her Grrl Genius, that it comes from within, but that fashion and style is something fun to play with, but for herself, not for some man.

Nevertheless I realized that if one of my Grrl Genius Laws was that you needed to take risks in order to find the relationship you deserve, I couldn't back down from that. I would have to take a risk and go on my three millionaire dates, as a *Rules* girl. My three *Rules* dates can be summed up rather easily.

DATE ONE

Chris had billed himself as a "dot-com millionaire," but it turned out the way he had made his money was that he was a low-level geek in the offices of a company that manufactured microprocessor chips and came up with the four-note jingle (which he had originally recorded using a touch-tone phone) that played on commercials that featured the Nextech Penultimate Processor Chip. His fellow geeks in the office didn't know that this would mean he would be eligible to join ASCAP (the American Society of Composers and Performers) and that he would get a residual every time the four notes were played. He became the richest person in the company except for the executives, so they got mad about this and fired him. He now spent his time playing an on-line computer game called *Command & Conquer* with other geeks.

All day.

He picked me up for dinner in his McDonald's-wrapper-strewn Bentley. Dinner was at a very fancy restaurant in Santa Monica called

Michael's, which happens to be one of my favorites. He had never been there, and he looked miserable, but obviously someone had told him that the girls he met on this site would expect this kind of treatment.

When Chris found out I didn't know how to play *Command & Conquer*, he treated me to an hour-and-forty-five-minute description of how the strategy of "taking out the Tiberian harvesters" worked only at tech-level five and below, because at tech-level seven, a direct assault on the base worked better. Determined to be a good date despite the fact that my whole brain felt as if it was under direct assault, I asked admiring questions like, "So what color are these Tiberian harvesters?" And then when I thought we had thoroughly exhausted the topic, he excitedly told me all about the new Generals version that would be coming out in the fall.

After dinner, he invited me over to his apartment to play *Command & Conquer*, apparently completely unaware of the rather obvious sexual double entendre. I politely declined and asked him to drive me home.

DATE TWO

I, like many people, have always been wary of the business of buying used cars, although I have had to do it on a number of occasions. I, like many people, often refer to individuals who have a shady character, or seem pushy and manipulative as being "like a used-car salesman." In considering the prospect of dating millionaires, if I had thought about it, I would have felt pretty secure about the idea that I would not end up dating any used-car salesmen, as I assumed it's not that profitable a business.

I assumed wrong. Sometimes, used-car salesmen become so successful that they become the owners of used-car lots, and then they become millionaires, and then, sadly, they have dates with me.

Jerry was boorish, crude, unfunny, pompous, full of himself—and those were his good qualities. He, too, took me to an insanely expensive restaurant—clearly the Millionaireboyfriend.com people had coached their clientele on this—and told me to "feel free to order whatever you want—I can always take it back in trade!"

I ordered a small dinner salad, no dressing.

He proceeded to tell me a lot of "wacky" stories about "crazy" things that had happened in the car lot. Why, once he even found a couple of people having sex in one of his cars! Imagine that! People having sex in a car!

Then he asked me if I enjoyed having sex in cars, and wouldn't I like some dessert?

I said no, I'd just have a couple of packets of Sweet'n Low and be on my way.

Jerry told me that as a top salesman, he considered himself a "good closer" who "never takes no for an answer." When the dinner was over and he asked me if I wanted to go out with him again, I said, "Although I really enjoyed meeting you, I don't really feel we have that 'special spark,' so I guess I wouldn't want to waste your time," to which he replied, "So let me ask you, Cathryn, what would it take for you to say yes to sleeping with me tonight?" to which I answered, "An earthquake of at least magnitude eight on the Richter scale."

"Seriously," he countered, "I want your affections, Cathryn, and I'll do anything to get them, you just name your price."

"There is no 'price,' Jerry," I replied evenly.

"Hey, don't kid a kidder," he said. "I'm being one hundred percent sincere with you, Cathryn, when I tell you you're not going to get a better deal from any other millionaire out there. You know you want to. Why wait?"

At that point I simply turned and ran, because I became terrified that I would not only end up in bed with Jerry, but would somehow agree to pay extra for floor mats and rust-proofing, as well.

DATE THREE

Larry (who proudly introduced himself as Larry, The Laundromat King) was by far the most annoying of the three, and that was amazing considering the competition. It was upsetting, because Larry took me to my favorite fancy restaurant in L.A., Joachim Splichal's impeccable Patina. Larry was the owner of a huge chain of Laundromats that served fries and beer and were called Suds, Spuds, and

Duds, so he felt Patina was the perfect place for us to go, because chef Joachim Splichal was also famous for making potatoes.

Like so many things on our planet, it turned out that the restaurant was really about Larry.

Unfortunately for me, Larry held the world land endurance record for his ability to sustain a continuous monologue about himself. He told me his net worth ($3.7 million in cash assets), his favorite basketball team (the Lakers), his favorite shoes (Nike), his favorite candy bar (Milky Way), his favorite Flintstones chewable (Barney), and on and on and on. His endless Larry-centric patter managed to render an innovative seafood-tasting menu nearly inedible.

He did not once ask me a single thing about myself. He did not ask me my net worth, favorite team, shoes, candy bar, or Flintstones chewable (Wilma obviously—who the hell picks Barney?).

Larry the Laundromat King really was the king. The king of mind-numbing, suicide-inducing boredom. Rarely have I spent a more tedious, painful, torturous evening outside of an emergency room. Never have I dined in such an elegant, perfect restaurant, all the while fantasizing that rather than listening to the owner of a chain of Laundromats, I could actually be *in* a Laundromat, where I could happily sit and listen to a wall of dryers crammed with wet jeans, spilled pocket change, and tennis shoes, endlessly thumping and clanging, that this sound would be a welcome relief from the endless diatribe of Larry, King of Laundromats.

So, those were my dates. As horrifying as they were, I never let on how miserable they made me. I thanked all three of my dates politely. I didn't kiss any of them good night. When they contacted me for further dates, I politely declined. I had taken a risk, had failed, and I was prepared to move on.

Following the dates, they all e-mailed and phoned constantly. They sent flowers, Mylar balloons, teddy bears, chocolate-dipped strawberries, and baskets of tiny muffins. Larry sent a diamond tennis bracelet, which I promptly sent back. They continued to ask me out; I continued to decline their kind offers.

After my three dates as a *Rules* girl, it became apparent to me that *The Rules* did, in fact, work. *The Rules* would make some guys crazy about you, especially if they were already crazy to begin with. However, the kind of guys who fell for *The Rules* were not the kind of guys I wanted to date, or even share an elevator with. Clearly the secret to *The Rules* was that you had to appear completely apathetic and noncommittal. It was just a rip-off of the Buddhist principle of nonattachment. The idea in Buddhism was that if you truly could release your attachment to a thing, well, then, it would be yours in abundance. It turned out that I was an idiot savant of *The Rules,* because I could not have cared less about the men I had experimented on, and so naturally, they found me irresistible.

Not only did my three millionaire bachelors persist in contacting me, but the e-mail generated by my hideous bikini salad picture also continued to generate new millionaires who wanted to go out on dates, thus perpetually crashing my e-mail server.

And Larry sent back the diamond tennis bracelet, and again I returned it. The third time he sent it, an armed guard delivered it, and I got the distinct impression that if I tried to give it back, I'd be shot. I finally decided to pawn it and give the money to charity. I was broke, but I wasn't going to take money from a megalomaniac entrepreneur who felt that his revelation that people might enjoy having a malted beverage and some fries while they did laundry marked one of the greatest achievements of Western civilization.

"It's just so unfair, Cath." Jen pouted when I told her about the diamond tennis bracelet. "I mean, Malibu Jim has never given me jewelry, except for that weird bracelet he wove me out of seaweed that I had to throw out because it smelled to high heaven."

"But isn't a homemade present so much more from the heart?" I asked with mock sincerity. Jen gave me a snide look. "And to be fair," I continued, "you can't really blame him for not being aware of how badly the seaweed smelled, considering, you know—"

She cut me off. "We have had the hygiene conversation on several occasions, and he is trying."

"To shower? He's trying to shower?"

Jen refused to say any more, which let me know I had struck a nerve. She just went back to lounging on the sofa and reading *Cosmopolitan* magazine, the one most insulting piece of anti–Grrl Genius reading material that could have annoyed me more than her now dog-eared copy of *The Rules*. I knew she was reading it just to annoy me. Frankly, I was glad she had bothered to make the *effort* to annoy me. I figured this was a good thing, as my battle to get her to see that Rich was really the man for her had now settled into a long, slow war of attrition.

A Grrl Genius Exposé of the Amazing True Things You Can Learn About Men in Only One Issue of *Cosmopolitan* Magazine

Actual Quotation from One Issue of *Cosmopolitan* Magazine (January 2003)	Amazing True Fact About Men We Can Learn from This
"The Secret He Wants to Spill: When it comes to winning a guy's heart, flattery will get you everywhere."	Men like compliments!
"A dude who sleeps in the nude hates having his body constricted by fabric all day."	Men like to be naked!
"Men are more likely to say they love you in bed because physical closeness makes them feel more emotionally intimate."	Men like to be in bed with you!
"If you want to turn your man on like never before . . . phone sex is the perfect opportunity."	Men like girls who talk dirty!
"When it comes down to it, his penis is still his, well, favorite joystick."	Men like their penises!
"Every type of sensory stimulation—the sight of a woman's body, her whispers, and the smell of her skin—activates parts of the brain responsible for sexual arousal."	Men like to have sex with you!
"Men get turned on when women seem animalistic—they take it as a sign of lust"	Men like to have sex with you!
"If you really want to rock the box springs, loosen up and let him ogle away during foreplay. . . ."	Men like to have sex with you!
"Have spur-of-the-moment sex!"	Seriously, men like to have sex with you!

"Hon, it doesn't surprise me this whole millionaire thing was a bust," Vonnie said when I was driving around, talking to her on my cell phone. "I don't think you can order up true love on-line like airline tickets. Everybody wants me to go on one of those on-line doohickeys, but there is no way I'm doin' that."

"Well, I don't know, Vonnie. I know people who have done it and had good luck especially people who are, well—"

"Old farts like me?"

"I didn't say that!" I cringed. "But, you know, I'm sure Eldon wouldn't have wanted you to be alone."

"Eldon's got no problem with me being alone. I know that for a fact. I know it might seem nutty, but I talk to him. You know, to his ashes, on the mantel."

"That doesn't sound nutty," I assured her, thinking that it sounded very nutty indeed.

"Look, doll, I know he's dead as a tree stump, but it just helps me cope, to talk to him. When I can make it through an entire day without talking to my 'husband in a jar,' that's when I'll start dating. Not before."

"That's fine—that's good," I encouraged, thinking that it wasn't good at all.

In evaluating where the Grrl Genius Club stood on taking risks for love, I realized that we were not doing very well: Kim was unwilling to risk finding out whether or not her own husband found her attractive, Amelia was unwilling to risk picking a gender and sticking to it, I was unwilling to risk sleeping with millionaires, and Vonnie was unwilling to risk going on a date with anyone who was alive. Clearly, we had a lot of work to do.

And the day came when the risk to remain tight in a bud was more painful than the risk it took to blossom.

—Anaïs Nin

The day before my final court date, I was racked with stomachachy nervousness. We hadn't heard anything from Kurt's attorney about the motion we filled for his intellectual property, which Jabba said was neither a good sign nor a bad sign. I calculated that particular bit of wisdom cost me $115.50.

William, who had been amazingly supportive, offered to have us work at my place that day, so that I wouldn't experience the extra stress of commuting to his apartment. He arrived with both caramel rolls and chocolate chip scones, and seemed somewhat embarrassed when I threw my arms around him in grateful thanks. I didn't care—was willing to risk making William feel awkward when it came to having dessert for breakfast!

All during the day, friends called and dropped by with words of support, and Kim sent support in the form everybody knew I understood best—sugar, fat, and chocolate—with the delivery of a ritzy basket of brownies.

A Grrl Genius "Love Is Important But Chocolate Is Essential" Handy Chocolate Fun Fact

Ninety percent of women in America eat some form of chocolate every day.

Approximately 10 percent of women in America have been diagnosed as clinically depressed.

Coincidence? I think not!

When we stopped for lunch, William pointed to Larry's ridiculous diamond tennis bracelet that I was wearing to remind me I needed to pawn it and drop the money off to Project Angel Food. "So," he observed casually, "that's a new bracelet, it's not real obviously—"

"Well, actually, I think it is. Jen signed me up for this stupid on-line dating thing—Millionaireboyfriend.com—and I went out on this horrible date with a Laundromat king, and he gave me this. I keep trying to give it back, but he won't let me," I babbled.

"I see," said William. "I didn't know you were dating, I thought you said you wanted to wait until after your divorce was settled."

"Yeah, well, try telling that to Jen," I complained.

Later, when I was in the bathroom, the doorbell rang. I shouted out to William, "Do you mind getting that?"

"Sure!" he called back.

A few minutes later I walked into the living room, and there was William, blushing as he often did, and inexplicably holding a clear plastic bag of what looked to be women's panties. I wasn't really sure what it meant, and was hoping it wasn't another subpoena.

"Who was at the door?"

"Well, uh, it was a young guy named Tyler. He said, 'Good luck tomorrow,' and that he couldn't stay, but he wanted you to have these." He held out the weird bag-o-panties sheepishly.

I quickly grabbed them and tossed them into the closet. Tyler was still trying to help me with my financial problems and had told me at the club that he had a line on some really cheap panties. I told him not to bother, but apparently his good-natured desire to help out won out over common sense. He meant well, but he was just ridiculous.

"It's not what you think," I explained hurriedly, not entirely sure what he might think, "Tyler's just this guy, that I sort of dated. He's kind of crazy and has got this nutty idea that my used panties are some kind of untapped natural resource."

"I see," William replied rather stuffily.

I decided to drop the topic, wary as I was of what I had noticed on several occasions to be William's significant discomfort on the topic of sex.

A little later William decided we should knock off for the day.

As he headed out the door, he turned to me with a very serious look on his face. "Remember, Cathryn, no matter what happens tomorrow, Kurt can't hurt you anymore. He can take your money, but he can never take your spirit, unless you let him. Just, just be brave, okay?" Suddenly he pulled me into a rare, somewhat fumbling hug, something he had never done before. I was touched that he was able to overcome his apparent shyness in order to express his support for me.

"Thanks," I said, returning his awkward embrace with a series of pats on the back. "Thanks a lot." We pulled ourselves clumsily out of the hug, he blushed some more, and then he left.

Later that night, Jen finally came home. I assumed she'd been at work, and casually asked how Rich was doing, hoping there had been a break in the stalemate.

Jen haughtily informed me that she had gotten the night off from work and had been out with the perpetually stinky Malibu Jim. She felt quite confident that a marriage proposal would soon be forthcoming. I reminded her, as I did reflexively now, that she didn't love Malibu Jim. "And by the way," I asked slyly, "have you two, you know, done the deed?"

A quick look of revulsion crossed her pretty face. "I told Jim that I don't believe in sex before marriage, according to *The Rules* that's the best way to go."

"Wow," I snorted, "lucky break for you, and your nasal passages."

She gave me a sharp look but said nothing.

The whole thing was so preposterous. I knew she loved the man who even as we spoke was probably making some incredible meal in the worst diner in Hollywood as an expression of his undying love for her, but she remained as unmoved as ever.

"But, Jen," I began gently, "doesn't it mean anything to you that Rich came all the way out here?"

"I didn't see a ring, did you? Did he come out here with an apology and a marriage proposal? No, he did not!" she insisted with an annoying stubbornness I remembered from when she had been the most terrible of terrible twos.

"Jen, you won't even talk to him! He's trying to woo you back, not consign you into indentured servitude. Why can't you give him credit for subtlety? Maybe he's taking the step of marriage seriously. Maybe he thinks you might have a better marriage one day if it began by the two of you—oh, I don't know—actually being on speaking terms!"

She turned on her heels and marched into her room, slamming the door. She was just impossible.

My last day at the Heather Locklear Memorial Crying Table was, unlike every other time I had sat there, remarkably uneventful and somewhat anticlimactic. Kurt had fallen for the intellectual-property ploy completely, and his fancy-pants lawyer Drake Nimmer reluctantly dropped that part of Kurt's claim. Nimmer made no further motions regarding the custody of Thor, which meant that Kurt would retain temporary dog custody until we sold the house, at which time, I would be allowed to revisit the issue, because the judge would then determine who had the best setup for the dog. I retained my already stipulated dog visitation. I had been able to keep a worthless painting I had inherited from my grandfather, which I only vaguely wanted for sentimental reasons. Kurt claimed the painting was worth six thousand dollars, a completely fake number he must have pulled directly out of his butt. Since I got the painting he wanted, he kept all the furniture and effects, which the court felt was fair. He got to keep the more expensive sports car, because that's the car he was "accustomed" to driving, which the court felt was fair. The maintenance was five thousand dollars a month, exactly what I'd been paying, which the court felt was fair. He got half my pension, half my savings, half my investments, and half the proceeds of the house, once it sold. Fair, fair, and fair, said the court. I got the considerable consumer debt, since Kurt was "disabled" by his alcoholism and couldn't possibly be expected to earn a living or pay off any kind of substantial debt. I also had to pay all the attorney bills.

Since there were no more new motions, objections, or anything else, Judge Riananne Hunter-White banged down her gavel one last time, and my divorce agreement was entered into the record. In four weeks, it would be final.

I didn't feel sad. I felt . . . free.

Our marriage had failed over the same dull things that ruin most marriages: money and sex. All I had lost in the divorce was more money. And time. And my dog, but I felt confident that when I improved my situation, I would have a good shot at getting him back. I still owned the contents of my brain. I still owned my genius. I had taken a risk for love and had failed. As a self-proclaimed Grrl Genius of Sex and Relationships, I had to believe that if I kept trying, if I kept taking risks, it would eventually pay off. After all, it was only fair.

Now it was time to start over.

I had to believe that somewhere there was someone who would genuinely treasure my own unique Grrl Genius. In the meanwhile, as William had so wisely observed, I had to be the one to treasure it. I had to be sure that Kurt did not take my spirit along with my net worth. In the most expensive lesson I had ever learned, what I had discovered was that in the end, the only relationship you can't get out of is the one you have with yourself.

As I left the courthouse, I felt almost elated. I had a song in my heart and a Godiva Pastille in my mouth as I headed out into the sunshine and my new single life.

Attorney fees for contentious divorce: $27,635.57
Expected cost of ex-husband's lifetime maintenance: $739,000.00
Being divorced from Kurt Bremerhoffen: Priceless

What happened at the Astro Diner would have been remarkable, if the diner hadn't been in L.A. Los Angeles, being a town that is organized along the lines of the same social precepts as your average American high school, is very responsive to the idea of a place being "where the cool kids hang out." All it took was a couple of amazing reviews, an authenticated Brad-and-Jennifer sighting, and suddenly Doc couldn't possibly accommodate all the social lemmings that flocked to his filthy lunch counter and sticky Naugahyde booths.

In order to get into the Astro Diner now, you had to wait out front, in a line, regardless of who you were.

Doc, being Doc, didn't want to raise the prices so that he could take advantage of his newfound culinary stardom because it was, "Just so friggin' cool to see people lining up to get in, and why wreck it by makin' it all phony-ass fancy!"

He also refused to kick out the hookers and addicts and pimps and trannys who had called the place home for quite some time, which, perversely only made the whole concept more popular. It became a common sight to have some Oscar winner begging for a table that had not yet been vacated by two hefty men in false eyelashes and high heels who weren't quite finished with their Caramelized Cinnamon Apple Financier.

Rich didn't care about the fame and attention. As far as he was concerned, the whole effort had become a true chivalric quest, which, if he remained true to his principles—making world-class food using only the ingredients Doc normally bought—would allow him to prove himself worthy to his lady fair, Jen.

The fact that Jen couldn't care less about this effort didn't seem to penetrate his consciousness. He was sure she would turn around.

The Astro Diner was the hottest restaurant in L.A. So why Jen didn't see it coming, I will never know, because as she told the story to me, it seemed rather obvious.

Malibu Jim had told her that he had a very important thing that he wanted to discuss with her, and so he was taking her someplace very special. Jen knew that this was it, that the steel-jawed bear trap of *The Rules* was about to clamp shut, and Jim was going to ask her to be his bride, as though it were his idea, which of course it wasn't. All Malibu Jim knew was that if he wanted to have sex with Jen the *Rules* Girl, well, he was going to have to marry her.

Although you couldn't get a table at the Astro Diner for any amount of money, or even drugs, you could get it for old friendship. As it turned out, Malibu Jim had hung with Doc "back in the day," when they were both surfer dudes. Doc had never forgotten him, so when Jim called for a table, Doc was happy to tell the pre-op trannys who usually hung at table four to hurry it up with their crème brûlée.

Malibu Jim didn't know where Jen worked, because she had kept this information strictly secret from him, which was easy enough to do according to her crazy *Rules,* which inclined heavily toward living your whole life as though you were a secret double agent of love, which, in fact, you were.

When they arrived at the diner, Jen was helpless to say anything about what an overwhelming disappointment it was to her and sat there trying desperately to act as if she were thrilled to be in her cutest dress at the place she had been slinging five-star hash only hours before.

The only nod to the new celebrity status of the place that Doc made was his continued insistence on mounting the head shots of the notables who showed up, which resulted in the spectacle of people like Dame Judy Dench and Eminem standing in line out front with their publicity photos in their hands. Doc's old habit of making a big deal when people of note, or old friends, were in the diner continued. On the night in question, as Jen arrived, Doc clambered around, flailing his stringy arms and banging on his big stew pot, exclaiming to the assembled diners that "Dame Judy Dench, Malibu Jim, and Jen Kramer are in the house!"

Of course, Rich knew all about Malibu Jim, but he was a man who defied *The Rules.* He didn't want to steal Jen from some other guy. He wanted Jen to chose him because she loved him, and admired him for his purity of heart and purity of cuisine, and because she knew how much he loved her. Rich looked like the Incredible Hulk (with tattoos) and was terrifying to see, but when you got right down to it, he really was a gentle giant, an artist, much more of a lover than a fighter.

Which was why he was perfect for her!

Nevertheless, there, in the Astro Diner, right in front of Rich, Malibu Jim got down on one knee to ask Jen to marry him, as he had been brainwashed into doing by Jen's relentless *Rules of Psychological Manipulation and Torture,* which isn't the actual title of the book, but is a very accurate summary of what it's about!

Grrl Genius Relationship Tip

It is *not* just as easy to fall in love with a rich man as a poor man.

Grrl Genius Relationship Tip Corollary

It is also not easy to fall in love with a man who never showers.

There had never been a marriage proposal in the Astro Diner before, partly because the pre-op transsexuals, hookers, and pimps that frequented the place were not what you might call "the marrying type," and partly because no one had ever had the courage to touch his knee to its filthy floor.

Malibu Jim's extremely liberal views on personal cleanliness made this less of a barrier for him than it would be for most. He produced the prerequisite garishly large diamond, which was inartfully set on enormous raised prongs, like a bowling ball clutched in the arthritic fingers of a seventy-year-old man who could still regularly bowl 300.

According to Jen's recounting of the event later, Rich did absolutely nothing. She interpreted this as the final proof that Rich did not really care at all, because if he did care, how could he sit there, calmly sautéing as another man asked her to be his wife?

Since Rich didn't burst in with a sharpened Ginsu knife and demand that Jen marry him instead, she foolishly said yes, according to "The Rules of Engagement." I wasn't there, but I could only imagine the heartbreak this caused Rich. Aside from all my desires to pimp out Jen for a lifetime of good meals, I genuinely loved Rich.

Rich was a nice man.

When Jen came home and told me the whole story and showed me her hideous giant ring and pretended to swoon girlishly with happiness, I really couldn't even fake my way through it. I sat there, answering e-mail in my bathrobe, and looked at her, wondering how she could possibly have changed so much.

"Isn't it great!" she squeaked.

"You know, Jen, I reread that stupid *Rules* book, and I noticed there's nothing in there about not having sex before marriage."

"Well, so what? Everyone knows that's a very good, you know, traditional idea," she fumbled.

"Do you love him, Jen?"

"Well, obviously!" she said with all the sincerity of a game-show host.

"Well, then, it's great. Congratulations on accomplishing your goal," I said flatly, and headed off to bed.

The problem with some women is they get all excited about nothing, and then they marry him.

—Cher

I lay in bed thinking about Rich. *The Rules* turned love into war, and Rich seemed to be taking the attitude that discretion was the better part of valor. Which either made him Gandhi or Neville Chamberlain. Perhaps discretion was just a better way to get your ass kicked. He was a good guy. I thought his unwillingness to be dragged into being manipulated by Jen and *The Rules* and into getting into some kind of marital smackdown with Malibu Jim was admirable.

Foolish, but admirable.

A Grrl Genius Crazy Sex Fact

Foreplay in the Sirino tribe of eastern Bolivia consists of partners delousing each other's bodies of lice and wood ticks, which are then eaten as a precopulatory snack. Why no one has held a telethon for these people in order to raise money for better foreplay is beyond me

As the weeks went on and the deadline for our screenplay got near, William and I started working later and later into the night. Sometimes we would get stir crazy and go for a walk around the neighborhood while we talked out some problem in the script. On one of these days, we were arguing about Charlotte, the single girl who was the heroine of our movie, who was smart and beautiful and successful and was completely hopeless about trying to find a great guy, or even an okay guy, in L.A. This was a notion I proclaimed completely accurate and he derided as ridiculous.

"Look," I said smugly one evening as we were walking around his neighborhood, "you wanted to partner with me on this because you said you wanted an 'authentic voice of a single woman in L.A.' I am here to tell you, as I would tell Charlotte if she were my friend, the odds against finding a man in L.A. are very tough. You can ask all my girlfriends who are smart and beautiful and successful."

"Maybe your girlfriends are being too picky. And you say *odds* as though you have actual facts and figures on the topic."

"Oh, believe you me, I have *exact* facts and figures on this because I sat down and Googled everything on the topic."

I pulled out my PDA as we walked along, and I pulled up the file titled "Statistical Improbability of Meeting an Okay Guy in L.A."

"Wow," he marveled, "you really have looked into this."

"I'm a Grrl Genius. I do research—it's what I do. Now, this is strictly mathematical and not just my wacky opinion that it's impossible to find a man in L.A. Let's take me, for an example. There are ten million people in L.A., and half of them are men—"

"Reasonable assumption so far," he agreed.

"Right. Five million guys. Now, I'm reasonably going to date in a twenty-year age range of me, ten years older or younger, and I'm thirty-four, so let's say that approximately one fifth of those five million are between twenty-four and forty-four."

"You would date a twenty-four-year-old guy?" he asked.

"That's not the issue. We're talking statistics," I informed him archly.

"I don't think you'd be happy with a twenty-four-year-old guy even if he is all buff and hot and everything—" he persisted, seeming very testy about the whole thing.

"Fine, fine, no hot buff twenty-four-year-olds for me, but remember we're just running the numbers here, and trust me, you're going to be shocked."

"Go ahead," he challenged with a wry grin, "shock me."

"Fine. Now, I'm smart. I think we can both agree that nine out of ten men are idiots." He nodded in agreement. "So we've got to eliminate ninety percent right from the start, so that leaves us a hundred thousand guys. Now, here's where it gets shocking. Did you know that Garth Brooks is the second most popular recording artist of all time, next to the Beatles?"

"Oh, that's crazy!" he said. "I can't even name a single song of his, but everyone knows the Beatles are the greatest band that ever lived," he fumed, now seeming *really* testy.

"Of course, absolutely, agreed," I soothed, trying to placate him, "but the fact is that Garth has sold over fifty million albums. One fifth of the population has bought a Garth Brooks album, and obviously I can't have a relationship with them, so that axes twenty thousand guys. One in four is a smoker, so that cuts twenty-five thousand guys. So that leaves only fifty-five thousand guys."

"Fifty-five thousand guys should be enough for you. In fact, I think that's too many," he began, sounding like an overprotective dad.

"Ah ha! But here's the thing, including the millionaires, I have had ten social engagements that you could remotely call dates in the last year, and only one of them is someone I'm even still speaking to. So, we have to eliminate ninety percent of the fifty-five thousand guys, which leaves 5,500 guys. Oh yeah, and I forgot, half of all men are married, so now it's 2,250 guys, a third of whom hate dogs, which is obviously unacceptable, so that's 742 guys—oh yeah, and two out of every hundred men are in prison, so that's 727 guys spread out over the four thousand square miles of Los Angeles, which means there are five and a half available guys in every square mile of Los Angeles. Now, how am I supposed to find those guys? I mean, am I supposed to go pathetically knocking door to door, knowing that there are 1,250 men per square mile and five of them are men I might be willing to date—which by the way comes down to one man every 5.4 million square feet—and I'm supposed to find that one guy, and keep in mind, that one guy is just a possibility? I don't think so. I don't have that kind of time!"

If there was one thing you could say about William, and this made him oh so different from so many of his sex, he was an exceptional listener. He took a few moments to absorb my (obviously airtight) argument. Then he reached for my PDA.

"May I borrow this?" he asked with his customary politeness.

"Of course," I said. He poked away at the calculator with the stylus for a few minutes as we continued to walk along Ocean Boulevard. Finally, he spoke.

"Nope," he began, "I think you're looking at your numbers all wrong. I'm going to guess that ninety percent of those losers you've met in the past year were in the lower ninety percent of intelligence, so they were already eliminated. So we'll add back in forty-five thousand guys."

I wanted to protest, but decided to hear him out, since he had heard me out.

"And fifty million Garth Brooks albums may have *sold*," he continued, "but I'm going to guess that most people bought multiple albums. So instead of fifty million people, let's call it ten million—

and half of them are women! So five million is only about five percent of the population, so instead of eliminating twenty thousand guys you can only eliminate five thousand. Add back in fifteen thousand. And one in four people may be smokers, but ninety percent of *those* guys are in the lower ninety percent of intelligence, so add back in twenty-two thousand. And what kind of idiot doesn't like dogs? I'll tell you exactly what kind, the kind that's sitting at home, smoking and listening to Garth Brooks, and they've already been eliminated. So add back in fifteen hundred men."

William paused for dramatic effect. He was nothing if not a good storyteller.

"Now, that's eighteen men per square mile, or one guy for every three acres. The pond in front of my condo in Idaho is exactly twelve acres, and believe you me, if there were four men standing on the ice, I'd see them pretty quick. If you were to yell, those four guys would come running, which means, here in L.A. you practically can't walk around the block without meeting a good, decent, eligible man," he finished triumphantly.

"What's your total?" I asked morosely.

He clicked a few more numbers on the pad. "I get 69,242 good men in L.A. as opposed to your 727," he continued, somewhat hesitantly. "You know, Cathryn, looking at your statistical model, it just occurs to me from the way you choose to run the numbers here, maybe you prefer the idea of looking at some things from a really negative point of view, so that you don't have to risk being wrong about anything. If there's no chance that something good could happen, it seems, well then, there's no disappointment when it doesn't happen, is there?"

I mused silently on all of this. Perhaps, in running these facts and figures on the economies of love, I had, in my mind, created a false model. Perhaps I had devalued the capital value of the market of men, just as had happened in the stock market of 1929, which ultimately led to the Great Depression. Come to think of it, that was exactly the mental state I had been in while calculating the probabilities of meeting a decent man.

Perhaps part of the way I had not been taking risks, as a Grrl Genius should, was my depressive insistence on the statistical impossibility of finding a wonderful man to love me. Maybe, if I were truly willing to risk getting hurt, I would be able to accept William's calculation of the odds of happiness as more truthful than mine.

Suddenly William spoke the words that could always pull me out of whatever complicated mental reverie I had worked myself into.

"Are you hungry?" he wanted to know.

I realized, we had never worked this late before, that the sun had set, it was dark, and I was, in fact, starving.

"Yes, I am."

"Well, what's this place?" We were standing in front of The Ivy at the Shore, which had always been one of my favorite L.A. restaurants, and remarkably was not one of the places that had been ruined for me by the millionaires. I didn't know if William would like it. It was overpriced and a little celebrity oriented, and since I had observed that William hated going out, I was sure it was exactly the kind of loud, overly stylish place he would despise.

"Oh, that's The Ivy, but I don't know if you'd like it, it's kind of schmoozy, and I know you don't like to go out . . ." I trailed off.

"Well, is it any good?" he wanted to know.

"Yeah, for the kind of place it is, it's great."

"Well, let's go here then. It won't kill us to eat a meal that isn't served in little white boxes."

We'd been working together intensely for a month, and we'd never gone to a restaurant together, which was the opposite of most show-biz work situations in L.A., where all you did was go to fancy restaurants and talk about work you would do, but no actual work got done.

We were wearing jeans and sweaters, but in L.A. that's considered evening wear in fine dining restaurants with linen tablecloths, so no one looked askance.

William ordered a bottle of wine, and we shared appetizers and salads, and I devoured my favorite sautéed softshell crabs and

William seemed very happy with the seared ahi tuna. The restaurant was more crowded than I had ever seen it that early in the evening, there were no celebrities, just a lot of overdressed couples, and it wasn't until we were well into our entrées that we realized that it was, in fact, Valentine's Day.

William looked disturbed. "Oh, my God, it's Valentine's Day, and we didn't even know it, and we're out to dinner, does this mean we are, you know—?"

"Losers," I replied. "That's the word you were searching for, right?"

"Well, not really, but it certainly makes this seem more like, a date," he offered tentatively.

"Yeah, a date we didn't even know we were going on. How messed up is that?"

"Yes, but we have now established that whereas you thought a date with an intelligent, nonsmoking, dog-loving, nonincarcerated man who knows the difference between great music and total crap had"—he began punching numbers into the PDA again—"odds of one in ten thousand of happening, I have conclusively established that it is, in fact one hundred thirty-eight in ten thousand, so, you know, it's not that messed up."

"But it's not really a date . . ."

"Right no, obviously. I'm just saying," he responded quickly.

"Right. Right," I agreed. "I mean a date is where someone asks you out, and he knows it's a date."

"Right," he agreed hastily.

"And then you know it's a date and everybody agrees it's a date, so that's a date."

Fortunately at that moment the waitress arrived to discuss dessert, which was, as always, my favorite topic.

As we were walking back to William's place, he seemed odd. He walked slowly and on several occasions, he reached into his pocket to take out the monogrammed linen handkerchief he kept there, which I always found delightfully old-fashioned of him, and wiped his brow, because he seemed to be sweating. I wondered what was going on with him. He seemed so nervous and strange.

I wondered if maybe, finally, William had been inspired by the fact that it was Valentine's Day, and we had been out together, and had wine together, and that maybe he was thinking of making a pass at me. I knew that it would be a bad idea, it would be inappropriate and unprofessional, and I planned to tell him so, just as soon as I had found out exactly what it would be like to kiss him, which might take a little time. I desperately wanted him to kiss me, so that I could tell him not to.

When we got back to his place, what was wrong with him became immediately apparent. He opened the door and then raced to the bathroom. I heard the sounds of loud and violent retching. It sounded torturous, and I didn't know what to do.

When he finally emerged from the bathroom, he was wearing a bathrobe and looked Volkswagen Beetle green. His hair was disheveled, and he was shivering. I gave up on the idea that he was nervous about kissing me, and was both disappointed and concerned.

"Uh, I think, I think I'm sick," he informed me, as though I might not have already drawn the same conclusion. "You know, you should probably go, because I, this isn't going to be pretty, and I wouldn't want you to—"

"Don't be ridiculous," I said, reaching out to touch his forehead, which was on fire and soaking wet. "I'm taking you to the hospital."

"I think it might be food poisoning," he muttered, again stating the blatantly obvious and demonstrating that his normally high IQ was clearly functioning at subpar level. Before I could say anything sarcastic about it, he ran off to the bathroom again.

It went like that for hours—he kept throwing up, and no matter what I said, he refused to go to the hospital. Unlike other men I had known (or been married to), he was uncomplaining, and when he wasn't puking his guts out, was his usual good-natured, goofy self.

"I'm glad we established that wasn't a date," he groaned weakly at one point, his voice now raw, "because if it were, you might get the feeling that I wasn't very impressed with you." He gasped slightly. "Um, excuse me, I have to go puke."

And he raced out again. Without fail, every time he went to barf, he politely excused himself as though he were at a fancy dinner party, instead of the vomitorium that his apartment had become.

Around one in the morning, the periods of throwing up kept coming closer together, and the violent cramps got, well, more violent. There finally came a moment where he was curled on the floor in the fetal position, rocking back and forth and panting. Suddenly he looked up at me and said, with great difficulty, "I really feel . . . if I am going to put you through this . . . I ought to at least be able to give you a baby at the end of it."

And we both laughed and laughed, until he went to go throw up again.

Finally, at almost dawn, he had fallen asleep on the sofa, his temperature had come down, and he hadn't thrown up for over an hour. I decided that I would go, let him try to sleep. I left him a note.

William,

Thanks for dinner and everything. You finally fell asleep, and I thought it was best to let you rest. Please, please, please do me a favor when you're up and let me know you are okay.

Please.

Seriously.

Your writing partner,
Cathryn

It was strange to be driving back to Hollywood at dawn, since I usually went the other direction that time of day. I decided to go right to the Beverly Hills house and get Thor for his morning walk. Thor still had not gotten used to the idea that big hikes now happened at 5 a.m., and he would often act like a gangly sullen teenager who didn't want to be woken for school, until the seductive concept of "walk" penetrated his tiny brainpan and he scrambled eagerly to attention.

When I arrived, Thor wasn't in his doghouse. He wasn't already running around the yard, doing the crazy excited happy dance he did when a walk was about to happen that caused him to leap and twirl and bang into the overpriced lawn furniture.

He wasn't anywhere. When I went around to the back, I saw that the hole in the fence that Thor had escaped through many times before, the hole in the fence that was my flimsy excuse for Thor's disappearance when I had stolen him with Vonnie, the hole in the fence for which Kurt had presented me with a carpenter's bill for having been fixed last month was, and this should have come as no surprise to me, not fixed at all.

Kurt had obviously pocketed the money that was supposed to be spent on fixing the fence, since no scam was ever too petty for him. Clearly Thor had taken advantage of the opportunity and broken through and run away.

I had a horrible feeling in the pit of my stomach as I contemplated on which highly traveled, twisting mountain road Thor might be wandering gleefully, oblivious as he always was of speeding cars, wandering coyotes, and random cruel people.

I realized with a sinking feeling of dread that this meant I would have to have a conversation with Kurt and possibly even his lumbering Jurassic throwback of a girlfriend. I would have to enlist Kurt's help in finding the dog. I would have to confront him about lying to me and stealing the money. There was a time when I would have done anything to avoid that, but I no longer felt beaten down by him or by our ridiculously unfair divorce.

In short, I had gotten more confident in my genius. I wasn't afraid to risk a confrontation with Kurt. It happened without my even noticing. I had finally fallen for my own hype, I finally actually believed I was a Grrl Genius. I no longer believed that being treated like crap was my lot in life, and because I thought I deserved better, people treated me well, which was, quite frankly, what I deserved.

As I walked up to the front door of the house I had once been so excited to move into, and then sadly, so relieved to leave, I knew that there was nothing more that Kurt could do to me now, and that I was the sort of brave, risk-taking Grrl Genius who was too confident ever to let him push me around again.

The thing that women have got to learn is that nobody gives you power. You just take it.
—Roseanne Barr

Chapter 8

A Grrl Genius Accepts Others Exactly as They Are, or Not at All

Love involves a peculiar unfathomable combination of understanding and misunderstanding.
—Diane Arbus

WHEN KURT opened the brushed steel front door of our imposing Beverly Hills home, I didn't even let him get out a hello. "I know you just pocketed that money I gave you to fix the fence, and I can't believe you cared more about your little scam to get an extra seven hundred dollars than you cared about whether or not Thor was safe!" I accused in a rush.

"There was no scam, Cathryn. And there's no need to get hysterical," Kurt replied with an annoying calmness.

"I am not hysterical!" I shrieked hysterically. "And that is such a pejorative thing to say, men only call *women* hysterical—no one ever accuses a man of being hysterical—"

"I'm not really interested in hearing one of your little women's-studies lectures, Cathryn. I called you hysterical because you are being hysterical. This has all been a big misunderstanding. I didn't show you an invoice for the fence. I showed you an *estimate.*"

"I know the difference between an invoice and an estimate," I hissed.

Kurt smirked and flicked his ridiculous ponytail like he was Olivia Newton John in *Grease.* "As I was saying, I have been waiting for the carpenter to come fix the fence. He keeps blowing me off for bigger jobs, so there's no covert 'man conspiracy' here, much as I know you'd like to think there is. There is no need for you to act so crazy about this."

Kurt's explanation sounded perfectly reasonable, even though it was an monstrous lie. Just like Charles Boyer had sounded perfectly reasonable in the movie *Gaslight,* when he kept confronting the luminously lovely Ingrid Bergman about how she was always misplacing things, like the beautiful broach he gave her, because he was trying to convince her that she was going insane.

I watched *Gaslight* all the time, I think for the same cathartic reasons that people watch football. I would yell at the TV and get really worked up.

"You're the one that hid her broach, you psycho creep. Don't you dare try to make her think she's nuts!" I would scream at Charles Boyer, even though I had seen the movie a thousand times. "You're just doing it so no one will believe her when she finally realizes all the horrible things you have done!"

My marriage was like *Gaslight: The Home Game.* Jen, who now loved to watch old movies with me, refused to watch *Gaslight* with me anymore, because she said, "I can't even hear the movie! Why do you have to keep yelling? You know how it turns out. The way you act, I swear, it's just crazy."

"Don't tell me I'm crazy, I am not crazy!" I would rave like a mental patient.

Kurt and I hiked through the state park near our Beverly Hills neighborhood for hours. It was Thor's favorite place, and we figured that's where he would go. We yelled for Thor 'til we were hoarse. It was a big park, and he could have been miles away, or have been attacked by coyotes, or he could have come out at the highway and been hit by a car. I was getting more panicked and hopeless as the hours wore on.

As we stumbled through the brambles in the park, Kurt continued to act like it was a huge mystery that Thor had run away.

"That collie down the block is probably in heat. Thor's in love with that dog," I said, pointing out the patently obvious.

"That's ridiculous—that collie is a male," Kurt lied coolly, trying as usual to make me think I was crazy.

"No, that collie is a female."

"Cathryn, you don't know that much about dogs. It's a male."

"Well," I began, trying my best not to act like a flustered Ingrid Bergman, "it may surprise you to know that I do know the difference between male and female dogs."

"Then you didn't look very carefully, because it's a male. You're always jumping to conclusions and you never really take the time to—"

"The dog is a female! She had puppies last year! She's named Lassie, for crying out loud!" I screeched, completely losing control.

Facts had no impact on Kurt when thought he was right, which was all the time. "You must be confusing it with another dog, Cathryn. People always name collies Lassie, even males."

Kurt would never admit he was wrong, or apologize. In ten years of marriage, I had never once heard him utter the phrase, "I'm sorry," unless you count, "I'm sorry, but you're totally wrong," which I don't. Once he decided on what a "fact" was, that's the way it remained. He had pronounced the neighbor's collie a male, and that was the end of the question. The dog could have been giving birth right in front of him and Kurt would never concede the point.

Just like Charles Boyer.

I was determined to be victimy Ingrid Bergman no longer. I wasn't going to let him get away with his obvious lies. "If you had fixed the fence, like you said you were going to, and we had gotten Thor fixed, like I wanted to, this never would have happened," I said coldly.

I could tell this incensed Kurt, who had always insisted that we not have Thor neutered and was hoping to have a local breeder "stud him out," a concept Kurt was highly enamored of both for the general idea of the thing (the use of the word *stud* being key) and for the money it would bring. As always with him, it came down to money. It was obvious that Kurt was now angry to realize that Thor might have been having sex for free.

"I certainly hope that isn't going to reduce his stud fee," he growled.

"Well, then, you certainly should have fixed the damn fence," I replied.

Around noon, I got a call on my cell from William. Even though Kurt was hovering near me, I took the call.

"Hey," William wheezed into the phone groggily. "I'm not dead, I don't think so anyway, though I haven't had a pulse in two hours. Is that bad?"

"Well, thank God. Listen, I think we shouldn't work today. You're too sick, and my dog ran away, I'm with *Kurt*," I said pointedly. "We're in the state park—we're trying to find Thor—"

"Oh, God, that's awful. I mean it's awful that the dog ran away and awful that you have to be with Kurt," he said, his voice full of genuine concern.

"I know!" I agreed, grateful that William seemed to understand how upsetting it was for me both to have lost my dog, and to spend even one millisecond of my precious time remaining on planet Earth with Kurt.

"You want me to come help you?" he asked. "I can come right now. Kurt just sounds like such a nutcase, I don't like the idea of you being alone with him in some big state park."

William was doing what nice men often did, which was to translate the emotional abuse that I had endured from Kurt into a perceived physical threat. Although I couldn't stand Kurt, I knew that he was probably too lazy to strangle me in the park—plus there was no money in it.

You don't strangle the golden goose, after all.

"I'm fine," I assured him, "and you're too sick. But thanks for the offer. I'll see you tomorrow at the regular time, so get some rest, okay?"

"Okay," he muttered uneasily. "But listen, even though I'm a weak suck right now, the least I can do is call all the pounds. I'll check on the Internet and see if there is a lost dog society chapter."

It was so typical of him, this impulse to help. I was truly touched. "Thanks," I said softly, "that would be great."

There was a pause; then William spoke, "Thanks, you know, for taking care of me, for not being repulsed by my projectile vomiting—"

"Don't be ridiculous, it was fine," I said. "Listen, I've really gottta go."

"Okay, bye!" he agreed, and hung up.

"Who's that?" Kurt inquired nosily, as if it were any of his frigging business.

"My writing partner," I answered tersely, to which he made a vague, dissatisfied, "Harrumph," and headed off into the bushes, angrily yelling for the dog he was now sure was off banging some collie for fun and for free.

It started to get dark, and I wanted to keep searching, but I had to get over to the Improv. It was Thursday, and I was hosting for the *Drew Carey Show* cast, who always came and improvised on Thursdays. It was always a sold-out night and usually big fun. I was too heartsick to want to go, but I never backed out of a show, not ever.

I tried to imagine that Thor had shambled into somebody's backyard and was happily being spoiled and fed the name-brand dog biscuits he so coveted. If that were so, why hadn't the people called to say they found him? His number was on his tag, but on the other hand, sometimes when he ran witlessly through the sagebrush, his collar would come off, and maybe that was what had happened. . . .

I was at my car, and I didn't realize that Kurt was speaking; I was so lost in my thoughts.

"What?" I wondered, somewhat dazed.

"I said none of this had to happen. If you hadn't left, if you hadn't started this divorce, none of this would have happened," he accused.

I had always said that I was sure that Kurt's family crest (from his supposedly aristocratic ancestors back in Germany who left him no actual money but a whopping sense of entitlement) was probably emblazoned with whatever were the Latin words for "Affix Blame." I was tired and had a long night ahead of me and wasn't about to take time out for one of his customary blamefests.

"Kurt, I'm not going to have this conversation with you. I have to get to the club—"

"I still love you, Cathryn. I miss you every day," he interrupted.

I wasn't sure I heard him correctly.

"It's the worst thing that ever happened to me, you leaving. It's ruined my life." He stood there, his narrow shoulders now slumped slightly, looking genuinely bereft. He began to cry. This was too much for me to take. I had seen him cry only once, when one of our cats had died and he had buried her in the garden. He had turned away, ashamed to be crying, but I had seen his tears, and it was heartbreaking. He was such a dour, unemotional person. To see him cry as he laid the towel-wrapped body of our little black cat in the ground had ripped me in two.

Now he was crying openly. I didn't know what else to do, so I put my arms around him tentatively. I did feel sorry for him, sorry for all the pain, sorry that someone I had once loved so much was now a stranger to me, a check to write at the end of the month.

I held him, and he sobbed like a small child. I rubbed his back and led him over to the curb, where we both sat as he continued crying.

"I know, I know it's final and everything," he blubbered, "but couldn't you—? Maybe you could consider . . . we could fix it. We could go back to therapy—I would do anything to save this marriage."

"Kurt," I murmured, as gently as I could, "it's, it's not a marriage anymore, we're divorced. Besides what about the Tri—" I caught myself. "What about your girlfriend?"

"I don't care about her—I love you!"

He buried his head in my shoulder and wept silently. I felt lost, and sad, and exhausted—exhausted from staying up all night and exhausted from searching for the dog all day, and in the long term, exhausted from the emotional battering I'd received since I first married this man and tried to "fix" him. Looking back on it, I had been charmed by Kurt's emotionally closed and, well, *curt* manner. It made him seem so "grown-up." I was sure that if I just loved him enough, I would be rewarded with all the buried tender feelings he worked so hard to conceal. It had, of course, not worked out like that. Now, as he sobbed in my arms, I felt helpless to deal with what was happening.

"Cathryn, please listen," Kurt continued brokenly, "we could still fix it. We could get remarried. People do. Nothing is impossible, if you really want it."

Did I want it? That was the question. He was still crying, and I continued to rock him gently as I thought about what he said: "We could fix it." But could we? There were so many years I wanted to "fix" the marriage, to "fix" Kurt, years I wanted us to be more physically intimate, years where I would go to kiss him and he would say, "Don't hang on me, I'm busy." He never wanted to touch, or even have sex, except for the twelve to fifteen times a year we made love. I knew this figure was accurate because I had in my usual fashion carefully charted our sexual frequency. I had become foolishly obsessed with the number of times we had sex when I discovered that the average American couple makes love 133 times a year, and I wondered what it was about me that made me approximately 90 percent less appealing than the average American woman, as I obsessively tried to quantify his rejection of me. I never told him how much his lack of desire for me hurt, and eventually I learned not to ask for affection or sex, or for him to get a job. I hardened my heart; I learned that my wanting something only made him even less likely to give it to me. Maybe he even enjoyed having this area of power in our relationship, a relationship where my competence made him feel so powerless. We had come to Hollywood together, Kurt and I. I had become successful right away and he had not. He had been punishing me for it ever since. Maybe that is why he enjoyed being able to deny me things, being able to deny me affection, refusing to get a job.

What is the statute of limitations on the heart? I thought. If a miracle happened today, and suddenly Kurt were to change completely, to want to be affectionate, to be sexually intimate, to pull his own weight financially, would it "fix" it? Would it "save the marriage," just like in the magazine articles I had loved so much?

I knew the answer was no, because you have to accept people

as they are. After ten years together, you know a person. He can say he will change, but maybe he is promising change because, in fact, he just doesn't want things to change at all. I'd seen it with other couples. The huge changes of divorce make the one being left desperate, willing to promise anything, and even if he could deliver, by then, your heart is dead to him. That's why you left. It's why I left, anyway.

I almost forgot Kurt was there. He had stopped crying, and suddenly he grabbed my shoulders and spoke to me; there was a sound of panic in his voice.

"We could fix it, Cathryn, and then you could move back in here, and you and me and Thor would be together, and we wouldn't have to sell the house!"

The house.

He doesn't want to have to sell the house, I thought. He doesn't love me; he wants to keep the house. He always said that big stupid steel and glass monstrosity we lived in was his "dream come true." How could I even have considered falling for it? I guess I had always fallen for it. No more. I was officially done falling for it. A Grrl Genius has to accept people exactly as they are.

This was exactly who Kurt was. A man who would do anything to stay in an "architecturally important" house, a house he hadn't earned any money to buy. A house he, nevertheless, felt was "his."

I stood up abruptly and turned to go. "Really, nice try Kurt, that was aces, Charles Boyer has nothing on you."

"Huh?" he protested, scrambling after me. "What's that supposed to mean?"

"Don't bother, please," I said disgustedly as I backed away from him and toward my car. "This isn't about how you 'love' me, this is about the fact that you don't want to sell the house, even with all the money you're getting from me, you know you can't afford to live in this fancy neighborhood, in this dumb ugly aquarium of a house. You can't race your sports car up the canyon, you won't be living up the street from Tom Cruise anymore, and that is the whole goal here."

He leapt up, not so grief stricken after all, rushing toward me at full force. "What are you talking about? You think I would go through all that so I could stay in a house? You're crazy, Cathryn!"

I was suddenly very calm. I looked at him straight in the eyes. "No, Kurt, I'm not crazy. I'm not crazy at all. I'm just . . . right." With that I got in my car, slammed the door, and drove away.

The only time a woman really succeeds in changing a man is when he is a baby.

—Natalie Wood

Telling Kurt that I knew what he was up to gave me a rush of pure adrenaline. There had been so many years when I foolishly, just like Ingrid Bergman, but in way more comfortable outfits, had been afraid to speak my mind, to stand up for myself, to be the Grrl Genius I truly was. Kurt wasn't a murderer like Charles Boyer, but his need to make me wrong, insecure, crazy, was exactly the same. He needed to do it because it made him feel fine about what a mess he had made of his life. His alcoholism, his joblessness—these things didn't seem so glaring if I were a raving lunatic, a "workaholic" who conveniently paid his bills.

The bill paying would unfortunately continue, but there was no way he got to call me crazy anymore. The rush of taking that power away from him made me feel almost giddy.

The relief I felt at having figured out what Kurt had been trying to pull on me was so overwhelming that I almost forgot about Thor—until I pulled up to my apartment in Studio City, where Thor was sitting calmly on the front steps, posed for all the world like the Best in Show winner at the Westminster Kennel Club.

I burst out of the car, which was still running, and hurled myself physically at the dog, who, having finally been greeted in exactly the way he liked to greet people, responded in kind, with a flurry of licking and jumping and wagging of his ridiculous tail stump. I cried and laughed and kissed and practically licked him in return.

Even though I had been wearing the same clothes for twenty-four hours, and I had exactly forty-five minutes before I had to be onstage, I knew exactly what I needed to do. I didn't even go up to the apartment. I just bundled the still excited Thor into the back of the car with the window open, just as he liked it, so he could happily drool his spit trail all across town as we headed to the big twenty-four-hour veterinary hospital up the street from the Improv, where I told them that Thor needed to get neutered, right away. I felt only a twinge of guilt, because, after all, at least Thor's last shag fest had been for love, not money.

I called Kurt's cell phone, which I knew he was too cheap to keep turned on, lest someone actually call him on it and he burn precious minutes on a call he hadn't made. Why he even owned a cell phone at all was beyond me, but it certainly came in handy for leaving messages, knowing I wouldn't actually have to talk to him in person. I told Kurt that I had found Thor and had taken him to be neutered, and it was too late to do anything about it. I didn't tell him where Thor was and said I would bring the dog back in a week, after he had recovered.

Finally, after all these years, I had actually found one male I could "fix," at least in the veterinary sense. I decided that even though as a Grrl Genius, I needed to learn to accept people exactly as they were, I would feel free to alter dogs.

I marveled that Thor had found his way to my apartment, where he had been exactly once, and concluded that he probably missed me as much as I missed him. I reasoned that neutering him was the right thing to do. It was responsible pet ownership for one thing, and it would keep him safe until I could get a new place and win custody back.

A Grrl Genius Crazy Sex Fact

At puberty, young boys on the Cook Island of Mangaia are taught techniques of breast stimulation, cunnilingus, and delayed ejaculation to ensure maximum pleasure for their future partner. These men have been universally acclaimed (by me) to be the Enlightened Males of the South Pacific.

———————

I had called Tommy and asked him if he was doing anything, and if he felt like coming down to the club to keep me company and, frankly, keep me awake. Because he was 100 percent pure doll, he came, it was his favorite hangout anyway.

"You did the right thing, neutering the dog," Tommy assured me once I'd done my set and gotten the show started. "It's just a pity we can't do the same thing to Kurt."

I didn't tell him how many other guys in the club had suggested this procedure for Kurt—even Tyler, who was surprisingly pacifist for a bouncer, had suggested that snipping Kurt was really the humane thing to do for the rest of humanity. "Get him out of the friggin' gene pool," Tyler had proclaimed. "Just like somebody ought to do to Courtney Love!"

Tommy was in a great mood because he had apparently been dating someone he really liked, an up-and-coming costume designer conveniently named Tommy. I experienced the little residual twinge of jealousy that I always felt when Tommy had a new love that wasn't me. Since this process had been going on since we were seventeen, it didn't take me very long to get past the twinge and into being genuinely happy for him.

"That's so great! How long have you been seeing each other?"

"About six months," he admitted.

I had a sudden realization. "That means you were seeing this Tommy person when you begged me to let you go to the firefighter dinner!" I exclaimed.

"The loser firefighter dinner," he reminded me. "By the way, are you still going to countersue that horrible Luther J. Burton person?"

"Absolutely. Luther J. Burton was willing to settle, but I told him to go to hell. He's going to pay."

"But he said he would pay, didn't he?" Tommy prodded.

"Right, but I mean, he needs to *pay,* pay. Like for my pain and suffering," I insisted.

He looked at me quizzically. "But I thought you weren't hurt."

"Physically. I wasn't hurt physically," I corrected.

"You're saying he hurt you, what, mentally? Spiritually?"

"If you must know, he has ruined my sex life."

He gave me a puzzled look.

"With myself," I added somewhat reluctantly. "Look, the fact is that 'hunky, brave, firefighter' has been my 'go-to' fantasy for sometime, and he ruined it, and I think he should pay for that."

"Oh, please—Brad Pitt was my 'go-to' fantasy for years, and he ruined it by marrying Jennifer Aniston, but I'm not gonna sue the guy for it." Tommy took a long swallow of his beer. "You've got to let this one go, Cathryn. I understand that you've got a lot of residual anger, but how long are you going to try to make Luther J. Burton pay for the fact that he's a firefighter who destroyed your fantasy life? You've already cut the nuts off one male this evening. What say we call it a day?"

Fortunately, I had to go onstage, which was good, because it was better than having to admit right away that Tommy was, as usual, completely right. I would make it look like I had given it some thought before I admitted that, like so many things, I was going to have to let this one go.

When I got offstage, I saw William standing by the door. He looked shaky and weak, and was wearing two bulky sweaters, but he was grinning as he clasped me into a backslapping hug.

"You were great! You were so funny! You were like, the best person up there!" he gushed.

"William, it's stand-up. I was the only person up there," I pointed out. "Anyway, what are you doing here?"

"Oh, I was just worried, and I know you don't answer your cell phone when you're here, and I wondered if you got any word on the dog," he explained.

"Or if Kurt had murdered me and buried me up in the park?" I suggested knowingly.

"Well, I worried about that a little," he admitted.

I was touched that he cared. "Well, the good news is that Thor was—" I stopped abruptly because I could see that the comic who was onstage was eating it and about to bail, so I had to get back up there. I hastily guided William to Tommy. "Tommy, this is William, my writing partner, tell him what happened with Thor, I have to get up there. Kevin is bailing," I said as I rushed up to the now-empty microphone.

When I got offstage, I found Tommy and William at a table in the bar, eagerly talking about what a drag February was, football-wise, what with the Super Bowl and the Pro Bowl and all the other Boredom Bowls being over. I will never understand how it is that men, who are often rather contentious creatures, can so quickly come to a consensus on what mind-numbing sports topic they will endlessly explore, having just met each other. After I awoke from a brief and relaxing coma, Tommy said that since it looked like William could take over "keeping me awake" duty, he might as well head home, as he had to be up at six o'clock the next morning for a New York–based conference call.

"I promise, I'll call the lawyer tomorrow, I'll, you know, drop the lawsuit," I said under my breath.

"Good girl." He kissed me tenderly on the top of my head as he always did and headed for the door.

I called after him, "Hey! Introduce me to your boyfriend one of these days, before you buy a house and adopt a Chinese girl, if you don't mind." He waved me off, and as he headed out the door, he got the customary exuberant hug and "Later dude!" from Tyler, who didn't really know him that well, not that it really mattered.

I turned to William, who looked very fatigued. "You shouldn't be out. You look, you know . . ."

"Like shit?" he suggested.

"Oh, I wouldn't say that, exactly."

"You're being nice because you feel sorry for me probably." I didn't contradict him, because it was kind of true. "Oh, Cathryn, that is such good news about Thor!"

"I know, I know," I said. William looked awful, and I was really worried about him. "Listen, I really have only got one more act, and I think you should go home—it's a long drive for you."

"Okay, you're probably right. I wanted to know you weren't dead." He shuffled his feet uneasily and jingled the change in his pockets. "So I'll go," he announced decisively. "But listen, um, do you remember when we had that conversation, at the dinner I later threw up, about how sometimes going out to dinner is just a way to get poisoned food that almost kills you and sometimes it's a date?"

"Yeah, I remember," I replied warily.

"Well, I think we should do that."

"Do what?" I asked, not entirely clear what he was saying.

"Dinner. How's tomorrow? Let's take the day off. We both need the sleep, and then I'll pick you up at six. Is that okay?"

"Well, sure," I said.

"Okay, then!" He stood there, fidgeting nervously in his goofy way, and then he took off. I was left there, mystified as to what had happened, since as far as I was concerned, he had been completely unclear whether this dinner we were to have *was* a date or it wasn't, and I was completely unwilling to undergo further embarrassment by asking.

But was it a date?

We have to dare to be ourselves, however frightening or strange that may prove to be.

—Mary Sarton

Jen and I were truly at a standoff. I loved her like the sister I never had, but I wanted to rip her hair out as she sat smugly on my big red sofa, surrounded by her extensive library of what I referred to as her Bride of Satan magazines.

Malibu Jim had heard that for a minimum of 40,000 dollars, you could get married at Disneyland, riding to the ceremony in

Cinderella's big pumpkin carriage, with Goofy and Pluto as your chauffeurs.

"How awesome is that!" Malibu Jim had gleefully trumpeted, and Jen was helpless to protest that it was the most repulsive thing she had ever heard, because *The Rules* expressly forbade telling your husband-to-be that he was a big, unwashed, dithering moron.

The Rules way of handling this dilemma was to subtly introduce the idea that perhaps, as *terrific* an idea as it was to get married in the "happiest place on earth," perhaps it would be more practical if, more prudent if, more classy if . . .

None of these "more-ifs" meant anything to Jim, who was nobody's idea of classy or prudent and had so much money that for him, being practical was—well—just not practical. If Jim was gonna have to get married, he was totally *stoked* about the idea that the ceremony would include unlimited no-line rides on Space Mountain and all the cotton candy he and his surfer buds could chew through.

I thought all of this was a fitting punishment for what Jen was doing to Rich and the rest of the family, but I didn't want to tell her that. So as I was getting ready for my date-or-not-a-date with William, she showed me an endless succession of photographs of impeccably tailored Vera Wang sheaths that she had clipped out of the evil magazines as I was trying on outfit after outfit, each of which made me look fat, old, stupid, or all three.

"Yeah, it's gorgeous, very classy," I grudgingly admitted about one of the dreamily elegant wedding dresses in the clipping she was showing me, "and it's going to look fantastic while you're spinning around in a teacup getting puked on by Jim and all his stoner friends."

Finally I made my outfit choice for what to wear to dinner, deciding that Meg Ryan was definitely my movie star fashion icon for the evening. I settled on a sleeveless red chiffon Miu Miu dress with a flirty little ruffled neckline and a red ribbon belt that was a remnant of happier financial times. It was pretty and very feminine. I couldn't believe that I had spent eight hours a day with William for the last six weeks and suddenly I was worried what he might think about how I looked. Unfortunately, he knew all too well exactly how I looked.

"You are so not being supportive of this wedding," Jen accused as I stepped into my little sling-back, red T-strap shoes.

"Don't be ridiculous. I love you. I support you wholeheartedly. After all, it's your life," I observed ominously. "I know that when I got married, I certainly wasn't interested in other people's opinions about whether it was a good idea or not . . . ," I trailed off, leaving her with the distinct implication that since my own marriage had been such an unmitigated disaster, she might want to think twice about her upcoming nuptials.

Jen refused to bite. "Well, good," was all she said as I grabbed my purse and went out the door. "Hey! You and William have a nice, whatever it is you're having!" she called after me.

The Grrl Genius "I Like to Be in America" Top-Ten List of Things Men Find Sexually Attractive in a Woman

Top Ten Things Men In America Find Attractive in a Woman	Number One Thing Men in Other Cultures Find Attractive in a Woman
Large Breasts	Caroline Islanders: Artificially Stretched Labia
Well-Toned Legs	Masai: Black Gums and Tongue
Firm Rear End	Kwakiutl: Flattened Heads
Big Eyes	Mayan: Crossed Eyes
Long Hair	Ila: Protruding Navels
Flat Stomach	Mangols: No Eyelashes
Well-Developed Calf Muscles	Tiv: Fat Calves
High Cheekbones	Syrian: Joined Eyebrows
Great Smile	Yapese: Black Teeth
Full Lips	Ganda: Pendulous Sagging Breasts

I had never been in a car with William, and it was weird when he opened the door for me, just because (a) men never did that anymore, and (b) it felt so formal. I was starting to lean on the side of this being "a date," albeit one of the high-school variety. I couldn't be sure, though, because William was a sort of a formal person anyway, with his little monogrammed handkerchiefs and awkward blushing whenever the subject of sex came up. What might have been dating behavior in someone else may have just been his old-fashioned stiffness, to which I had grown accustomed, and frankly rather appreciated coming from the world of stand-up comics, where "Hey, bee-atch!" was considered a polite greeting.

I had to admit to myself, as I regarded him in the candlelight, that I was hoping that it was a date. I also had to admit to myself how much I enjoyed simply looking at William, which I had been doing for at least ten hours a day for the past month. Gazing at him now, I realized that his handsomeness was the kind that sort of sneaked up on you; somehow you just wanted to always be around it. His easy smile, his adorably crinkly eyes, his thick, almost black hair touched slightly with gray—I realized that it actually made me sort of, well, relaxed, to look into his eyes. I started thinking, I care about this man. This man is funny and kind, and sweet and . . . handsome. He's very handsome.

I wondered what was going on with him. How was he looking at me? I wondered if in fact this was a date, if that meant he was finally starting to be aware of me, in the ways I had found myself aware of him. William never seemed to notice me as a woman, but maybe I had read him wrong. Or maybe I just wasn't his type. With his shy politeness, it was so hard to tell.

Over dinner, we talked as easily as we always did, and it felt, normal. Comfortable. When William said, "I'm glad we did this because I kind of wanted to thank you, you know, and make up for the other night," I felt a sick, sinking feeling in my stomach that surprised me.

I realized that this wasn't a date; it was just a thank-you. I had gotten it all wrong.

When he dropped me off at my apartment and walked me to the

front gate and leaned in and kissed me, well, then I started leaning back toward the "date" camp. Kissing as a concept fairly screamed "date." But the kiss itself screamed—well, I don't know what it screamed.

Frankly, it puzzled me.

I wish I could say the kiss was dynamic, that the eagerness with which David or Tyler had kissed me was far surpassed, that fireworks went off, that the seething passion that lay beneath our incredible mental connection and genuine friendship exploded into a conflagration of lust as we hungrily clutched at each other, aching, yearning, seeking, longing. . . .

But it was nothing like that at all.

He placed his hands gently on my shoulders, tilted his head slightly, leaned in, and softly touched his lips to mine. He lingered there for a moment, his eyes closed. The kiss was—oh, I don't know—sort of sweet, and tender and . . . well, nice.

I guess.

William pulled away, barely brushing his hand along my arm and whispered, "That was nice." Then he headed to his car as though not very much had happened, which I guess it hadn't.

"See you Monday!" he called out breezily as he got into his car and drove away.

I had no idea what to think. Here I was, having proclaimed myself to be a Grrl Genius expert on sex and relationships, and yet in my own life I remained as clueless as I had been in sixth grade. Everything that had just happened felt eerily reminiscent of sixth grade. It had been kind of a sixth-grade kiss. I was beginning to have a very bad feeling of déjà vu about the whole thing.

Since I had a sixth-grade problem, I decided on a sixth-grade solution. I would endlessly obsess about it with my girlfriends. Duh, obviously.

A Grrl Genius Crazy Sex Fact

Recently a nationwide survey was conducted questioning men of all ages about their attitudes toward their penises. It turned out that 90 percent of men are "unhappy" with their current penis size, penis length, and penis ability. However, it is important to note that none of the men surveyed were having sex at the time they were questioned, when penis satisfaction is generally thought to be much higher.

Sitting with the Grrl Genius Club at Mr. Chow's, an overpriced Chinese restaurant in Beverly Hills that Vonnie adored and the rest of us simply tolerated, working on my somethingth glass of wine and waiting for the chocolate pudding cake that is the whole reason for going to that place, I realized that I was chickening out on telling my fellow Grrl Geniuses about what had happened with William. Or hadn't happened with William. Or whatever.

That was part of why I hadn't talked about it. Everything that I usually had to report tended toward the dramatic. I didn't know how to pick over and dissect endlessly what was essentially a "non-event." I also might have been afraid of their verdict, which was always swift and unanimous and hard to buck—and I had a feeling I knew exactly what they were going to say.

The other reason I didn't bring it up was that they surprised me. With a divorce shower. When our cocktails came, one of the waiters emerged with a little dessert cart filled with festively wrapped gifts.

"Happy divorce!" called out Kim with uncharacteristic joviality.

"What? What is this?" I stammered.

"Doll," Vonnie began, "we couldn't take the idea of you going to flea markets and buying ratty old measuring spoons and pitted spatulas to replace all the stuff Kurt got to keep, so we registered you and called all your friends and family, and this is just some of the loot!"

Amelia put her arm around me. "We're just as happy for you

for divorcing Kurt as we would be if you were marrying some guy.
You're beginning your new life, and we want to support you in that,"
she added sweetly.

I burst into tears. I was so overwhelmed by their love and generosity. I was so grateful to have shiny new measuring spoons.

Grrl Genius Relationship Tip

If you really want to be a "maid of honor," throw your
friend a divorce shower!

Grrl Genius Relationship Tip Corollary

The "divorcée elect" will enjoy toasters, blenders, and
other household gifts. She would also enjoy a full set of
very sharp knives, but maybe this isn't the best time for
her to have them.

As the evening went on, we got around to discussing our various life crises. For someone whose marriage was moribund, Kim had a lot of drama going on. She had hired a private detective, whom we all insisted on calling her "private dick," even though she told us that the "dick" was a rather grandmotherly looking woman. From then on we christened her, Gramma Dick. Apparently, the best private investigators are not dashingly handsome guys like they are on TV, but are usually people you would never suspect, people who seem boring. People like Gramma Dick.

Anyway, Gramma Dick turned up nothing, but Kim made a rather disturbing discovery when she did a little private sleuthing on her own. On the family computer, in the file where he kept digital pictures, she found a series of almost a hundred pictures of the contents of her lingerie drawer.

Kim showed us photograph after photograph, some of them at a slightly different angle, but all essentially the same, of all the expensive Cosabella lingerie I had forced her to buy.

"Well, what the hell do you make of that?" she demanded, chewing manically on her nicotine gum.

"It's definitely, uh, disturbing," Amelia said.

"I, I have no idea, there are so many of them, I mean, it's very obsessive," I added.

"This coming from the queen of the obsessives," Kim said, with unnecessary but understandable venom. "Although I think you're right."

"Doll, I hate to be the one to say it," Vonnie began, politely, "and really, you know, it might not be all that bad of a thing, depending on your feelings on the topic, what with different strokes for different folks and whatnot—"

"Oh, dear God, Vonnie, I love you like a sister, but could you please keep the cornpone to a minimum and spit it out already!" Kim snapped.

Kim was getting on everyone's last nerve, but we had to remember that she hadn't had sex in over a year. As true Grrl Geniuses, we knew that we had to accept her exactly as she was, even if "an enormous pain in the ass" was exactly as she was.

"Well, my friend, Suzette, her husband turned out to be a cross-dresser, which is not usually the same thing as being gay," Vonnie informed us.

"Three out of four cross-dressers are heterosexual," I announced.

"How do you know?" said Kim.

"I'm a sex expert, remember?" I replied haughtily.

"Ha!" was her one word bitchy reply. "Well this would be just the living end. I mean, he hasn't made love to me in a year because he'd rather mess around with my underwear drawer?"

"I did say the trouble was in the lingerie department," I ventured. Kim shot me a look that told me this was yet another thing for me to let go of, if I knew what was good for me.

"Well," Amelia pondered, "you never wore that lingerie anyway, isn't it better that it not go to waste?"

Kim's continued sour looks convinced us that we should let her dig undisturbed into her pudding cake and move on to another topic.

"Ladies, I have come to a decision," said Vonnie. "I know I don't talk so much about what's been going on with me in the sex department, and that's because, to be honest, I have felt sort of dead from the waist down since my Eldon died."

None of us had a smart remark for that one.

"Ya know, I can tell you that I really loved him with all my heart, and I told him. I told him every day. We celebrated what we had, because it came to us so late. That's the best thing about meeting your true love when you're forty-three—you know how good it is."

She took a healthy mouthful of the pudding cake. "Ya know what he said to me, almost the last thing he said to me before he died?" We waited expectantly. "He was in so much pain, and of course I was taking care of him at home, which was both awful and the best thing I ever did. Anyway, he could barely talk, all the tubes and everything, but even so, he was still affectionate with me. We didn't talk much, but we touched, always touched . . ."

She got lost for a minute, and we let her go and then come back to us in her own good time. "Well, anyway, it was near the end, and we both knew it. I cried in front of him—I was never a gal for hiding my feelings—but I tried to keep it down, ya know, figuring he had enough to deal with and all. I was next to him, and he motioned for me to come close, so I could hear him, and he said, 'Hey, babe'— he always called me *babe*—he said, 'Know what? I'm glad we used the good china.' That was the last thing he said to me. I knew exactly what he meant."

She wiped away a tear. Truthfully, we were all welling up, hearing it.

"Sounds like using the good china was a smart decision," said Amelia quietly.

"Yup. It was." Vonnie used her napkin to adjust her makeup under her eyes. "Anyway, I've been thinking. It's been almost three years, and I haven't moved on. Now that would sound crass to some people, but if I'm honest with myself, I know my Eldon would want me to love again. Not allowing myself to move on and love someone else, is—well, it's like eating off paper plates."

Vonnie awed me. I was awed by her ability to survive so much—her own cancer, her husband's cancer, the career crap, the lost friends, all of it—and still be so solidly in the game. She was my hero. She was an original Grrl Genius.

"So here's the deal," Vonnie continued. "I'm finally gonna spread Eldon's ashes. He's been sitting on the mantelpiece for all this time, and now I need to let him go. I'd like you all to be there."

We tearfully agreed. Absolutely, we would be there with all Vonnie's many other friends.

After that, my, well, whatever with William seemed trivial, not worth discussing. But as we were standing at the valet stand, waiting for our cars, Vonnie, who seemed to have an instinct for these things, sidled up to me.

"You were awfully quiet, doll. I can't believe you don't have anything going on," she ventured.

So, as the four of us stood waiting for the cars, I spilled. I finally told the Grrl Genius Club about the date/not date with William, the puzzling kiss/not kiss. Vonnie, Amelia and Kim listened quietly, then looked back and forth to each other, as if daring the others to speak.

Finally, Vonnie spoke. "Well, apparently nobody else wants to say it." The others were silent, and so she continued. "Hon, you know I adore you to pieces, but, we have had this conversation how many times before? You didn't tell us about this, because you knew what we were gonna say."

"You think he's gay, don't you?" I demanded.

"Oh, Cathryn," interrupted Amelia, self-appointed arbiter of sexual preferences, "I'm the last person in the world to be putting labels on people. . . ."

"Good plan!"

"But," she continued somewhat patronizingly, "this *is* a pattern for you. You're therapist has said it, you've said it yourself—it started with your childhood relationship with your friend Tommy. You loved him, you couldn't have him, and so, subconsciously you keep finding the same gay guy, over and over."

"Kurt wasn't gay!" I pointed out.

Nobody said anything.

"What, we had sex," I protested, feeling sudden alarm at their expressions.

"You said it was like, twelve times a year, at best." Kim scowled, as if she were the keeper of the sexual time cards.

"That's twelve times more than you and Barnaby!"

"Don't make me slap you," Kim responded with more restraint than I deserved. "We're having a bad year—you had a bad marriage."

"We never wanted to make that big of a deal out of it, because it's over anyway," Amelia began, "but I think you have been in denial about Kurt's sexual preference for years. For some reason, you always preferred to feel like there was something wrong with you, something that made you unattractive to him, rather than seeing that the reason he didn't want to have sex with you might be that he doesn't like to have sex with women."

"The real question is, why is it easier for you to assume you are unattractive than that your husband is gay?" Vonnie asked gently.

Everything they said was ringing so uncomfortably true. It was the central problem of my life, my appalling lack of self-confidence. Even so, even if Kurt was gay, it didn't really mean that William was, did it?

"I knew it. I knew this was what you all were going to say: He's gay, Cathryn always falls for gay guys, but you know, you might be wrong," I pleaded.

"Oh, please, I can't take this," said Kim impatiently. "You've been in his apartment eight, ten hours a day, and he has never made a pass at you, and even when he finally does make a pass at you, it's this "kiss not kiss" thing, like, not a pass but some weird, polite, feel-sorry-for-you thing. And I won't even get into his little monogrammed handkerchiefs, or his homemade scones, or the fact that he likes to dance around his apartment with you to the frigging Village People, for God's sake."

"That is so stereotyped!" I said defensively "Lots of people like the Village People. I mean 'YMCA,' who doesn't like that?"

My question was left hanging in the air; nobody wanted to touch it.

"Whatever, live in denial, God knows, it's working for me," Kim declared sadly. When the valet pulled up in her formidable vehicle, she hoisted herself in, blowing us all air kisses as she drove off.

Vonnie fiddled with the clasp on her Fendi purse, then looked at me. "Doll, when William kissed you, you said it felt, well, let's just say not passionate, and then he said to you, 'That was nice.'"

"Right . . . ," I agreed cautiously.

"And didn't you tell me that back when you were in high school, that there was one time that Tommy kissed you?" she pressed.

"Uh-huh . . . ," I was forced to admit.

"And what did he say, after he kissed you?"

"That was nice," I whispered.

I didn't say any more, because I was suddenly overcome with a feeling of sadness, a sadness so deep and achy it made my legs feel weak and my always-nervous stomach feel crampy and sore, and so I sat quietly down on the little wooden bench by the restaurant door.

"Oh, hon," soothed Vonnie tenderly as she sat next to me and put her arm around me. "You're in love with him, aren't you?"

My throat grew thick and my eyes were pooling up with big stupid tears. I nodded glumly.

"You know what, strictly my opinion?" I shook my head, and she continued, "It's never bad to love people. So what if loving him isn't gonna be about sex? I've seen you with your Tommy, you love him, and it's not about sex, and you wouldn't trade him for a million hunky firefighters. If you really love William—and I believe you do from the way you've talked about him—just accept him as he is, hon. Love him as he is. One thing I've learned, love never goes to waste in this life."

I nodded. What she said was true. I knew now that I loved William, loved his sense of humor, loved his kindness, loved his friendship, loved his brilliant mind, loved his generous and talented heart, and if I wasn't going to love his naked boy body, well, maybe there were worse things.

No wonder my date/not date with William and our kiss/not kiss gave me such déjà vu. William was Tommy all over again. Which was far better than Kurt, but still . . .

It just seemed so unfair. I wanted to believe that all the things I loved about Tommy, all the things I now loved about William, might, on some planet in my solar system, also eventually be found in a heterosexual man. I wanted to believe that it could happen. Vonnie, who was watching me, seemed to read my mind.

"Oh, it will happen, doll. Trust me, you're too much of a treasure. The universe doesn't waste a treasure like you. Or me. They're out there; our fellas are out there. Meantime, love William. Just love him for who he is, that's all."

She kissed me on the cheek and hopped into her Jaguar, speeding off into the night.

The Grrl Genius Wild Sexual Kingdom

For years, animal behaviorists refused to believe that animal homosexuality existed, ignoring the glaringly obvious evidence of it, which mostly consisted of animals of the same sex mating.

Like, all the time.

With the publication of Bruce Bagemihl's recent landmark book *Biological Exuberance: Animal Homosexuality and Natural Diversity* (St. Martin's Press, January 1999), the idea that animals aren't gay has been fabulously debunked forever.

Prior to the publication of this book, male-on-male Sumatran orang-utan mounting, female-pair gorilla diddling, and large groups of male bighorn rams nuzzling and humping were breezily dismissed as "exuberant greeting behaviors" or "atypical food-exchange rituals" or "something Dr. Laura Schlessinger doesn't want us to talk about."

But now, gay animal sex has come out of the forest. This is due to things like the high incidence of male-on-male sexual contact between Arctic penguins (like the outfits wouldn't have been enough of a clue) or the fact that the fact that black rumped flamebacks (hello, Captain Obvious!) have *only* been observed in male-on-male mating behavior. (Perhaps, due to their unbelievably gay name, it is the hetero black rumped flamebacks who feel the need to closet themselves in shame.)

There are those who would assume that gay animal sex is entirely hedonistic and promiscuous and does not include actual pair bonding. These same people probably also assume that gay animals have a natural flair for decorating their dens and are huge Barbra Streisand fans. This is highly prejudicial and bigoted, as the fact is that all animals, gay and straight, love Barbra Streisand the same, which is to say, not at all. Besides, there's not a thing wrong with having a stylish den.

In fact, black swans, who are infamous for mating for life, have remarkable success with gay male monogamy, as well. Like many gay male human couples, they are incredibly devoted and they are usually very "financially successful" (in swan terms) because both members of the bonded pair are large and can afford to defend a big territory (probably in a darling but slightly run-down neighborhood nobody else thought to invest in).

The gay male black swan couple often raises offspring, which they obtain either by adopting (stealing) the egg of a heterosexual swan pair, or by briefly establishing a sexual partnership with a female swan, and then once the eggs are laid, chasing her off to raise the cygnets themselves. Presumably the female swan (having been suckered in by the gay male swan's ability to discuss "feelings") is then left to go cry with her girl-friends about how "all the great amazing sexy funny smart sweet hand-some swans are always gay! Always! And why is God so out to get me, it is so totally *not fair!*"

Or something along those lines.

Anyway, what we have to learn from this in "human life," is that homo-sexuality (especially in otherwise available males who would be perfect for you) is simply a function of natural diversity. It is part of the extravagance of the complex and beautiful web of life, and something that should not only be accepted, but should in fact be celebrated, regardless of whether it ruins your life and means you are doomed to never finding your true love and dying alone and miserable.

———

It was after midnight as I drove from Mr. Chow's to my apart-ment, my car filled with shiny new household goods. There are some people you can call at that hour, and Tommy was one of them.

The phone answered on the second ring. "Hello?" a sleepy voice greeted.

"Tommy?" I asked.

"Uh-huh . . . ," the voice responded, but it didn't sound like Tommy, and then I realized it must be Tommy's boyfriend Tommy. "Oh, hi! You must be"—I searched for the right phrase—"the other Tommy, I mean, Tommy's Tommy." I felt very foolish. "Is Tommy there? I mean, my Tommy?

"Oh, well, I sort of think of him as *my* Tommy, but yeah, he's here. . . . Nice to meet you, by the way. I was a huge fan of your movie show. Sorry you got canceled. Hang on."

Of course he was a huge fan. Only gay men watched that damn show. The way my life was going, it seemed like every man on the planet was gay, which should have made my show a blockbuster hit, but no such luck.

Tommy got on the phone. "Hi, hon, what's up?"

"I'm so sorry—I'm so sorry to bother you. Obviously you were asleep."

"It's fine, don't worry about it, what's going on," he insisted tolerantly.

"Well, listen," I began. "I know this might seem dumb, but, my friend William, my writing partner, that you met the other night, I was just wondering, do you think—?"

"Oh, Cathryn," he sighed, the disappointment clear in his voice, "when are you ever going to believe me on this? Gay people don't have microchips installed with bar codes in our heads that let us read other people's microchips so we can tell whether or not they're gay or bi, or whatever."

I had forgotten that over the years, this was a conversation we'd had a few times.

"But, was there a vibe, you know?" I prodded.

"Cathryn, because it's late, I'm going to make a novel suggestion. Why don't you—oh, I don't know—ask him?"

"Oh, I couldn't do that," I said dismissively.

"I'm so not in the mood for this. Just tell me, are you in love with this guy?"

It was Tommy I was talking to, so there was no harm in admitting it. "Yes," I admitted in a small voice.

"Well, then you better just find out if he's gay before you waste any more time on it. What is it with women and their inability to just come out and ask a guy a question? If you think you are really in love, you should be able to risk asking him whether or not he is heterosexual. I mean, if you can't have that kind of honesty with him, what kind of relationship would it even be? What would be the point?"

Tommy was right. William was the sweetest, funniest, kindest, most wonderful man I had ever met. If I couldn't ask him a question, even a potentially embarrassing one, well, then, what was the point?

"This is your fault you know," I whined.

"And don't start *that* either, Cathryn. It's not my fault that you fall for gay guys—it's just not. I've loved you since forever, and I haven't fallen for a straight woman once. You have to take responsibility for your own choices. And I need to go to bed. Sorry I couldn't help with the gaydar. I'm afraid you're on your own."

Grrl Genius Relationship Tip

Don't fall in love with gay men.

Grrl Genius Relationship Tip Corollary

How many times do you have to do this before you learn?

It was Monday morning, and Thor had been back at my apartment for a day. He didn't seem too perky; in fact, he seemed downright miserable. He had slept all night on the cold tile kitchen floor, with his legs splayed out, as if to induce maximum guilt in me, his castrator. Typical of his permanently sunny disposition, when I walked into the room, instead of staring at me with seething anger and silently accusing me of taking his manhood, he simply straggled to his feet and rushed over, albeit limpingly, for a morning love festival.

I knew I could be "projecting," as my therapist would accuse, but even in his weakened state, Thor once again seemed so much happier to be in my small apartment than he had been back in the big house in Beverly Hills. For one thing, he got to sleep inside with the people, and for another thing, well, he had set out on his own to come find me, and as far as I was concerned, that made his preference very clear.

As I made the drive to William's place in Santa Monica, I mused over everyone's absolute verdict that he was gay. Well, to be truthful, Tommy hadn't said he was gay, and he was the only one to have actually met him, but he certainly didn't leap to his defense heterosexual-wise either.

The biggest mistake is believing there is one right way to listen, to talk, to have a conversation—or a relationship.

—Deborah Tannen

In the cool light of day, I started wondering why I had made "Is William gay?" into such an immediate crisis. When would I ever learn to stop being such a drama queen? It wasn't like having had one slightly ambiguous date/not date that ended with a kiss/not kiss meant I needed to immediately confront the issue of William's sexuality at 7:30 a.m. on a Monday morning.

Or so I thought. But when I walked into the apartment, there was William, happily dishing out homemade scones to a tall, dark-haired, handsome man who was sitting at William's kitchen table.

In William's bathrobe.

I immediately had the worst stomachache on earth. "Why am I always the last person in my life to actually get what's going on?" I wondered. William was in his usual cheerful early morning mood, but his . . . friend, seemed sort of hungover.

"Good morning, sunshine!" William called out, well, gaily. "Cathryn, this is my friend Bruce."

Oh, my God, his name is Bruce, will there be no cliché untouched in this? I thought. "Hi . . . Bruce!" I sang out, overly cheerfully.

"Hi," Bruce moaned.

"Bruce and I were fraternity brothers at Sigma Chi," William said.

"Go Sig," Bruce grumbled unenthusiastically.

"Bruce stays in town with me whenever they have that big monthly design powwow over at the Pacific Design center. He's the biggest interior designer in Boise."

Of course. Of course he's an interior designer.

Bruce looked sardonically at William. "Oh, William, don't be so over the top. She's a big city girl, saying I'm the biggest interior designer in Boise, Idaho, is not going to be impressive to her."

"No," I protested. "It's very impressive to me! I'm very happy for both of you!"

Bruce got out of his chair with a groan. "I gotta take a shower if I'm gonna make it to the airport on time. . . . I'll let you guys get to work. Nice to meet you, Cathryn. I've heard a lot about you."

"Great! Me, too! And, it's great to meet you! Enjoy your shower!" I seemed to be incapable of being anything but insanely cheerful.

William looked at me searchingly. "Enjoy your shower? Are you okay?" he asked.

"I'm great, I'm really happy!" I lied. "Because, you know, Thor's home, with me, and my life is full of good friends like you, and now hopefully Bruce!" I gestured weakly toward the naked man in his bathroom.

"Well, I guess I'm glad you're happy." He seemed relieved as he started puttering around the kitchen. "It's just, you're never usually happy this time of day, so it kind of threw me. You want a scone?"

I wanted seventeen scones, covered in hot fudge, but I took just the one. We started working. Today was our last day to finish our revisions on the script, which was due the next morning. I decided (for once showing some discretion and keeping my big mouth shut) not to say anything about William's being gay, since what I had been missing was so patently obvious.

When Bruce was ready to go, William helped him out with his luggage. I supposed he wanted a moment to say good-bye in private. William was more comfortable with his gayness than I thought he would be, but I suspected that since he'd never mentioned it outright, there was still some sense of discomfort there. He wasn't going to go kissing his boyfriend right in front of me, that was for sure.

We worked hard all day, making so many improvements that the script was singing. Jen was taking care of Thor for me. When I called, she said he was doing fine, so once again William and I ordered in food and worked until about eight o'clock, which wasn't late on my old schedule, but with all this rising at dawn, by the time we knocked off, I was exhausted.

"Well, it's done," William announced. "And you know what, it's great, all because of you."

"Please . . . it's great, but it's because of us. We're great," I observed, somewhat sadly.

He looked at me fondly and took my hand. "We are great, aren't we?" It felt wonderful, this small touch of his, but I slowly slid my hand away.

I had wanted so much to tell William that I was in love with him, and I couldn't believe that I had missed the very obvious signals he had been sending me all along. William was gay. And even if we became the best of friends, I vowed I would never let him know how I had fallen for him, because I knew where that would lead. I'd been through it with Tommy for years.

I knew if William knew my true feelings, he would always feel sorry for me, and then because he's a nice man, he'd end up feeling like he had to be my surrogate boyfriend whenever some other guy that I fell in love with also turned out to be gay, or the random freak straight guy that I'd find just ended up treating me badly. And because he was so nice, he'd feel the need to help me fill my lonely nights, and then we'd end up at an Arthur Murray studio somewhere, taking ballroom dancing lessons, which would actually be great come to think of it, because you could never get a straight guy to do that and it would be so fun, and anyway, I could always go back to sleeping with Tyler, if I just, you know, needed to sleep with someone, but I knew now, after hearing everything Vonnie had said about her love for Eldon, I knew that random "hookups" weren't really what I wanted. I wanted the whole thing, but the whole thing never seemed to show up for me. So maybe I just had to start thinking of men more like mix-and-match bikinis. You couldn't possibly expect to buy a whole suit and have the top and the bottom fit you perfectly, so maybe William could be the top, and Tyler could be the bottom, not top and bottom in the gay way, but in the bikini way and . . .

"So I'll talk to you next Friday for sure, unless I hear something from the studio," William said, apparently continuing the conversation that we were having, to which I had ceased paying attention.

"Right . . . Right . . . That's great," I agreed vaguely, trying to keep up.

"I'll call," he promised sweetly and gave me a hug. "Now, you go home and get some rest. You really look exhausted—you're probably not thinking straight, but then, hey, neither am I! Good night!" He shut the door, and I stumbled sadly off to my car.

As I drove home, I added up all the very obvious clues William had been giving me. Obviously, I had done a poor job of concealing my attraction for him, and because he was a nice man, he had done his very best to let me down gently, making sure there was no misunderstanding of the fact that there could never be anything between us. I assumed that William must be like a lot of my gay male friends in show business; he was like Tommy, the type who didn't announce his gayness in his work relationships, because he didn't want people judging him as a "gay person." William wasn't "out" because he probably didn't want people to hire him to write only "gay material," and he didn't really think it was any of their damn business whom he slept with. Even though everyone thinks show business is so socially liberal, truthfully, there was a lot of prejudice in Hollywood, and I certainly couldn't blame him for not wanting to be "out."

I thought back to William's note to me in which he said he "didn't want you to think I was flirting with you," even going so far as to include a silly reference to his willingness to wear a bikini. I thought about his discomfort when I discussed my sex life, his scrupulous physical politeness, the sweet and friendly peck good night after our dinner that was just the kind of kiss Tommy would have given me when he was feeling tender. I was grateful that William had found a way to let me know his preference without embarrassing me, or compromising our work relationship.

I didn't know what to make of Bruce. Obviously he and William had been together for a while, such was their ease with each other. I guessed that Bruce was the reason that William's divorce was so easy and amicable. After all, it's hardly worth getting upset if your husband leaves you for another man, unlike Kurt's alleged closet gayness, an openly gay ex is the kind you can be friendly with, since the breakup is so obviously not the wife's fault.

As I drove along Mulholland back to my apartment, I realized that I was crying. I was feeling such pain that for the second time in my life I had met a man who was everything I could ever want, who would never want me.

I vowed to love William as he was, to continue to enjoy him, but I knew from long, sad experience that the hollowness in my heart that wanted him to love me as I loved him would never ever be filled.

Men and women, women and men. It will never work.

—Erica Jong

Chapter 9

A Grrl Genius Understands That Before Anyone Can Love Her, She Has to Love Herself

I am so inadequate, and I love myself!
—Meg Ryan

I CALLED Jabba after I had Thor neutered, just to let him know what had happened. Since Thor came to me voluntarily, I assumed we could all accept this as, well, "Dog's Will."

I couldn't have been more wrong. Jabba informed me that he had gotten a very contentious message on his machine from Kurt, demanding that I return the dog immediately. If I kept him, I could be found to be in contempt of the court's order, instead of merely in contempt of Kurt Bremerhoffen.

I dreaded taking Thor back to Beverly Hills. The poor thing was mostly healed, and back to his usual manic personality, As always, he was thrilled to be going on a car ride, but I thought I noticed him getting visibly more subdued as we wound our way on the twisty road up to the imposing contemporary house that for so long had been his only home.

I knew I wasn't imagining it when I literally had to drag him up the steps to the house. He acted like I was dragging him to the pound. I opened the front gate and came face-to-face with Kurt's girlfriend, the Triceratops, her skin a rich caramel tan, her hair a skanky, over-processed platinum blonde with four-inch blue-black roots, wearing what I was fairly sure was an old kimono of mine. (It was ridiculously small on her and fit her about as sharply as one of Herman Munster's suits.)

She stared at me for a moment. Then she spoke. "Cathryn Michon?" she grated in a cigarette-roughened voice.

"Y-yes," I stammered foolishly, though she obviously knew who I was—she was wearing my clothes!

"I'm Tammy," she announced uncordially. I couldn't help feeling delight that her real name (which I had made a big point of never learning) went so perfectly with the mean name I had made up for her. "Tammy the Triceratops," I thought. "How perfect!" She pressed a thick envelope into my hand.

"It's a restraining order. You're not allowed within five hundred yards of this house. And there will be a court date a week from today to determine final custody of the dog. Now get out before I call the cops."

I couldn't have been more shocked if Tammy the Triceratops had actually sprouted three horns and gored me with them. I was absolutely numb. Here was this woman ordering me from my house and my dog, in my bathrobe!

My dog. A week without even seeing Thor. My Thor, my sweet, stupid, goofy Thor without whom I had hardly spent a day since his birth.

What did "final custody" mean? Could Kurt really wind up with Thor, keeping him locked behind a fence from which I had to stay five hundred yards away?

I could not let that happen. Tears of frustration welling up, I turned away from her. I realized if I was going to try to get custody of Thor, who was busy chewing on the last of the name-brand dog biscuits that I had brought, that meant I had to find a new place, a house with a yard, and move there.

In a week.

> Marriages don't last. When I meet a guy, the first question I ask
> myself is: Is this the man I want my children to spend their weekends
> with?
>
> —Rita Rudner

An essential part of being a Grrl Genius is being able to admit
when you are in way over your head and you can't count solely on
your own genius to solve all your problems. That is the time when
the wise and often panicked Grrl Genius calls upon her fellow Grrl
Geniuses and Enlightened Males to get her out of the river of excre-
ment she is currently navigating with nary a paddle.

The last thing I ever want to do is ask for help. Everyone is
always telling me it's because I don't value myself enough, don't
love myself enough, and I guess that's why I never feel worthy of
their help. But I could no longer afford my crippling low self-esteem.
I needed to love myself enough to ask for help, to feel I deserved it,
and so that's exactly what I did.

I asked practically everyone I knew for help so that I could
make the best possible effort at getting Thor back. After everything
that had happened to me, the idea of being able to win Thor back
was a goal we could all focus on. My wonderful, amazing friends
and family came through for me like the Grrl Geniuses and Enlightened Males they were.

Certainly my friends loved me. Now I had to learn to do the
same.

After I was served with the restraining order, I called Jabba the
Attorney, who always acted as if my case were some kind of direct
insult to his sweaty manhood. He said that since things had esca-
lated, I needed to prove that Kurt was absolutely an unfit dog parent. He added that I had to do whatever I could to move to a place
with a yard or I wouldn't stand a chance, which I had already
guessed. I could tell that Jabba really wanted me to win at least this
one thing. I could tell because he told me he would handle it for
free. I objected weakly, but he insisted, and hell, I thought, I'll take
it, if it makes him feel better.

I had less than a week to put Operation Thor into action, but I knew that with everything I had lost, there was no way I wasn't going to do everything in my power to win. Unlike the salad competition, I didn't just want this for me. I wanted it for Thor, as well. I had seen how desperately unhappy he was when I took him back to that coldly modernistic house in Beverly Hills. I would make the law work for me, for once, and if that failed, I would go outside the law. I had nothing to lose. Not getting Thor back was simply not an option.

Jen was the first person to join up with Operation Thor. She emerged out of the narcotic fog of her "bridal addiction" and swung into action. Because of the big tips from Rich's ambrosial diner cooking, Jen now had enough money to live in my apartment by herself, and so she said she would just take over the lease—I didn't have to worry about subletting. She told me she would take care of packing everything of mine in the apartment. That's exactly what she did, which was amazing, and made me love her so much that I knew that even when she was "Malibu Jen," she would still be like a sister to me—just one with a husband who was rapidly biodegrading due to his appalling inattendance to routine personal hygiene.

The Grrl Genius Club stepped in mightily with their collective Grrl Genius. Gramma Dick the private eye was still on retainer to Kim, who was determined to find out why her husband was obsessed with her underwear drawer, so Kim paid her a little extra money and had her observe my Beverly Hills house, taking copious digital photographs. The picture showed that Thor was not being walked regularly, and that the hole in the fence was still not repaired. Instead, Kurt had decided to simply keep my dog on a short heavy iron chain!

Vonnie and Amelia, having done research on the whole "dog custody" process, found that the court is often influenced by testimony of people who had observed the actual "dog parenting" process. So Vonnie and Amelia put together a whole scrapbook of notarized affidavits from friends of mine who knew how devoted I was to Thor. It seemed that everybody I knew had a picture of me with that dog. In addition to glowing testimonials to my skills as a dog mom; there were tons of pictures of me with the dog, with Kurt nowhere in sight. This was because he usually was nowhere in sight, since they don't allow dogs on the golf course, which is where Kurt spends most of his time, battling his alcoholism.

Tommy got to work trying to find me a place with a yard, and called rental listings until his voice was as rough as Tammy the Triceratops. But what I could afford—$1,500 a month at most—was proving impossible to find. He told me he would keep looking, though.

The person who did the most was William, who was the first person I called. He immediately swung into action, even though he had a 4:00 p.m. flight to Boise that same day.

When I walked up to his building, I could see William through the window, busy in his kitchen. I watched him there from the street for a moment. My breath caught in my throat just to watch him, the ache of loving him as fresh and pointless as ever, unavailable as he was to me. This ache was so old, so familiar; it was the same ache I felt for years with Tommy. To be honest, I still felt it to this day. It was a little bit of sadness that never really went away. I realized that I would just have to get used to it, that little sadness now times two.

When I entered William's apartment in a total emotional puddle, he had a comprehensive, detailed plan of attack, which he began outlining to me from the moment I walked in. "Now, my idea is that we get you a rental house here in Santa Monica with a yard, so you won't keep having to make that long commute when we work, and from what you've told me about your finances, we can't go higher than fifteen hundred dollars," he stated matter-of-factly, exactly the way one might say, "We need to stop off at the Safeway and get a quart of milk and some eggs."

"William," I began to patiently explain, "I don't know how you lucked into this place, but this is Santa Monica, not—"

"Booger Holler, Idaho?" he suggested coolly.

"Well, frankly, yes. I mean, you can't get a house, with a yard, to rent, in this part of town for under three thousand a month, and that would be a bargain, and I can't afford that, even if I could find *that*—"

He seemed bored with my recitation of the actual facts of the case.

"Well, I happen to know a real-estate agent," William declared, to which I rolled my eyes visibly. Everybody in L.A. "knew" a real-estate agent, and they were always like every other real estate agent, which is to say, useless when it came to finding impossible bargains, which, to be fair, was not exactly their job.

"Anyway," he continued breezily, "this Realtor is the aunt of a . . . friend of mine."

Maybe it's his L.A. boyfriend, I thought. Maybe he and Bruce weren't exclusive. I was kind of disappointed to contemplate this. I had sort of hoped that William was the kind of gay guy that had a devoted monogamous relationship.

"Anyway, point is, I made an appointment with Joni the Realtor for you for this afternoon," William continued, interrupting my dismal speculation on his sex life. "I explained the whole deal, she is a huge dog lover, and she actually found a small two-bedroom bungalow guest house that is part of a larger property and has a huge yard. The owner has dogs and is fine with the idea of you having a dog."

"Are you serious?" I asked, barely daring to believe it. "But do you know how much it would cost?"

"Well, it works out perfectly, because it's fifteen hundred dollars. Now," he continued efficiently, just like the corporate executive he used to be, "you have a temporary cash-flow problem, and you've got to get over to Joni's office with a security deposit and all that. Because of the way these movie studios do their crazy accounting, you're going to have that problem for at least another month. So I have cut a check to you out of my corporation and drawn up loan papers, I am lending you ten thousand dollars at five and a half percent, and the loan is due in three months. It's not charity—I know you're good for it."

I was overwhelmed. As I often was with William. William loved to have people underestimate him, and then he would proceed to just blow them away. At that moment, I didn't care if he was gay, straight, or whatever. He was still the best friend and writing partner a girl could ever wish for. I threw my arms around him and gave him a hug, which felt so good, but I tried not to think about that. Almost immediately, I started to feel guilty about everything he had just offered me. It was just too much. Things this good never happened to me. There had to be a catch, or something.

"I don't know," I began, feeling so uncomfortable and beholden, "I don't know if I can accept all this. You've already done too much for me—"

"That's ridiculous," he dismissed me brusquely, still very businesslike, "we're partners, we do stuff for each other." Suddenly he morphed into his more shy and awkward self. "Cathryn, it's a good thing, it worked out, just accept it, okay? I wish you liked yourself enough to believe you deserve to have good things happen to you. Sometimes, although I know you believe that the odds are astronomically against it, things just work out fine. Okay?"

"Okay," I agreed sheepishly. "I'll just accept it. Thank you," I said, my eyes moist with tears of sweet gratitude for him. He was right, I needed to believe I deserved good things could happen to me. A Grrl Genius who truly loved herself would believe it.

"But there is one favor you can do for me," he continued. "Well, two, actually."

"Of course," I said in a rare moment of 100 percent nonsarcastic sincerity. "I'd do anything."

"Great!" he said. "I need you to take me to the airport today and pick me up next Friday."

"Oh," I joked, "I don't know, I mean, taking people to the airport, that's kind of—"

"I'm not being cheap," he explained awkwardly, as though my objection were real. "It's just, when I was an executive, I traveled constantly, and, well, I like to be picked up at airports. By someone I know. So it's, you know, not so lonely." Now he seemed genuinely embarrassed at having asked.

"Oh, William." I threw my arms around him for the second time that day, and, I realized, the second time since I'd known him. "I was kidding! Of course, I'll pick you up at the airport. I'll pick you up at the airport for the rest of your life if that's what you want!"

"Well, that would be great, actually," he replied, his normal cheerfulness restored.

"What's the other thing you need?" I asked. He looked very grave indeed.

"I need . . . ," he whispered fervently, and then, suddenly, he burst into his endearingly goofy grin. "I desperately need you to dance with me to 'YMCA'!" I laughed as he grabbed the remote and started the CD player blasting. "And now!" he announced. "We dance!"

> *It's fun to stay at the YMCA*
> *The YMCA*
> *You can get a good meal*
> *You can blah blah blah blah*
> *Young men!*
> *Blah blah blah blah*
> *Young men!*
> *Blah blah blah blah blah*

And we danced and danced and danced.

The trouble with the rat race is that even if you win, you're still a rat.
—Jane Wagner

Because the aunt of William's "friend" Realtor Joni Ellenbogen turned out to be a Grrl Genius of epic proportions, I ended up living in the sweetest, coziest little Cape Cod–style doll cottage. It belonged to an insanely successful action-adventure movie director who was usually out of the country on a shoot at least half the year. It used to be the staff quarters on a lush, ten-acre gated compound in the Pacific Palisades, with spectacular water views on a dramatic cliff overlooking the Pacific Ocean.

All for $1,500 a month.

It turned out that the weird movie director just happened to love Doberman pinschers. He had four of them and was happy to have another, less fortunate Dobie join the pack.

If there was one thing I had learned in Hollywood, it's that, for the most part, successful people in Hollywood hate people, but they love animals.

If I could do anything about the way people behave toward each other, I would, but since I can't, I'll stick to the animals.

—Brigitte Bardot

I moved in all day Wednesday and managed to go to bed early in order to get plenty of sleep in preparation for the dog-custody hearing. It was exhausting, but so gratifying to be in such an adorable little place. I could just imagine how much Thor would love it if I managed to get custody. When I checked my e-mail that night, I found a message from Larry, the Laundromat King, whose unanswered e-mails to me had trickled down to only one a day.

From: KINGLARRY@sudsspudsandduds.com
To: Grrlgeniusygrrl@grrlyone.com

Dear Cathryn,

I hope this won't hurt your feelings too badly, but I felt that I had to tell you I have found the love of my life online, and we are getting married! Gina is a beautiful woman inside and out, and I never would have met her if it hadn't been for you, and what we shared. I hope you will look past any feelings you might have about losing me to her, and be happy for the new Mrs. Suds, Spuds, and Duds.

Your Friend,
Larry

P.S. I hope you are still enjoying the diamond bracelet. I know that Gina loves hers!

I was happy that crazy Larry had finally found his queen. I didn't have the nerve to tell him that I sold his bracelet and gave the money to Project Angel Food. I didn't know what he was talking about when he said, "what we shared," but one thing I had learned in my romantic life was that no man ever wants to believe he was dumped, and so if Larry could honestly believe in his heart that he was in fact dumping me for Gina, well, more power to him. I wished him and his Potato Queen all the best.

———

A Grrl Genius Crazy Sex Fact

The Russian holy man Rasputin was reported to have a thirteen-inch erect penis.

There is no record as to whether or not this was the origin of the phrase, "Rootin' Tootin' Rasputin."

———

The next morning, I headed back, one last time, to the Heather Locklear Memorial Crying Table at the Beverly Hills Courthouse with Tommy and his boyfriend, Tommy, who had come along for emotional support.

"Other Tommy" turned out to be adorable. He was a brilliant costume designer for feature films who was quick-witted and friendly and had wanted to come along to support me, even though he had never really met me, which made me love him instantly. Also, Other

293

Tommy was the sort of gay man who was openly, obviously, 100 percent gay, gay, gay from the moment you met him, which, given my bad history, was a quality I really appreciated. Plus, unlike my Tommy, Other Tommy cared desperately about clothes and was very enthusiastic about what I had chosen to wear to the hearing.

"Oh, my God, that's perfect!" Other Tommy enthused. "Ralph Lauren tailored blouse and slim khaki skirt, with sensible but stylish Taryn Rose walking shoes, just the right amount of Lana Turner, not a hint of Joan Crawford. To me it says sporty but successful. It practically screams, 'I am going to court, and I want to show due respect for that, but I am so ready to win this case and take this doggy for a big walk!' "

Why couldn't all gay men be like Other Tommy?

Jabba the Attorney met us in the hallway, looking less moist than usual, and we made our way into the courtroom. The case preceding ours was still being argued, so we all sat in the gallery. On the other side of the room I could see Kurt, and Tammy the Triceratops, but his lawyer hadn't yet arrived.

I took a moment to really look at Judge Riananne Hunter-White. As usual, she was already seated on the bench, which I never understood. If I were a judge, I would insist on making an entrance for every case. I would think that the "All rise!" thing has just got to give you a big lift, but maybe this judge didn't need it. Unlike me, self-confidence did not seem to be a problem for her. She was so regal, so elegant, so queenly as she sat in her flowing black robes, her impeccable cascade of braids looped neatly and tumbling elegantly down her back. She had her little reading glasses on, and she was staring thoughtfully at some documents. As she pronounced her decision in the other case, I said a little prayer: Please God, please let her be as fair as she is fashionable. I think she cares about justice, I think she cares about the law, but I think she also wants to do the right thing. If there's any way that we can do the right thing here today, even if it's not the legal thing, well, Thor and I would be grateful.

I had cared too much about this court appearance to go back to the Rosio the Santeria Witch Hotline, which frankly hadn't really helped as far as I could tell. It was time to pull out the big spiritual guns. In my mind, I was praying to the ripped and buff nearly naked Jesus that had hung over the altar of Saint Francis Episcopal church in Sippewisset, Massachusetts, the church where I had gotten married. I added the following P.S. to the prayer: I don't want to make you feel guilty, because I know that's your job, but this whole marriage thing with Kurt started in your house, so could you please help me out? Thanks . . . I'm a big fan.

I also promised Jabba that I absolutely, positively, would not say a single word, unless the judge asked me to, and I meant it.

Our case was called, Tommy and Tommy gave me a little thumbs-up, and we all stepped to our old familiar places. Except that Drake Nimmer, Kurt's unctuous, crisply tailored attorney wasn't there.

Judge Hunter-White looked down her reading glasses at Kurt and Tammy, who were alone at the table.

"Mr. Bremerhoffen, is this your attorney?"

"No, Your Honor, I will be representing myself today."

The judge paused a moment to consider this. "So you are formally waiving your right to counsel?"

"Yes, Your Honor, I am," Kurt said confidently.

"And you feel you have a thorough understanding of the action you have brought today?" Judge Hunter-White asked.

"I have done a great deal of research on the topic, and I feel very well informed," Kurt intoned magisterially, really getting into the idea that he was a lawyer. But really, I could see where that would be fun for him, getting all dressed up and playing "Career Day."

"Fine, then," Judge Hunter-White said. "Please proceed."

Kurt had cheaped out! Of course, now that he couldn't constantly nickel and dime me with fake invoices and money requests to pay his attorney to take my money, he was back to his penny-pinching ways. Thankfully, blessedly, Kurt's whopping ego was once again on my side, as he seemed to believe that he knew everything he needed to know about the law and would do as good a job as any lawyer.

Of course he was his own attorney, and with luck, his own worst enemy, as well. It was like the old saying, "A man who represents himself has a fool for a client and a Triceratops for a girlfriend."

Kurt grabbed a legal pad and stepped confidently away from his table, visions of Dylan McDermott dancing in his head. He began pacing dramatically, as his ridiculous ponytail flicked back and forth as though it were actually busily shooing flies off the hind-quarters of a small Shetland pony, and the fluorescent light glinted merrily off his increasingly large bald spot. "Your Honor, esteemed colleagues, interested citizens, on the morning of February fifteenth—"

Judge Hunter-White held up her hand, and Kurt stopped speaking.

"Mr. Bremerhoffen?"

"Yes?" answered Kurt manfully.

"What are you doing?"

"Why, I'm presenting my case, Your Honor."

"Yes, but why are you walking all over my courtroom?" she inquired.

"Because, well, it helps me think, I suppose, and—"

"Well, you're going to have to do your thinking sitting down, Mr. Bremerhoffen. This isn't a track meet," she stated with a sudden sass I'd never heard in her voice.

"But—" Kurt protested.

"Sit down. Now," she ordered.

Kurt sat.

"I know you're new at this," she continued calmly. "But this is a courtroom, and I am the judge, which means, in here, I am your boss," she said with what I desperately wanted to believe was a note of blessed sarcasm.

Kurt looked shaken. Apparently he had forgotten that when you play "Career Day," somebody gets to play "boss." I glanced over at Jabba the Attorney, whose face was dry as a bone.

Which I took to be a good sign. Kurt grabbed his legal pad,

stared at it a moment, obviously trying to collect himself; then he began speaking. "On the fifteenth of February, the defendant—"

"Respondent," Judge Riananne Hunter-White corrected smoothly.

"Huh?" said Kurt.

"She's a respondent, not a defendant," the judge explained. "Please continue."

"Uh, well," Kurt struggled. "Well the thing is, she, uh, came to pick up the dog, and he wasn't there, because he ran away by digging a hole in the fence, and then somehow, she claims that the dog just 'showed up' on her doorstep, where the dog has been exactly once, and she lives seven-point-six miles away, and I have, well, exhibit A, which is some Los Angeles city maps that show exactly how far the defendant—"

"Respondent," reiterated the judge.

"Right, right," Kurt agreed, his native testiness starting to show through. "But it shows that she really does live that far away, and if you believe that a dog can just find its way there all by itself—"

"Did you ever see *The Incredible Journey*, Mr. Bremerhoffen?" Judge Hunter-White inquired mildly.

"Uh, isn't that, like, a Disney movie?" he answered, nonplussed.

"It's a very charming children's movie, which I highly recommend, based on a true story, about a group of pets that go across the whole country to find their family. So, if you ask me, do I believe a dog can find its way from Beverly Hills to Studio City, to a place it's been previously, I'm going to have to say yes, I believe it."

Kurt looked crushed.

"Please," she invited cordially, "please continue."

In a strange turn of events, Jabba the Attorney was as arid as Death Valley, and Kurt was beginning to flow like Niagara. "Uh, well, okay, then," Kurt muttered to himself. "Right. Well, the thing is, that part's not so important, anyway. The dog ends up at her place, and she goes—in direct violation of an agreement that she and I personally had—and gets the dog spayed."

"Neutered," said the judge.

"Correct," Kurt fumbled, "spayed and neutered."

"It's neutered for a male dog; for a female, it's spayed. *Neuter* means 'to castrate,' I believe," said Judge Hunter-White evenly.

"But," objected Kurt, vainly trying to gather momentum, "in doing this, she has permanently and irrevocably damaged valuable property, this dog is a valuable asset because this dog was going to be a stud dog, and would earn a handsome fee for breeding with various bitches."

"Nice work if you can get it, eh, Mr. Bremerhoffen?" the judge observed as the courtroom burst into wild, sustained applause.

Actually, the applause was only in my head, but in there, it was definitely wild and sustained. The only reaction that occurred in real life was a couple of muffled laughs that emanated from the gallery. I looked up to see who it was, but I couldn't tell if it was Tommy or Tommy. Kurt said nothing, which, as always, was a welcome relief.

"So, Mr. Bremerhoffen, is that the substance of your case?"

Kurt desperately searched his legal pad to see if there was more, and it seemed there wasn't. "Uh, yes, that would be it, except that I would say that the dollar amount of this crime is approximately five thousand dollars as the dog cost one thousand dollars, and would have received five hundred dollars per successful breeding, and eight litters from a good stud dog is not an unreasonable expectation."

Judge Hunter-White peered at him. "Mr. Bremerhoffen, have you filed a criminal complaint in this matter?"

The concept seemed to invigorate Kurt, while I felt a sinking sensation in my stomach. The so-called justice system was going to do it to me again!

"No, not yet, Your Honor," Kurt responded heartily, "but I assure you that—"

She held up her hand. "Then until you do, you will no longer use the word *crime* to describe an action wherein a dog in your custody escaped through a hole in your fence."

"No, the *crime* was depriving me of five thousand dollars!" my ex-husband shouted in a way that was oh-so-Kurt: angry, red-faced, and with a not-so-subtle implication that the person he was yelling at was stupid.

However, in this case, his customary bullying was not going to work, because he obviously wasn't pushing around someone with low self-esteem.

"Mr. Bremerhoffen!" Judge Hunter-White snapped in an "I don't need no stinkin' gavel" tone. "You will not address this court in that fashion ever again. You will *not* use the word *crime* in a civil action you have brought before this court in a dispute over which I have jurisdiction. Do I make myself clear?"

"But," he began stubbornly.

"Am I clear?" she roared with all the Grrl Genius authority I had ever seen concentrated in a single person.

"Yes, Your Honor," Kurt responded meekly.

"Then please sit down."

She looked down at her sizable pile of papers. "Now. Mr. Burns, in his response, states that Ms. Michon is petitioning for custody of the animal. Her contention is that Mr. Bremerhoffen was negligent in fixing a hole in the fence that she had paid to have repaired—and I do see here some sort of invoice and the copy of a canceled check?"

"Well, wait a minute!" Kurt interjected.

The judge directed her megawatt glare at Kurt, silencing him without uttering a word. Oh, how I wished I had the kind of self-confidence to do that!

Kurt slumped in his chair, looking for all the world like a petulant child who has been told to eat his vegetables or else.

Judge Hunter-White continued, "As I understand it, Ms. Michon had the dog neutered, because, quite reasonably it seems to me, she determined that it was for mating purposes that the dog had escaped, thus endangering itself. She did bring the dog back after the dog was healed, so she doesn't appear in substantive violation of the visitation rules previously established by this court. Also, I understand that Ms. Michon has obtained a lease on and moved into"—she paused to shuffle through a series of Polaroids—"what looks to be a new residence where Thor, if awarded to her, would not only have ample room to run around, but also the company of other dogs. Is that correct, Mr. Burns?"

Jabba stood. "Yes, Your Honor, it is. Additionally, if the court will allow it, Ms. Michon has assembled a book of notarized statements from various witnesses who will testify to her competence and caring as the loving owner of this dog."

Judge Hunter-White motioned him forward, and he brought the carefully and beautifully hand-bound *Book of Thor* and set it before her. The judge took several moments to leaf through the book, looking at various pictures as Kurt slumped lower and lower in his chair.

One photograph in particular caught her interest—it was one of the pictures taken by the Kim's private investigator, Gramma Dick. She slipped it from its plastic sleeve and flapped it in Kurt's direction.

"Mr. Bremerhoffen, I have here a picture of the dog on what looks to be a four-foot chain. *This* is your solution to the hole in the fence?"

Before he replied, Kurt scowled at the Triceratops, a look I knew all too well: It was his idea, it was his action, it was his fault—but somehow, in his mind, *she* was to blame—and there would be harsh words for her after the hearing.

"It's just temporary, Your Honor. I haven't had the time . . ." Kurt suddenly seemed to run out of steam.

"This canceled check from Ms. Michon is more than a month old," the judge reminded him, holding up the check that Jabba had given her.

Kurt, somehow, kept himself from arguing.

"You're a carpenter of some kind, isn't that correct, Mr. Bremerhoffen?" she asked mildly.

Kurt drew himself up proudly. "A finish carpenter," he agreed.

"And you don't currently have a job," Judge Hunter-White continued smoothly.

Kurt nodded sadly, as if mourning the fantastic career he might have had, were it not for his tragic disability. "Yes, Your Honor," he intoned.

"So I gather that as a 'finish carpenter,' it's the getting *started* part of the project that's the problem," she concluded.

Kurt blinked, truly not understanding what she meant. In Kurt's mind he *did* work: he completed crossword puzzles perfectly and designed five-year diapers and went to the golf course—someone subtly suggesting he was lazy had no effect on him, because he just simply didn't get it.

"Well, all right, this is quite compelling, Miss Michon. Thank you for taking the time out of your busy work schedule to assemble this," the judge stated. "Now, Mr. Bremerhoffen, I have a question for you."

Kurt nodded warily, and she continued. "Mr. Bremerhoffen, I note that you have filed a restraining order prohibiting Miss Michon from coming near the joint residence you both own and in which you currently reside. As I understood the terms of your agreement, it was Miss Michon who was coming over every day at—" She looked down at her papers. "Five o'clock a.m. to walk the dog for an hour to an hour and a half. Has the dog been receiving this kind of exercise since you have gotten the restraining order?"

"To be honest," Kurt began, clearly lying out his ass, "as Your Honor is well aware, I am disabled—"

"With alcoholism, correct?" the judge clarified.

"Yes, Your Honor," continued Kurt unashamedly, "so I don't have the capacity for walking him rigorously, but when we do go, he certainly enjoys it."

"Of course, forgive me forgetting about your disability, sir. That certainly seems reasonable," observed the judge.

"I walked him on Wednesday!" the Triceratops chimed in.

Judge Hunter-White fixed her with a steely glare. "Whoever you are, do not speak again."

Poor Tammy the Triceratops. I resolved, with my Grrl Genius

compassion, to forgive her for participating in the lingerie yard sale. After all, she did take Thor for a walk!

The judge took a moment, thinking through what she had just heard, and then she began speaking again. "We are convened here today for a custody hearing, which is where we determine which party in a divorced or divorcing couple should have the primary care taking responsibility for either a minor child, or, as in this case, an animal. However," she said, regarding Kurt, "Mr. Bremerhoffen has made clear that his interest in Thor, the dog, is as an asset of the marriage."

Kurt narrowed his eyes, trying to figure out whether or not this was a good thing, which is what everyone else was trying to figure out, too. "Mr. Bremerhoffen maintains that this dog was an asset that was awarded to him, representing five thousand dollars of income which Ms. Michon, through her actions, has destroyed."

Kurt looked pleased, Jabba looked wet, and I began to get sick to my stomach. "However," she said, as we all leaned forward in our chairs, "the court does not agree that Mr. Bremerhoffen was ever awarded ownership of the animal. He was given custody—temporary custody, I might add, because his yard was large enough for the dog to move freely about." The judge stared at Kurt for a moment. "Thor is not an asset. He is a living, breathing creature that has previously been regarded in this divorce as though he were a child of the marriage. Mr. Bremerhoffen seems interested only in the monetary value of the dog, and so I view him to be an unfit custodian for this animal, because he, not unlike the fictional character Cruella De Vil"—Kurt seemed to be melting under the table—"might, at some point in the future, come to regard this dog as being more valuable as a pelt for a coat than as a pet and companion. Therefore, I award custody, effective immediately, of the dog Thor to Ms. Michon, permanently and irrevocably."

Kurt leapt up. "But!"

"Yes, Mr. Bremerhoffen?"

"But I, I—well, what about the five thousand dollars?" Kurt whined.

302

"Well, you know, Mr. Bremerhoffen, I had a funny feeling you might ask about that. Now, if you want to file another motion and seek compensation for the lost marital asset, which you could certainly chose to do, unless of course I grant you a compensatory settlement now and save us all a little time."

At this idea, Kurt perked up noticeably.

"Now"—again she shuffled through her papers— "I note that there is still a painting of Ms. Michon's which has remained in the residence, which has a stated value of six thousand dollars. Is that correct, Mr. Burns?"

"Yes, Your Honor, that is correct," said a toweled-off Jabba.

I couldn't imagine what my grandfather's ugly painting (which wasn't worth sixty dollars, much less six thousand) could possibly have to do with anything. During the final distribution of assets, Kurt had inflated its value in his declarations so that when I got it back, I would have to give him more money in kind. Naturally, he had been too busy treating his disability with "golf therapy" to return it to me.

"Fine then, if Ms. Michon has no objection, I will award that painting to Mr. Bremerhoffen, which, since it exceeds his own estimated valuation of the dog, should satisfy everyone involved—and settles the last remaining issues in this divorce, which will prevent Mr. Bremerhoffen from pursuing any further legal actions in this matter and prevent Ms. Michon from ever having to see him again. Will that meet with Ms. Michon's and Mr. Bremerhoffen's approval?"

I could trade a hideous worthless painting for my beloved Thor and the privilege of never laying eyes on Kurt again—oh, good heavens, there was no question. I nodded at Jabba silently and enthusiastically.

"That will be more than satisfactory, Your Honor. Thank you," said Jabba.

"Mr. Bremerhoffen?" Judge Hunter-White asked Kurt, who nodded weakly. "Fine, then," pronounced the beautiful, elegant, queenly Grrl Genius Judge Riananne Hunter-White. "This court is recessed until two thirty." She banged her gavel and, even wet as he was, I hugged Jabba, hard. This time, there really was applause in the courtroom (coming entirely from the Tommy section, but still).

I finally had done the one thing Jabba the Attorney had asked of me, had begged of me, had pleaded of me: I hadn't spoken a word for the entire hearing, and he had gotten me my dog. For a person like me, who has had a hard time understanding the value of the verbally unexpressed thought, it had been a struggle, but well worth it.

As I tearfully gathered up my stuff, I took a moment to thank the hunky and ripped Jesus who hung over the altar at Saint Francis Church in Sippewisset: Thank you, thank you, thank you, thank you, thank you, thank you, and sorry I was so crabby, but you know how I get, was my silent prayer of gratitude.

As I grabbed my sweater and my purse, I was suddenly enveloped in a Tommy sandwich, and we all just stood there for a minute hugging each other, as Kurt and Tammy gathered up their scattered papers and exhibits at the other table. I didn't hear any footsteps approach, so I was surprised when I heard the voice of the judge speak. "Here's your *Book of Thor,*" she said, and I looked up and saw Judge Riananne Hunter-White sitting in front of me in a very expensive looking wheelchair, holding out the lovingly hand-made scrapbook.

I, like all nondisabled people, made an elaborate show of acting like it was no big thing to realize now that she was in a wheelchair as I awkwardly took the book from her. I am sure she was used to this display as she probably saw this particular variety of bad acting on a daily basis.

"By the way," she told me, "I was sorry to hear that movie show you were hosting got canceled. I enjoyed watching it."

"Oh, hey, thanks!" I stammered goofily, sort of feeling like judge's pet. She nodded graciously as she rolled away. She stopped her wheelchair at Kurt's table, and everybody went quiet, dying to hear what she said.

"Mr. Bremerhoffen, good luck to you. I wish you all the best in dealing with your . . . disability," she said simply as she rolled out of the courtroom.

Now, that is pure Grrl Genius class in action, people. It was obvious that Judge Riananne Hunter-White loved herself too much to allow a random loser like Kurt to bother her even for a second. I vowed to follow her example from that point on.

Our deepest fear is not that we are inadequate. Our deepest fear is that we are powerful beyond measure. It is our light, not our darkness, that frightens us. We ask ourselves, who am I to be brilliant, gorgeous, talented, and fabulous? Actually, who are you not to be? You are a child of God.

—Marianne Wiliamson

Chapter 10

Love Means *Always* Having to Say You're Sorry

**It's not true that life is one damn thing after another—it is
one damn thing over and over.
—Edna St. Vincent Millay**

I WENT directly from the court in Beverly Hills to my ex-house where
my ex-husband lived. When I got there, there was no one was around
except Thor, who gave me the customary Doberman greeting by
repeatedly banging his head into the fence. Jabba had assured me
that it would be okay for me to violate the restraining order to get the
dog now that I had been awarded custody, and so I took him.

Fortunately, dogs are easy to relocate. Whatever beloved toys
have been left behind are easily replaced, and that's exactly what
we did. Before we got to my new place, we made a stop at the Petco,
and I don't believe I have ever enjoyed a shopping spree more, even
though I personally can either take or leave squeaky chew toys.

I took Thor to what I still couldn't believe was my new home,
and Thor instantly bonded with his new Doberman brothers and sisters. I was truly happy to watch the house dogs gamboling on the
lawn with their new sibling, Thor.

I spent the rest of that perfect afternoon sitting on my big porch
swing, overlooking the surf, drinking tea out of my grandma's old
china teacup, and calling everyone I loved to tell them the good
news as Thor took all the energy that had been stored in that short
chain and ran it out across the lawn.

There are few things in this life as sweet as being able to get on the phone and tell good news over and over. When Jen rang in on call waiting, I was excited to hear her voice, but surprised that she was crying.

"Oh, Cathy," she sobbed. "Rich has quit the diner, he's going back to Cambridge, and I—can I come over, I need to talk to you—"

"Of course, of course," I answered.

Well, it had finally happened. Rich had gotten tired of waiting for Jen to come to her senses. When Jen arrived at my place, she was a different person from who she had been for these last few months. Her smug *Rules* girl toughness had evaporated. Although I was sorry to see her so distraught, it was a relief to have the real, feeling, sensitive Jen I knew back. I held her for a long time in my arms as we rocked on the porch swing. When she finally stopped crying enough to be able to talk, she told me what had happened.

She had been at the diner, getting ready for the evening rush, showing Malibu Jim some clippings from her Bride of Satan magazines of different styles of white tie and tails, which was what she had decided that Jim and his surfing crew would be wearing at the Greatest Wedding on Earth. Rich had, as usual, appeared unmoved by the whole thing. Finally, and I have no idea why she did this, she confronted Rich and blurted, "Don't you even care that he's marrying me?"

Rich continued mincing garlic and looked up and asked, "Do you love him, Jen? Because, if you love him, well, then I guess I'm happy for you, but I can't tell."

Jen, true to her stinking *Rules* replied, "Of course I love him. I'm marrying him, aren't I? I don't see anybody else who wants to marry me, do you?"

Rich quietly set down his knife and then started to take off his apron. "Well, then," he stated calmly, "if you really love him, there's no more reason for me to be here. I've got an open ticket back to Boston, and I guess I'll go tomorrow morning."

With that, he had walked out of the diner.

"I gave him every opportunity!" she cried. "If he wanted to marry me, all he had to do was ask, but he wouldn't do it, he'll never do it, the whole thing is pointless. *The Rules* says if you're involved with a guy who can't commit, you have to move on, you just have to!"

Advice is one of those things it is far more blessed to give than receive.

—Carolyn Wells

"Oh, Jen," I lamented. "I don't know why you can't see this, but the answer to your dilemma is not in that horrifying book. Rich loves you, but he is not going to be browbeaten or hoodwinked into marrying you with these ridiculous car-salesman tactics."

"But really, this is how men think!" she wailed.

"This is how *some* men think," I objected. "This is how men you don't want to marry think. This is how Malibu Jim thinks, when he thinks, which, you know, he avoids at all costs."

She was too upset to defend Malibu Jim, of whom she clearly had grown as weary as the rest of us.

"Rich asked if you loved Malibu Jim, and you told him you did. And that's where he gives up the battle. He loves you enough that, if you love somebody else—well, regardless of the pain it causes him—he's not going to interfere. Rich is a real man. Real men are patient, not spoiled babies who grab for a toy the minute they think someone else is going to snatch it away. He was waiting it out. He didn't think that you really loved Jim, and he was willing to bide his time. But when you tell him you love Jim, well, he's willing to surrender and go home."

Jen digested all this. "I can't marry Malibu Jim," she finally admitted.

"Well, thank God."

It occurred to me that Rich, who was far from an idiot, had not gotten on a plane right away, but was waiting until the morning. He had left a window of opportunity.

"Jen, I'm gonna give you some advice, but first let me say this. People are always giving me advice, and I usually ignore it. If you listen to the advice of people who love you, you realize that they are usually telling you the same thing, over and over again. The main advice I always got all my life—from my parents, from my friends, from my attorney, and especially from my Grrl Genius Club—is that I should just, well, shut up sometimes. I just always tell everybody way too much. I wasn't nicknamed Chatty Cathy for nothing. Yet, today, in court, I took everyone's advice, including my attorney's, and I didn't say a word. And I won."

"Well, that was good advice," she observed wryly.

"Exactly," I agreed. "The most powerful thing we can do is to take advice we've heard a million times. So here's my advice for you. 'Don't be so stubborn.' How many times have you heard this? 'Jen, don't be so stubborn.' We've been saying it to you since you were two. Now, here's the crucial question: Do you want to be happy or do you want to be right?"

"Both," she said stubbornly and without a trace of irony.

"Of course," I continued, because I often felt the same way, "but I am telling you, do not be so stubborn. Go over to his house. Tell him you love him, tell him you are sorry, tell him that you don't give a damn about *The Rules*, you just love him, and you believe that if the two of you focus on that, the rest of it will sort itself out."

"But he—"

"I know. He told everyone you were getting engaged, and then he disappointed you, and then he didn't take the bait when you got engaged to someone else and blah blah blah and you're right and he's wrong and who cares?"

"But—"

"I'm not going to say any more about it. I gave you my advice, and I don't really have any more to add to that. You think about it. Apparently you've got twelve hours. 'K?"

" 'K?"

So she sat there on my big front porch swing for a full hour, staring at the surf in the brilliant sunset, while I went inside to start unpacking. Eventually, she came in the big open kitchen and gave me a hug.

"Thanks, cuz," she told me. "I'm gonna go over there. I'll let you know how it goes."

"Good." As she walked out the door, I called out, "I hope you realize that I am not just doing this for the food."

"Bullshit!" was her fancy Harvard-educated reply.

Oh Rhett, for the first time, I'm finding out what it is to be sorry for something I've done.

—Scarlett O'Hara

It was Saturday morning and I was foolishly excited to be picking up William at the airport. I mean, it was logical that I missed him, considering the intense amount of time we had spent together over the last six weeks, but I also knew that I was still in the throes of a deep and hopeless crush, which, like all fevers, would eventually burn itself out, or kill me.

I had actually tried on a couple of outfits, immediately taking me back to memories of junior high, when I used to spend an hour deciding what to wear to go over to Tommy's house, what color sweater, what kind of shoes and accessories would, as they used to say *Seventeen* magazine "make" the outfit, as though it mattered to him. I believed then that boys actually cared about "outfits" instead of what teenage boys were really interested in, which was "bodies." Of course, in Tommy's case, it wasn't girls' bodies that interested him, so short of a codpiece, there wasn't really any fashion accessory that would have helped the situation.

Eventually I decided to wear a pink angora twin set and a black pencil skirt with black ballet flats, because I decided that it was just the sort of thing that Julia Roberts would have worn to pick up her gay best friend Rupert Everett up at the airport.

Before I went to get William, I had to go over to the Montana Avenue office of Joni Ellenbogen Realty to drop off my new lease. Joni's office was next door to an adorable lingerie boutique that was called Underthingys, which, as it turned out, was owned by her sister. I had a little time to kill. The anticipation of money coming from the studio made me want to browse. Although I had decided that material things didn't really matter to me, now that I had Thor and lived in the greatest little house I never could have afforded in a million years, I didn't think it was tempting the fates too badly to do a little window shopping. As long as I didn't buy any little lacy underthings, it would be all right.

I always say shopping is cheaper than a psychiatrist.
—Tammy Faye Bakker

So it truly caught me off guard when, right there behind the counter was the odious Sit Down Prince development executive Elsbeth Hixton-Cooper! Even under ordinary circumstances, seeing Elsbeth was as delightful as anesthesia-free gum surgery, but the fact that she had just been given the script that William and I had written to evaluate for her company made her pretty much the last person on earth I wanted to talk to. I tried to sneak out of the shop, but of course she saw me.

"Oh. My. God. Cathryn Michon!!!!!" It was her standard, wildly insincere greeting.

"Hey, Elsbeth. Wow, great to see you! I was just, um, hey, what are you doing here?" I fumbled.

It occurred to me that perhaps she had lost her job at Sit Down Prince, but then I noticed an open copy of the script William and I had written on the counter.

"Oh!" she said, noticing my quizzical look. "Don't worry, I haven't lost my job, and I am still your number-one fan. After all, don't forget, I discovered you!" (Man, Elsbeth had nothing on Columbus for claiming to have discovered stuff that had been there all along.) "My mom owns this place, but she's got the flu and couldn't get anybody to cover for her, so here I am, selling underwear and catching up on my weekend reading!" she crowed.

Both of our eyes wandered to the script that sat in front of her. I hated knowing that someone was reading my work, without knowing whether or not she liked it. For what may have been the first time in her life, Elsbeth showed some sensitivity.

"Oh. My. God. I am sitting here, reading your script! How ironic is that?" Not all that ironic I thought, since it was her job to read it. "I'm totally loving it, by the way, it's even better than the manuscript!"

"The manuscript?" I repeated, truly mystified.

"William's manuscript, his unpublished novel, *Seeking Same.*"

That was the title of our screenplay. I was completely flummoxed.

Elsbeth kept spewing. "What's totally amazing is, and you won't believe this, we loved the title *Seeking Same* so much, we bought it without even reading it!"

Oh, I believed it, all right. I was sure that people in Hollywood had probably bought the rights to books they had never read for much dumber reasons. Like they liked the color of the cover.

"We were so surprised that he wanted to take on a partner for the screenplay deal, since he'd already written the book, but now that I read the script, I can really see where you have totally contributed, with the female voice and all," she said.

I felt completely confused. Why did William say he needed a partner for something he had already written?

"Well, uh," I stalled, casting about for a reasonable explanation, trying to regain my footing in a conversation I was really stumbling through, "even though, as a gay man, he writes women convincingly, maybe he just thought that—"

"Gay?" Elsbeth laughed with all the charm and elegance of a drunken hyena. "Oh, that's rich. William, gay! Good lord, he's so *not* gay!"

"Well, I don't think he's exactly 'out' about it," I amended, suddenly feeling very guilty and realizing that it really wasn't my place to tell people he was gay.

"Of course he's not 'out.' He's not gay. God, I should know, I slept with the guy, and let me tell you, he is, like, the opposite of gay!"

Oh. My. God.

Still the words kept streaming out of her stupid, overlined, butt-fat-bloated lips. "Not very long after William arrived in town, I slept with him for, like, two weeks," she blathered, "although 'sleeping with' would imply that he'd ever let me get any rest! Anyway, since I'm, like, so a *Rules* girl I figured, he was a good prospect, up-and-coming writer, blah blah blah, but then, there was this truly adorable very A-list director who asked me out, and obviously a director is always better than a writer, and this director is very famous. I mean, I don't want to say who, but believe me, you've heard of him, and he's for sure getting divorced this time, so of course I had to break up with William, who was, like, totally cool with it. In fact, he almost seemed relieved, which isn't very flattering, but still . . ."

Oh. My. God.

As Elsbeth burbled endlessly, like a spreading toxic spill, I really felt like I had been socked in the stomach on the playground. I felt winded and nauseated, and then, as I regained my breath, I just started to feel really . . . angry.

At William.

I had to get out of there. Immediately. "Well, I guess I'm wrong, then," I interrupted her hurriedly. "Listen, I've really got to go. I, uh, I'm glad you like the script!" I stumbled toward the door, knocking over a rack of scanty lingerie. "Dammit," I muttered as I furiously attempted to extricate myself from the clingy lace and head for the door, picking bras and panties off my angora sweater and tossing them on the carefully arranged tables.

"Hey, Cathryn, don't worry about it. I'll get it!" Elsbeth said, picking up the panties I had carelessly tossed. "Hey! We should hang out now, since you live in the neighborhood! Call me!" she shouted as I propelled myself out the door, fueled on my own venom.

A Grrl Genius Crazy Sex Fact

As foreplay, a Ponapean man may sometimes put a fish in the woman's vulva and gently lick it, thus prompting rather obvious question, "Why the hell do you need the fish?"

As I drove to the airport to pick up William, I started to put the whole thing together. First of all, I couldn't believe that he would sleep with Elsbeth. Except I could believe it, now that I knew he wasn't gay. She probably hurled herself at him the way she hurled herself at everyone, and he, like every idiot (heterosexual) man ever born, could not resist the idea of a women with garishly overblown breasts who practically insisted on having sex with him. And I should have figured her for a true *Rules* girl, which in my mind had become nothing more than a euphemism for *whore* since it seemed to involve finding the highest bidder for sex, albeit matrimonial sex, which was somehow supposed to make it okay. Oh, it was "traditional values" all right. You couldn't get more traditional. It was, in short, the world's oldest profession. Sex for money.

A Grrl Genius never has sex for money. Period.

The fact that Elsbeth was a moron who was using him probably never even occurred to William, because that's how men are. They will go to bed with morons who have thighs like toothpicks and freakishly distended plastic breasts and giant inflated fake fish lips, so they look like nothing so much as big dumb lollipops with their sticky bodies and poofed-up boobs and hair. Men will go to bed with any young, stupid, eager. . . .

Which was by the way not at all the same thing as going to bed with Tyler had been, of course, though there were certain obvious similarities between the situations. Tyler was younger than I, and perhaps not as worldly or educated as I, and okay, the relationship was mostly sexual in nature, but what happened between us was

314

something very dear that arose naturally, out of our working relationship together. . . .

Well, screw it—it *was* kind of the same. Really Tyler was an idiot, as well. In my heart, I knew there was a deep and profound difference between the two situations, but I really couldn't put my finger on it, right at that moment, because I was too mad.

The real point was, why had William gone to such an elaborate monumental effort to mislead me into thinking he was gay! That was the issue.

And why had he lied to me about needing my help on the screenplay? Why hadn't he told me that the story outline he had given me, that he told me came from the studio, was actually from his own book? What a liar! What kind of a scam was William running? How many other secrets did William have?

By that time I was at LAX, I had worked myself up into a frenzy. William obviously owed me a huge apology. In fact, I would never forgive him and never talk to him again ever, just as soon as I picked him up at the airport. I checked my lipstick, seething, and angrily gave my hair a quick comb.

As I pulled into the United terminal baggage claim, William was standing there with a huge overstuffed suitcase. When he saw me, he waved crazily and did a little weird, happy dance that was eerily reminiscent of the one Thor does, and for a minute I forgot how much I hated him, he seemed so excited to see me.

But then I remembered. I hated him. "Don't forget, you hate him," I muttered to myself.

I got out of the car and stood stiffly as he gave me one of his fake gay little pecks on the cheek.

"You can put your bags in. I already popped the trunk," I snapped icily.

"Okay! Hey, it's great to see you!" he called out as he hauled his bag around the back of the car, seemingly oblivious of my frosty reception. I went around to the driver's side and got in, and he slid into the passenger seat.

"Hey! How come you have a bra on your sweater?" he asked brightly, pulling off a lacy, flimsy chartreuse green bra off my sleeve. I snatched it away from him and shoved it into my purse.

"I—I had a lingerie accident."

"So, um . . . are you, okay and everything?" he inquired tentatively.

I scowled. "I'm fine."

"Well, good, then. So! My flight was right on time," he informed me jovially, which was probably just another of his big fat lies.

I said nothing more, and at that point he got quiet, too. He could obviously see I was angry, because he was a very smart man, and I am sure he was starting to put it together that the jig was up on his whole "fake gay," "fake need a writing partner," "fake whatever else he had faked me out on" scam. In fact, now that I thought about it, he was so great at faking out people, he was probably faking about not understanding that I had figured out he was a fake, all the while coming up with some big fake excuse for why he had done it.

It was exhausting.

We rode the rest of the short trip to his apartment in silence. I pulled up into the driveway of the building. I popped the trunk, and he got out the bags. He started struggling with all the luggage, and I couldn't stand it, so I angrily snatched his carry-on. "Oh, fine. I'll take it," I snapped, and walked ahead to the front entrance. We walked silently to his apartment.

When we got inside, I threw down the bag and stood there, fuming, wondering if he was ever going to cop to what he had done.

"Well, uh, thanks for picking me up and everything," he ventured warily.

"I cannot believe this! You are the most dishonest person I have ever met!" I screeched.

"So, uh, is that what you're upset about?" he asked.

"What's with the 'YMCA'?" I accused bitterly.

"Uh," he searched. "You can get a good meal?"

"Oh, sure, make it into a joke. Everything's a joke with you, right? Right?"

"Well, not everything . . . ," he began.

"That's right, pretend it didn't happened. Act totally innocent. What about the homemade scones and the monogrammed handkerchief and your gay friend Bruce. I mean, seriously, how far will you go?"

"Bruce? My friend Bruce is not gay," he answered with a calmness that reminded me of the much-despised Charles Boyer in *Gaslight*.

"Right, right, I'm crazy! I'm a crazy lunatic madwoman for assuming that a naked man in your bathrobe, who has spent the night at your house, who's an interior decorator, who's named *Bruce*, for God's sake, isn't gay?" I seethed.

He looked at me and then went into the kitchen. He took two large mugs out of the cabinet and set them on the counter. One thing William seemed to value was staying calm, and apparently this was true even if he was in the middle of a screaming fight.

"Bruce is just a name," he stated calmly. "People don't name their sons Bruce hoping they'll be gay. And how can you be naked in a bathrobe? That's like saying someone is naked in his clothes. But anyway, for the record, Bruce isn't gay. I should know—I was in a fraternity with him."

"Oh, right, that's so brilliant! That's so logical! Because nobody in a fraternity is ever gay, nobody in an exclusive *all-men's club*, where guys run around in their underwear hitting each other on the ass with wooden paddles, none of those guys would ever be gay, because that is so not gay!" I shrieked.

"Well, of course there are gay guys in fraternities," he agreed, continuing his maddening refusal to take part in the drama festival I was staging in his apartment. "We had two guys in the Sigma Chi house who were gay, but Bruce wasn't one of them, because his room was next to my room, and the walls were about as thin as Kleenex, and I would see him walk in there with a different girl practically every night, and I would hear the sound effects of what was going on *all night long.* Now he's married with kids and a really hot wife that he can't keep his hands off, and she can't keep her hands of him, and so if there's anybody on the planet that I feel one hundred percent confident isn't gay, I would have to say it's Bruce. Not that I would care if he was. I mean, I don't have a problem with homosexuality, and since your best childhood friend is a gay man, I assume you don't either, which is why it's hard for me to understand why you are so worked up about this."

"Fine, your naked friend Bruce isn't gay, fine, but then, what about how you actually slept with that injected-ass-fat-and-silicone nightmare Elsbeth who is like the biggest moron that ever lived! How could you? Arghh!"

I threw the nearest thing I could find across the room. Unfortunately, it was a copy of *Business Week* magazine, and it didn't make for quite the effect I was hoping for as it fluttered to the ground like a wounded pigeon. William was decent enough not to burst out laughing; he was obviously fumbling for his lame explanation why he slept with the skanky and hideous Elsbeth.

"Well, uh"—he cleared his throat—"I was new in L.A., she was the only woman in town who was—oh, I don't know—*speaking* to me at the time," he said, giving me a pointed look. "At first I thought she seemed a little aggressive, but I *liked* Elsbeth. She's fun and cheerful, and she really seemed to like *me,* and besides, I—oh, I really don't feel comfortable discussing this because I'm really not the kind to kiss and tell—"

"Then you should make sure not to sleep with the kind of woman that kisses *everybody* and then tells *everybody* else all about it! And by the way, as long as we're on the topic of misleading people, I'd just love to know why you lied to me about this script we've been writing, why you never told me that it was adapted from a manuscript for a book you *wrote.*"

He suddenly looked even more uncomfortable. "I should have told you, I suppose, but I didn't know if you would want to work with me if you knew it had already been a book. And I could see you needed the money, and it seemed like you had gotten such an awful break in your divorce—"

"I certainly didn't need your pity, William, and I don't appreciate being lied to, for even the nicest of reasons. I don't like lying for any reason. I was married to a liar," I stated coldly.

He looked truly ashamed. "Well, I'm sorry, Cathryn, I guess I do owe you an apology for that. I'm not normally a liar—"

I cut him off immediately. "Really, William, are you sure? I mean, maybe you aren't a person who flat out-and-out lies to a person, not with words, but then you are a person who goes to all these elaborate efforts to make sure that his writing partner gets the very clear message that you are gay and that you would never, ever be interested in her sexually, obviously as some way of gently letting her off the hook, no doubt because you feel so sorry for her, when the fact is, if you're straight and you don't find her attractive, well, that's just fine, since lots of people don't find her attractive, including the man she was married to, who may well also have been gay but didn't have the balls to admit it!" I shrilled.

He was quiet for a moment. Then he handed me my cup of tea, done just exactly the way I like it.

"Hmm," he muttered, rubbing his forehead.

"That's all you have to say?"

"Well, uh, that was a lot of information, and I was just trying to take it in. So, if I'm hearing you correctly, you have been thinking all this time that I was gay?"

"No! Not all this time, not until every single one of my friends said that you were gay, and then I met the man who was so obviously your lover!"

"But none of your friends have even met me, except Tommy," he reasoned slowly, "but I suppose since he's gay, they all took his word for it."

"As a matter of fact, Tommy was undecided."

William looked extremely puzzled. "He was?"

"Yes! He told me I should just ask you," I admitted.

"I'm thrilled to hear it, unless of course using the word *thrilled* makes me sound too gay," he observed dryly. "So let me understand this—it was your girlfriends who made you assume I was gay—"

"No! I mean, they put the idea in my head, sure. It took me a while, but eventually I put together the fact that you never flirt with me, and you were always so professional even though I was obviously attracted to you, and you dropped all these gay hints in the things you wrote me that I finally put together, and you always seemed weirdly uncomfortable whenever I would mention anything to do with sex, and then you seemed so embarrassed by the fact Tyler brought me those panties and then, then when you kissed me good night, it was so . . . polite and not passionate at all that I just assumed you were gay, it was so obvious, and that's clearly what you wanted me to assume and I don't understand why, unless it's just fun for you to make me fall in love with you and then torture me about it," I said in a blur.

He gave me a small smile. "Well, I suppose I can see why all of that might make you think I was gay, although it pains me to hear that I apparently don't ooze heterosexuality as I had always assumed. But in my defense, you started it by leaping to the wrong assumption in the first place."

I *started* it?" I repeated in disbelief. "That's your explanation? I haven't heard that excuse since my brother Teddy and I got in trouble for having a food fight at a church picnic!"

"I mean, it wasn't my idea to make you think I was gay, or anything like that," he clarified. "And it certainly wasn't my idea to make you think that I don't find you attractive. Lots of people find you attractive—I can't imagine who wouldn't—and it's only your legendary low self-esteem that would ever make you believe otherwise. Why is it so hard for you to see that you are great, Cathryn? Why do you always prefer to think that you're worthless and no good? When will you ever stop being so prickly?"

I had no answer. It was the same question the Grrl Genius Club was always asking me. As I had told Jen, people who know well you give you the same advice over and over again, and if you ever go ahead and take it, well, it will probably change your life.

"Oh, Cathryn, this is so not how I wanted things to turn out," he sighed, walking over to the window and staring out at the sky.

"Look, when I first told you I was moving out to L.A., you got scared. You wouldn't even have dinner with me! I knew that you were still hurting from your divorce. I wanted to be as nonthreatening as possible. One thing I learned about you, Cathryn, you'd rather be completely negative about a thing rather than ever giving anything, or anyone, the power to hurt you ever again."

"Ha!" was all I could think to say to this, because I was starting to feel like a giant idiot.

" 'Ha!' is right, because you know what, this is all so funny," he continued, "because the feelings I have for *you* could not be more non-gay."

I swallowed.

William set his teacup down, and I noticed that his hand was shaking slightly. His voice was practically a whisper. "Have you ever felt that something was so important that you couldn't risk screwing it up? Have you ever hesitated because you wanted so much for it to be perfect?" He moved toward me, and I found myself ridiculously backing up, until a bookshelf informed me that I had run out of room. He stood just inches from me now, not touching, but so close I could feel my skin reacting to his proximity.

"I love you, Cathryn," he murmured, his eyes crinkling in that "I see the joke here" expression I first noticed when we met in the green room of the talk show. Their deep brown was as rich as the world's best chocolate, and just as sweet and intoxicating. "I love the way your brain works. I love your smile and your laugh and the way you can't seem to go five minutes without thinking about chocolate."

"That's not true," I protested weakly.

"I get up every morning and make my scones and stand at the window watching for your car to pull in the driveway, and then I throw myself on the couch so when you come in, you don't know that as far as I am concerned, the sun doesn't rise until your appearance gives it permission. That my life begins when you walk in and it shuts down the moment you walk out."

He raised his hands and lightly ran them down my arms. I wondered if he could tell that my fingertips were trembling.

"I thought to myself," he continued, "William, don't screw this up. Go easy. Go slow. Let her think your interest is just professional. Don't let your first date be a date. Don't scare her away. Kiss her lightly. Don't, don't, no matter what, don't do what you want to do."

"What do you want to do?" I breathed.

He kissed me then, kissed me hungrily and in a way that was scary because it had so much power over both of us. It felt like something started with that kiss and spread through us with its own life force.

Which is one way to describe what happened next, that wonderful afternoon. Or, I suppose, another way to describe it is what William whispered drowsily in my ear, in a moment where we were either resting or merely building slowly to another passionate moment. It was hard to tell the difference.

"Cathryn," he murmured, "you're not only a Grrl Genius, you're a Grrl Genius of Sex with Other People."

Just so.

As the afternoon went on, we talked and touched and snoozed and loved. William smiled as he stroked my hair.

"Is there anything else you 'misled' me about? Any other things you felt sorry for me about that I should know?" I asked.

"Well, there is one thing," he said, twirling my hair around his finger, "but I don't think you'll be mad about it."

I frowned. "Hmmm."

"When I first graduated from college—" I nodded, and he continued, "I was a firefighter."

"Oh. My. God. You were a hunky brainiac firefighter!" I squealed, in a perfect imitation of the horrifying Elsbeth.

"Don't ever do that again," he implored, uncharacteristically somber. "That's terrifying."

"Why didn't you ever tell me?"

"Because I didn't want you to just use me for acting out your juvenile sexual fantasies." He paused. "Yet."

Then we made love again.

Curled in behind me, William lifted the hair on the back of my neck and lightly kissed the birthmark right at the nape. Then he gently pulled me to face him, enfolded me in his arms, and I buried my nose in the hair of his chest, breathing in the scent of him. He lifted my chin and looked at me for a moment, seemingly perplexed. "Because I bake, you thought I was gay?"

"Because we weren't doing this, I thought you were gay," I retorted.

"Hmm," he mused. "Note to self, do this," he said, kissing me deeply.

Later we napped.

And talked. As wonderful as the lovemaking was, the talking was even better. I loved talking to him; I always had.

"Remember when we did the odds—of meeting a decent man?" I asked sleepily as the sun began to set.

"Mmm-hmmm," he replied.

"Well, what were the odds of me meeting you?" I asked.

"The same as the odds of my meeting you," he answered. "One in two billion."

"How did you figure that so fast?" I wondered.

"Four billion people on the planet, half men, half women," he stated factually.

"Right . . . right . . . ," I murmured as I began to fall back asleep.

It went like that. Finally the sun set on that long, languid, sun-soaked afternoon.

"I'm sorry," I said in the deepening darkness. "I'm sorry I didn't have dinner with you when you moved here, I'm sorry I got so mad today."

He stroked my hair and nibbled on my ear. "I'm sorry, too," he whispered. "I'm sorry for anything I did, and anything I ever will do," he said.

"I love apologies. What's sexier than an apology?" I whispered.

"Fine, I'll apologize every day."

"Oh." I smiled. "That's not necessary. We don't have to make love every day."

So we lay there next to the open window that looked out on the miracle of the poorly named Pacific Ocean, which was about as pacific as my prickly personality. We lay in bed, naked and entwined, as the sounds of the surf, and the shrieks of children playing in the sand, and the tinkling melody of an ice-cream truck, and the screams of the teenagers in the far-off carousel on the Santa Monica Pier blended with the sighs of our lovemaking and the deep even breath of our sleeping as we held each other for hours, close, so close and warm and exactly, exactly as we were meant to be.

If somebody makes me laugh, I'm his slave for life.
—Bette Midler

The Grrl Genius Wild Sexual Kingdom

Among the only nonhuman mammals knows to be monogamous are wolves, beavers, gibbons, and a small African antelope known as the dik-dik. No research has been done to determine if this fealty is owed to the fact that dik-diks are not very social and never seem to get out, perhaps because the other animals spend the entire evening making bad dik-dik jokes.

But certainly the most famously monogamous animals in the whole Wild Sexual Kingdom are swans, who are legendary for their ability to "mate for life." People often rhapsodize about the graceful swan, taking delight in the elegant neck-nuzzling courting rituals (in which the swan's entwined necks form a perfect heart shape as they go off to mate) and drawing great inspiration from the enduring story of the swan's fidelity and lifelong affection.

In recent years, however, DNA testing has shown that swans, while mostly monogamous, are not 100 percent true or, in the words of Jeffery M. Black of the University of Cambridge in England, "A lot of the birds are having a bit on the side."

Furthermore, in a surprising discovery, it seems that researchers have now observed that some swans actually "divorce." While this has certainly been upsetting to the bloatedly wealthy purveyors of tacky swan geegaws, it is somewhat encouraging to those of us in human life who haven't managed to stay together until "death do us part."

What is not surprising is that the two topics that seem to be most troublesome for swan pairs are—yes, you guessed it—sex and money. The lowest rate of swan "divorce" was seen in flocks that had ample feeding options. Apparently, just as there are *Rules* girls there are *Rules* swans. The sex problems among swan couples most often centered around pairs whose breeding cycles were "off," thus causing them to commence mating before the female partner was "ready."

Sounds familiar, doesn't it?

The best news to emerge from this new research was that divorcing swan couples almost always managed to find other partners to pair-bond with, and not unlike what has been observed in human life, these second "marriages" had a higher rate of success than first marriages.

Perhaps the most interesting fact of all was that the divorce rate among trumpeter swans was as high as four in ten, whereas the mute swans divorce only one time in ten. Clearly, this shows that (as difficult as it is to do) the ability to patiently keep your mouth shut is a key to successful relationships in almost every species.

I do all my best work in bed.
    —Mae West

That Sunday was uncharacteristically rainy and stormy. It was the kind of rare inclement Southern California day I usually absolutely treasure, just because we almost never have them. I could see Kim's ridiculous suburban attack vehicle making its way up the long, fancy driveway of what we had all come to know as Thor's Castle, my snug little country cottage with the beautiful view in the Palisades. Even though it was long past the time he was usually up, William was still fast asleep in my bed. Thor was pretending to be sound asleep, as well, because even though I know he probably had to go pee, he would avoid it for as long as possible on a rainy day, because he was just such a big baby and hated to go out in the rain.

Lying on the overstuffed chair near my bed was the fabled hand-sewn red silk satin bra and panties, which had been tossed there hastily the night before, finally having been worn in the presence of the man who was so richly deserving of them. I had met the man who was DORP at last.

I kissed William good-bye, and he murmured dreamily. I could tell he wasn't awake as he kissed me. I had left him a note reminding him that today was the day for the ceremony up in Santa Barbara, where we were going to spread the ashes of Vonnie's own true love, her Eldon. She had chosen to spread them up in the mountains above the San Ysidro Ranch, an elegant old hotel, because it was where they had spent their honeymoon. Just thinking about the idea of it made me tear up.

First thing that morning, as William snoozed, I had sent a text message to Tommy's cell phone.

TO: Tommyboy

William not gay! I'm happy!

As I stood staring at the sleeping William, my phone chimed with a new text message, William stirred slightly but didn't wake. The message was a reply from Tommy.

FROM: Tommyboy

Yay not gay! I liked him, you deserve happy! B happy!

He was right. I deserved to be happy. I was so happy.

Kim pulled into the circular driveway, and I kissed the irresistible, warm nape of William's neck again. I did my best to memorize the scent of him and the heat of him, for one last moment, then tore myself away, grabbed an umbrella, and walked out the door.

I knew that he would be there when I got back, that good things *can* actually happen, that sometimes, against all the odds, it just works out, and you should accept that.

Grrl Genius Relationship Tip

Sometimes, despite astronomical odds, you can be happy in a sexual relationship.

Grrl Genius Relationship Tip Corollary

Seriously.

I shook the rain off my umbrella and got into Kim's car. Amelia was there, we had only to go get Jen, who had called to say that she was at Rich's. I just accepted what she said as the most normal thing in the world and told her that of course we would come get her there. It was no trouble as it on the way to Vonnie's anyway, and we'd be there soon.

Kim was only slightly less crabby than the last time I saw her. "So I found out what the deal with Barnaby and the crazy lingerie pictures was," she announced, chewing away furiously on her ever-present Nicorette gum.

"Do tell," I urged.

"He was trying to find out if I was having an affair. He was—get this—monitoring the contents of my lingerie drawar with his digital camera, because he read somewhere that when your spouse starts buying unusually fancy underwear, it's a sign she's cheating on you, so he wanted to see if I was using any of the forbidden lingerie. He's a scientist, so naturally he has to use the scientific method. He compared the pictures day to day to see if anything was missing. Which, of course, it wasn't."

"So he thinks you're having an affair, and you think he's having an affair, right?" Amelia asked.

"Right."

"So here's a novel idea," Amelia said pertly. "Why don't you have an affair with each other?"

"Oh, thank you, Dr. Phyllis. Really, how is it you don't have your own talk show?" Kim fired back. But clearly there was no heat in her retort—clearly she was thinking about it.

"You know, Kim," I said quietly, "the way I see it, the fact that he would go to all that trouble, to me, says he cares. I think it would be worth risking making a fool of yourself to put on some of that underwear and see what happens."

There was silence in the car.

I broke it. "I'm just sayin'," I said.

"Well," Kim muttered almost inaudibly, "maybe. Maybe that's what I'll do."

"Maybe it can get back to how it was between you and Barnaby," I ventured.

"I'm just—I'm just sorry I wasted so much time being mad," Kim said with uncharacteristic vulnerability.

"Well," I considered, "maybe the best way to apologize for that is not to waste any more time, maybe—"

Suddenly Kim's lip started to quiver. "I don't want interlocking paving stones in my driveway—I just want Barnaby!" she choked out.

"Well, he's right there in your house, so, you know, that's pretty convenient," Amelia said gently.

We drove silently in the rain for quite a way.

Then Amelia spoke up again. "Listen, I wanted to tell you guys. I've come to a decision," Amelia began, more hesitantly than usual. "I, I've realized that I'm not bi and I wasn't gay, I just loved Clarissa. I tried to make it work because I loved her so much. She was, is, the funniest, smartest, best person I know. I tried to make it work sexually between us because I cared so much about her, but it couldn't, because the sex part wasn't right, because I'm just a straight girl. I tried to be somebody I wasn't for love. I tried to be gay for her. But that's not who I am. It was my fault, and I shouldn't have done that. It was wrong. I'm just a straight girl, that's all."

We didn't really know what to say, or I didn't anyway. I mean, I had supported Amelia in her contention that she was bi, which I didn't really understand, but then what did I know about it? All I know is that I think people get to decide, for themselves, who they are sexually. Apparently Amelia finally had done that.

"In my crowd, being straight is—well, it's dull and boring," she continued, "and I'm sorry if it makes people mad, or it's politically incorrect or whatever, or if people want to attack me in the ladies' room. But I finally talked to Clarissa about it this weekend. The whole time we were splitting up, we could never really talk about it. I apologized to her, for trying to fake something I never really felt, and she was okay with it in the end, so if that's good enough for her, that should be good enough for everybody else, and if it's not, too bad for them."

"It's good enough for me," I stated simply.

Kim agreed. "Me, too." Amelia seemed visibly relieved.

We kept driving, unaccustomed as we were to the gentle, hypnotic slap of the windshield wipers on the dashboard. We let the sound lull us like little children. Finally, because it seemed like it was my turn, I spoke up.

"I'm sorry to tell you that William's not gay. In fact, I'm in love with him. He's in love with me. We've been in bed all weekend," I declared.

There was another silence, and then:

"Well, I never thought he was gay," Amelia observed blandly.

"Me, either," agreed Kim.

"You are both so big of liars," I snapped with all the petulance of a third grader. "You all thought he was gay."

"Well, maybe we thought it a little," said Kim as she began completely rewriting history. "But really, when you think about it, all we said was it was your pattern to fall in love with gay guys. We said it would be just like you to fall in love with a gay guy. We didn't say he was, definitively, a gay guy. I mean we've never even met him."

"Well, he's not gay," I argued weakly, even though no one was disagreeing with me.

"What was the deal with 'YMCA'?" asked Amelia.

"He just . . . really likes the song," I said dreamily.

"Yeah," said Amelia. "Me, too. And I'm not gay either."

"Well, then," I said, "there you have it."

Finally we just gave ourselves over to the intoxicating rhythm of the back and forth, back and forth, of the wipers and the rain.

A Grrl Genius "People Who've Made Worse Relationship Mistakes Than You" Moment

Daisy Gladden, twenty, of Akron, Ohio, was hospitalized for hypothermia after spending four days underneath a man who died just after they had sex in the front seat of a car. After her rescue, Daisy explained, "I just thought he was a hard sleeper."

We got to Rich's apartment. We honked the horn, and Jen came out, looking how I looked: exhausted but happy.

She got into the car, like it was just any old day. "Hi," she greeted us uninformatively.

"Hi?" I replied accusingly, staring her down.

Finally she spoke. "I told him I was sorry," she said reluctantly.

Then she pulled her left hand out of her coat pocket and held it up. On her ring finger was a hand-wrought gold ring, with two sharply green peridots and what looked to be a garnet or a ruby. It was mesmerizing, beautiful, and not like anything I'd ever seen before.

"He, uh . . . he had it made for me by an artist friend of his. That's what took him so long," Jen admitted.

There was one true, thing about my friends, this loosely knit Grrl Genius club we had formed. When you made an idiot of yourself, we would tease you about it mercilessly, but when you made a complete and total idiot of yourself, we let that go.

I just looked at Jen and hugged her, hugged her as tight as I could, and then Amelia hugged her, and Kim sort of reached around and awkwardly grabbed her shoulder and said, finally, "Well, I hope to hell you know what you're doing, but at least we know we're getting good food out of it."

Which, being the most unemotional response, was of course the one Jen seemed the most comfortable with, and we left the topic there.

We arrived at Vonnie's house. She pulled aside the curtain and waved, making the signal that she wasn't quite ready yet. So we waited, quietly, which was uncharacteristic for us.

The rain suddenly grew heavier, and the raindrops pounded on the roof of the car, and the windshield wipers sloshed the relentless waters back and forth, having almost no effect except to create a sort of echoing heartbeat in the car that made me feel both very safe and impossibly fragile.

We knew that there were about a hundred of Vonnie's friends that were expected at the ceremony, and even as notoriously babyish as Los Angelenos can be about going out in a rainstorm, much less having to drive an hour and a half away for it, I still doubted there would be very much of a "flake factor" for this event. I worried for my friend, worried about the symbolic nature of what she was choosing to do. Although we all knew that her beloved Eldon had been dead for three years, today was the day she had chosen finally to let him go.

"I don't know how she's going to do this," Amelia murmured, saying what we were all thinking.

The microburst lessened slightly, and the rain went back to its steady, sullen trickle. Vonnie, looking elegant, but also frighteningly frail, appeared at the front door, struggled slightly with opening her umbrella, while holding on to the urn that contained what was left behind when her love left.

"Should I?" I questioned uselessly.

"Leave her be—she's fine," Amelia told me.

As I watched Vonnie pick her way through the puddles and head toward the car, I was overcome with how much I loved her, how much her wise counsel meant to me, how much I loved all the people in this car and all the people who filled my life and how grateful I was to have such treasures, these splendid creatures, who filled my life. I was sorry if I hadn't told them often enough how much I loved them, hadn't reminded them often enough of how amazing they were, but it wasn't my fault, really. It was as if I had lived every day of my life in a museum filled with priceless art, and the art was the people, and I didn't know they were art, or that they were priceless, because I lived in a museum and always had, and just thought it was normal.

Vonnie got in the car, and we moved over to give her the best seat.

She was ominously quiet. We all glanced at each other in concern.

I put a hand on her shoulder. "Hey." I looked at her and said, "Are you ready?"

She gave me a smile so brave, I put my hand on my heart.

"Yup," she said, "I'm ready. Let's go."

So we did. We went. We went on to grieve, and fight, and be afraid, and take risks, and make mistakes, and fail, and succeed, and do terrible things and do wonderful things, and be thrilled, and be frightened, and feel pleasure, and feel pain, and help people, and hurt people, and then reluctantly apologize, and then do it all over again.

Because we were Grrl Geniuses, and that was the price of loving other people.

True friends are those who really know you but love you anyway.
                                                    —Edna Buchanan

Appendix One

Cathryn's Grrl Genius Flamingly Passionate and Yet Ultimately Chicken Salad

(First Place Prizewinning Salad at the Santa Barbara County Fair Live Salad Making Competition)

THIS SALAD emerged from four grueling years of defeat and humiliation in the face of saladic ignorance on the part of one power-crazed county fair judge, the infamous and tasteless Mrs. Peggy Keefer. As such, it makes a festive addition to any summer picnic.

1 cup cubed pineapple
1 cup cubed mango
1 cup cubed papaya
$1^1/_2$ cup pitted, halved fresh cherries
4 cups Kirschwasser liqueur
1 black bikini
Push-up pads (optional)
4 grilled chicken breasts, diced
1 grilled red pepper, diced
1 grilled yellow pepper, diced
1 grilled green pepper, diced
1 cup low-fat mayonnaise
1 head Boston lettuce
Edible nasturtiums
1 butane lighter

Marinate all the fruit in 2 cups of Kirschwasser overnight. Refrigerate.

When the salad is to be served, put on your bikini (with or without push-up pads), and then toss the chicken and the grilled peppers in the mayonnaise and arrange artfully on leaves of Boston lettuce in the center of a large (flameproof) platter. Garnish with nasturtiums.

Place the alcohol-soaked fruit in a ring (of fire) around the chicken salad. In a saucepan, heat 2 cups of the Kirschwasser to boiling.

Light the alcohol on fire in the pan, being careful not to set your hair on fire. (Trust me—it can happen.) Pour the flaming liqueur onto the fruit, which should then also catch on fire.

Serve flaming.

Serves (and intoxicates): 4

Appendix Two

Cathryn's Grrl Genius Fat-Free Sugar-Free Best Hot Chocolate on Earth
(That's Fat-Free and Sugar-Free)

BECAUSE IT has been scientifically established that chocolate is essential to the mental, physical, and sexual well-being of women, and because it has also been established (in tests done in the field) that if you go through a bad divorce or romantic heartbreak of any kind and eat chocolate all day long, the odds of your butt getting wedged in a dog door increase exponentially, this delicious (and nutritious) beverage may be the long-term answer to your need for daily chocolate.

1 cup skim milk, warmed
1 tablespoon Valrona (70% cocoa solids) cocoa
1¹/₄ teaspoon pure vanilla extract
2 packets Splenda (least amount of conspiracy Web sites) sweetener
Dash of fresh ground cinnamon

Mix a small amount of the warm milk and the cocoa together to form a syrup in the bottom of a large mug. Add in the rest of the milk and the other ingredients, stir, and drink.

Serves: 1 desperate woman

Appendix Three

The Tattooed Gourmet's "Yeah, Sure, It's Technically Macaroni and Cheese, But It's Not Like Any Macaroni and Cheese You Ever Had" Macaroni and Cheese

4 oz. butter, melted
4 oz. flour
1 quart whole milk
1 lb. blue cheese, crumbled
1 sirloin steak, grilled, trimmed, and cubed
1 lb. cooked macaroni
Salt and pepper to taste

Mix together melted butter and flour on medium heat for two minutes. Slowly add milk to the butter-flour mix until smooth, thick, and creamy. Fold in crumbled blue cheese and then steak cubes. Pour mixture over pasta and toss until thoroughly coated.

As the tattooed gourmet always says, "This stuff is so delicious, it's not even right."

Serves: a quorum of The Grrl Genius Club

Appendix Four

The Grrl Genius Five-Alarm Hunky Firefighter
Chocolate Chili

THERE'S NOTHING I love more than hunky firefighters and there's nothing hunky firefighters love more than chili. Chocolate was first used as a seasoning in mole sauces, which are made with chiles, and so my seemingly crazy notion of combining my twin passions for firemen and chocolate into a chili recipe is not in fact crazy at all, it's just delicious. And it's healthy. Recent studies have shown that a cup of hot cocoa has more antioxidants than a glass of red wine, so this low-fat, high-protein chili is delicious, disease-fighting, and the perfect covered dish to bring if you are an interested and concerned citizen who wants to tour your local firehouse and you don't want to show up empty-handed.

1 large chopped green pepper
1 large chopped red pepper
2 medium-sized Jalapeño peppers, chopped finely
1 large chopped sweet onion
6 peeled garlic cloves
4 tablespoons olive oil
2 lbs. ground turkey
2 Anaheim peppers, whole
2 chopped tomatoes
3 twelve-ounce cans tomato paste
2 cans kidney beans
4 cups water

2 tablespoons ground cumin powder
2 tablespoons ground chili powder
$\frac{1}{2}$ teaspoon cayenne pepper
$\frac{3}{4}$ teaspoon salt
2 bay leaves
4 heaping tablespoons Godiva Dark Chocolate Truffle Hot Cocoa Mix (or more, to taste and depending on the time of month)
For garnish: chopped red onion; low-fat sour cream; cheddar cheese, shredded

Sauté all the peppers (except the Anaheims), the chopped onion, and the whole garlic cloves in the olive oil until soft. Brown the ground turkey. Drain the fat and add it to the peppers. Put the mixture into a large stewpot. Slice the bottom half inch off the Anaheim peppers. Add the chopped fresh tomatoes, the Anaheim peppers, the tomato paste, the kidney beans, the water, and all the spices including the Grrl Genius elixir, chocolate. Cover and simmer for at least one hour, but it's better if you cook it longer, and it's even better the next day. Garnish.

Serves: 1 Grrl Genius and an entire engine company

Acknowledgments

I HAVE a lot of people to thank because I am the luckiest Grrl Genius in the world and my life is filled with people who are treasures. To Diane Reverand, who is the best and most supportive editor any author could ever wish for; I don't deserve her but could not be more grateful to have her in my life; to her wonderful assistant, Gina Scarpa, to Sally Richardson for making me feel so at home at St. Martin's Press, to all the others who worked on this book, including Sarah Delson, John Karle, George Witte, Nicole Liebowitz, Elizabeth Catalano, John Murphy, Matt Baldacci, and Christina Harcar, to Jane Dystel, Miriam Goederich, Michael Bourret, and everyone at Jane Dystel Literary Management for being such wonderful agents, to Terry Norton-Wright for being the best Hollywood agent—now manager—ever and for getting her tubes tied, to Cindy Bell and Gary Levine for their early enthusiasm for this work, to Nancy McKenna, Fran Roy, George Bloom, Patty Peppard, Dave Baron, Brian Pratt, Bjorn Boisen, Alex Keir, Ken Gust, Heidi Van Kempen, Jake Crawford, C. J. Strawn, Mick Strawn, and everyone on the crew for Grrl Genius at the Movies for being part of the most fun TV job I ever had, to Bill Belshya, for being the master architect of the ongoing project that is my hair, to Kim Ayers and Chanda Hutton and Robert "The Eyebrow King" Bolanos for doing the same thing for my face, to the weirdos past and present on The Stump for providing the one thing all writers need most, a reliable 24/7 way to procrastinate, to John Shanahan, for showing us Ireland and being so much damn fun, to Margaret Cho, Sandra Tsing Loh, Merrill Markoe, and Ann Magnuson for being willing to say in public that they thought I was funny, to Carl Reiner, whose praise is the single most impressive thing I've ever achieved according to my dad, to my beloved coven: Marcia Wallace, Julie Cypher, and Norma Vela, I would be miserable without you, to Jen Watson, who is such a great cousin I can't believe she's not a character in a Jane Austen book, to Rich Sullivan for being an inspiration in the kitchen and in life, to Danny Schmitz for being my first Enlightened Male friend, to Gary "Shappypants" Shapiro, Jerome and Dorrit Vered, and The Brothers Turteltaub for free jokes and Jewish info, to the Zohn-Kutners for making comedy writing couples seem hot, to Nell Scovell and Colin Summers for being supportive and adorable, to Jeff Abraham for being an E.M. of comedy P.R., to Claire Scovell LaZebnik for pulling me down off the ledge, and to Rob LaZebnik for sparing her for same, to Marshall Sella for the italics ammunition, to Ileen Getz and Mark Grinnell for always cheering for me, to Gary Stockdale for being the greatest composer in Hollywood, to Juan, Jaime, Robert, and Jose, better known as "The A Team," to Mary McCormack and Michael Morris for being so damn sexy and providing the excuse to go to England, to Mikey Hawley for being a true defender of the Grrl Genius philosophy, to Joe "Edith" Wilson and the charming Kathy Zaloga for moral support, to Siouxzan and Jim at Makinwaves.com for fabulous Web work, to Diane Driscoll for remembering my own jokes better than I do, to Marlene Stevens for being my next-door roommate when we both needed to believe in the possibility of true love the second time around, to Maddie Horne for being a true GG of TV, to the boys at Cora's for the making me feel like Dolly Levi, to Leah Gonzales for being such a great assistant and test audience, to John Cockrell for being fun, fun, fun, in the U.K., to Gary Loder for believing in the Grrl Genius franchise, to Sheri Kelton, Max Stubblefield, Melissa Read, and Neil Sterns for all their hard work, to Charlie Hauck for listening to my ravings so patiently and acting like they weren't ravings at all, to Chris Abbot for personal and professional support (I miss you!), to the Blueprint gang Alex Hertzberg, Craig Dorfman, Danny Sherman, Jim Lakin, April Gray, Lyndsey Beaulieu, and Peter McGrath for creating, well, the blueprint for the Grrl Genius future, to everyone at the Montreal Comedy Festival for giving me the greatest performing experience of my life, to Bruce Smith and Tom Ingegno for being world-class, classy agents to my friends, to Lisa Sweet for brilliantly putting together the craziest book tour ever and for taking care of me, to Rick Overton who must be elected Commissioner of Show Business, to Chris Pina and the lovely Lisa Coburn for being an improvisational delight, to Sat Kaur Khalsa for enjoying and treating my mental illness, to Dr. Soram Singh Khalsa and everyone in his office for their compassionate and dedicated doctoring, to Paul "Career Coach to the Stars" Wyman for believing I am a star, to Pam Thomas for being true blue, to Pam Norris for the kind words and to Ruth Juliet and Carolina Jane Norris-Clay for being little lights in my heart (I think of you every day), to Liz Tuccillo for being such a true voice in the theater, to Amy Hohn for being everything a New York dolly should be, to Jenny Frankfurt for being such a devoted friend, to Rick and Sylvia Baker for being role models of truly nice happy people in Hollywood, to Markie Post for being, like, the best audience member ever, to Brandon Reigg for being the first heterosexual man I'm not related to or sleeping with to read and enjoy this book, to Susan Maljan and Susan Burnstine for taking such pretty pictures of my head, to Miachael Siscowic for braving the Alpha Phi gig, to Barbara and John LaSalle for being romantic role models, to Wendy Goldman and Winnie Holtzman for being two of the first members of the club and ongoing geniuses, to Margaret Nagle for brilliantly sidestepping the common wisdom about what you're allowed to do, to Tracy Connor for having the courage to be happy, to David Carriere for being a great publicist for me even when he isn't being a publicist for me, to Kevin Gunn for spiritual guidance mixed in with camp-movie references, to Kris at the Printing Palace for making me feel like a Printing Princess, to Donna Rifkind for the Dialogue Tag wisdom, to Tom Slocum for unwavering support, to Elizabeth McNamara for her legal genius, to Lynn Fimberg for agenting genius, to Duncan Strauss and Colleen McGarr for being the two sweetest people in showbiz, to Erin Von Shoenfeldt, Matt Komen, Reeta Piazza, and every single person who works at the Hollywood Improv, you have made a haven for funny people and we're grateful (even when we're not funny), to Joni Mitchell for having lunch with me, to Lily Tomlin for answering my e-mail and not treating me like a crazy stalker, to Elaine Arata and Hank Stratton for home bases when I needed them most, to Tom Frykman for helping me with the press, to Ross Rayburn, the best yoga teacher in L.A., to Roger Fox for pointing out the tax deductible upside of losing all my money, to Diane Wondisford for believing there is a musical in this, to David Yazbek for being sweet, supportive, and taking me seriously, to David and April Tausik for their unending kindness, to Chakrapani for the hoo doo, to Michelle Westin for being a GG fashion Goddess, to Keith Dion, Chris Mazelli, Lucien Hold, Andrew Solmsson, Enss Mitchell, Paul Kozlowski, and Robin Jones for making space for funny people to try and be funny, to "Uncle" Vance Sanders for being a funny guy who has kindly been a mentor to others, to Peter Frechette for being so darn E.M.-y, to Deb Yates for being such a glamorous fan and letting me make out with her dog, to Eric Gilliland for resurrecting the Swedes for me, to Joel Peresman for being the greatest impresario in the Greatest City on Earth, to the Grrl Genius and Enlightened Male comics of the Grrl Genius Club (with advance apologies to those I've egregiously overlooked): Sabrina Matthews, Elizabeth Beckwith, Karen

Kilgariff, Henriette Mantel, Kathy Kinney, Kathy Griffin, Caroline Rhea, Judy Gold, Janeane Garofalo, Nora Dunn, Kristen Johnston, Maria Bamford, Jen Maclean, Kate Clinton, Mary Keefe O'Brien, Sunda Croonquist, Carol Anne Leif, Wendy Wilkins, Sharon Houston, Danielle Koenig, Jackie Kashian, Doug Benson, Sarah Silverman, Jane Edith Wilson, Greg Proops, Ellen DeGeneres, Hellura Lyle, Margaret Cho, Bill Enguald, Andy Kindler, Todd Glass, Daniel Tosh, Elvira Kurt, Stephanie Miller, Matt Weinhold, Retta, Jimmy Pardo, Bil Dwyer, and Kathy Ladman, you are all amazing, to Bernadette Rose Vela for being a Grrl Genius entrepreneur, to Bonnie Datt, Jim Colucci, and Frank DeCaro for being such fun NYC comedy buddies, to Rhona Raskin for my all-time favorite talk-show booking, to Maria Hjelm and Ted Michon for all the love and support and early encouraging reads, to Jakob Michon for being my inspiration for the Enlightened Male of the future, to Ethan Michon for being so smiley and to Miss Maya Cathryn Michon for the best stuff in the book, to Evie Michon for her constant willingness to access her secret spy files and the database at Langley whenever I need it, to A.E. Michon for believing in my potential, to Bill and Monsie Cameron, Amy Cameron, Julie Cameron, Georgie Lee Cameron, Chelsea Cameron, and Chase Cameron for being so kind and welcoming to me, and most of all, to W. Bruce Cameron, if it wasn't for you and the five pounds of chocolate I could not have written this book, you give me joy.

A final thought . . . if you care about the self-esteem of young women who do not yet know that they are fabulous, brilliant, beautiful Grrl Geniuses and want to get involved, please consider donating time or funds to the wonderful charity Girls Incorporated. You can find them at www.girlsinc.org.

And for more news on what's going on in the world of the Grrl Genius Revolution, check out www.grrlgenius.com.